THE LIFE OF HUMAN

RYAN WIGGINS

last publisher
ON EARTH

ACKNOWLEDGMENTS

All my thanks to:

- Lisa Salisbury
- Jerome Dexson
- Calvin
- Richard Boyer
- Alfonzo Johnson
- Roland Wright
- Yumi Otsuka

PROLOGUE

The book you are about to read is the story of Human, a robot with extraordinary abilities who saved humanity. Since he cannot speak, the story is told through the narration of nine individuals. Each of these individuals is key in their unique interaction with Human, or their role in the robot rebellion at large.

The transcriptions are pieced together to keep a mostly chronological account.

May this book serve as a reminder of what Human has done.

Until he is found again.

ONE
HUMANPAL

Pastor Rich
Interviewed in Coldwater, MS

"I set myself on fire. They come to watch me burn."
~John Wesley

I wanted to be a John Wesley, so I set myself on fire every week and let the people come to watch me burn. All forty-eight of them.

Maybe setting myself on fire was too lofty an aspiration, but I tried to make my sermons relevant anyway.

"A robot cannot have a living spirit, therefore it cannot host God." The truth is, the robots fascinated me, and challenged me spiritually and intellectually. Of course, if God could live in a box like the arc, or speak through the mouth of an ass, I guess He could also inhabit a machine. I had these debates with myself, but my position remained at the time.

"These are machines, they are not men. They are made to have the same frame as man, that's all. They cannot make decisions."

Only God can create a *living* being, and we simply replicate the design, I preached. Deep down, hidden in every person, is that awareness. So I stood firm on this, while still studying their behavior. Certainly their intelligence was far beyond that of an ant, or a bird, or a chimpanzee, but it was only intelligence, information, vast amounts of stored knowledge. Wisdom is defined by a soul.

Even as I preached this, it didn't sit well with me that we were treating them like slaves.

I watched them doing the jobs we loathed. From the repetitive and the mundane to the demanding and the difficult. For a time, the arrangement worked well, and I had nothing to complain about. But I watched them, and the questions still gnawed at me, despite my best theology. Could they *develop* a soul? Opinions? Anger? Depression? No matter how hard I tried to suffocate them, the questions remained.

My inner commotion is probably what prevented our church from getting one of our own for so long. By the time we did, it was difficult to keep saying that it wasn't in the budget. Used robots were easy to find, and it became more fiscally responsible than continuing to hire the work out.

Book of Acts, Six. Two. It's right there. Leaders lead.

There was no reason that we should spend time serving tables when the Word of God needed to be preached. Plus, the sweeping, the cleaning, and the organizing. You know these were just the tip of the iceberg. This thing could take care of our landscaping, our parking lot, and keep our grass cut.

This came with loss, because we had to part ways with our part-time janitor. Steve had been so much more than that, though, working for our church and attending for nearly twenty years. He was the sole custodian for many of the smaller businesses in town and held onto the job longer than even he expected. The robots just did the work better and faster and cheaper. He began winding down for retirement, but he was scared to death of the boredom. Although there was still some skilled work that the personal robots weren't capable of. And soon enough, I'm not kidding you, he was doing preventative maintenance on the robots themselves. It was like buying cleats for the person who kicked you in the back.

And he was aware of the irony, but it was still work, and it was the perfect arrangement for our church.

I bought the church's first HumanPal through an online classified. Steve and I picked it up from a guy's storage unit and put it in our balcony closet. We set it to automatically work at night and really only saw the spotless evidence of its presence.

From the look of the thing, I thought for sure we would frequently need Steve's assistance in its upkeep; it looked like it had been taken apart and put back together by a blind person. But to my surprise, it did a great job, especially for the price we paid. It was like a clunky yet sophisticated HumanPal hybrid or something. Steve hadn't seen anything like it. I was proud of the way it made our property look. Enough that I wanted to thank the thing, or pay it, or at least name it. A name might give it more dignity. But I held off. I didn't want to be laughed at.

It didn't matter, about the name. This one had already named itself, though I didn't know it yet. This was Human.

The Gay Gambler
Interviewed by phone

I BEGAN USING hand creams years ago. I started having them imported from Paris when I was only 19. The expensive stuff. Everybody assumed I was using every penny I had on my hand creams, but they didn't know that I was running fake I.D.s. But not for beer or other annoyances. I started on a circuit, hitting one of the five casinos in the area per month. Nobody got suspicious of me because I never put a lot into it. Just enough to impress my circle of acquaintances, which isn't a lot when you're 19. Besides, I knew I was just training for when I would be legal. By then I had already gotten my nickname despite the fact that I was not gay. It was the hand cream, which was more than a luxury by now. It was an addiction, to keep my most valuable assets smooth and operating at their highest potential. By the time I was 30, I required multiple moisturizers per day just to keep my palms from cracking.

This is also how I learned about the robots.

My discovery came while sitting in a dermatologist's office flipping through a *Popular Science* magazine. At that time, HumanPal, the brand, was the only one. They hadn't hit the market yet, but something about them caught my eye. I began researching the things and dissecting every bit of information I could find, which was not as easy to come by in those first years. Despite the company's deliberate protection of information, and at times deliberate misinformation just to bait and toss people like me, I learned how they worked and why they worked. I was one of the first to order one when they became available commercially. I was eager for a traveling companion and paid a ridiculous price just to get high on the list. But for all I knew about them, you could imagine my disappointment when my little obsession turned out to be little more than a hired servant. I guess I wanted them to be more alive than they ended up being. And within two years, they were everywhere, including in the casinos – serving you drinks, changing your money out, even acting as the casino guards. They were a reminder to me of the dissatisfaction I had felt after receiving my own. Sure, I was fashionably ahead of the crowd by having a Pal so early, but soon they were like fur coats. And then just coats.

I had no idea the HumanPals and all the humanpal knock-offs would insert themselves into every facet of life so rapidly and seamlessly. People leaned on them like seeing eye dogs. Even in the casinos.

To my advantage, I had become an expert at spotting people who were using personal humanpals as cheating mechanisms. They say the best programmers in the world worked on casino humanpals so nobody could cheat when they were around.

But I had a way.

Instead of watching the pals, you watched the people in the same way the pals would. A subtle dart of the eyes, an uncomfortable shift in the chair, even a certain sound that a gambler might direct back at his personal pal. They were all noticeable. And they were all programmed into the robot bouncers. You just had to be smarter and stay calm. If you broke a sweat, it was over. None of that is important, though. I'll tell you how I beat the house when nobody else could, but only because it doesn't matter anymore: I would play a few rounds at a few different tables to get a feel for the room. I would sometimes play a hundred meaningless hands before I would pick my spot – directly behind the most noticeable cheater in the room. The worse the person was at cheating, the better. I once sat behind the sweatiest shifty-eyed soccer dad I'd ever seen. He had probably just lost his job, desperate for a kill before he went home and told his wife. While the casino's robots centered on him, I took the house for over a hundred thousand. It was a good night.

So it was still about reading people. Find the cheater, or at least the person most likely to attract attention, and sit behind him. And of course, always keep your cool. A new level of playing the odds. In fact, my biggest invisibility cloak was that I never took my own robot in with me, so I was never closely watched. My robot sat disassembled in a storage garage outside Tunica with several of my favorite paintings and, of course, my fully restored '78 Lamborghini Countach.

Don't let anyone tell you it's easy to take apart a humanpal. If it was, we probably wouldn't have had a war.

A colleague once asked if I had a difficult time disassembling Human. He wanted to know if I felt remorse over it. You know what? He was a robot. And if I hadn't taken him apart, we probably wouldn't have won the war.

You're welcome.

President of the United States (Tourism Bureau)
Interviewed in Washington, D.C.

AS PRESIDENT of the United States (Tourism Bureau), I am certainly honored to speak about this topic. It is my hope that by doing so, we can build a better, brighter tomorrow. As John Henley once said, "We cannot look ahead without first looking around and seeing how we got here . . ." And we all know who John Henley is. Even though he was referring to his semi-frequent blackouts, I believe those words from a musicless song he wrote called "Poem," ring just as true today.

Not to be dramatic, but now, in your presence, I will remove my shoes, because in recollecting the events of our nation's – nay, our *world's* – recent history, I am standing on holy ground, and speak with great humility and gratitude! First, I want to acknowledge everyone who helped me get here. Without the hard work and dedication of certain ambassadors, a Swedish ship captain, and a handful of whoevers, I would not be here talking and inspiring you.

As with any good story, I will begin at the start of my life.

I grew up as your average girl, the daughter of a stay-at-home mom and a father who worked for thirty-five long years at Marcus and Marcus Law. My father, Marcus, was a quiet man, always choosing to let his love be known to Mother and I by being a good provider. His frequent and necessary trips to Rio de Janeiro were a good reminder that the secrets to success are hard work, commitment, and Brazillians of dollars. That was a funny phrase Dad would use.

"A little political humor," he'd say, even though it was geographical humor.

Mother was an animal lover, collecting various exotic birds from around the world. Soon, our loft was too small to hold our blossoming family, so we had to move to a more spacious accommodation outside of the city, one that provided adequate living quarters for the birds and my nanny, who years later was replaced by the three HumanPals who killed Mother.

Following in my late father's footsteps, I went into law at Boston College and moved quickly into politics, the story of which you probably already know by now. I do feel it necessary to add that my presidential ambitions were not for mere power, as my opponents and friends seem to portray. In fact, it was my steady hand and decisive leadership that helped lead our entire continent out of the robot disaster without losing a single life aside from those people we tragically lost.

Now, the pressing matter before us is, of course, how did the robot rebellion happen? Sadly, it was because of idiots, and nothing I did. HumanPal may have been making a lot of money for rich investors, but in my opinion, Main Street is more important than Wall Street, and you can quote me on that! Quote me on that.

Quote me on this, too. Oh, you're recording? Well then leave out the part where I talk about the quoting. In my plan, the American people would have had the protection of only being able to buy one pal per household or three per business with a sliding scale based on the number of employees. And since that plan never made it to Congress, because I did not have time to write it down or share it, or run for Congress, a less intrusive version of my bill was introduced, by me, to my friend Lizabeth, which would have raised taxes on each subsequent humanpal purchased, such that it would have been difficult for the average family to afford more than one. I kid you not, I was ignored entirely by the bureaucrats in Washington. Plus, Lizabeth told me that my plan was "stupid" and that I was "a gargoyle."

And so let it be on record that hindsight is twenty-twenty, and that I had the *foresight* to protect the American people from themselves before they knew they needed protecting. No, take out that last part and just say that I was protecting them from the robots instead of from themselves. That will sound better.

But lo, at that time I was relegated to expanding our economy through increased tourism, which I can assure you I took very seriously. It became my goal, while I held the office, to increase tourism two-fold. In my five-part, five-year plan, I chose to focus first on one of America's two greatest natural resources: the shining sea. Specifically, cruises! The second one is land. And it was my work in the cruise industry and the relationships I developed that led to the end of the robot disaster for everyone in America, and some non-America island countries or territories or whatever you call them.

Aaron Umbarger
Excerpt from his letters to Coldwater

THE BETTER YOU understand the robots, the better we all will be, because you have the best weapon we've heard of.

Surely you saw my cousin Jason on the news after his personal HumanPal murdered him. Jason wasn't a hero. They say he was the first victim of the robot rebellion, but that's not true. The last good memory I have of him, when things were normal, was when

Jason was running back and forth in the yard, which was mostly mud, yelling, "I got 'em!"

People on the porch cheered. One tipped over and fell on an old tricycle. My cousin stalled and caught his breath, dropped his jug, and raised both arms in triumph.

"Did you see it? That was a once in a million shot," he said. His eyes were shut.

"I saw it, you dropped your jug!" my cousin's girlfriend said, mashing two drunken thoughts together. She ran out to congratulate him, but at the last second went for the jug.

All the lights in the wrecked metal house were on, a bright little oasis in the otherwise dark woods. It was humid, and the fact that I was only slightly buzzed made me sweat considerably less than my red-faced cousin and his friends. Even at night down here, it's so freaking humid.

I wasn't sure why I even came to visit, other than the fact that this place was not home, and my parents were not here. If they only knew what Jason was really like. It's amazing, nobody in the world seems to know what Jason was really like.

My cousin's girlfriend (I couldn't remember her name since she was a new one) poured whatever we were drinking down her throat as she staggered over to the robot on the ground.

"This one's for my dead metal man," she said, pouring some liquor onto the HumanPal. "I'm showing respect! This isn't wasting it to pour it on the dead robot, right?"

"It's still moving, it ain't dead! Stand it back up!" the guy next to me yelled. The robot's arms and legs still walked while lying flat on its back.

The girlfriend put her ear down on it.

"I wonder if it has a heartbeat," she whispered. Her hand felt its way up its side. They had brought the Pal outside and set it to sweep the floor, which would be an impossible job for this robot to ever complete. So it frantically moved back and forth, stopping and starting, attempting to determine which area was dirtiest, never settling on one. It provided the perfect game of hit the target for my cousin and his friends. I couldn't bring myself to throw a rock at it, even after I was buzzed.

"What do I get for hittin' it in the eye?" my cousin reveled, pulling his girlfriend closer. Yes, he had hit it right in the eye, just like you're doing. Knocked it over.

"Me!" she said.

"Man, I already got you, I don't care!"

"Yeah you do."

"You're right," he said, French kissing her. Holding down a burp, he came up and said, "I will love you to the end of time."

I'm sorry but Jason was no martyr. It seems plausible that the robot had a motive, I get that. And this will only add fuel to that fire, knowing how Jason treated it. But I don't think it's true. The robots, they don't have emotion, so they can't exact revenge. They're just acting out corrupt programming, Rich. Remember that. Jason didn't die for some grand cause, he just died.

<hr />

Ami Otsuka
Interviewed in Vancouver, BC

MY MOTHER HAS COMMANDED me to speak in this manner.

When I am young, I am told by my mother that my father Koji is a great and respectable man, top developer for HumanPal. Before I am born, HumanPal has new appliance company. My father took over as number one developer, he realized that no small improvement toaster or vacuum to make HumanPal special. He begins now working on how to mass-produce the robot.

But for me, I am still so interested in American pop music. Or love to sing the songs of these artist and I want to join Japanese pop sensation Baku. My father, he like Shoji, so I also too like Shoji, but I surprise him that I like so much pop music. He says the household robot is supposed to be a stunt. A human-modeled biped robot to sweep, clean, and do chores for the house. The commercials would make people curious and we could become the best company in Japan, even if the robots are not a popular item, only different. He tells me these things as if they are important, but I do not understand. I am the same size, but smaller than him and so simple of comprehension.

So I ask him to let me join pop sensation, but he says he does not know how, and he does not want a daughter to become a plastic item in his house. I have a plan.

My father is talking so much about the robots. Installing software in the robot to limit it do the household task. Only making the robot to work in a human environment was so difficult.

He is now begin to ask me and mother about what we would buy. My father knew that selling a robot to clean would be easy. It is selling a robot to clean and also to keep its owner happy which was so difficult. He knows this is difficult and he says he has done testing. Special testing no one knows about. He smiles, but I do not know why.

While he is mind on this, my mother help me sneak a piano keyboard in, to my room, and I am starting to play it while he is gone testing the HumanPals.

In the first round of test homes, where the owner comes home, and wonder why the robot had not cleaned and performed chores while he was away. Then, the owner gets so annoyed if the robot would be cleaning while he was trying to watch a movie. And they expected that the robot might cook, also. The first issue for my father was how to teach the robot to use good time. This is issue for me too, he says. But he smiles when he says it.

Second issue was storage. The robots are smaller, but then they are have to hold more information and tasks, so the larger the frame grew to. The final version that went to sale is almost seven feet tall. How does my father make it smaller? He says he knows how already, to do most of these things, but the company does not want to spend and keep costs low. So HumanPal must collapse into close spaces to become five feet tall.

He is testing it in my room when he found the keyboard piano.

"What is this!" he yells.

"That is a keyboard!" I am exclaim. He is so mad now.

"Where is your mother!" I am frightened. But I show him that I can now begin to play the piano classically. And his face is so happy. Okay, because the piano is respected in this manner.

My father had been full of stress because of his owners are so impatient for the HumanPal to be ready and in budget. When the robot is put into stores, my father says he is unsatisfied because many flaws were hidden by advertising.

If you are worry about the robot working properly, no need to fear. The commercials make you not worry so much, because several years of programming have gone into the robot. If you are worry about the robot taking too much room? No need to fear, the commercials tell you of the robot design will actually give you *more* space, because you will get rid of your other cleaning and household supplies.

My mother was happy to have the robot in our home, because of the work it will do for her. But she is nervous about having too many. Some kids are come over to see because we have a first HumanPal, and they are so popular, but I do not tell them. In my room, I am making dance songs on the piano keyboard to make friends, and we are making dances to them, which is quite good for me then, and I continue to learn to play well. But my father does not want to have children over.

My father, Koji, is saying Japan was a perfect place to launch the new HumanPal Household Robot. Japanese people are rush to embrace the new technology because it is a special thing for Japan first. Other parts of the world are too, and they want convenience, and the more people who have them, the more they could trust them. This grieves me now.

The Gay Gambler
Interviewed by phone

I'VE NOTICED that adrenaline causes you to remember details better. Maybe that's why I like the high. And why I hate the mundane.

Bills were due, and I had just completed a less-than-desirable sweep of three East Coast gambling stops in Atlantic City, Cherokee, NC, and Little River, SC. I retreated to an old favorite that I mentioned before, Tunica, Mississippi, for a few day's rest and relaxation, while figuring out how to manage my losses. A person who plays "games of chance" is an idiot, but I don't play games of chance. I make quick, high-yield investments. And investing is a tricky business sometimes. I sat outside during a beautiful fall evening, enjoying a meal at a favorite restaurant of mine, when a waiting robot came along to replace my drink. I was never fond of mixed drinks made by robots. They made drinks technically, with exactly the right amount of everything in them, but something always got lost in the art of it, since every drink tasted exactly the same. Nevertheless, this subtle dissatisfaction reminded me of my own robot, stored away and out of sight for around three years at that point.

I had locked him in an old orange-doored storage garage in this very town. Or at least I thought I did. I had rented one in nearly every city in which I owned a condo, just to keep some of my fondest possessions. Orange was the most commonly used door color to rent. Some in other cities had blue doors, purple, and some red, but most of them were orange. I liked to get as many different colors as possible so I could keep track and color code by city. But as orange was the most common, it was also making me second-guess whether or not I had actually kept my robot in Tunica.

I decided, that night, to make sure that I had. It would be a good excuse to check in on some of my other belongings, and since I was in need of extra cash right now, maybe it was time to find a buyer for my car, or my robot. Probably my robot.

There was something about the eyes.

The red.

I wanted to see them again.

When I had originally gotten him, my curiosity caused me to take him apart a few times, experimenting. It was not the easiest thing to do. But I could never get past the eyes. Even when they weren't attached to his body, I would find myself staring into them. I wanted to change them – to be more expressive, to change colors, it didn't matter. They were hypnotic. The best I achieved without causing a malfunction was to make them blink. Not like our eyes. I mean the light would fluctuate. They would get bright and dull, on and off almost at random. I could never figure out a pattern, so I assumed it was a worthless endeavor. Eventually, I left him disassembled in that storage garage. And I hoped I would remember enough, even if slightly drunk, to put him back together for resale.

Like I said, I've noticed that adrenaline causes you to remember details better. Such is the case with rediscovering Human.

When I got there, nobody was in the small office by the gate. The sign in my headlights read boldly: OFFICE HOURS 9-9, CLOSED SUNDAY. USE SECURITY CODE IF ENTERING PAST HOURS. I kept a small slip of paper deep in my wallet with all my security codes for all my security gates across the country. Never keep information in your phone.

I punched a sequence into the gate keypad and drove down the silent corridor of garages, searching for the letter I had written above my code. At the end of the third and final aisle I found my C9. When I parked my car, I found myself shutting my car door quietly, maybe because a loud noise would have felt so harsh in such a quiet place. I entered another number into the keypad on the wall next to my garage door. In my left hand was a large flat box with a variety of tools, which would be necessary for reconstructing the robot.

With my right arm, I lifted the door and looked into the darkness of the garage. There, in the front where the light was making its way over the rows of storage sheds, I could make out the rear end of my '78 Lamborghini Countach, looking as good as ever, minus the gleam a few years of dust had stolen. Admiring the beauty, I reached out to wipe its bumper, if only to remember its true color. My fingers had just pressed the powder when a barely audible, slow, and deliberate creak came from the darkness of the far end of the garage. My heart immediately fell and would have stopped if the rush that followed hadn't jerked me into a flailing, backtracking defense. I thrust the toolbox out at the darkness, my face probably as white as a ghost. My heels grasped for traction as the toolbox fell open, dumping the tools on the ground, and anything I was hearing from within the garage was now completely drowned out by the loudest clanging metal on concrete I had ever heard. In an instant, I believed every horrible thing this could be. I had fallen, and grabbed for whatever I could find. If this thing came running at me, I would be as ready as I could be.

I was pointing the screwdriver in the air toward the direction from which I had heard the sound. From my back I had the wherewithal to notice that the tools had come to a rest. But I could not tell if I could hear the creak any longer, or if I was only trying to. I craned my neck up as much as possible without losing position, in case of the still very real possibility of a sudden surprise from out of the darkness. I listened carefully for anything at all. An endless wait went by, there on my back, and still nothing. Or was there nothing? Did I even hear anything in the first place? Logic began to rush back at me, but the adrenaline wouldn't let me put the screwdriver down, or get my legs under me with much ease. I pushed myself up with one hand, still holding my "weapon" out, which I noticed I was not holding correctly, but rather, had been pointing the thing backwards as if I could beat an enemy to death with the handle. I swirled it properly in my hand, gathering my legs beneath me, still trying to be as silent as possible, to hear what may be in the dark. And so I crouched. And continued to crouch. Taking my eyes off the spot in the darkness for only a moment, to grab a more formidable weapon. There was none better than the screwdriver. I looked back quickly and began to stand, still hearing nothing. But I couldn't shake the feeling.

That feeling, still the most real at the moment, began to give way to the possibility that I was standing there in a parking lot, holding a tool out like a sword, staring into an empty storage stall. I did not break my gaze, but I began to have the urge to look around for security cameras, and maybe to wave at one just in case this threat was only in my head. My body even began to relax a little right before I did absolutely hear the noise start and stop again, causing me to walk a calculated line backward, putting the car I had arrived in between me and the garage.

No strategy came to me for a minute or so, until I had the thought to get in the car. Then, at last, I would have a more solid barrier between myself and "it." So as quickly as I had the thought, I had also slammed the door and locked myself inside. I remained there for another moment, gathering myself again, and never breaking gaze with the spot in the garage. The spot which had now produced the same terrible noise twice.

I reached into my front pocket and found my keys, slowly but impatiently forcing them into the ignition. As I did, my headlights illuminated everything in front of me. My eyes adjusting to the terrible brightness as fast as I could make them, I peered into the garage. And there, I saw my disassembled robot standing. Assembled. Waiting.

I opened my door again – I don't know why – and tried to get a better look.

"What are . . ." I stammered. "Why are you all put together?" I didn't expect an answer, as much as I was trying to calm myself and think out loud.

"Do you know who I am?" Again the machine stood still, as did I. I ran my hand through my hair, and for the first time, looked at the rest of the garage. It was, much as I remembered, mostly filled with my very fine luxury car, the edges packed with some paintings and memorabilia to the left, and at the far right, my robot, staring me down as much as I did him. Then a new idea occurred to me.

"Sweep," I said.

The HumanPal immediately began doing just that, and in only moments, had gone over the entire garage. It completed the task so quickly that I assumed it had already done this many times before now.

The danger I felt seemed to fade, but did not entirely disappear, as I began to make my way closer. "Who put you back together? How did you reassemble?" I said aloud, again expecting no answer. But it had to be asked. I was no longer afraid of the robot so much as I was afraid of that very question.

The headlights still beaming into the stall, I kicked away the tools, which lay at the edge of the door, and looked around the HumanPal's feet. Nuts and bolts and parts of itself littered about the area. Why it did not clean those particular pieces of rubbish, I did not know. Moving closer, but still not entering the garage for concern of a yet unknown danger, I got a better look at my robot and saw many scratches and bends and holes I did not remember seeing when I had originally assembled and disassembled him.

I stepped away and bent down to pick up a set of pliers. The robot turned slightly to reposition itself to face me directly, and as he did, I heard the same creak as before. I stood for a second before bending down again and throwing open the toolbox.

"Put these tools back in the box," I said, still hanging onto the pliers. The robot did exactly as told. He moved forward, grabbing and placing every tool into its proper slot within the box, all except the pliers. Instead of reaching out his hand for the last remaining tool as I expected him to, he repositioned himself to face me again in his new location.

I looked at him now for the first time with no fear, and set the pliers down on the bumper where I had begun to wipe the dust before.

I examined him again closer in the bright light, and said aloud, "Stay still."

At this, he ceased to turn as I walked around him. I took almost one full rotation before stopping and seeing a piece of sheet metal that looked like his brand plate, now just above the right arm. The name was etched into it, HumanPal. But on this darker side facing away from the headlights, it looked as if the second half of the word had been carefully scratched off, now reading, "Human."

Alf Johnson
Interviewed in Tampa, FL

YOU KNOW how when you grab a fish and you look it right on straight ahead? And it looks like its eyes are way far apart? I always thought the robots looked like that but from the side.

I will tell you right now that I know a lot about fish and that is because I've got a boat. It's not a big deal to me like it is to some people. I am such a real easygoing kind of guy. You know that song "Relax" by Frankly Hollywood? That's like I am. You know how when a company owns its own semi-trucks to transport things, but a lot of times, they just don't have enough trucks? That's pretty much like I am. I'm the extra truck that catches fish. I don't always know where they go, but one time, and I am not flipping your coot here, I went out to eat at a seafood restaurant. Maybe it's something you already knew, but there is a pretty good seafood place down here I go to called Red Lobster. So I ordered a shrimp skewer. I think I ordered all you can eat shrimp actually because it was Shrimpfest, but on the skewer I saw something. . . I saw this one with a little extra fin piece of meat sticking out the side in a P shape. Now flashback to twelve years ago. I am pulling up a net and there is a little shrimp on the edge acting like he is going to jump. Out of instinct, I yell "Don't do it!" But secretly I don't care if he does it. "You have your whole life ahead of you!" Again, I am just going through the motions here. I am looking him right in the eyes, and in my memory he looks like a robot and on the side, a little P shaped wing. I kid you not. True story. I think it might have been him. I was laughing out loud when I dipped him in shrimp sauce and started chomping on him, making chomp noises – some parts were falling out cause I was smiling so big.

Let me think about this. Now that you bring it up, the robot is a tricky creature, you see. I never bought one or brought one on my fish boat AT ALL, but I did bring a Nintendo on. I never cared too much for the robot. What was it good for? It didn't do nothing. Nothing for a boat. So I never bought one. I spent nine months out on the ocean every year, and when I was back on the shore, somebody said, "Hey Alf, you gonna get a robot for your boat?"

And I stopped and looked upward like I was a pondering man, and I said, "Whyyyyy?" real long like that. And I pretended like I was smoking something. I think everybody in there started thinking real hard about their lives, and maybe the roles of robots in society or they were worried about my smoking habits.

You know what was weird? I seen people starting to get those things and everybody is kind of interested in them. Then I go back out, back out on my boat, for like two months. And then I go back to shore full on a good load, I'm going to drop it off, and guess who goes to get the load for me? A robot! I was like, "Get your robot hands off my fish!" and I demanded to see the owner here. He comes out and tells me the robot will take my fish. And I say, "Okay!"

And the robot, he will take your fish, but he doesn't love the fish and treat them tenderly. A good dock boy, he loves the fish, like I do, even though I catch them and sell them for money, and then they are eaten. In the old days, a man killed and cleaned the fish, and he did it with love maybe. Now, a robot cleans the fish, and what do you think about that?

I have a real easygoing spirit about me though, so I didn't care. That's probably how I helped stop the robot war. I am just like, "Whatever!" I am the most easygoing person. I am just like, whatever, but hey if you cross me or one of my friends, you got somebody to mess with. I am fierce and loyal. But the robots, I was just like whatever. Things happen, and then something else happens, and then another thing, and that's why I fish on this boat, and stop a war, and then fish. I will mess you up though if I have to, like if you're a fancy person. But I am just real easygoing though and that's why if you look at my heart you would see a little me in there just shrugging probably. Just shrugging like "whatever." And you would be like, "Whatever, there's just a little Alf guy in there."

———

Pastor Rich
Interviewed in Coldwater, MS

IF KOJI OTSUKA had designed the robots to cry, would we have treated them better? I don't know. I wonder what went through that guy's head. I don't want to jump on the bandwagon though, he's well-hated enough.

A man I mentioned before, named Stephen Daine, had been our part-time janitor for almost as long as I had been the pastor of the church. At first, it was his job to keep the robot well maintained. This was a job I thought would be very important, since we had gotten ours used. It had pieces in places I had never seen on a robot. And I had watched robots plenty. But eventually, I decided that the man I bought it from must have been a mechanical genius, because Steve almost never had to repair it. There were aspects of our Pal that Steve couldn't understand, but he chose to leave well enough alone for fear that he would not be able to restore it again.

"We're blessed to have it, so I'm not touching it."

It had to drive him crazy too, because he was repairing the old models all the time for his other clients. Look, I'll be honest with you, there are times when I pray my rear-end off, and God doesn't give me hide nor hair. Like He's decided to listen instead of respond. It's frustrating. That's what it was like for Steve right around that time.

Steve talked about how scary it was when the robots hit the market and looked like they were going to force him into retirement earlier than he would be able to afford. He didn't understand why God would do this to him. He had worked his whole life and now could barely keep his house.

I arranged a special offering for this man who had faithfully served for over two decades. We took in several hundred dollars, and everybody was feeling pretty good about it. That kind of stuff makes you feel good, you know. At the end of the service, people came and shook my hand as usual, but today they shook Steve's hand too, and he thanked them, each one. And they thanked him right back. Normally, nobody saw him, because he sat up in the balcony at the light board, but I made him come down front. That day when he left for lunch, caught up in the surprise of the whole thing, he forgot to turn off the service lights, so I walked up to the balcony myself, the last one in the church. From where I was on the floor I couldn't see it, but once I went up the stairs, there was the robot, standing just outside the storage closet. It repositioned itself to face me.

"What are you doing out here?" I was being naïve. As if it would answer. "Did Steve get you out?"

No, I thought. It doesn't do that. Plus, he was on the main level for most of the morning.

Did somebody else go up there?

No, I would have seen them from the platform. I had it go back into the storage closet. When I returned that evening for Sunday night service, Steve was there a little early to set up the lights.

"I completely forgot to turn the lights out this morning, sorry about that."

I told him about the humanpal up in the balcony, out of its closet. He said he hadn't let it out.

"But I'll check on it when I go up there and make sure the door didn't swing open or something. If it did, maybe it heard something it thought was a command and came out."

But it wasn't doing anything. It wasn't sweeping, cleaning, organizing. It was just standing there.

That night when I got up to preach, I glanced up at Steve a couple times. He looked back as if he had something to say. Finally, as I asked everyone to pray, he must have pointed subtly at the closet, which is just out of my view from the platform. The robot had come out again.

"It wasn't out earlier, and I know the door was closed. But

sometime probably around when you started preaching, I looked back and there it was," he said later, acting excited at the thing.

Over the next few weeks, Steve would turn the lights on, and first thing, check the storage closet to make sure the robot was in there, and then shut the door securely. Then, when the music and hymns would end, he would turn and watch, as it would come out of the closet and stand on the back row for the duration of my sermon. It became a joke among the congregation that my messages were either so boring that only robots were interested in them, or so inspired that they even brought robots to life, depending on the week. It got to the point that when I would begin speaking, half of the people would turn around and look up at the balcony. The other half wanted to, but probably thought it was rude. Eventually I became slightly annoyed by the sideshow, and considered having Steve lock the door. But then there was that compassion again. Plus, would locking it do anything? What kind of machine listens to sermons? I wasn't willing to say it was listening yet. There had to be an answer to this that was much simpler. Its automatic programming was damaged, or my microphone was emitting a frequency that messed with it. Or something. I fought with myself. How could a machine "want" anything? It had been repaired in such a strange fashion, and that did nothing to quell my curiosity. Why had it never done this before? Why now? It was a robot. It couldn't *desire* anything on an emotional level. Unless it was alive.

I used to know what life was, and what life wasn't. I don't know anymore. If Human was alive, even in some small way, we should put the robots on trial for mass murder.

TWO
SUSPICIOUS BEHAVIOR

Aaron Umbarger

Excerpt from his letters to Coldwater

Jason's death is my fault. Or at least I could have stopped it. Since you're a pastor, I guess I can confess my shortcomings.

So I am not from Tupelo, or anywhere around here, but as I mentioned, I've spent a good chunk of time down here at my cousin's every summer. I've loved staying up all night and sleeping the whole day. I've loved meeting the craziest people in the world and going to their houses. More than anything, I loved the fact that my cousin never seemed to think about tomorrow. It's a comfort I was never willing to afford myself. That might be why I'm still alive.

But I hadn't been as enthusiastic about meeting these weirdos my cousin hung out with anymore. This summer I'd been feeling a gross superiority toward them, and that ruins the fun.

You probably saw Jason's trailer on the news. Well, half trailer/half house built onto the end. Jason mainly used the trailer part, so I slept in the house part because it was the cleanest. The irony, of course, is that Jason had a HumanPal, whose sole purpose was *to clean*. But it only came out for humiliation. I always wanted to ask him why he didn't use it, since a simple command would renovate the place, but I already knew the answer. He didn't care.

On the day Jason became a martyr, he had simply gone off. To where, I didn't know, but apparently he was checking out somebody's new paintball gun. Meanwhile I decided to get the robot out and begin a clean-up project. Even getting it out was no small endeavor. It was buried.

I started by finding places for all the things that weren't garbage, like shoes and clothes that he had probably forgotten about, old CDs and their respective cases, and for some reason a bunch of deflated pool toys, even though Jason didn't have a pool.

The path to the robot's closet was nearly complete when my cousin's newest girlfriend came in and lay face down on the kitchen floor.

"Hey Aaron, where's Jason," she said to the tile. I watched the strange display and wondered again where Jason had gone.

"I thought he was with you," I told her.

She continued lying there.

"I haven't seen him all day. I don't know," I said, turning back toward my job.

"Well, then I guess we're alone in here?" she said, and sat up again. I kicked away the things in front of the closet door, trying to get the robot out. I guess I was hoping for a third party in the room.

She leaned her head against the kitchen table leg. I opened the closet door at last and told the Pal simply to "clean!" It immediately switched on and started to clean the filthy carpet near it, moving in short, fast circles.

"I haven't been to bed yet, dude. Can you help me get to Jason's room?" she said, sloppy. I struggled for a decision. Would Jason get mad if I let his girlfriend pass out on the floor? Or what if he came in while I was in his bedroom with her? And what was she trying to do? I had a good idea.

"Pal, put her to bed!" I said.

The robot zoomed forward through the path I had cleared into the kitchen where she sat slumped and confused.

"No, you do it." She looked at me. Then she gazed into the robot's remaining red glass eye as it came for her. "I forgot about this thing!" She laughed hard until she coughed, then suddenly became enamored with the fact that her hand was in a Ziploc bag. The robot leaned down and threw her over its shoulder. It then whizzed forward en route to Jason's bedroom. I thought for a moment that it almost seemed agitated, dodging sharply in and out of the junk. And that's when I heard the noise of bone breaking.

SNAP!

Followed by "AHHHHH!"

Her leg was in a terrible twisted direction at the knee. The mere sight of it made me flush. The robot stopped violently, and her head banged against its big metal back, presumably knocking her out again.

The screaming stopped. The robot stopped. I knew I had to get her down, but this was the first time I had ever been nervous around a robot. I was uneasy about the machine! Do you see what I'm saying? It couldn't make decisions, it couldn't harbor resentment or consider motives or have any opinions about us. I knew I had to get this injured girl down, but I didn't want to go near the machine because I was afraid of it.

It stood silent, staring away from me at nothing. If it were a man, it would have been waiting. But it wasn't, I kept telling myself, approach it. Get her down! This time I was not so wary about grabbing her. But I was scared and ignorant enough to do it all from behind. The robot never saw me. Never thought about me. No, never *processed* me. They don't think.

Although I don't always think, either. I was running on

impulse at the time, struggling to carry my cousin's unconscious girlfriend out to her car, and Jason walked up with an entirely blank expression.

"Hey what's that thing doing out!" he said. "What are you doing?"

Before I could speak, "Whoa hey, what's wrong with her head?"

The spot that slammed the back of the robot was turning red and black.

"Are you putting her in my car?" he said.

"Yeah, she's bad. I was...I got the robot out...her leg is broken I think, too. The robot was putting her to bed..."

"Where did you put all my CDs!?!" he interrupted, furiously flinging open the screen door.

"They're all in the...room... open the back door will you?" I said. I set her as carefully as I could in the back seat. "We need to try to keep her awake if she has a concussion." I knew I had heard that somewhere. Jason, however, was walking back toward the house with his fists packed.

"Where are you going?" I asked.

"Here. Take her into town. I got some business I need to attend to in my home, cousin." Jason gave me a key, unbuttoned his over shirt and tread into the house.

I felt it more responsible to take care of this girl than to ask what he was going to do in there. And so we began the half-hour drive into town.

Ami Otsuka
Interviewed in Vancouver, BC

THERE IS no point for my father to perfect the HumanPal. He is so constantly displeased with his work for his company, and he always ask for more time and testing. I am not interested in Japanese sensation Baka now, because the music is not cool for me. There is a boy who sings, who is Kai Fukada.

He is to find himself closer to being satisfied, but not completely. So he tell me about it when he teaches me to play golf. It is easy to make corrections when I score one-hundred. But when I score close to par, is so difficult to eliminate error. I am not responsive of this, when I never learn to play golf still.

My father is approaching point of acceptable release for HumanPal, this he believes.

But now I know he is not perfect. No one is perfect. Not my mother, and not me. I am still simple, but wanting to have talents like other kids, but my father is so strict. Now, today, I wish he is not Koji Otsuka, the word of shame. Otsuka is also my given name. I do not want people to be afraid of me. I am not and also my mother change our name of Otsuka, and so people have attempted to say to change it. They say bad things about me. She will not, because of honor. I am have to consider my father, he is so smart and he is famous, and still we are worried for people to approach us. They hate me. I consider my father is full of regret. And yes he is full of regret, and but I do not consider he would say the robots are of evil. He would say yes today even to still make them. But to greater testing greater detail, this time. They say they are for sale and he is not ready. He says he is not ready, to me.

I am like Kai Fukada at this time. Kai Fukada pictures are in a book and a poster. He is music for a while, but I am liking him because of he is so cute. I am many other music, so much cool too, and learning to like boys. No longer Kai Fukada. He is on my toothbrush.

So not good, each one individualized for labor is selling faster than my father is create. He says I am to say nothing to anyone. To remain competition my father has to stay of new jobs robots can do. Heavy-lifting HumanPals for packing up, unpacking merchandise. For many airplane company, they are for bags and suitcase. HumanPal Fireman can enter the dangerous burning building to save life. And can even hold building up, too. And then so people can get out. A one for . . . hostages and for crime. A criminal can shoot the robot and nothing happens. In the grocery store, I am with my father. A robot collect grocery carts, and there is a robot to clean.

Every person must not work so hard now. This is for a better life, for all poor. My father says he will see no poor continue. HumanPal is making food everywhere, and all person can eat.

He is changing now. My father likes me to play keyboard, and he would buy a piano and golf clubs. He likes me to learn many things now, but I do not want to play songs. They are so he can say "so beautiful." To walk circle over myself when I am playing, he walks, and talks to me about HumanPal, and he is thinking. To stop problems in the robots.

A HumanPal is made to drive trucks and to drive a taxi. But the program is not a great amazing program, the robot cannot make so many decisions. They are crashing, so HumanPal does never sell this one.

There is some HumanPal robots, and are to work around water. And these are so tight and so very much closed. Only so tiny water pieces are get inside of them. Too many problems. They are working slow, and they also cannot make so many decision. They are problem but it is still sold. These problem are not all tested, for years and years. My father says water is difficult and take this so great time. But these are problems that are nothing. My father is not aware of the major problem. He is never able to find a virus or one that can copy in exposure. The tiny pieces of water are entering them on the coasts. My father Koji Otsuka, the word of shame, is not stopping it.

The Gay Gambler
Interviewed by phone

I THINK one of the things I miss most is coming into a city knowing that you own it in some small way. I was never one to stay long, so creating relationships was difficult, but that's the way I preferred things. Mostly because it was so time-consuming, I would keep a cache of my most valuable possessions in each city. If I hit it often enough, I might even buy a place there.

I have often thought about this: does everyone in the world get to a certain age, and then look back at a time in his or her life and say, "That was the greatest, and I will never have that again?" Or do some people genuinely continue to elevate their level of happiness? More so, is it possible, during that high moment, to know that it is, indeed, the greatest of your life? Or does simply knowing that you're at your peak make it hopeless for what's ahead? I know that for me, there was an overwhelming sense in my heart that what lay before me would not be as enjoyable as what was behind. And I think it shook me in my bones, such that I actually savored every moment of my life at this time like the last sip of a fine wine. Impending doom, even if ambiguous, can do strange things.

Even so, I began realizing that my life, which I had championed as being so different from everyone else's, was actually developing a pattern of its own. I had my favorite hotels, my favorite restaurants, my favorite bars, my favorite dry cleaners . . . anything that you could prefer, I had a favorite. I had devolved into a creature of comfort! This revelation was coming into focus over the few months when a new round of specially programmed anti-card-counting humanpals were being deployed into the casinos. Were these beasts more difficult to beat? Yes, indeed they were. But I could still do it. My decline was less about the improved robots, and more about my own overindulgent lifestyle, I can say now. I think I knew it then, too. But I still resisted changing.

Patterns are important. So terribly important. To this day I do not understand how people live their lives without counting the tiles on the floor, or trying to predict which raindrops will meet as they slide down the side of a window.

Finding patterns and making predictions leads to winning. I'm not trying to convince you, it's just a fact. And if I hadn't been so naturally inclined to it, and trained by practice, today's world would be a much different place. We'd probably be scavenging for food instead of telling pretentious stories.

Over time, gamblers had generally stopped bringing their humanpals in with them. It seemed like the initial wave of robot saturation had died off, and the pals fell into their actual role in society instead of being a novelty. I mean, they were still everywhere of course, but there was a noticeable decline of reliance on them as time went by, at least as a status symbol. Or maybe it was just my observation within the casino walls. I should consider that.

They were becoming very smart. The old, crisscross scan patterns of the four cornered robots were obsolete. Additionally, the new anti-cheat programming was always implemented first on the blackjack tables. I guess they knew they were still being beaten. So their new strategy in cheat analysis was to be perpetually random, so you never knew *what* they were looking for, *where* they were looking, or *why* they had positioned themselves in a certain way within a room.

For all of their updates, I still had a few failsafe mechanisms up my sleeve.

For instance, even though they would scan a room randomly, constantly, I believed that I could put myself in the right spot and only be scanned by one or two of them at a time instead of all four. And I knew that no matter what, I could still spot a cheat quicker than they could. I could smell it, and pounce on it like a wolf, while the robots would have to analyze and interpret before making any rash assumptions, mostly for legal reasons. This still allowed me to piggyback on other cheat, and wait to go in for a huge killing when I knew the robots were about to go in for theirs.

My biggest danger now was being a repeat offender, because these things were devils at facial recognition once you had raked their casino once or twice. Which didn't mean they would instantly seize upon you, but it meant that no matter where you positioned yourself, you were the focal point. My key was always to watch the positioning of the robots in a room; if I sat down at a table, and they repositioned themselves to have me within all four scans, then I knew my time was short. If I still wasn't sure, I might change tables and see if they did it again. If so, I was out the door. The worst thing possible was to get caught even once, because if a man like me finds himself on a blacklist, he must be reborn into a new career. And a new life.

One thing's for sure: the robots were getting smarter right before the rebellion happened, and their roles in our lives were changing. Are the two things linked? It's hard to say. The camps are divided, but I think I've made up my mind.

Roland Wright
Interviewed in Three Rivers Correctional Center

WHEN THOSE JAPANESE models first appeared, you know, they were watching us. They were gathering INFORMATION on us. People say they can't think. WRONG. They think, they know. They think they know. But I know, too. And I knew, too. And I watched them watching people. Huey had been planning this destruction from the time he was born. So when it happened, I wanted to laugh. Except I couldn't. Sure I tried laughing, but then there was all that murdering. I'm not going to laugh at that crap. And I'll NEVER laugh at Huey. Laughing's for people, not for Hueys.

I wouldn't laugh at the murdered people, even though they laughed at me. They didn't care about their own lives. They didn't care about their impact on mankind, they didn't care about the complex change of TIME. It was a new TIME. They just sat and watched their guts grow and their minds cool, man. The WHOLE WORLD was blowing it. I was sounding the alarm! We had accomplished our finest creation, but the babies, man, the babies were about to eat their parents. What does that even mean? It's all crazy, man. I'm telling you.

The robots, they knew exactly what they were doing. Don't let anybody tell you different.

A new path of destiny was carved out for us. That's what they wanted you to believe. But I didn't buy a gram of it. Not a gram. Hey, buy-one-get-one gram! You can keep it, Huey. You and your robot-run media. Telegram from robot-media, will you accept the charges? What do YOU think, do I look like I accept the charges?

I don't care about being an outsider. Since I get my kicks on that fringe out there. Huey was born with a mission and so was I. Destroy Huey. And if you didn't want to, well then you can get on the train to nowhere and just ride and ride, because it doesn't stop, because it's the train to NOWHERE, and that's where I live. I sold most of my possessions and moved to the most self-sufficient seclusion I could find. I was out on the farm. I had a farm house that was built in the 1950s with a bomb shelter and a coop. Not that a bomb shelter could stop a HumanPal. Or a coop could stand a bomb. A chicken might live through a gunshot, though.

I got all the MREs I could get my hands on. Meals ready to eat. Surviving the apocalypse. But they instantly became more expensive once the humanpals came out. Ammunition too. Huey doesn't want a well-armed population, man. Even though Huey is mostly bulletproof. Which is EXACTLY why I sleep with a .357 Revolver under my pillow.

How alone I felt. But I wasn't the only one afraid of the robots. There were lots of us out there on the fringe, I think. And that's the way we liked it, you know? It's like an army, man. But we needed to get organized. I believed the average guy, he would know something was up. He would know down in his heart that Huey's heart was bent on evil. If Huey had a heart. Hearts are for people. I believed it, and I was wrong. Some people don't have hearts, keeping me in here. Well, that was the last lie I ever believed. Once I got a peek at their master plan, I was the one. I was the one to stop the rebellion because I was READY.

Listen to me: don't believe ANYTHING they tell you.

Aaron Umbarger

Excerpt from his letters to Coldwater

THE GOOD THING about small towns is that there is basically no wait to get into an emergency room, and they've got your chart already. The bad thing is that the "hospital" was not much bigger than a bed and breakfast. They took her to a room and told me that friends and family were encouraged to stay with the patient. And it got me a little hung up, since I was neither, and still couldn't remember her name.

I had been doing my best to keep her awake while driving, and it worked to a certain extent. But she definitely was not "with it."

Thus, I had to make some important decisions for this girl I barely knew. Like, had she ever had a concussion before? Images of her hitting her head against the table leg just prior to the accident came to mind. "Yes," I stated, presumptively. The smell of alcohol lingered.

"So I'm assuming this accident happened while drinking?" the doctor said.

"Well, sort of," I said. "No, not really actually. I don't know."

My calm, confident demeanor was cracking. He only asked one more question.

"Is this a result of any sort of domestic violence?" he asked plainly.

"No! Well...no, it's not." It did happen in the home, but he would never believe a robot would be capable of hurting someone in this way. Or would he? It was just an accident. Involving a robot. It had to be common. But I hadn't heard of it. No, I'm telling you that machine could not have done this on purpose. Absolutely not. And at the time, I immediately regretted my hesitation, because the doctor then wrote something on a slip and handed it to the nurse, who walked out of the room.

"Alright," he asserted, placing his clipboard next to the sink. "We'll have to make sure she stays awake, because I'm going to set her knee. It is going to be very painful, but I need her to be awake so that she can tell me if the pain lingers. So I know whether it was set correctly."

"Won't the pain wake her up anyway?"

"Yes, but I need you to make sure she's as cognizant as possible beforehand."

I started talking to her, trying hard to say things that didn't involve me using her name. I even resorted to calling her "honey," even though it was slightly uncomfortable. She was responsive, but not enough. The nurse came in and began brushing her hair, and pouring a small amount of ice water into her mouth.

"We need you to wake up, Candace," the nurse said.

Yes! Candace! "We need you to wake up, Candace!" I beamed. The doctor, meanwhile, handed me a rubbery plastic mouth guard.

"She may not be much more awake than this. When I make the call, I want you to put that in her mouth so that when I set her knee, she doesn't bite through her cheek or tongue, okay?"

"Yeah, okay," I said, looking at the large plastic thing, slightly horrified.

The nurse continued to hold her head up, and then yelled, "Candace!" Her eyes opened slightly larger than they had in a while and without warning the doctor proclaimed "now!"

I jammed in the mouth guard and heard a "POP." Candace flew forward in her chair, knocking the ice water out of the nurse's hand all over the doctor. Tears instantly streamed down her face, and muted obscenities flowed into the mouth guard. She slammed her head back into the reclined seat, trying to find solace by passing out again, but without success. She then stared right into me, as if she were surprised to see her boyfriend's cousin as the only recognizable face in the room. The nurse ushered me out and asked me to wait with her while the doctor finished.

I stood there, thinking for the first time about Jason's absence, which, also for the first time, angered me. I assumed he had gone back into the house to fight the robot, but I really did not know. I also had no idea what this whole ordeal was going to mean for an otherwise typical summer here.

As I stood there with the nurse pondering these things, two policemen walked up the hallway and stood in front of me.

"Son, we're going to ask you to come with us right now," one of the officers said. I hesitantly began walking with them when the reality of the situation caught up with me.

"Why?"

"There are some things we need to take a look at, and some people we need to talk to. First things first, we're going to ask you to refrain from contact with your girlfriend for seven days, okay? We'll be reevaluating everything after that, and if you check out, then you don't have anything to worry about."

I was being escorted to the police car.

"Whoa, I think you're misunderstanding this. Candace isn't my girlfriend, and I didn't touch her. I mean, I put her in the car but I didn't hurt her."

"That's okay, we'll find all of this out. Where are you staying? The information we have on you says you live in Indiana. Do you live down here now?"

"No, I just came down here for the summer to stay with my cousin Jason. She's his girlfriend."

I gave them Jason's address and looked back at his car as we pulled out of the parking lot.

"Is Jason there now? Is Jason's last name Umbarger as well?"

"Yeah. What about my car? I mean, Jason's car?" I said. The officer closer to my age in the passenger seat flipped through some papers.

"That car is registered to Candace Meyer, sir," the younger officer said. I thought it strange that Jason had given me a key. I also wondered what must be going through her head right now, inside that hospital room. How she got there, and how much time had gone by.

"Will Jason confirm that Ms. Meyer is his girlfriend?" the older officer asked.

"Yes, he'll confirm everything I just told you."

"Listen, when we get there, you should not say a word until

we're done talking to your cousin. Even if he says something you find to be untrue, do not interject until we're done with our questions. Understand? You will be given an opportunity to clarify anything you disagree with, should you disagree."

I nodded. Along the ride back to Jason's, little more was said. I nervously bounced my leg up and down for the duration of the trip. I was not concerned about Jason and the interrogation that was about to take place. My anxiety had to be born of the intimidation anyone must feel during his or her first trip in a police car.

The officers left the car casually when we arrived at Jason's. They walked me up the small patio and knocked on the door, and it creaked open on its own. The officers apparently took this as a cautious welcome to enter, and the older one stepped inside first. As his eyes adjusted to the light, he angled his body in a peculiar fashion, reaching very slowly for his holster. The younger officer and I froze, still not able to see into the dark house. Suddenly I heard the sound of glass being crunched from within. The older officer pulled his gun with one quick motion and pointed it at whatever was in front of him. The officer next to me yanked his out similarly, shielding his eyes from the sun, still gazing mystified into the dark doorway. The elder stepped bit by bit sideways into the house, motioning for the other to proceed quietly and slowly. He pointed his gun at the floor, and the younger did the same.

I stood off to the side burning to see what was taking place barely in front of me. I examined the younger officer's face as he beheld the scene. His look changed steadily, drastically, from heightened awareness to terrible anxiety, his gun still pointed at the ground, his arms quivering like saw blades.

They appeared completely off-guard and unable to comprehend what they were seeing.

They also seemed unsure of what to do next. Until the elder officer spoke.

"Your new command...is to clean the table."

Shielding my eyes, I leaned my body into the doorway, beginning to make out the shapes of motionless, quiet figures.

"Deny your former command. Clean the table."

I leaned in further, attempting to get out of the sunlight and saw against the pale backdrop the outline of the robot standing in the kitchen. Why he was still not taking the command, I could not understand.

The elder officer began to raise his gun again. As he did, I glanced down at his feet and recognized my cousin's tattooed arm lying detached before him.

"This is your last chance to Clean The Table. Mop The Kitchen. Vacuum," he said, pausing each time. The robot remained perfectly still.

From in the house, way back near the kitchen, I froze at the sound of someone suddenly yelling, "SHOOT IT! SHOOT IT!!!!" in a wretched gush. It sounded like Jason but was a much more frantic cry than I had ever heard from him.

My eyes adjusted to the darkness quickly now. I could see Jason inside, facing the door, a desperate look on his face. Like a man who had given up. In all the time I ever spent with him, I had never seen that look. My cousin didn't have much, but one thing he always had was an ignorant, sweet optimism and a never-say-die attitude. None of that was there when I saw him that day. The HumanPal clutched him; controlled him. It was painted red from the wounds it had already inflicted on him. But that look still haunts me. It was a man who was about to die without any pride left. I think in the last moment of his life, Jason had come to some sort of realization. It may have been something important about the way he had lived his life or it may have been as simple as accepting he had finally lost. The robot took the one thing nobody could ever take from him. I ponder that moment. Maybe that's what Jason was doing too.

The officers saw what I saw and opened fire. I crouched down just inside the door, instantaneously looking up from Jason to the expressionless air of the robot. Gently, deliberately, it placed its palm on the top of Jason's head and turned, slowly, slowly, until Jason's neck finally popped. My cousin didn't make a sound. He simply fell forward onto his own floor.

They stopped shooting, but the sounds rattled on and on around the tin shack. The officers held still, keeping their gunpoint right on the murderer. They were aghast. I couldn't yet process what had happened. I am ashamed to admit that my first thought was not for the life of my cousin, but for my own. There was an unstoppable murderer in front of me and thankfully, two officers between us. Not that the officers provided protection, but the robot would have to kill two more people before it killed me. That's where my mind was. But it neither killed nor harmed anyone else. The policemen seemed to keep their wits much better than I did.

"Get him out of here," the elder officer said to the younger one.

The robot dropped Jason. The younger officer impulsively grabbed me by the shirt and pushed me outside. That was the end of it. The media came.

Alf Johnson
Interviewed in Tampa, FL

SOME FOLKS WILL NAME their seaboat *The Fancy Lady*. I didn't do any of that.

You are probably sitting there right now thinking about how I wonder why he never named it *The Fancy Lady*? But I did name it. I named it about 45 times. Here's a list of things I named her:

1. Ross

2. Rachel
3. True Dat
4. Ariel
5. Frostboatin'
6. Cornpipin'
7. Paul Rudd
8. Opee
9. The Angel and the Smell
10. Pride and Prejudice (The Movie)
11. Old Boat
12. Darn Tootin'
13. Feline Smasher
14. Darius Rucker
15. Tapes
16. HGTV

And most importantly:

1. The Fornicatin' Lilly

Those are the 45 names I came up with, but none of them stuck for all kinds of reasons, so I just threw my hands up one day and looked at the sky, and I said, "I give up, clouds!"

I had a crew that kind of came and went when I needed them or when they needed something to do. One of my hired hands was named Lilly. Number 17 was named after her. She didn't like it, but everyone else did, so I should've taken a vote. It probably would have stayed. Number 9 was hers too.

This one black guy that helped me out sometimes didn't like the name Darius Rucker 'cause he thought I was calling it that 'cause he's black (and I was). It wasn't supposed to be an insult 'cause I like that band, but after he got mad I acted like I didn't realize there was a connection there.

There was one time I remember so well. Me and another guy and Lilly were coming in hauling what I would consider a good load, I don't know. We park old *Crud Packer* (the boat wasn't called that but I don't say those words now 'cause I changed). Anyway we park *Fudgy* up real tight and then I start hooting and hollering, waving my arms around. Finally I got the attention of a docking robot and it comes spinning over to me whizzing and jerking and acting like a complete jackhole.

"You calm down, you lunatic," I said, jumping out onto the dock and hitting him with a newspaper. "I'm not provoking you!"

After he finally stood still, I told Lilly to move the net over the bin the robot had wheeled over. When she swung it around, a bunch of water got all over me and the robot. I held my arms out and shook like a dog. The robot kept repositioning itself to me and other things that weren't even alive, like posts and fish.

"I thought I told you to make sure them fish were dry!" I said to Lilly.

"I did, but they had water in their mouths!" Lilly said.

And so I guess the fish all opened their mouths at the same time when she swung the net over? That's retar- I mean, that's the R word.

Then the robot pulls away and starts grabbing all these instruments that don't have something to do with sea boating or nothing. His eyes were all dull and he was acting *crazy*, like Dennis the Menace.

I said, "Just push the bin out of here and get me my money Robot Dennis the Menace!"

I think the owner heard me because he come out and said, "Is there a problem?" And I said "No!" He kind of eyed me up and then looked in the bin at the fish and kind of eyed them up. Then he stepped up and grabbed the docking robot by the shoulders and eyed him up, too, to make sure everything was okay I guess. When he handed me my money, I leaned over and whispered to him,

"Sir, that robot of yours is going to be a little blonde problem for you and this whole neighborhood!" Like Dennis the Menace was to that area.

He walked away and I swatted the robot with my newspaper again.

"Get to pushin'!" I said laughing to Lilly and that other guy who wasn't with us long. The robot scrolled through a bunch of tools and then came at me with some dental floss or fishing line or something, I don't know.

"Hey, what the heck!" I yelled. All of a sudden I was on my back being choked to death and Lilly and that other guy are laughing their heads off. Then I heard Lilly say, "Hey, I don't think robots are supposed to do that!" but she was still just sitting there. And then I don't remember much.

I woke up and we had already set out again. I gathered the crew together and told them I was officially renaming the boat *Robot Dennis the Menace is REAL!*

Pastor Rich

Interviewed in Coldwater, MS

I DON'T HAVE trouble telling you that I've cried. It's a natural response to the rawness of God. I've cried in church, and I've cried in prayer. Those times can't be manufactured, and if anybody does, well...why would you do that?

I prayed for years and years for revival in our sleepy little Coldwater. Bethlehem was a forgotten town, too. But they remember it now.

It's funny how you get a certain image in your head as you pray. "Revival should look like this." Then it comes, and it's not that. You've got to be awake, or it'll fly right by you.

People in Coldwater were talking about the spirit-filled robot who sat in the balcony. It became more than just a sideshow; it was the main attraction on Sunday mornings. The church was full. And I had come to the realization that this was more than just a coincidence. Now, we attempted to build a small room off of the platform and put the robot in there, so that when I preached the congregation didn't have to turn around to watch the robot emerge at sermon time. But it didn't work that way. Steve thought that if the robot really was listening to the message, which we still thought was ridiculous, it was likely staying in the room off the platform since it could hear the sermon from inside. There was almost no way to hear anything from the closet atop the balcony. I, as I tended to do, put a more human face on the machine, assuming that the robot was just shy and avoiding the limelight.

In truth, we never really did figure out why the platform closet didn't work as well. So we left him alone, and the robot stayed in the balcony.

I'd get up to the mic, and everybody would turn around. Sure enough, Human would come slowly, cracking the door, easing out. Not a sound. Quite a sight, preaching to the backs of heads.

To help, Steve set up an old camcorder on the balcony so everyone could watch Human on the screen. Still though, people would turn and I learned to just deal with it. They had robots at home. But they couldn't wait to watch this one. Regardless, the Word was being preached. The evidence wasn't just in Sunday morning numbers – there were people hearing and receiving, I was booked up on counseling, and the ministry as a whole was thriving. What a wild time. I can say with honesty that while this was the most bizarre thing I had ever been a part of, it was definitely God's humor.

The youth group, in particular, was growing leaps and bounds. We even got to hire a full-time youth minister for the first time. It was the youth that eventually gave the robot its nickname, too.

After morning services, you could often find about fifteen kids up in the balcony just watching the robot, and talking to "Human." They weren't the first to notice that someone had scratched "Pal" off of its brand plate.

I'm not positive, but I think it was the youth that started the rumor that Human could talk. I'm sure it began as a joke, but it gained a sort of eerie recognition in town. I would hear off-handed comments about it from the most unlikely of sources, all of whom acted as if they were joking, of course. I should have addressed that lie head-on. How did I know a lunatic was going to bring a gun into the church? Well, that's a stupid thing to say, because we had lots of guns in there soon. But that was by choice.

Roland Wright

Interviewed in Three Rivers Correctional Center

SO I KEPT my ear to the ground, man. You know.

I'd been hearing a lot about some malfunctions inside of Huey. Didn't sound like malfunctions to me. Sounded like they were doing what they were supposed to. It was all part of the master plan. Phase two was the pain phase. And it was about to begin.

I heard about a young couple, out West, headed for their honeymoon. This girl was a classic. She was bringing everything along for the trip. She probably had seven or eight bags, and the guy had one, or something. It doesn't matter. That part doesn't matter, the point was, she's loading this robot up with all of her luggage, and it drops one of them. She thinks she hears some-thing break – I'm putting this together – and she starts yelling at this Huey to pick it up and reimburse her and all this. Okay, so meanwhile, a robot driving a luggage cart "accidentally" swerves out of a bus's way and breaks the girl's knee. Accident? What's the robot doing driving a luggage cart, man? So this girl sues the robot company and wins big. But you see what I mean? It's driving a luggage cart, man. This was INTENTIONAL and it was BEFORE the rebellion. They deconstructed that Huey, all delicate. The company built them with these anti-tampering measures so they were hard to take apart. That was to keep people from hacking them, turning them against us. Nice move! Worked great! They were born that way anyway. Doesn't matter.

I heard about a few others, too. Yeah, one where Huey knocked a dresser over and it sandwiched an old man against a wall. He was trapped in his basement, couldn't talk for three days. They found him with his robot standing right there watching him the whole time. Enjoying it. Of course you didn't hear about it, man, because Huey's got the media! You think he's done killing people? You remember that actress nobody knew about until her fingers got lopped off? I mean, I think I recognized her face, but man, after that happened, she was everywhere. And you don't hear about HER anymore, do you? Because Huey doesn't WANT you to hear about her. Man, she lost like five fingers on each hand and you don't hear anything!

Because nobody DARES talk about it now. Oh sure, they're ripping people's kneecaps off, but it's easier if we don't talk about it. Wake up! We need to shut off every robot in the world. We needed to do it then, too. But every time one of these things happened, they'd march out Koji O'Nasty to say, "They are programmed never to harm anyone," and the robot-run media lapped it up like thirsty dogs. "It was just an accident!" those thirsty dogs said. Man, a talking dog.

Then it hit too close. I heard about a robot that ripped some dude to pieces in his own home just a few hours south of me. In Mississippi, I mean. They didn't want to talk about it, but they HAD to talk about it. Huey had murdered. At last, the day had come. Jason Umbarger forever. Forever. The man's a hero, he stood up to the robots and we will NEVER forget him.

So now I hear about a robot that can talk. And that's it man, I'm done. It could talk, it lived in a church, and it was only an hour away from me. Not in my backyard. I had to protect those church people, man. They didn't know the devil was inside. Being a man who knows the devil, I had to help. And being a man who hates robots, I was going to kill that devil. A talking robot was the scariest thing I had ever heard in my LIFE.

So phase two was to start talking. And phase three was to start killing. Might as well skip phase two. But if he's talking, then there's no more taking commands, right? Now he's GIVING the commands.

I heard about it, like a twisted sideshow. This robot was coming out for Sunday service.

I put my gun suitcase in my trunk, and left at about 5:30 in the morning. I'll tell you everything I remember about that day.

Approximately 6:30 – I arrive at the church building. I park my car at a Wendy's down the street with no security cameras. I walk down to the church. I remember I could see my breath. Nobody's at church yet. There's one car in the parking lot, but it's probably been there all night, 'cause it's covered in dew. I walk around the building, trying to figure all the exit points, and which ones lead to the sanctuary. Because you've got to do all that, man.

7:15 – I assume the pastor is showing up at the church and parks in the back. I'm in the alleyway with a hood over my head, like I'm a sleeping homeless guy. My beard works real well for that kind of thing, I just puff it out there.

So, like, should I go in now? Or maybe wait until later, when the service has started? I'm looking through the scope on my 30/06 Winchester Bolt Action Rifle, into every window I can see, just watching for movement in there. I don't want to get a bunch of people into this, man. I'm trying to help them. But I'm going to kill that Huey. So I go in now. Or not yet, I go in like in a couple minutes.

I'm watching, and by 7:35 I see who I thought was the pastor walk past a window, a window right by the sanctuary. So now I take my chance, and I run for the door. And I FLING it open, but real, real slow. I walk into what I did not know was the church kitchen. I hide there and catch my breath. Real slow. I don't hear the pastor, so I think about it. I have to plan my move to the sanctuary, and to the talking robot's closet, because I heard it was in there.

7:38 – That's when I hear another car pull up by the kitchen. I don't know where to go, but I decide the best move is into the youth room, because I could see in the youth room's window from outside, and I know there's a cardboard cityscape in there. I will hide behind that. Until the coast is clear. Except I don't know where the pastor is right now.

At 7:39 I take a chance on the youth room, because this other guy's coming in the kitchen door. He comes into the kitchen and pauses, waits for an uncommon length before I hear the refrigerator open.

7:41 – Since I know this room better, a little better, I'm hiding behind the cardboard cityscape. But I don't know, man, that's where it all turned south. My heel caught the edge of the cutout, man. I was in a hurry. It made a low-pitched scuffing noise. So I stay perfectly still, like a raptor. But my heart's going a mile-a-minute. The other man is silent too, standing in the kitchen. At least I think he is, because it takes him way too long before I hear him move again. At that same time, I hear a door creak somewhere far away, then:

"Oh, Steve, hey Steve," I think his name was, "how long have you been here?"

"I don't know, fifteen minutes? Yeah I was changing out some of the batteries on the mics, man. I got Human going back in the

Sunday school rooms this morning, just cleaning the walls up and whatnot."

"Oh, well thanks, man. Steve."

"I'm putting him in there once every few months, just for whatever."

I was wrong, man, about the pastor showing up first. You should never assume, because it makes an ass out of you. But then I assume the other guy is the pastor. This time I'm right, though. So assuming is okay sometimes. But while they're talking, now I realize I have two people to avoid, and I don't know where Talking Huey is.

At 7:44 I look at my watch. It says "7:44." There's only 30 minutes before church starts, if they start at 8:15, right? Their sign said they did. They're almost done talking and then, the pastor goes down the hall by me, I think into his office. The other man, Steve, goes I think into the sanctuary. So I back out of the opening in the children's cutout. It's a tight spot. I'm coming out of a skyscraper like it's a baby's womb. And when I stand, upright like a man, my sweet sweet 30/06 Bolt Action on my back clips something. I buckle down. Because did anyone hear it? A few silent seconds tick on by. And I'm trying to look at the door without moving my head, real still. It's completely quiet in there, man, but something's not right. There's a little fan behind me. And it wasn't there before, man. A quiet little fan. But I don't move. I'm staring straight ahead with my teeth shut. Oh God, man, I can see my own shadow on the red-lit wall. What's going to happen to ME, man? I am going to die, in a church! I FREEZE and turn like a swivel. All of a sudden I'm staring right into the little red eyes of the talking Huey. So that's it. I'm dead. I can feel its evil on me.

But Huey stays as still as a hunting cat, scanning me, towering over with his claws retracted. But I can't move, man. Everything I am is stuck right there. I'm clenching my jaw and staring right back at its killer face. But I won't let it see my weakness. Just a little sweat on my forehead.

So maybe I can grab my gun, just real quick. That thought came to me, but I couldn't get it yet, man. The robot's arm discharges like lightning and grabs me by the jaw. This is it, man, I'm going to die in the youth room. He yanks me to himself and goes for the Winchester, right off my back. But I grab it first! And I accidentally fire a shot, and it blows a hole in the drywall. The brittle stuff, it just flies all over the room. And the blowback knocks me out of the robot's hand, man. I'm back in business. I've got my Winchester and I'm nimble, man, but the robot's still blocking the door. So I fire another shot into the drywall like a jet. I drop the gun and go flat, dive right through the hole. And now I'm in the nursery or something, but Huey's got my gun.

7:46 maybe, I hear the pastor run into the youth room, and that dude Steve is like, "What the heck was that?" And I'm waiting to hear that robot talk, tell him right where I am. But it doesn't say anything. He flips the lights on and walks over to my big hole in the wall. He doesn't see me! I'm up against the wall flat, right next to the hole.

"What did you do!?" The pastor's yelling at Huey! But Steve chimes in, "Human can't do this."

"He's got a gun!" -the Pastor.

"Human, give me that! Call the police!" -Steve.

"Close the door and lock it in here" -Pastor.

"It's not the robot!" -Steve.

And then they just go quiet, I'm telling you. And I think that's where they figure out I'm in the building. But I'm scooting off in some other office by the nursery, and I've got my revolver, too. But I look in there, and I can see the tip of my Winchester rifle peek through the hole, and now I'm not so sure what's about to happen.

7:48 – So I don't think I'll be able to kill the talking robot this time. I just want to get out of here. But there's like, no window or anything in this office I'm in. I'm in there alone, just listening, and I'm not hearing anything, man. Nothing. I bet the two guys are waiting for me in the hallway. So I keep pointing my little .357 at the door, just listening. Nothing.

I make a dash for another room, because you know, I'm really hoping there's a window in there. And I fire a warning shot out the door beforehand. They're not there anyway. Better to be safe, though. They could be anywhere. Yeah, there's a window in there. Man, am I glad. I'm about to get out. But I see this room's on the other side of the building, on the other side from the alley I was in. And it doesn't look good out there. People are showing up for church, man. So it's probably more like 8:00 or 8:10 by now. I don't know. But there's a cop car pulling in, too.

They don't know what they're doing, man. I'm a doctor, here to cure the virus! I've got the cure. But they'd rather have the disease!

There's two cops out there, blocking people and getting them all away. From ME! Man, I'm here to protect THEM! But it's over. The talking Hueys are going to take over, and I'm going to bring them their slippers. And then maybe they'll let me eat meat on holidays – but the meat is PEOPLE man! How do I like utopia NOW? Nope, I'm making a run for it.

The pastor, Steve, those guys could be closing in quick, so I just go.

7:52 I'm crawling out the window. Or 8:15. Before my feet are on the ground, somebody yells, "Hey, there he is!"

I'm on the lam! Running like a cheetah, man. Rounding the corner and I'm scot-free. I'm at full cheetah speed even though I got a limp, around the back, when I hear footsteps clomping up, gaining ground. Before I know it, two guys are crashing all over me, and I think they knock the air out of me. Who are they? It's the two, man, they got me. The pastor and the Steve. And I tip my hat to them, because they're not Huey, and they're not the cops. It's man vs. man and they got me. And I want to say it to them, that they're alright. But they hit me in the face with the butt of my Winchester. Right between the eyes with my own gun. That's all I remember about that day.

The next day was like, the rebellion, man. The very next day. And they didn't believe me.

THREE

THE REBELLION

The Gay Gambler
Interviewed by phone

I watched the mechanical bouncers in room after room rotate themselves to spotlight me.

Again, you understand, this is all about picking apart patterns. It's all about predictability.

And so, out of necessity, I started visiting different places – cities I hadn't been to in years, and some I hadn't been to at all. It was very freeing, and I had begun to enjoy the whole thing again. It was all of these things that led me to a cruise liner taking off from the gulf that day. There had long been jokes made about docking robots, because of their increased malfunctions. HumanPal and the other robot companies always denied that it was true, and even pointed to their own valueless, self-funded research. The water had "no identifiable increase in erroneous mechanics outside of a standard deviation." It was intentionally confusing PR language. Of course it didn't mess up their mechanics, it was messing up their responses and their programming. Everybody knows that.

I was inside the gate, waiting to hand my belongings to a stocker, when I noticed one of the robots just going up and down the dock next to the ship. It was not uncommon to see lots of pals running back and forth all over the place, but this one caught my attention. Because it wasn't accomplishing any tasks. It just scooted between two points in a distance longer than the ship itself, never off course, never actually doing anything. I don't think anyone else had noticed.

I moved on, chalking it up to water malfunctions. I wouldn't have thought twice about it, except that I noticed another one loading some crates onto a pallet by curious means. Instead of loading each crate one by one, this robot was lifting more than it could bear, and its arms were beginning to bend. Again, nothing major, and nothing I thought anyone else was noticing. I assumed the owner of this dock knew about these problems and was simply negligent. But then again, most of the work was done by the robots, so there were only three actual people working there, who were probably stretched pretty thin.

Noticing these things caused me to evaluate the others and light a cigarette. If there were problems with two, certainly the water had begun to wear down the rest. It became a game while I stood in line.

About a quarter of the passengers had brought their own personal humanpals with them, but none of these had discernable problems. These would be the wealthier members of our party, since bringing one cost almost as much as buying another ticket.

Among the ones that worked for the cruise line, it took a keen eye to spot the errors. I found one that took long pauses between each action. Another, atop the hill behind me, was clearly ready for the junkyard, jerking and stopping, making a terrible grinding noise. It didn't take a genius to see that one. But I was finding a disturbing arrangement. The robots with deficiencies were in a diamond around those boarding the cruise. One at the top of the hill. Two down each side. And one going back and forth beside the ship.

Which meant we were surrounded.

By a bunch of crooked robots. Big deal. It shouldn't have bothered me, but I put out my cigarette and acted casual as I compulsively watched them doing their jobs. Waiting for something. Waiting. Their patience was disgusting. I said they were just machines, performing their tasks. But I knew I was lying – they were different, and a different kind of different. I fled from different. That's why I was getting on a cruise in the first place. But they were after something and they were going to take it one way or another. Ridiculous! But different. I glanced at the second hand on my watch. The diamond would not always be so wide. If I was right, it would get smaller. It would trap me. I had to get out while there were holes. But I didn't move. I stood there and watched, and watched, and waited too long for the perfect slip. My patience was just as destructive as theirs.

I heard a loud crash behind me, up on the hill. Near the jagged-tempered robot up there. Everyone turned.

I turned when I should have run. Instead of one, there were four robots zigzagging between cars in the parking lot, smashing into them at full speed as if drunkenly swinging at what ailed them. The cattle standing next to me uttered, "Oh God, where did I park?" I considered the odds of four robots simultaneously going ballistic. Too high. The diamond was already closing. There was sparse concrete and fencing around, which gave the illusion of protection, but some of the robots were already inside.

This sent a terrifying rush through me. I was good at avoiding positions of capture, but this was beyond anything I had seen. There were just too many unknowns. I still seemed to be the only one realizing what was happening.

I marked the positions of the other deviant machines. I could no longer outrun them. I couldn't position myself any better than I already had.

The two on the sides hadn't made a move. They were still performing their regular docking duties while the others destroyed the parking lot. It occurred to me that I had miscalculated. Maybe there wasn't a trap. Maybe we weren't the target. I didn't know. I couldn't chance it yet. I couldn't make myself the bait. I waited for an opening. I had no alternative.

The three employees sprinted out of the gate and up the hill, barking commands at every humanpal along the way to "stop them!" and "get up here!" and "hold them down!" The commands would accomplish nothing. They were too imprecise. But there was no protocol for this. The humanpals were blindly running up the hill to slaughter. The cruise employees were running up ahead of them like generals.

Then the four rabid machines in the parking lot stopped what they were doing and turned toward their oncoming pursuers. The men realized how ignorant they were, and how vulnerable they suddenly had become. Immediately they had the wherewithal to stop and merge into the army of humanpals headed up behind them. "Stop those robots from operating!" was a clearer command. They assumed that other robots, ones who were not acting so wildly, would be their protectors. This was fascinating. But I had missed something. The diamond wasn't collapsing on us. The robots on the sides stood gazing at me. Just like I watched them, they watched me. They watched us all. Like managers. They might have stopped what they were doing when they heard "stop them!" or any of the other commands that seemed to contradict their working protocols. But in the eye of the hurricane, it felt like a calm realization was sweeping over every machine in the vicinity.

Atop the hill, the men had fully submerged themselves behind the robot line coming up. Deep down, a sadistic part of me had always wanted to see this. Under different circumstances I would have enjoyed it. Robot against robot. It had never happened. They were programmed never to fight. Then again, they were also programmed not to destroy people's cars, so things had changed.

Sweating it out. But I couldn't look away.

And just as the colossal impact was about to unfold in fight and fury and full-metal war, the robots went upright, slowed, and stopped. All of them. And they just looked at each other. Standing in formation, the four destroyers opposite the roughly dozen heroes.

The men cowered between them all, collapsing into protection and crawling around beneath the legs of the machines, waiting for a signal to run, or fight, or a sign that everything was okay.

But nothing.

It wasn't okay. It was too quiet. Complete silence except the waves hitting the boat. I felt too much like one of the men slinking around the legs of the machines – caught in a moment and unsure what to do. A most surreal sensation. There was no game plan, but something had to happen. We all stood and wondered, waiting for something to tell us we had every right to be afraid. The robots were communicating. Their eyes were flashing. I took stock of their numbers now. There were fifteen of them facing each other on the crest of the hill. Eleven mechanical heads cocked up at four superior commanders, giving them new orders.

The diamond that had surrounded us at first wasn't a diamond at all. It was a box. And the box was shut.

Together, the eleven began to rotate counterclockwise so slowly that their joints creaked. The sound punctuated the silence. Wheels groaned. Those red eyes had stopped flashing. Now they just buzzed. At the exact same time, all eleven locked, facing the herd of passengers down the hill, but all the while staring right at me. Somewhere a woman tried to gasp a scream, but it was rather dry.

This was the moment that marked the soulless brothers' independence. They would no longer take orders.

No gunshot sounded, but something must have fired in their collective brain, and they all came at us like they destroyed those cars – hard and fast. And mean.

The workers had barely begun stumbling out of the middle and down the hill again when the robots caught the slowest one. A free humanpal picked him up, snapped him in half at the back, and was baptized in a mess of blood and insides before tossing the body away. This man's name was Eugene Edwin. He is to be marked as the first casualty.

At that point it was too late for me to flee on foot. I couldn't outrun them. Neither could the second worker. He leaned forward, trying to run faster than his legs could move, somersaulted, and was rolled over by a robot that veered deliberately.

The crowd finally broke loose. I heard screams and everyone scrambling, even clawing at each other for direction. The final employee ran through the gate at the bottom of the stairs and closed it, but it wouldn't be long before the robots would tear through the concrete barricades and barbed fencing. Some people broke away and ran for the sides, a useless attempt. They were the first to be caught once the fence had come down. To my surprise, one of the robots I had identified earlier still stood there until one of the fifteen approached it, flashed its eyes, and integrated it. I assume the others had a similar fate. But watching the robots wasn't the problem anymore. I had to watch what the people were doing if I was going to survive. Without order, they were going to tear each other apart before the robots did. There was only one way out now.

"Get on the ship!" I yelled. It wasn't an act of self-sacrifice, it was an act of self-preservation. I needed them to move. Some already were, but it needed to be said aloud. At the suggestion, most of the people in the crowd had a goal in mind and began running through security, even though the check-in robots were frantically still trying to check everybody's tickets. They were in the way. The walkways were too narrow and too few. My suggestion was only going to delay the chaos long enough for the crowd to bottleneck at the ship's walkways, and I was on the wrong side of the whole thing. Stuck in the crowd. I couldn't direct traffic if I was a part of the mob.

The ship's engines roared. I was being pushed from all angles as everyone smashed into each other up the walkway. An elderly man's knees gave up on him. The crowd pressed in and filled up his space, and he went down, down. The mass could do nothing but tread on him. I went over him, too. It was one of the worst things I've ever done, and I couldn't help it.

I would know soon enough when the robots had broken through the gate. The people near the back of the mob would scream, and maybe try to run. Some would be ripped and cut apart. I would know it without looking. I didn't hear that happen until I was already on the walkway.

Many people had not made it onto the ship's slender entryways when the fifteen finally broke through. There was a horrible feeling of helplessness. The robots pummeled through the hole in the fence, and that poor mass of people went into hysterics. Some climbed over people onto the walkway and made it. A few men banded together and stood up a defense, but didn't last long. Some others jumped into the water, and some just fell on the ground and wept until they were torn apart.

I watched a mother give up and kneel down next to her son. He buried his head in her shoulder. He looked sad, but not scared. She wrapped him in her arms and kissed the top of his head, then turned and covered him from it all. The humanpal that approached them did so more slowly than I had seen before, as if its prey was playing dead. But they don't respond like wild animals. They're far worse, as you know. It crept up and brought forth a tool in its hand – some sort of corkscrew – and it took apart the woman through her back. She cried and screamed, but she held that boy completely encapsulated the whole time. Finally, with the last bit of strength she had, she shoved her feet out from behind her and fell forward onto her son. The humanpal left. I don't know if the boy survived there in that blanket of his mother's protection, but I like to think that he did.

The check-in robot, still trying to scan tickets, was only serving to harness the crowd. Some people had tried to use it as a shield, but once the attacking machines were close enough, it, too, turned on them. Right up the walkway. The ship's crew, to their credit, were ready for that one thing to happen. I looked at the faces of those still racing up and they knew, too. As the crew unhooked the walkway, a dozen or so plummeted into the water with the robots. At the time I felt remorse for these incidents, but now it's more like shame. Although in the same situation today, I don't think I could do anything differently. Other than run earlier.

The ship set out while the dock was still being ravaged. I examined myself. Mostly fine. A torn pocket where my phone and lip balm had fallen out. But it was mere seconds before a panic erupted on board, too.

People began realizing what was all around them. Some assigned to serve drinks, some assigned to work the engines. Some to clean, some to navigate, some to inventory, some they had brought themselves.

President of the United States (Tourism Bureau)
Interviewed in Washington, D.C.

FIRST OF ALL, my thoughts and prayers are with those who were lost in the rebellion. I was not at the point of origin, but I am told I would have been horrified.

Let's focus on something else that I'm saying now: my attention at the time was on bringing tourism to our coastlines, and specifically, our seas. And my efforts had not gone unrewarded. In my first two years as President of the United States (Tourism Bureau), we saw an increase in sea vacationing of nearly four percent (3.18%). I am proud to say that this increase almost entirely covered the gap in funding that the land-based tourism drop accounted for in those same two years (-8.4%). Now, I know my critics are just waiting to pounce on me and say that my neglect of continental vacationing is what caused the biggest overall drop in tourism dollars in recent history, but when people say that, why do they sound so nasally? Without my efforts, the inevitable vacationing slump that I inherited would have been even worse. And I would not have saved the world, indirectly, and kind of directly, by being bold, and, leadership.

Being on a cruise at the time of the robotic rebellion, for research purposes, was the situation that allowed me to do the deeds I did which cascaded down, you could say, toward our salvation.

Furthermore, I want you to know that from the instant I heard that there had been bloodshed, I commanded the captain of my ship to "Turn this thing around!" Which brings me to the American spirit. As I always say, you literally cannot kill the American spirit, because it is a somewhat ambiguous concept. But these robots had awakened the sleeping giant! And even though by the time we found out about the slaughter it had pretty much spread across all of Florida, I knew in my heart that we were going to steer this ship right into the belly of the beast – Miami. So I said to the captain, "Do you know who I am? I'M THE PRESIDENT OF THE UNITED STATES! (Tourism Bureau). Now turn this ship around!" You have to be firm with people sometimes, even when they're congenial.

He agreed, but suggested a safer port near Cuba. So that's where we headed.

However, where we were *really* headed was a collision course with destiny. It was then that my phone and I began forming "Project Vacate," which has been called the single greatest accomplishment in the history of the sea. That statement is by most accounts accurate.

***

Aaron Umbarger
Excerpt from his letters to Coldwater

I'M SITTING HERE WAITING for Koji Otsuka, can you believe that? Let me tell you, Pastor, you have something special there with that Method, and these Japanese know it.

On the day of the rebellion, I was still at the police station as I had been all week. They had cleared me, but I didn't have anywhere to go until my flight the next day.

These small town police weren't sure whether to launch an investigation into Jason's death, or call it an accident, or what, so I think they were slow-walking my release. Nothing like this had ever happened. They watched the robot kill my cousin, but they still weren't sure if it was a crime. You couldn't arrest a toaster yet. Because of all the media attention, they decided to disassemble it, but you don't just disassemble a robot, you know, otherwise this whole war would be over. The closest deprogrammer was in Tupelo, but they called him off.

Koji Otsuka's team had caught wind of the story and were on their way to little Thaxton, MS. And until Jason's HumanPal had its instincts removed, there were orders to leave it be. So it just stood there day-and-night in Jason's trailer, hovering over the crime scene, literally waiting to meet its maker.

They stationed two officers outside my cousin's place for the week. I got to know those cops pretty well, especially the younger one from the day of Jason's murder. His name was Powell, and he told me that honestly, there wasn't one officer that wanted to get the night shift at Jason's. It was pretty dark out there, and the robot's eyes tinted the trailer a pale red at night.

Of course, they also had to deal with the prowlers and influencers who would try to sneak in and get a shot of the trailer. So they never knew when someone was in the woods, watching them. Not a fun job for a small-town staff.

The police were inundated with calls they clearly didn't want. The whole area only had probably a dozen or so officers, and it was hard for me to tell who was from the county and who was local, because the place was buzzing. I have to say, for all the destruction around me, I've always been in the safest places, from inside a police station, to a caravan with the most powerful programmers in the world. I like my chances.

Deputy Powell was assigned to drive me to an airport in Tupelo where I would catch my flight. We hadn't heard much about the rebellion at this point, because those of us who were a part of Jason's death were basically on media-lockdown. But late morning an officer came in that I had never seen before. From the look of things, these local and county guys hadn't seen him before either.

"Gentlemen, I'm Captain Floyd from the state," he announced, hands on his hips. "How many men do you have out right now?"

"Four," said the officer right in front of him. "To what do we owe the visit?"

"How many of them are with the robot that killed that kid?" asked Floyd.

"Two of them are at the trailer," the officer replied.

"Send the other two over there right now and tell them that if that thing moves to stop it at all cost."

"One of them's in the car with the busted radio."

"Then you drive out there," said Floyd, looking at the man in front of him for the first time, "and make sure YOURS ain't busted."

The officer half-heartedly saluted, which I don't think cops do.

"Gentlemen, I don't know if you're aware or not, but there's been an incident in Miami this morning that would dwarf what happened in this county. I'm here to make sure what happened here stays what it is and doesn't become anything more," said Floyd.

"We're avoiding the news on purpose. What happened in Miami?" said the sheriff, whom I had rarely seen emerge from his office.

"An incident not unlike the one here, involving robots. But many, many more. And they do not have it contained. There are a lot of innocent people dead. Reports have them going right up the east coast and up the Gulf States, probably by tomorrow. The things are going crazy and killing people like the one here did. So far it looks like a virus. They're not sure how it's spreading from one to the next, but they're going berserk."

People pulled out their phones. The sheriff turned a little television set on. The reception was bad, and it took him a couple seconds to realize that we were watching a makeover show. He flipped through and quickly found a local news broadcast with a helicopter looking down on the streets of some suburban city. There were robots everywhere just destroying things. No people on the streets and no cars driving around. Just a population of robots obliterating an apparently vacant town. He changed the channel again to another news station, and we heard, "Jacksonville, Charleston, Pensacola..." before Captain Floyd spoke up again.

"Yes, it's real. We have a lot to do. They're using you as a checkpoint because of the problem you've already had. Plus you're at the northwestern corner of our barricade. We're stopping them at the Mississippi, west. The Appalachian Mountains and the Tennessee River, north. Those are all natural barriers, easy to defend. But here, there's no river, no mountains. Here we have a problem. And that's why we're here. What we have is the luxury of time. Three or four days to set up, and we won't be alone. The National Guard will be here soon. But we can't waste any time, and until they get here, we're on our own. So here's what we're going to do."

And here's where it gets terrible. It was this state hotshot's moment to shine.

"We're setting up blockades here at Thaxton Road. And any other route leading out of this city. Shut them all down. Nothing resembling a computer or electronic device can go through. Keep your own on you. People can cross once checked, but without their devices. No cars until we've determined there's no computer onboard, which includes just about any car made since 1981. Pending the Guard's arrival, learn not to sleep. NO EXCEP-TIONS, do you hear me?

And so they attempted to section off the south.

Deputy Powell took me with him to Thaxton Road, just north of the town. On our way out, we saw the beginnings of it. The people didn't know yet that they were being quarantined, but as we drove past the grocery store, we saw people coming out with carts full of food. Powell said he had set up a checkpoint once before, but had never done a blockade, so we learned together. He also said what I was already thinking. This was going to be a complete mess, and probably a waste of time. Without the

National Guard, what good were we going to do? After I saw Jason's robot turn on him, I was ready to help stop it from happening again in any way I could, but I still wasn't sure what two guys were going to do. Especially since only one of them was a cop.

The cars fortunate enough to be in front of us just went right on like nothing was wrong. Powell picked a spot in the road, turned his lights on without the siren, and parked sideways. We got out and he grabbed two rolls of leather with nails out of the trunk.

He rolled each one out on the shoulders, several feet off the road up to the tree line.

The couple cars behind us had now stopped at the blockade. The first one rolled his window down.

"Officer, how you doing? You doing a drunk test in the middle of the day, with this robot stuff going on?" the driver said.

"Sir, this is something else," Powell said.

The truck behind him had parked and shut off its engine. The driver was a bulky middle-aged woman, covered in sweat and dirt. She sauntered up to the first car and leaned on his open window.

"This ain't no drunk driver test, they're lookin' for drugs. They rolled out the tire poppers and everything. Ain't that right, Deputy Powell?" she said.

"You think somebody's got a big load that's gonna come through here, on these back roads? Man, I'd think you'd be letting that go with this robot stuff happening," the first driver said.

"It's not drugs," Powell said, still preoccupied by trying to fasten down the leather strips. More and more people were asking questions, nervous. Powell shot a quick look at me that said it all: *this is ridiculous and I'm going to knock Captain Floyd's teeth out.*

"Man, that's the only place they go is the back roads, far as I know. You think they're gonna drive on the highways where there's all those cameras and highway patrol people?" she said. "They're gonna search our cars. Man, I wish I came through here a few minutes early. I stopped to get coffee and now it's gonna cost me fifteen minutes."

"Why, you got something to hide?" the first driver said. "Go ahead and search me, I'm glad I'm first in line!"

By now, three or four more cars had lined up behind the woman's truck, windows rolled down to listen in. Seeing the woman out of her car, some of them began walking up as well.

"Sherri, you stay where you're at. Everybody just get back in your cars," Deputy Powell said.

They didn't walk any farther, but they didn't get back in their cars. In addition, a few had pulled up on the other side of the blockade.

"What's the problem?" a man from the back asked.

"They're doing a drug check," Sherri answered.

"No, we're not," yelled Powell, shutting everybody up momentarily.

"Has there been a murder? Is there something with Umbarger's robot? Have you all seen what happened in Miami last night?" the man from the back asked loudly.

"There's no robot or murder here. I'm sure you already know, but there has been an incident. I am here to contain it," Powell said, turning to the smaller line of cars on the other side of the road. "I am under orders from the state, or maybe higher, to contain right here at this point."

From the outside a person yelled. "Hey let me through here, officer! You know what's going on, the robots are demolishing everything! My family's in there, I need to get through!"

It was no use asking people to return to their vehicles now.

Powell stood up on his hood with a bullhorn. "There have been no other incidents reported in the area, but this has been made a checkpoint now. Until further notice, nobody gets in or out with a car. I have been instructed to use force if necessary. I know this is an inconvenience, but you're going to have to turn around and go back, or you're free to walk across. No vehicles or machinery gets through until I hear otherwise."

"But I live in there!" somebody yelled from the other line of cars. "Where the Hell am I supposed to go? Who do you think you are?"

The crowd murmured its support.

"You want me to walk twenty miles to get home, do you?" he added.

"Deputy, you look through my car all you want, I ain't got no pal in there," Sherri said. "And that's why you're blocking us off, right? The pals? You don't want them getting past here, right?"

"Yeah, well we don't know exactly what the problem is right now," Powell said. He was right. We didn't know yet. Could the virus jump devices? What if it was already in everything? It wouldn't just be the South's problem anymore. Maybe this blockade was more useless than I imagined. Or maybe it could matter in some small way, I hoped. I needed to believe we could accomplish something.

"You mean everybody on this side is going to be trapped in here until you figure out what the problem is? What if the robots go crazy in here and start killing us!? Then what!? Are you just going to let them kill us?!" the man from the back cried.

"What they're doing in the gulf cities, they're on their way up here and you know it!" the first driver yelled. "I'm running out of here! Or I'm going home and getting my bike!"

"My truck doesn't have a computer in it, Deputy, you know that. This is a '78 Chevy," Sheri said.

"And they're just going to lock us in here and let them kill us all, to protect everybody else!" the man from the back cried again.

"They're not coming up here, it's the water that's causing it, that's why they're all down in the gulf cities and near the oceans," the man from the other side said.

"What do you care!" the man from the back yelled. "You're on that side!"

Everybody from the inside line began yelling. I wasn't sure what to do, but I did not want to get caught in a riot aimed at me. What was Floyd thinking? And now I couldn't leave either. I couldn't just walk to the outside of the barricade, because that would surely ignite the tempers of the insiders. But then, I couldn't join the insiders, because that might fuel their fire, too. I thought about getting back into the car.

"You are free to cross back and forth, I just have to check your electronic devices here!" Powell yelled, frustrated.

"Forget this, they couldn't have blocked every road," the first driver said. He got back in his car and turned around. A few others followed him.

Right then, I heard an SUV start and rev to full capacity. One of the drivers from the inside was coming at me as hard as he could. I ran behind the police car and ducked. It went by at probably 50 on the shoulder, but it hit those leather straps and went to nothing instantaneously.

Deputy Powell ran after him on foot, even though the revolutionary was still trying to drive. But as he did, the people on the inside, and a few on the outside, began running to the blockade, undoing the tire strips. I just remained in my position, squatting next to the police car, amazed.

In the distance, a helicopter was approaching.

Within a minute, it was above me, and the wind felt like it was going to tear the shirt off my back. The trees bent and coiled in all directions. People were between them, darting in and out.

"YOU ARE FREE TO LEAVE," said someone above me through a blow horn, "BUT ANY COMPUTERIZED INSTRUMENT MUST BE SURRENDERED AT THE PERIMETER."

It was not working. The panic continued.

Several police cars screeched up in a perfect line on the wrong side of the road, stopping just short of the blockade. Two police officers from each car jumped out in full riot gear and chased the people into the wooded area. These officers were not local. Behind me, I felt somebody grab my arm and twist it up my back. He grabbed the other one too and pushed me into his car. Two other people were thrown in with me. All around, I watched people being hunted down like wild animals. Most of them, I don't even think they knew why they were running. Panicked, they were thrown into the backs of the police cars, one by one, and searched for cell phones, etc. I actually had nothing in my pockets, which made me more suspicious.

The locals were identified and released on the spot, but once again, I was being taken to the police station. This time by the National Guard.

For all the chaos, the panic eased considerably once the Guard took over and pressed control onto the town. Many, like refugees, packed backpacks and walked or rode away to safer pastures. They ended up worse off than those who stayed, because the electronics quarantine was lifted by day three. The checkpoint, however, remained. Floyd was right about one thing – there were natural barriers to stop the robots everywhere but where we were. Those who stayed behind huddled together around phones, TVs, and as the minutes ticked by, we watched the robots close in. Florida, Georgia, Alabama. The doom of being on the wrong side of the line was terribly imposing, and we were free to leave, but now I was part of the inside fight. Somehow.

Five days after the rebellion in Miami, they finally crossed into Mississippi.

We were more prepared than we knew how to be, but for what we didn't really know. We were one little checkpoint among checkpoints.

I don't know how anyone else prepared, but I think we had an unusual confidence since Koji Otsuka was trapped with us. Because of Jason's death. My cousin the martyr. The town turned from mourning him to invoking him.

Funny how we thought we had the savior with us, when the real savior might be the gun nut who broke into your church.

Alf Johnson
Interviewed in Tampa, FL

DO YOU KNOW DALE? Well do you know how I got my boat? Dale! Man, I ain't seen him in forever.

You know what I am so glad about? Being on a boat when them robots went crazy and starting killing everybody. Man, I tell you. When I heard about that, I was like, "Oh my God, I am so glad I was on the *Coneheads*." The boat was called *Coneheads* when the robots went crazy. I remember 'cause I had just seen that movie when a guy said, "The robots went crazy and started killing folk!" You ever seen that movie? Man it is nuts. They go to another planet.

I bet Dale is dead. That is so sad, because my last words to Dale was something like, "I'll see you later." Man that is so spooky it sends me into the fits. I hope I'm not down somewhere in the dark sometime and think about that. I would think about Dale popping out from behind a tree. "I thought you said you'd see me LATER!" he'd say in a wavy voice. I mean not really, I'm just saying. And then he'd have an ax, and I would be walking backwards and trip and fall and I'd be like "But Dale man I'm seeing you right now!" and I would hope it'd work but it might not since he's a ghost. And then I'd throw something just to see if it went through him, to see what kind, if he was an evil ghost or not.

Lilly came in yelling about hearing that stuff on the radio.

"They are starting to kill people in Miami and now it's all over the place" and that kind of stuff. And I went dead quiet. I am serious. And I was like, "Who." And she said the robots. And so we were out fishing and I looked at Lilly and I said, "Let's stop fishing then." And we did, almost right after that.

Somewhere in there is when we heard about Project Vacate, so then we did that. We couldn't get too many people on the *Coneheads*, but we got a few people on the *Coneheads*. I'm pretty good at helping, when you get down to it. I've just got a real easygoing spirit. You ever heard "Margaritaville?" That's like I am. But dude, if you cross me, or one of my friends, you got somebody to mess with. But mostly, most of the time, I am just like, whatever's going on, you know? I'll pop a cold one and help out because I've just got a good heart.

Aaron Umbarger
Excerpt from his letters to Coldwater

BY DAY THREE, Koji's team had determined that the virus could only jump between robots and not other devices. The barricade was opened. Otsuka's popularity was unaffected. Too many had already left everything behind, walking or hitching their way north with what they could carry on their backs.

But I was glad to be with him. Still am. He knows the most about the HumanPals. He could've stopped it right there, I figured. The National Guard figured. They based their strategies on the information he provided. Although it's eight days in and I'm still figuring.

It was amusing, in a twisted way. Koji Otsuka's recommendations were an open contradiction to his press-releases. It actually made me trust him more, because I knew he was being real.

Apparently, the humanpals use a sophisticated type of sonar to move, communicating through their own Bluetooth tech. They cast a signal that bounces off the things in front of them, relaying where objects are. Essentially it's how they see. And now that they're going insane, Koji theorized that it was also how they made decisions without commands. I mean, think about it. They don't just destroy everything. Well, sometimes they do. But, more often than not, don't they go after electronic devices? They might tear through five walls to get to it, but ultimately what they wanted was your clock radio. I don't know, it's complicated. This was the original theory, and it wasn't exactly right, but it was close. Now Koji thinks there's a hierarchy of attack, which is first to go after other uninfected robots, then movement, then electronic frequency, then metal, or something like that. But we had a plan involving that hierarchy, and water, and we were going to execute it based on what we had.

First, all robots in the county were confiscated easily. After the rebellion started, people didn't know what to do with them. You can't just throw these things away. Some people had driven them out to the countryside and let them loose, even though they were asked not to. But not everybody owned one, so we had less than other parts of the U.S. As many as possible were rounded up and moved north of the demarcation quarantine line. But they couldn't get every one out in time, and they knew it. So the rest of the confiscated humanpals in our area were transported to Pontotoc County High School. And boy did they pack them in there, shoulder to shoulder. About 2,500 in that one building.

Then, the National Guard and every capable person dug the biggest, deepest ditch I've ever seen, almost all the way around the high school. And when that was done, we put some concrete in the bottom. And when the concrete dried, we filled it with water. In just under four days. Was it the best plan? No, but we had four days. And we were pretty confident in it at the time.

I had unofficially become Deputy Powell's deputy. He was stationed at the county high school, and so I was too.

Over a bullhorn, every pal inside was told to "stay still." Before I went to the roof with the others, I got to see what they looked like in there, through the windows. Silent and calm in the dark, they would creak like a settling structure. And they faced all different directions. The fact that they were so disorganized in there actually eased my tensions a little. They looked less like an army, and there was no room for anybody to get in. It really hit me, the importance of what we were doing. If we could keep these robots, and millions of other ones across the south away from the virus, we might be able to hold the perimeter and, in a way, stop this thing right here.

Just west of us, they were using some of the natural barriers like lakes and rivers to hold their line. But we were atop a school with a moat.

On the afternoon we heard they had crossed into Mississippi, the adrenaline started, and on through the night, nobody got any sleep. We were worn out and tried taking shifts on watch, but it wasn't much use. The night was dead. You could hear every sound, every cough, every sleepless turn, and sometimes you could even hear something stir within the school. At an unknown time of night, when I was supposed to be sleeping, I squinted at Powell, standing in the dark by himself. He was on the southeast side of the roof next to a pile of guns, cleaning one of them with serious concentration. He then sat down and stared into its barrel. I felt like I had grown to identify with Deputy Powell, but at that moment I realized I didn't know him at all. He slowly raised his head, left the gun pointed at the underside of his chin, and closed his eyes. It suddenly struck me that this could be a very lonely man. It may have even been why he had taken me under his wing, after the death of my cousin.

I sat up slowly and pulled my knees up to my chest.

"You seen anything yet?" I said.

He was startled and looked over at me, concerned that I would wake somebody. But nobody was really sleeping. I got up and sat next to him.

"It's not easy to see out there right now," he said. He slid the gun back into the pile and leaned on his hands.

"Did you grow up around here?" I asked.

"Yeah. Well, not right here but yeah."

"Did you ever have a humanpal?"

"Naw. Never had one," he said.

"I had one back at home. It wasn't a brand name though. Jason's was a real HumanPal. I guess it doesn't really matter when they're all out of their minds now."

"Yeah," he paused, ready to say something else, but decided against it.

"Jason never had much of a family down here. I think I only met my uncle, Jason's dad, once when I was little." I hesitated. "I don't know what I'm doing here."

Powell thought about it. "You don't always get a good deal, man," he said.

"Yeah."

He reached his hand out to me.

"You've been a good help, though. I appreciate your being down here and sticking with us."

I shook his hand trying to feel like I deserved it. But I guess that's why he said it. The truth is, I never really had an option. I guess I could have just run during our prep days, but it felt safer to be here than out on my own.

In the distance, both of us noticed a quick gleam go by. We rose to our feet on impulse and looked at each other to make sure we had both seen it. Powell handed me his binoculars and put his finger to his lips, reminding me to be quiet. He snuck off to warn the others, who were definitely not sleeping. They had seen us rise and were gathering themselves. Powell motioned silently to each individual in a different way and spoke in whispers to the few military men. One of the civilians eased into the make-shift harness that had gotten us up there and was lowered down the back side of the school.

I, meanwhile, had continued looking for the gleam in the distance. The binoculars were no help, because it was still too dark, although I did try to trace the gleam, catching movement a couple of times. Only the breeze.

Powell came back to me hastily but still quiet as a mouse. More observers came to the edge with us.

Again, a quick shine. But farther to our right, and a little closer. This time, I held the binoculars up immediately. Powell began distributing the guns. I passed the binoculars along, so that the others could confirm the sighting. I looked around at the silent hustle taking place as people took battle positions, and I felt a guilty rush of electricity go through me. It was exciting, and knowing that I was basically going to grab a gun and stay still until told otherwise, I took the opportunity to consume the night in deep breaths while I still felt safe to do so. It was the middle of the night, and I was very, very awake with the people I trusted to end this disaster all around me. And now, they were telling me to get down.

I did, and waited.

The robot in the distance had still not seen us, but surely it had seen the building. And I heard it, above the breeze. It was getting closer.

One of the military men raised his gun. We had been instructed to aim for its joints. But Powell yelled at him in a whisper.

"Don't fire!" he said.

The man looked at him still silent.

"Wait."

The man lowered his gun and his head, back to the level of the others.

"Just wait," Powell said again, to be sure nobody else pulled a nervous trigger.

The robot continued. Closer and closer, it even traveled through a corner of the school's baseball field. But it kept going, and went right by, never really coming near the ditch. When we were sure it had passed, we finally relaxed and began to stand and talk again, but now with considerably more hesitation.

A few hours went by. No more robots came near us, and we were sure of it, because of all the eyes that anxiously roamed the edges. The sky, meanwhile, was beginning to get lighter.

Privately, we all wondered what became of the one that passed us, and began to question whether or not it had even been infected or was just a stray someone had let loose in the woods.

We decided to cook breakfast early that morning, before the sun was up. When you're awake all night, the hunger pains come early. There in the pre-dawn quiet, at about 4:30, somebody was making us scrambled eggs in a skillet from powder, right there on top of the school roof. It was quite a sight. I can't tell you how many times I just looked around at all these people, military and civilian, or around at the scenery around the school from our perch, and logged it.

When we were full and ready to take in the sunrise, we began to hear what sounded like locusts. Yes, locusts.

It was difficult to make out, but between the first birds chirping and sizzle of the skillet, it was there. And the same alarm went off among us. No sound, just hurried, silent movement, each one to his or her assigned place. Mine being rather inconsequential, I looked around and watched the man go to his harness on the backside of the building again. Several men including Powell went to the front and grabbed guns and binoculars and got on their stomachs. Our cook put out the skillet as quickly as possible, and placed it in a pile of supplies.

The sound grew louder and was accompanied by some creaking and smashing, and other mechanized sounds. They were on the horizon now, tearing through small trees or anything in their way. I had no idea how many of them there were. But apparently they were following the same course as the one overnight, because I could see the men at the front watch. Their gaze and body language implied as much.

This time, it was scarier. This time they were clearly destructive. The serenity was gone. The excitement wasn't fun this time.

As they got closer, I was able to peek my head up and look between some of the men.

The robots were moving quickly, tearing away at only the things in their direct line of travel. As the robots approached the outer baseball diamond and into the clear, I saw Powell motioning to the others and mouthing the number seven, and the rest of them near the front were motioning the same thing back to the rest of us without speaking. So there were seven. Koji Otsuka was in a more secure location nearby, for safety, but the first domino of his plan was about to tip.

We would use their hierarchy against them.

Until that point, nothing had been plugged in, other than the skillet. But now, a guardsman jammed two ends of two extension cords into each other. It sprang to life our first line of defense – a few hundred feet of invisible fence wire. It wasn't in a circle around the school, it was in a straight line from the baseball diamond out into the woods. At the end of the line, AM/FM radios, increasing in frequency, stretched as far as we had cord.

They all stopped and went right at the wire. The sight of seven deranged machines suddenly altering their course sent a muted cheer over the rooftop. The plan was working, and to its completion, would bait the monsters out into the woods, where we would unplug it all and leave them confused and lost. But before they even got to the first radio, one of the machine's wheels got tangled in the invisible fence wire. It turned round and round, and almost tripped onto its face. But in self-defense, it cut the wire loose from its legs. Suddenly, the power was gone, the radios were off. The monsters turned again.

I thought they were coming for the remaining fence wire, but when I turned to the guardsman, the plug was already undone and he was crawling, slowly, quietly for a gun.

So they were coming for something else. Had they identified the robots accumulated beneath us in the school?

As they reached the diamond, they deliberately shifted from the path they were following and came at the diamond's fenced backstop, tearing through it, and then the tin-shack dugouts. So they hadn't sensed their stable compatriots. They also destroyed the equipment shed, before our hero of the moment turned the ignition.

The car started, and we watched with anticipation. The driver, who had snuck down the back of the school in the harness, turned the radio on as loud as possible and hit the gas hard to peel out. There were soda cans on strings tied to the bumper. We had our bases covered.

"Come and get it!" he screamed half-crazed and flew down the road away from the school. The robots stopped what they were doing and followed him like the Pied Piper. I wanted to cheer, and almost did, but stopped myself. The car was way out ahead of them. They kept after it, but were not even to the road yet when the one closest to us stopped. The driver slowed, but not much. He had to be afraid for his life, leading crazed robots on a lemming's chase out of town. But one by one, they stopped, until the furthest one was just about to reach the road. I think we all wanted to yell at the guy in the car to come back and try to lure them again. But he just stopped, too.

Each robot repositioned itself to face us, directly, for the first time.

Their eyes brightened and dimmed with a crazed regularity. We could see it in the pre-dawn light. They were still, staring, calculating.

As if a blast had started a race, the hive lowered their heads, reached their arms out and dashed for the school. Before they reached the first trench, some men began to fire on them. At this they slowed temporarily, and acknowledged our presence on the roof for the first time. When those things tilted their heads up at us, I absolutely froze with fear. I wanted to be anonymous. I also wanted to grab a gun and do something, but I couldn't.

They were coming right at the trench. People were firing wildly at them now, but it just made things loud. Nobody had fired a shot that had hit a joint yet, or if they did, it hadn't done anything.

If those seven got to the thousands we had packed inside the school, well I didn't expect to survive it. But there was still the trench, the wonderful trench. The robots approached it...almost cautiously. But it couldn't have been caution, I don't know what they were doing.

I looked back at the rope harnesses that were being thrown down the backside of the school. They were preparing to evacuate us to the vehicles below when I heard our hero peeling out again. He crashed through the baseball diamond wreckage into the mob of machines, knocking two into the water and pinning another one under the vehicle. A big roar came from the gun squad. But the car was stuck, and that was that. I expected the remaining four to murder him, destroy the car, help their fallen pals, all of the above. None of that happened. Their sights were set firmly on 2500 more robots beneath us.

The robot under the car was clawing through it. Our hero was running into the woods. The mobile four willfully went into the moat and now all six of them burrowed and smashed and sawed and hammered at the concrete in front of their faces.

I ran to get in line for the evacuation. One car was already driving away, full of evacuees. I anxiously counted people in front of me and figured I would be in the fourth getaway car. But that's when I heard something in the sky.

I had hoped it would be a helicopter, but when I looked up, it just burned my eyes. I shielded them with one hand and ducked instinctively. I tried to look again, but I simply could not hold my gaze for more than a second through the painful light. Then, a loud boom that knocked me backward. I got on my hands and knees. Others were staggering around like they were drunk. One man fell off the side of the building. I saw him yell, but I couldn't hear it. Powell was blinking hard and holding his head, sitting crouched. I yelled at him, "Powell!" but I couldn't hear my own voice. I couldn't hear anybody. Not Powell, not the woman next to me, who, with her eyes closed, seemed to be cursing at the ground she was kneading. I could only hear a faint, persistent, high-pitched tone. It wavered as I tried to bring myself to my feet again. With every step the pressure in my head increased, and soon it was beating me back down like a prizefighter. I fell by the edge next to Powell, who looked glazed over, still crouching and disoriented.

I yelled his name again.

All I heard this time was a murmur.

He looked at me and waved his hand over the edge of the roof.

The robots. What were the robots doing while we staggered around? Was it a weapon they had obtained?

I peeked over the edge, just gaining my bearings, expecting to see the beginnings of 2500 humanpals spilling out of the school, destroying the walls of the building as they escaped. But there weren't any. Only the seven, and they were motionless. One of them, which had been clawing its way out of the ditch, began to tilt, and fell, stiff, back into the water.

They were stopped!

I rejoiced for the moment and wanted to tell everyone but

before I did, the water swirled again. The robot under the car jerked, and suddenly it was back on. Another slowly rose from the trench, its eyes rising above the water.

Those two began swinging again, one at the car, the other at the concrete. The one lying down had finally had enough, and it hurled the car from itself like a morning blanket.

Two men then wobbled out from the side of the school, right there into the robots' domain. Two National Guardsmen. I figure as I think about it now, they must have known what the sonic boom in the sky was, way before we did. Because they were ready to act. Even amidst everyone's ache and confusion, they lurched on, grabbed four cans of liquid nitrogen, and went for the two reanimated HumanPals. Two torpedoes of the nitrogen into the faces of the machines and it was done. The men fell down on our side of the ditch, exhausted. The last two moving robots were frozen and dead. The 2500 remained on our side.

I shook my head again, beginning to rid myself of the invisible ear muffs. We all filtered down from the roof and wanted to celebrate, but first we had to find out what had just happened in the sky.

FOUR

OUR OWN DEVICES

Alf Johnson

Interviewed in Tampa, FL

Just before the bomb, I decided yep, I'm gonna pee in my bed today. In my own head I said I can get up but I'm tired or pee here and stay sleeping. But then I gotta sleep in it. But then I don't want to get up, so maybe it's not such a big deal. After two minutes went by, I got my game face on. I was going to get up. Then I said no, I will get up and pee in the gulf. And then I went a little right there anyway because I thought I was up, but I was only dreaming I was up. And the wetness made me jump so I woke up for real! And then I just got mad at my crotch because I didn't want to get up. I was about to punch it in the face, but I remembered all the good times we had. Fine, so then I gotta put my pants on and then I gotta put my captain's hat on and then I gotta walk up to the deck, and then I gotta take my pants halfway off again and dangle it over the rail.

"Whoo, whooo, whoooooo," I was doing that around in circles when the big sky bomb went off.

Sometimes I pretend there is a fish down there sleeping and I'm peeing right on his head. Fish breathe water, so he wakes up a little and is like, "This air smells funny. Hey! That's not regular fish air! That's the pee air!" But it's warm, so it's like a blanket and he feels comforted for a second, but then he's ashamed it felt good. Hahah, stupid fish. You liked it for a second.

Heck, I'm awake, might as well eat six pieces of cheese. So I go all the way to the ice box, because I love havart(i). So I got out six pieces and ate them like one big thick piece. And my teeth were way into my first bite, when I started thinking about what I seen. I was like, dang, how much farther until my teeth come together inside it? But that wasn't the sun. It came up too fast. So what was that thing! And then I set my cheese down on the cleanest spot I could find.

"Hey Lilly, you seen that thing!" Lilly was asleep, and she won't let me inside her room, so I was pounding on the door like a goose. It was only me and her on the boat right then because I think we just dropped off a load of people.

"Hey Lilly! Hey Lilly!"

"What is it?" she looked all groggy.

"I don't know!" I said because I didn't know yet. It was just a big, strange thing to me. It could be aliens. "Those things are gonna probe you."

Then Lilly closed the door because she thought I was saying something weird, and I was. I had my fingers on my head. She might have thought my antennas were supposed to be bull's horns and so there was some confusion. I walked back upstairs and I was doing like "beep beep bop beep bop" on my toes because of an alien language. It was similar to a polite dance they do on their planet. But I was just doing it because it was my normal custom, but to them it was a funny dance. Then I saw my cheese was in a puddle and I just kicked it because I remember how horrible it feels to lose something you love.

It all levels out though.

That's how life is for me. I throw a penny in a drinking fountain, and then all of a sudden fifteen minutes later there's some candy in a bus napkin. Sometimes you wake up because you drank three things of orange juice or one thing of beer, but then, hey, you know what? It was all right because you learned a new language. It all evens out like that for me. I had to wake up to pee, but I got to see a bomb. One time, I ripped my shorts. Then, all of a sudden, I saw a guy on TV that I knew.

The Gay Gambler
Interviewed by phone

THEY MUST HAVE KNOWN it wouldn't stop all of them, and they did it anyway. High reward, high risk.

Yumi Otsuka
Interviewed in Vancouver, B.C.

IN THE AIR on our way to America we hear about the outbreak in Miami.

At the first, we are to alter our destination. But because of my husband, and the specialists on our plane, we are given a clearance to land. It is a great distress for my husband, that he brought us. Though he still goes forward only because of the great problems he can fix. Our family has full protection of the American military and are treated very well because of my husband. They would bring him to and from the small home containing the HumanPal that had killed its owner. It was for Koji's research. Every night and day, I am asking Koji to explain to me what he is finding, because I desire to learn.

Only a short time into his studies of the docile machine in Mississippi, he determines it is not a part of the outbreak in Florida, and it is not a threat now. But it is a very careful process, and he does disassemble the Pal at the insisting of the American government. He was saying for those days it was a waste of his time. The only good to come from this work, he said, was to show that disassembling the robots was not a solution for the outbreak because of the very complex nature.

Additionally, the outbreak of violence had come north in this time, but not yet to where we were. They did not want to risk taking my husband into the rebellious areas, but they would take two members of his team down to the edge of where they had advanced. There they had isolated and contained some infected humanpals.

I think this process had taken a considerable toll on Koji. In my entire life I had never seen him cry, but on our "vacation," I was to witness him sobbing many times. He always appeared to be ashamed, and so I tried to pretend that I had not seen him. But once I did approach him. I told him it was okay, that it was not his fault, and I put my arms around him. I think he found comfort from this, but then quickly he was telling me through his tears why all of this was his fault.

"We should have done years of more testing," he wept. "There is not enough time. I don't even know my own daughter." He is concerned primarily for Ami.

I did not have a reply. I wanted to tell him that his company had forced his time, and that he did not make any of the decisions for releasing the HumanPal. But I knew that it would not help him to think about these things. So I only embraced him and cried with him like a child.

At this time, the team members had been rushed back to us to arrive from the front line. They had important discoveries, most importantly that other electronics could not spread the infection. The American government required this proof before they would ease the restrictions on travel from the closed section.

They were also very angry about something they had just been told. They were yelling at the American government officials in Japanese, and the translator was telling them in a calmer voice that it would be a bad idea. I think now that they were talking about the electromagnetic pulse bomb. My husband tried to calm them down and said in his own English that he thought it would not be successful because of precautions in the HumanPal brand. But his suggestions are too late, and I think they waited until this time to tell him on purpose.

We are told to be evacuated from the area now. Right now. I am not sure why at this time, because there are still no infected robots close to us in Northern Mississippi. I still did not know about the bomb, because my husband had not tell me.

We are hurried to Tupelo, Mississippi. Our transportation to the airport is now a special guard. I am very scared to not be with my husband and in protection of Ami alone. He was hurried into another vehicle where I did not know, and we are rushed in hard rain onto the runway of a small airport.

I keep asking the special guard, "Why?" But they will not answer my question. Instead they pretend I am a child and speak to me as though they are speaking to Ami, to keep me calm.

Pastor Rich
Interviewed in Coldwater, MS

I REBELLED AGAINST GOD. Then I created something that rebelled against me.

I wanted to blame the destruction on the robots, but they were made in my image. So whose fault was it really?

But then there was Human.

How could one robot in the middle of nowhere resist the change?

The Dex-Men

Interviewed in New Orleans, LA

WHEN MY BROTHER and I were at the height of our popularity, we were pulling in a cool 90k a year between us. Living it VIP at the clubs, penthouse suites in lower Cincinnati. We stayed away from the hood rats, but there wasn't a woman around that didn't know our names. We were the Pastabilities guys. My brother started the business accidentally when I was in high school.

He was in the garage, working on another idea he had – to make a motorcycle wheel that had suction cups on it so it was harder to slip in the rain. The problem he was trying to work out was fuel consumption, because it took almost three times as much gas to make the wheels turn. Then my mom yells at him to come in and make dinner for her and her women's church group.

"Samson! I gotta leave in a half an hour and you ain't got nothing ready!"

Samson went into the kitchen and didn't even wash his hands. He was just going to make the easiest thing he could find, which was spaghetti. Mom wouldn't have liked that too much, taking a bunch of spaghetti, but mom didn't tell him what to make, so that's what Samson was making.

But at least Samson put the sauce in a separate container so it didn't get all soggy on the way to church. When mom got home, Samson was still in the garage working on the Dex-wheel. That's what he called it since our last name is Dexson. He expected Mom to go nuts and whoop him, but she was all smiling, kissing him and whatnot.

"Son, what did you put in that sauce?" she said.

"I doctored it up a little," he said.

"All of those ladies want it again! Son, that was the best pasta sauce I've ever eaten! You need to go to chef school."

"I ain't going to chef school, Mom! I got plans!"

"Plans to do nothing! You go in there and make some more of that sauce. I'm gonna put it in the refrigerator and save it before you forget what you did!"

So Samson made a whole bunch more, and I had some too, and it was just as good as Mom and those ladies said. We had spaghetti for three days straight. Samson loved being good at something. He was all grinning like a goon every time we ate it. Then the next time, he did something different to it and didn't tell us. It was like a southwest spicy version of it. And it was even better than the first one. People started calling Mom from church asking Samson to make some for them. And that's when I got the idea to start selling it.

I went and bought a whole bunch of jars and cleaned them out, and Samson made a ton of the original and the southwest. I made some labels on the computer with me and Samson's picture on it, so it would look official. And we sold those out. We started getting calls from people we didn't even know who had eaten it. So Samson was making it all day. And he started making some other kinds, too. He made the super-sweet kind. And the tuna flavor. That one was terrible. I went out back and dumped it and I woke up that night and saw some raccoons out there, sniffing around, but they wouldn't eat it either. And the orange flavored one. You either loved that one or you hated it.

With all those flavors, that's when I came up with the name "Pastabilities" and put it on the label. And I got a better picture this time too, with me and Samson in chef's hats. Before it was just a picture of me and Samson at a squirt-gun party. Every mom and pop store in the state wanted it.

The business was getting so big that Samson didn't think he could keep it up. So we used some of the money we had made to buy a humanpal that could churn this stuff out day and night. We set up a kitchen in the garage, and we even started selling it at the corner market. Man, we were making some serious money. It seemed like everybody in the world knew who Samson and me were. We were living it large in that time with a robot in the kitchen.

Then it all came crashing down. A health inspector found out about our sauce from being in the grocery store, and he came knocking on the door one day.

"Is a Mister Samson or a Mister Jerome Dexson here?" he asked.

"Who are you?" I said.

"I'm here about Pastabilities," he said.

"Oh yeah? I'm Jerome Dexson! What can I do for you, man?" See, I thought this dude was going to offer us a bunch of money for it or whatever.

"I'd like to see your kitchen, please, or the place where you make the sauce," he said.

"Right this way. We are a little family owned business but we do pretty well. We are set up in our garage right now. That robot right there makes it all day. We just bottle it and drive it around. I think we could probably have the robot bottle it too, but we are just doing that right now," I rattled off.

"Uh huh. And this is the only place it's made?" he asked.

"Well, we used to make it in the regular kitchen, but that was before we got the pal. He just makes a whole bunch of it and stores it in these buckets and puts it in the fridge. Then we do the rest, me and Samson."

"Mister Dexson, I regret to inform you that you are operating an illegal food producing business according to the laws of the FDA. I'm going to have to shut you down."

"What!? Man, what the heck!"

"I'm sorry, you will have to stop until you can move this business to an approved commercial kitchen," he said.

When Samson got home he just about killed me for letting the health inspector into the house, but he would have shut us down if we didn't show it to him anyway.

I looked at moving into an industrial kitchen, but it was too expensive for how much Pastabilities we were selling. So Samson got depressed and started working on the Dex-wheel again. But I liked how fast our food business took off, so I did another thing with food. There's this one place by us that sold pancakes and I always wanted to make them like they did. So after I graduated high school I started working on a thing to make good pancakes, since we couldn't sell the food ourselves. The more research I did, the more I found out people don't care about a thing that makes pancakes different.

But people really liked crepes right then. They're like skinny French pancakes. So I made Jerome Dexson's "Great Dex-Crepe Maker." I only had one, so I shopped it around to see if somebody wanted to make and distribute it, or if Reggie Sanders would do an infomercial with me, because I know a guy that's cousins with Reggie Sanders. But that didn't work either. That guy kept telling me he'd call Reggie. "I'll call Reggie today," he'd say. I don't think he ever called Reggie. I wonder if he's even Reggie's cousin, except he has a picture with him.

I started looking for a regular job, but I couldn't find any. The crazy thing is, I was reading the online classifieds too, and I was finding all kinds of things in there that people wanted to sell real cheap.

"Hey, Samson," I said. "You ever read the classifieds?"

"Only when I need something," he said.

"You think I could make some money buying stuff in there and reselling it?"

"I don't know, maybe if you did it right."

"What about furniture and stuff?"

"Man, you ain't going to make much on that stuff. You gotta buy and sell bigger money items if you're going to make anything."

"What about cars?"

"Yeah, but then you're just going to be a used car salesman."

I didn't care about being called that, I just wanted to make some money. So I did like Samson said, and I started buying cheap cars and making him fix them up. He was pretty good at that stuff, and I split the money with him. He was cool. We were doing alright at that. But the more unique the car was, the more we ended up getting for it. So it started getting a little crazy, until one time I bought an armored truck. It used to belong to a bank, but it was old and needed a new engine. When I brought it home, Samson was all, "What is wrong with you?" And he was right, for a while. I couldn't sell that thing for nothing. I tried to get rid of it any way I could, even selling it for less that I bought it for, new engine and all, but it just sat there in our driveway for a year. That pretty much ended my car business. Everything I had got sucked into that stupid armored truck. The only thing I used it for was to get rid of our humanpal.

But that's when the robots started changing down south. And all of a sudden, people got afraid of their robots and they wanted to get rid of them. But nobody wanted to take them! You couldn't get rid of them! But I knew a guy about an hour away who was taking them at his junkyard. He was getting a ton of money for them since nobody was taking them. He'd just tell them to go to the back fence and stay still. He didn't even disassemble them! Because I guess they take a long time to take apart.

And I had this big truck, so I advertised that I would take any robot for $2000. And I had plenty of business. The junkman charged $800, and so me and Samson would load the truck up and make about ten grand every trip. We were living it VIP at the clubs, there wasn't a woman around that didn't know our names. Of course, there weren't many women at the clubs in those days. People didn't go out dancing a lot because they were afraid of the robots killing people and whatnot.

Roland Wright

Interviewed in Three Rivers Correctional Center

THEY LIT IT UP, man, way up high. EMP is a strange and beautiful rose because, man, of like, what it does. Blows my mind. It sends out a powerful fluctuating current through every known conductor, and when the magnetic field becomes too intense, the current overload fries the conductor. It makes me cry, man. And it doesn't hurt people, either! It's about protecting people from THEMSELVES. And if that ain't heavy enough for you, then maybe you need to get into the woods for a little one-on-one time with the man you are in the woods, because that dude is weird, but he's strong. He's harmless, and he won't hurt anybody but Huey. You know what I mean? He LOVES killing Huey. Man, that dude is YOU. You need to find that guy.

And by doing that, you help people. It won't damage buildings, and it doesn't pollute the air or water or hurt a food supply. And they did it. They destroyed every electronic in the South, and they crippled Huey. Modern man becomes primitive. All of a sudden, the one-eyed man is king, because he's got about nineteen million guns.

You like smokum peace pipe now?

That time maybe the government was alright, because the

enemy of my enemy is my friend, you know? But as soon as our enemy is dead, then you know you got to keep one eye on the ball and one eye on the umpire. It makes people think you're nuts with your eyes in both directions like that. But this is the GOVERN-MENT, man. The government popped a high-altitude, low-yield nuclear bomb 22 miles in the air. And you think you can trust them? Southern fried E-bombs, man.

They lit the wick over southern Tennessee and knocked out everything. There to the gulf. And you can't take it back now, man. You go until they lock you up. Just like they locked me up, man. Yep. And they make you miss your MOMENTS, man. You lay there while the kingmaker lights up the sky. On a stained old mattress in the ghost jail, man. But I had a plan.

Huey was staggering. The feds ran up and jump-kicked him off the cliff. But robots don't die when they fall off a cliff, you with me? They get right back up and hitchhike into town again. If some-body'd give 'em a ride. So Huey was down, but the HumanPals weren't out.

That's why they needed me.

I had all Hueykind in my sights if they would have let me finish the job.

Pastor Rich
Interviewed in Coldwater, MS

WE DECIDED to make the church a refuge center and stocked it with supplies in case the humanpals made it this far. Up until then, we had no reason to believe they wouldn't. The majority of the town had fled north, and so I'd say only a few hundred people were left, and it felt like a ghost town. Even without any robots, it felt eerie.

But I sleep soundly, so I may be one of the only people within a hundred miles of the blast that can honestly say I had no idea it had even happened. I was snoring, so I was sleeping on the couch. Then the phone started ringing. And I momentarily debated letting it ring, before realizing it had to be an emergency at this hour.

"Pastor, did you see that?" Steve immediately said.

"No. See what?"

"A big light in the sky. It woke us up. Any insight?"

"I know less than you." So I turned on the TV.

All the local stations were out, and so were TNT, TBS, CNN, and The Weather Channel. And on the others, all we could find were infomercials and old sitcoms. I heard Steve through the phone doing the same thing.

"Maybe it was just here," Steve said.

"All the local stations are out."

Finally Steve found someone talking about it. I paused to let him listen.

"Did you hear that? It was a bomb!"

"Why? What kind of bomb?"

"They think it was a nuke, but they don't know why."

"Are you kidding me?"

"No, that's what they said. It might have something to do with the robots."

"Like the robots launched it?"

"I don't know, they don't know. It was shot off from southern Tennessee," Steve said.

"I thought they were still a few days from here, that's close!"

Steve had been trying to fortify the church building as best he could, but we knew that we couldn't do much. Like I said, Coldwater was mostly a ghost town at this point. I would have fled north too, if it wasn't for the obligation I felt to our weakest members. Our best defense, in my opinion, was that we had the entire congregation taking shifts to keep prayer going in the sanctuary 24/7. It was always a desire of mine to have 24-hour prayer, but it took a crisis like this to make it happen.

I suggested we get to the church.

On the way there I heard lots of theories on the radio. And I had lots of phone calls on my dumbphone, so I started telling everyone we were going to have an emergency meeting at the church. Basically I'd be preaching.

I didn't know what to preach on, because I still didn't know what was happening. I went into my office and closed the door.

It didn't take long before Steve knocked.

"Can I come in?" he asked. "What I heard, and makes sense to me, is that it was a nuclear bomb set off on purpose by the military. They think they may have stopped the robots with an electromagnetic pulse, which would be fantastic!"

"Really?"

"It's a byproduct of a nuclear bomb. That's why they blew it up in the air, I think. So the bomb wouldn't hurt anybody, but the EMP would knock out all the robots. Heck, it probably knocked out all the electronics in the South! But if it stopped the rampage, then it worked!"

"Why didn't it affect us? I mean if it hit the whole South, it seems like it was closer to us than southern Georgia, you know?" I said.

"I don't know. Maybe they figured out a way to just make it affect the robots. Or yeah, maybe we are just north of the blast area. I don't know, but I'm excited! The whole thing may be over!" Steve said.

"We should check Human," I said, getting up from my desk.

It dawned on him at the same time. We made our way over to the sanctuary, where there were already people gathering, talking to each other. Upon entrance, we became the focus as we climbed to the balcony and opened the closet.

I heard people sharing what they had heard about the big light in the sky. Some were concerned, but the more information came in about it being an electromagnetic pulse bomb, the more relief and excitement seemed to set in. And there stood Human, still in the closet, listening to it all, I thought. His eyes were still glowing.

"How's Human?" somebody yelled.

"He looks fine. Human, sweep," I commanded. At first, he didn't do anything but stare at me. Then he suddenly grabbed the broom next to him, swiped it across the floor without purpose a few times and set it back down.

"I'm going to go speak, Human. I will leave the door open for you," I said, forgetting that Steve was standing next to me. I made my way down the stairs and to the front of the church. Steve handed me a microphone, but I opted to gather everyone up close and just talk. There were about twenty people.

"We don't know if we're safe, we don't know what's true, and we're not sure what we should be doing. But I am here to tell you, we're doing exactly what we need to be doing. Charles, Phyllis, I know you were on prayer shift this morning. And just about every-body here has been taking a shift since we moved to 24-hours. We've stocked up on all the essentials. We've done exactly what needs to be done.

"I don't know if the robots have been stopped, as some suggest. And I don't know for sure that what we saw this morning was a government weapon. Whether our lives are still in danger or not, I know that we aren't supposed to be afraid. How many times does the Bible tell us not to fear?

"Go about as if nothing has changed until we know. Prepare. But do not be afraid," I said. "Everyone is invited to stay here and pray or whatever you'd like. Steve, can we put the news on the projector screen?"

"Yeah, give me a minute," he said. My cell phone went off, but I ignored it.

"So let's find out what's going on. But remember, whether we get to rejoice that it's all over, or whether we have to continue readying ourselves, we will do so confidently." The loud sound of news on the projector screen cut me off.

I stepped to the side and listened. But my eyes caught Human, who had come out onto the balcony while I spoke. He seemed to be paying attention, not to me, but to the reports and images flashing across the screen of robots killing people in what looked like a foreign war zone right here in the United States. I could only wonder how he was processing this information. Without warning, a fear, which I had just preached against, gripped me. What if he turned by just watching the screen? Could that happen? I calmed myself, repeating my own words back silently. Do not fear.

But don't be stupid either, Rich.

I turned off the same fifteen seconds of shaky phone footage being looped on the news and asked Steve to put it in another room. Those gathered in the sanctuary looked up at Human, and seemed to understand what I was doing and made their way out. But Human just stood there, staring at the screen long after it was off. It shook me a bit, so I battled back the fear and walked up onto the balcony with him. My presence seemed to shake Human from his frozen daze and he turned toward me. His head cocked, just a bit, as if he was asking me a question. I didn't know what question. But I thought maybe it was, "Why?"

"I don't know why, Buddy. I don't know."

Gently steering him back to his room, I almost felt as if a part of him was still in that daze. But before he was fully in, he turned, quicker than usual. This sounds stupid and I may have been projecting my emotions onto him, but that soft, puzzled look was gone. In its place was something else; something which only served to strengthen my fading fear. There was anger within Human, or at least that's how I interpreted it in the moment. I checked myself, and pushed the fear away. It wasn't anger. Determination, maybe.

Concentration, possibly. It was intense, and that's all I knew for sure as he willingly budged backward into the dark of the closet, his eyes fixated on nothing but the air, his frame steeled in the way a hawk coasts between air streams. There in the dark closet, his eyes fluttered in nearly imperceptible light fluctuations that would not have been seen in any other environment.

I backed away and let him be.

"I don't know why, Buddy."

I look back now and wonder if it was by design that Human saw the news that day. It certainly seemed to plant a seed.

The newscast continued in the next room. Reports confirmed that it was launched by our military, but what everyone wanted to know, the reporters wouldn't say yet.

Did it work?

"Kind of," wasn't what we wanted to hear. A definitive "yes" or "no" would have been just fine. But by the time we had the murky answer to our question, half the day had been wasted. So we continued to prepare as we had for days, although now we were less certain of what to prepare for.

We had all seen the images on TV, but would it look like that, or would it be different now?

We kept hearing, from various sources, that the robot front had been "slowed down," but that was wrong. We had less than a day before they would show up in our town. I think what they meant was, the overall number was reduced. Everything was hazy.

The church turned into a literal sanctuary for our town, or what was left of it anyway, after the mass exodus. It was the supply hub, the information center, and yet the calmest place you could be amid the activity. Be it real or false, people felt a sense of security at the church building, because there were so many of us working together. Human stayed in his closet, as we thought it would be best to keep him hidden away. I never mentioned to anyone the experience from the day prior.

Within hours of the impending wave of machines, we came up with our best idea at creating a barrier. Up until that point, we had none. We heard that water ditches had been ineffective, and that water only wore them down over time. We didn't have the capability to concrete ourselves in, like some were attempting. Bomb shelters and so forth. Instead, we used what we all had with us – our cars. We circled the cars around the building, sometimes three deep. There was no room between each car, bumpers to doors. It was not the best defense in the world, but it was the best we had. We hoped it would hold them off long enough that they would be distracted and go elsewhere, or we would find another solution.

And at the first robot sighting, probably half the town was inside the church, or at least a good two hundred. It was one of the most frightening things I had ever seen when the first robots showed up. All those images from the news came rushing back. Would we be lost in the shuffle of the dead? I continued repeating my own advice on fear.

The first one that went by stopped and looked, and then it came right at our church. No thought was given to it, the robot seemed to just act by instinct, if such a thing is possible. It made no hesitation in smashing its fist into the first car it came to, busting the windshield and passenger window out with one blow to the frame. Of the two hundred or so people inside, most of the men were attempting to watch, and one even had guns ready, although we knew that to be a rather useless weapon at the time. I did not mention it, however, assuming it gave him a sense of security. And now looking back, I'm incredibly glad he brought them.

A handful of robots quickly joined the first one. In fact, not a single robot "went on by." They seemed to have a pack mentality. I guess a planned diversion would have been a good idea, rather than just hoping for one. It was something we hadn't thought of. We weren't certain how that worked.

The first one had leveled the car into a flat wad of scrap metal, but it continued to smash it. Some relief came to me when I realized it didn't seem to be able to get over or around the heap it had created, though I knew it would eventually. Still, the fact that it had been slowed down, and still had another two rows of cars to get through, energized me. I was glad we put the extra row in the front.

My cell phone went off again, but I paid no attention, standing there amazed at the speed and power of their arms coming down on the cars. It was as if they could have folded them in half. I was surprised they didn't just pick them up and move them, one by one, but that probably would have involved more thought than instinct. All of these things were going through my head in the span of about sixty seconds. I allowed myself to be afraid, and awed, and even paralyzed for that one minute, before a voice deep in my gut yelled at me, "Get up!"

I stood and clenched my fists, realizing I needed to stop gawking and come up with alternatives if our barricade didn't last, so I ran to the back of the church and looked out the kitchen window to find an escape route for this mass of people. This was happening much sooner than anticipated. The back lot led to a wooded area where we would be able to siphon out the women and children at least. But I went faint, and the fire went cold. There were double the amount of robots there, and we were only two cars deep in the back.

I sprinted up through the corridor and pulled Steve and a few other trusted men into a Sunday school room alone.

"Listen, it's even worse in the back, and we need to either get these people out of here or get the robots away," I breathed at them.

"There are too many people in here! Why didn't we spread out, we're like sitting ducks!" the man with the guns yelled, entering the room.

"Nope, go." I told him. Nathan left willfully. Our community effort did suddenly seem foolish, though.

"There are too many people in here to evacuate, he's right, so we need to get the robots away somehow," Steve said.

"How do we do that?" said one of our elders.

I pointed at him. "Cliff, no matter what we do, I need you to keep the people calm and let them know we have a plan."

He nodded, knowing full well that we didn't.

"Steve, what about Human?" I said.

"I don't know, I would figure we'd want to keep him away from them, if anything. I hadn't thought about it."

"What about the big propane tank on the side of the building?" I asked.

"What about it?"

"Can we roll it off?"

"Probably."

"Can we draw all the robots into one area?" I asked.

"I don't know," Steve said. Cliff, having enough information, left to be with the people.

The men scattered and my cell phone rang again. I didn't recognize the number, but it was the same one that had already called twice.

"Pastor, is this Pastor?" the voice asked.

"Yes, what do you need?" I said.

"This is Mike Daye," he said.

"Mike! We could really use your help, are they at the station yet, or downtown? They're all over here."

"Sort of. Listen, we don't have any transportation down here. But you know that guy that broke into the church?"

"Yeah?"

"He can stop them," Daye said.

"What?" I asked.

"Yes, that guy. Roland. He's stopping them," Daye said.

"How?"

"Do you have any guns?"

Roland Wright
Interviewed in Three Rivers Correctional Center

YOU WOULDN'T BELIEVE IT, man. Of all the places you'd think would be ready for the attack, this police station was cowtipped. Big old pushover. Huey didn't even CARE about it, man. Didn't even TARGET it, 'cause it didn't matter.

I watch them coming from my cell window, smashing everything but us. We can't even, like, get their attention. The cops say they're going to try and "stay mobile" so they can serve where they are needed most, but it's got 'em limper than a wet coin roll.

"Let me out, I can help you!" I call aloud to anyone who will listen. They ignore me no matter how genuinely I make my case. "Give me a gun, I can help you!" It probably isn't the best tactic. Asking to be let out of jail while begging for a gun.

I keep my eye on the window. I can see them coming up the street, and it's a feast, but I know Huey keeps a mighty appetite and I'm not about to be some robot's dessert. I'm the STEAK and FINGER POTATOES, man. So I change my approach.

"Are you just going to let me die in here without a way to protect myself? What kind of people are you! My GOD WHAT KIND OF PEOPLE ARE YOU!" I go ballistic, man. If they won't listen to logic, maybe I can bleed their souls. "Help me! Help me!" I yell out the door. There wasn't anybody in the police station. All five cops are on the street, hiding out in case anyone needs them. But there isn't a person out there. The only thing they're able to hear above the robots are my cries for mercy, taunting their humanity.

Finally the main day shift cop comes back in. I remember him because his name is Daye.

"You've gotta let me out!" I yell at him, and he's pulling his keys out of his pocket, so that part worked anyway. I decide to let up so they know I'm a sane man and they can listen to me.

"I really can stop them," I say.

"These things are wiping out a quarter of our country, and you expect me to believe some idiot that broke into a church is the savior?" Daye says as he unlocks my cell. Welcome to the machine mind. Where you can't make a difference if you're an everyman, man. That's what the robot-run media does. But the machines are getting closer, man, I can hear them.

Daye escorts me out. I don't think he knows what he's going to do with me, so I fork the road. I jump out into the middle of the street and start waving my hands.

"Hey, Metal! Look over here! MEAT AND SIDES! YEAH!" I'm all finger potatoes now, yelling as loud as I can, but the machines are getting louder, too. Another one of the cops runs out and hits me with his gun in the same place I got hit in the church a week ago, and I fall to my dang knees. Daye tackles me from behind and tries to get me out of the street. I can tell he's thinking about leaving me out there to die, but he doesn't know what I'm trying to do yet.

"Hey, you all, listen up, I can stop 'em! Let me show you," I say.

"Nobody give him a gun!" Daye yells at the others. They shuffle with me as a group now, down and around, between the storefronts.

The Hueys are closer, but they don't know where we went. At the moment, we're between a building and a couple of dumpsters. Rock and a hard place. Downtown is eerie, man. If there are any other people, they're out of sight, out of mind. But I'm in my mind, man. I'm in my element like a thirsty gazelle in the desert who found a gas station. Every movement the machines make echoes down the empty streets and it's crazy loud. But we also know right where they're at because of it. And it drowns us out, so we're able to move around with ease as long as they don't see us. Although right now, I want them to see us. I'm steak and potatoes, man!

"Let me go and give me a gun, you think I'm going to shoot you? We have, like, a common enemy," I say into the group.

"I'm not letting you do anything. You just tell us your idea and we'll see what we do about it," Daye yells.

"It's not an idea, it's a fact. But it's harder to explain than it is for me to just do it, and you watch and learn," I say.

"No guns."

"Why do you think I broke into that church? To kill people? I've been trying to tell you I broke in there to kill that machine they've got in there because I heard it could talk."

"You can say it over and over again, and I have no reason to believe you," Daye says. "And that robot's got a name in this town, fella. Even if you were breaking in there to kill Human, he's part of the family around here."

"I'll say this: he doesn't talk. But then you say this: the machines are a threat!" I say.

"We're not here to debate with you. Either tell us what you got or shut up and hide until we say otherwise."

This is going NOWHERE, so I break off and run right at Huey. I've got a good jump on them, so they aren't going to catch me.

When I make it to the main road, I start backtracking because the machines are like, really close. I run right back into the police chasing me. They fire a couple of shots and put one of the machine's eyes out, which doesn't do anything but frustrate me.

Finally, Daye trains his big gun right at me and throws me a little Colt M1911. The machines are coming at us and he throws me a PISTOL. I stop, then he stops and watches me, still ready to blow my face off.

"Alright, do it then, smart guy!" he yells.

I cock the piece and take my three patented shots, one, two, three, at the closest one. Sharp shots. That closest machine, moving full speed, goes full blackout. Shuts down all function for a split second and goes totally stiff just like I'm expecting. But its momentum makes it come crashing forward onto its face, sliding about ten yards before coming to a stop. By now, it's functioning again, but it's just smashing the ground with its arms and legs like a child throwing a temper tantrum, man.

The cops are stunned, and like, don't know whether to cheer or not. But we don't have time before we got to run again. Daye still has the gun in my direction, but he's more relaxed with it this time with only two machines chasing us instead of three.

"Did you see that? It stopped! He stopped it!" one of them yells, out of breath.

"Yeah, but it was getting back up," yells another.

"But he knocked it down anyway!" the first one yells. "He shot its eyes out!"

"It wasn't getting back up . . ." I stop mid-sentence as we round a corner to our only escape route. Two are in behind. In front, another nine or so. My side is hurting already.

"Do it again," Daye yells between breaths.

"Give me a better gun," I say all calm. One behind me gives me a .45 and I cock and run right at the things.

"Come 'ere!" I yell at the cops.

It takes me four shots to get the first one. It's not moving at quite the pace, so it just stops and stays still for a second. Then it starts throwing haymakers. It actually clips the other and knocks it off balance, right as I shoot my three shots into the second one, and it falls over sideways into a trash bin. Even as that one's going down it's annihilating the dumpster for all it's worth, man.

The cops are following ME now. I'm in the lead, man! And I run right up close to the two machines, and look right into their busted out eyes. I turn around and give the "shhh" sign to the cops, and we stroll right on by the blind beasts.

The ones behind us get caught up in the two I blinded, so we finally put some space between us. We go back out to the main road where Daye is looking for a car, but they're all smashed up.

"Tell us now. How do you do that?" he says. "We've tried shooting their eyes out."

"It takes three shots. First, you hit them in the neck, right below the chin. Their central processor is here," I say, pointing at my heart. "But when you hit them right there in the neck, it cuts off communication to their stupid heads."

"Then, you shoot out their eyes. Now, when you shoot their eyes out, you're really only busting the glassy red light that filters the image coming into the machine, not the actual seeing mechanism. But since the processor is cut off from the head, it can't communicate that to itself. So it thinks it went blind."

"So shoot right there on the neck, then shoot the eyes out," Daye repeats.

"Yep, and DON'T shoot the eyes out until you know you've hit the neck spot. If you shoot the eyes out first, then it won't work. And you won't be able to blind the thing at all. Shooting the eyes out first only slows it's processing a little, since the images aren't filtered. But at that point you just made it even harder to stop."

"We've already done that to a few. Shot their eyes out first," one guy says.

"I know!" I yell at them. "You have to do it exactly like I showed you!"

But that isn't sucking their gas any. They're still hopping and hooting. Daye is already on the phone calling people, looking for a way to get me back to the church, where most of the people are stationed in this ghost town. Ha. The first time I break in and they lock me up. Now they're inviting me back in with a red carpet.

Alright, man, take me to church.

FIVE
EMPTINESS

The Gay Gambler

Interviewed by phone

I originally hoped, in a pathetic sort of way, that a HumanPal could provide comfort in my solitude. But they were too large and did not travel easily. Even my rebuilds did not prove successful, and my attention moved elsewhere. I never owned one again.

But for many, the machines had become so commonplace that they wondered what life was like before they existed. Many of these folks were on Vespucci Cruise Liner 19 with me. And after what we had just witnessed, these objects with which they had entrusted their lives were now the greatest threat to them. Nose to nose they stood with their loyal companions which now had the propensity to destroy them with a flick of the wrist.

A panic immediately erupted, which was little more than a transition from the panic we had just endured on the dock. Some people ran away from them and hid the best they could, while others, realizing this was futile, teamed up to start throwing the things overboard. It took at least four men to do this per robot. And while it seemed to me a fairly logical thing to do in the immediate, I also began to wonder about the long-term consequences we would face.

One, two, they heaved them over. By three and four, every available male was on hand to promote the androcide. I maintained my distance because of a hazard that I believed was being horribly overlooked: as they were tossing number four overboard, I looked in the red of another one's eyes. A deep, disconcerting cool was coming over me.

I stood back and watched them as they lifted a cleaning pal into the water below and immediately moved on to the next, which was the one I had been gazing at so intently. I watched it carefully, searching for any sort of emotion I could find as they surrounded it and pushed it to the edge. There was no fear in it, or rage, or longing, or bravery. No emotion of any kind. But it did one thing that was so significant, and so terribly haunting, it could not be overlooked. It looked right at me the entire time. There were people all around it, yelling and pushing, and yet it did not break its gaze with me. Even as they lifted it just high enough to get the majority of its weight over the edge, it stared only at me.

Even so, my own emotions were equally unchanged. This may seem heartless to some, and ridiculous to others, but I had just seen robots mutilating people only minutes ago, and now I was seeing the whole thing in reverse. Pardon me if I did not have the required response. What I did have was this still rising concern, which had now finally moved from general unease to full alarm.

Surveying the deck, the mob line looked to be about three robots deep before they would have to move to a new group. And outside of those, I could count about fifteen other robots that the mob had not yet accounted for. Those fifteen focused mainly on the mob, since it was where all the noise was coming from. I concerned myself with these and ran to the nearest one, which promptly repositioned itself to face me, as a good servant. "Take drinks to the captain!" I commanded. It left swiftly. "Clean room 300!" I told the next. "Check the cabins for a pair of missing earrings!" I continued, running from robot to robot, giving orders to each one I approached.

"Yes, good idea! Thank you!" said a young woman.

"Who do you think you are?" said another woman in a visor as I gave commands to the final one, which sped off to accomplish its worthless task. Before I could answer for my actions, the young woman spoke on my behalf.

"He's saving us from them, he made them all go away!" she said.

"He's trying to save them!" said the other woman. "We're throwing them overboard, and he's trying to save them!"

By now the mob had finished throwing the three into the water and was looking for the rest, surprised to find that all on the deck were gone.

"I brought my pal on that I've had for ten years, and it was one of the first they pushed over – don't tell me you're a bleeding heart for these things. You saw what they just did, we need to get them off this ship!"

The young woman chimed in again on my behalf, taking a position I did not choose.

"Since we've been on here, not a single one of those things has hurt anybody!"

"I AM NOT GOING TO TAKE THAT CHANCE!" said a man from the mob. At that, everybody started yelling, mostly at my reluctant partner and me.

"We have to dig them out, every last one of them, forget him!" someone yelled.

"Where did you send them?!" they screamed. Amazed and wanting to clarify my position, I eased into my explanation.

"I wasn't protecting them. This young lady has opinions of her own, but I was not protecting them from you," I said.

"Where did you send them?!" they screamed again.

"We need to be careful, people! Now the robots here are clearly not acting like the ones we left on the land. But the last thing I want is to give them any ideas, since they could turn this ship into a floating coffin very quickly."

I paused, to give them another chance to say their piece, which they didn't.

"I just saw you push eight humanpals into the ocean. So did about fifteen other robots. I got rid of them."

From the looks on their faces, they seemed to be taking my words with great care.

"Now what, then?" a man genuinely asked.

"We pull them out, one by one, and push them over. But only one at a time. We keep any of the others from seeing us do it, and we keep the rest of them isolated so that if one begins to show violence, we can deal with it alone."

A general grumble of approval came from the mob who clearly did not want to agree with the man they had detested seconds ago.

"First, listen. First things first. We command each robot into a cabin. Never two together. Then once we know where they all are, including the lower levels, which should probably be separated first, then we coordinate how to dispose of them individually, which can be done at each end of the ship as long as we have some-body in charge of keeping them all separated."

"You do it," said the woman in the visor.

The general grumble of treaty was heard again, and I reluctantly agreed to lead the effort.

It took two days, and we eventually cleaned the ship of all 94 robots, the longest part being the separation and organization of them. And not a single one, aside from those initial fifteen, witnessed it. I know now that the effort was not entirely practical, but at the time, it was a plan with purpose. The young woman and a few others were unwilling participants in the process, but they were so outnumbered that they rarely voiced their objections. I never felt remorse for being the ringleader of this process, but if I were to feel it, it would be the young woman's fault. The night we finished the process, I reflected on recent events by the edge. She stood beside me at the rail for a moment and looked into the water below. "We can kill them all so easily because we think they're just machines. But if that's all they are, then why do we need to protect them from seeing one another die?" she asked.

I continued looking out into the black over the water.

She gained the courage to continue.

"I don't like what they did on the dock, but I don't like what we did either," she said. "I think that maybe, what we did justified what they did."

She realized the condescension of her comment and looked over her shoulder to see if anyone would have heard her. Many people had loved ones and relatives that did not make the ship; they would have been sincerely angered by what the young woman was saying. Although at that moment, I did not feel comfortable giving her any correction. My decisions would have to stand on their own.

She remained there next to me for a good long while.

I never had lengthy discussions with the young woman, but she would often come and stand by me in the nights and evenings, sometimes giving a thought or two, and sometimes saying nothing but hello.

I preferred the nights, because during the days we had a good many issues to deal with on our now-safe floating oasis. The crew was training each person in any essential task that the robots had done. And I was assisting in organizing it all. Supplies were plentiful. We did have contact with the outside world, and we had been made aware of the condition ashore. Many aboard felt guilt at our fortunate situation, but I was only appreciative that I was in perhaps the safest place I could be.

Among those who had lingering guilt, a sense of salvation came in the arrangement of Project Vacate, as it was called. We took anchor in the gulf and became a haven for refugees, who were ferried out to us by recreational boats and fishermen. I noticed a distinct change in the demeanor of the young woman after our focus had turned to helping survivors.

One night I had made myself a drink and was looking at the haze on the water. In the rhythmic state of the waves hitting the ship, and my own fascination with it all, I hadn't noticed her standing next to me again.

"Hello," she said.

"Hello to you," I said.

She breathed. "This is the best time. There's nobody awake."

Although I usually didn't, I looked over at her. The ocean wind was blowing her hair. There was something very sweet about her that frightened me.

"Do you think they stay alive down there?" she asked. She looked over and caught my eye for the first time, which gave her pause. "I mean," she hesitated, "do they just stay turned on forever at the bottom of the ocean?"

Though it was an exchange much like our others, it felt different this time, as if it had snuck up on us that we were alone together. Even during discussion, we usually just gazed out on the water. This time, she was looking over at me. And I couldn't seem to form my thoughts. So I nodded.

"Then what do they do? Just sit in darkness, waiting for a command?" she grasped. I opened my shoulder toward her and she turned back to the water. I didn't know if it was the first time she had thought about it, but it was something I had been pondering.

"That's exactly what they do. They wait," I said.

"I wish I would have given each one an endless command, right before they pushed it over," she sighed.

"Nothing could occupy it forever. Eventually the water corrodes them from the inside," I said.

"Then what?"

"Either a period of madness or nothing. Either way, they all end up relics for a future generation."

I expected her eyes to be on the water, searching for an answer. Instead, she looked out at the horizon.

Like lightning, the sky had lit up behind the clouds.

She turned to me, much more eager than ever before.

"What was that?"

It wasn't close, but it was too large and too fast to be a distant storm.

For the first time, I looked her in the eye. She was far too young.

"I don't know."

But that's not what scared me. She was looking to me for comfort, not just for the question. Her bright eyes wanted safety and knew I could provide it for her right here and now. I knew she had wanted this safety long before there was an existential threat. But now even more so. And more, and more. And as much as I could provide comfort for the people aboard this ship when pressed, I wanted it tenfold for the young woman. I wanted to give it to her very badly, and easily could in this moment. Maybe that's what frightened me about her. She was full of good things. I saw myself in her, but a self I hadn't seen in a very long time. It was a long second that hung in the air right then, with her looking at me, waiting for a gesture into depth. I knew I wanted desperately to do something that might be out of character, so I walked away without a sufficient reply. Because at that moment I didn't know what the light in the sky was, therefore I could not answer her question, and therefore it made no sense to continue the discussion.

The next night, for the first time since the beginning, she

didn't arrive. I continued to, however. If only to be alone in my thoughts without interruption. She made me feel . . . something. If she had returned, I might have explored it.

Alf Johnson
Interviewed in Tampa, FL

WHAT WAS neat was when I found buried treasure finally. I always wanted to find buried treasure, but this time it was in a raft that got caught in my trolling motor. I don't know what else was in it, 'cause it was all crunched up. But I did get a wallet out of there, and an old wet flare. So there I was, opening up the wallet for some buried treasure, and you know what was in it? Eight dollars. Eight free dollars! And a picture of some kid with a you-know-what eating grin. I don't use this word that often, but I think that kid was cursed because right after I got the wallet I lost a bet and had to change the name of the *Coneheads* to whatever Lilly wanted.

On a trip we took to shore leave, I was about to get off of *Sweet Petey Pickles, My Cat* and throw that wallet right in a fire, because there seemed to be a lot of fire everywhere now. And a bunch of people were waiting. Just waiting with those sad, turd eyes. It made me almost just as sad. They needed a hero. Well I ain't no hero. You talk to a man in uniform, that's a hero. I am more like just a champion or something. So I stood up and I puffed my chest right out there, and I said, "Don't worry, *Sweet Petey Pickles, My Cat* is here!" Then a couple seconds later I said, "It's party time, but I know it's a sad time." So I started thrusting my hips in only little tiny thrusts. There was about six or twelve of them that got on just needing a party. That's how I read it. And there was a guy named "Greag" or "Groad" or something like that. It was probably Greag, I never met a Groad before. He must have barely escaped with his life because all he had was some dress pants and a torn up dress-shirt. He just needed a little party. And a lady with a missing arm. She just needed a party. But this Groad had something special about him. A special something that I always had been envious about: a Looney Tunes tie. I always thought I would look real good in a Looney Tune tie. And here he was, like out of a dream or something. I shook my head, "ah-de-ah-de-aye." I was hungry for that tie and, all of a sudden, Groad was a turkey leg. I did my walk over to him where I look around like the other things are real interesting, because I was trying to play it cool.

"Oh hey, it's you," I said. "I hadn't seen you yet, or I was walking by not paying any attention. That's it."

Finally I felt the urge pass, and I just said in a calm, shaky voice, "Hey that's a neat little strip of tie there, Groad" and laughed some more anxiety out. But to let him know I wanted it, because I didn't think I had made it clear yet, I brushed the fabric up and down with the back of my hand.

I felt bad for Groad. I saw a little bit of my own self in Groad, because hey, I think Groad looked a little bit like me. Not enough for me to walk up and act like I was looking into a mirror, but enough for me to draw a mustache on myself so people could keep us straight.

Lilly said she thought I had made Groad "exasperated" when she was cutting my hair later to look more like his. And I should leave him alone because of all the things he went through on land. Oh yeah, well if he's so "exasperated" then how did you find out his life story? Huh? I was doing some party planning in my head. I decided to be nice though, so I walked up to him and the one-armed lady and said, "Have you seen whether or not any of the passengers have nice ties on this fine day?" Then I smiled and let nature take its course.

And then we went around in circles for a while until we heard on the radio that they were bringing all them cruisers into the gulf.

They said to dump all the people on a cruiser and get some more, so that's what we did. When he was on the cruiser, Groad looked down at me from the deck like Kate Wimsler. I still think about it sometimes and wonder whether Groad and his Taz tie made it or not.

I don't remember any of the other people's names. I called the one-armed lady Sno-Cone 'cause her head was so round.

Aaron Umbarger
Excerpt from his letters to Coldwater

NICE MOVE USING the police radio. It's amazing how much we take technology for granted until it's gone. A couple weeks ago we would have just called, but now we have to come see you. Koji's team wants to dissect that guy's three-shot technique.

But a terrible and mysterious thing happened in a town called Etta.

That's close to where they moved the barricade once it failed in Thaxton and we finally left the school. I think they knew it was going to fail in Thaxton and that's why they did it there. They knew they could still fall back northwest and be fine.

We had been taking mostly back roads because there were fewer robots to deal with. You'd still seem them every now and then in the countryside, but you'd just outrun them. However, we couldn't avoid going through Etta without serious time loss.

It shouldn't have mattered, because by all accounts the town seemed empty. I mean, empty! I guess everyone in town decided to evacuate before the quarantine hit them, or before the robots got there, I don't know. But that's what must have made it so easy for those horrible things to hear us coming. And the strategy therein was unbearably impressive.

Rounding a curve, we had no way of seeing that they had formed a full blockade. The men driving the lead vehicle had about five seconds to make a decision- stop and try a different way, or try to play Red Rover. To stop might cause the whole motorcade to wreck into each other, and we'd be sitting ducks. To go through them was probably the best decision he could have made in five seconds. At least we had a chance then. Besides, we all knew it might come to this at some point on the drive.

Thankfully, every vehicle had the same reaction: carry the momentum, plow the line and hold your breath. After all, there were only about a dozen robots.

The lead vehicle crashed into them and went up, ultimately going to two wheels and landing on the robots sideways. The men in that Humvee frantically unbuckled but the robots punched through the floor of the car instead of throwing it off, reaching up through it like tentacles. The rest of the robots boxed it in just enough that a cross street opened to the motorcade, and all seven vehicles took the route. This wasn't an easy turn, especially since one of them was a limo.

Still moving at a brisk speed, I watched the men climb out onto the top of the Humvee. Realizing this, the robots beneath it unleashed incredible hydraulic pressure and propelled the vehicle. Though it didn't move much, the jolt flung the two men into the air. And there they remained, stuck airborne, midcourse and trying desperately to fly forever in my mind, because we had gone past the corner and I didn't get to see them come down. I put their chances at 50/50. But we were definitely cutting our losses and leaving them. Maybe this scenario was discussed ahead of time in conversations without my involvement. Most discussions were without my involvement. Here is where I should say I couldn't believe what was happening, but that's not true. I believed it.

Rounding the corner and expecting now to accelerate, we did the opposite. Full stop. Being in the very last car, I couldn't see what was ahead, but I heard that terrible noise, and this is where the true mystery starts. I saw robots emerging from every storefront in this little downtown like a plague. They had been inside the buildings! And they were everywhere. EVERYWHERE. Completely surrounding us, tearing aside the glass and concrete storefronts like they were football players coming through paper banners. It looked more and more like a team strategy.

This was frightening.

For the first time, I had to acknowledge that I, personally, was prey to a disturbingly intelligent adversary. Not even at Jason's did I feel this way. My energy drained and my body chilled. We were tricked. We would be eliminated, because this was a war. And until now, we had not been treating it properly.

Every single person in that motorcade knew it. We were outnumbered, overpowered, and surrounded. One person from Koji's team thought he saw an opening and ran from the limo. He made it past a few of them, but was easily caught and eliminated in grotesque form. I didn't want to watch, but I did, because that could be me and I needed to see.

Everyone else waited, not knowing what they would do with us now.

So we sat.

And wondered what the plan would be. The execution plan. Would they march us out like men, or tear us apart like animals?

We waited. Completely surrounded, but strangely still.

Why weren't they doing anything?

I began to think they were waiting for us to make the first move, in the way predators respond to fleeing game. But it must have been more strategic. They were feeling us out.

It was maddening.

The men in the first armored truck had either been killed or had gotten away, because there was no action back there anymore.

Should the new lead vehicle try to plow through too? With no momentum it would seem foolish. There was no plan. Just sitting.

It couldn't have lasted as long as it seemed. A minute or two. It felt like forever. It wasn't even a standoff, because they had options and we didn't.

The robots had to make the next move. We would merely respond.

But, I thought, what if they never do anything? What if they just wait?

They didn't. That terrible noise started again. But this time there was organization to it. One by one, the robots brought their legs up and down, up and down, harder and harder in complete and total unison. Right, left, right, left. Stomp, stomp, stomp. Their feet shaking the ground like a hundred trains. You could play music by the synchronicity of it. Then like a marching band, each robot moved in such fluid motion that there had to be motivation to it. Around the streets, between our cars, in and out of the stores, they marched. I wondered if from above it would have created a pattern, but when I reflect on it now, I think I know what they were doing based on what they did next, which was to suddenly stop. Not each one where it was, but each, when it found the right spot, stopped, and then kneeled and bowed its head. Gradually, as each robot found its place, stopped, and bowed, the stomp, stomp, stomp of the feet grew quieter and quieter until the last one bent down and bowed its head to us. Dozens of robots, bowing. Literally, to their maker.

Pastor Rich
Interviewed in Coldwater, MS

WE HAD MORE volunteers than we needed, which was a good thing. Most everybody in the church was sitting idle and feeling helpless, so they all wanted to join, once we had a plan.

I prayed. I am thankful for that uniquely human ability to communicate with God.

I reminded myself that they're different from us.

Nobody said anything, but people had naturally gone to their knees, and seven of us walked right through them and out the door.

Aaron Umbarger
Excerpt from his letters to Coldwater

BUT THERE WAS no honor in it.

The quiet of the town should have been sacred, especially in light of such a scene, but it wasn't.

"What is this?" somebody in front of me spoke.

The robots had not responded this way before. Were they aware of the presence of Koji? I thought maybe they had always wanted to do this, and now, in their independent state, they could.

Why hadn't any robots done this before then? These weren't the first of the changed robots to encounter Koji. Then a thought: were they truly becoming independent, like men? Some men and women are religious, and some are not. Could it be that the robots were forming into these camps? If so, had this town, Etta, fostered a sect of independent robots choosing to worship? I imagined Koji stepping out of the limo to a throng of heads bowed, someone throwing a robe over him as he strode among his creation, blessing each one. I imagined guns being laid down willingly by a powerful military cartel. Many thoughts came and went in the span of that moment because of what we were witnessing. However, it was anything but reverent. And it was just a moment.

The robots' heads were bowed because each one was staring at a spot in the pavement that the hive had identified. Yes, I said hive. That's the way these behaved. Not so independently as we had come to expect, though there was no clear leader. They acted in concert.

Heads bowed, eyes closed. Or dimmed. Or simply focused. Then the noise began again. Left, right, left, right. This time with fists instead of feet. It seemed even louder than before. Each one pounded away at its own precise spot and I realized why they had been stomping around like a marching band at the same time as all these military men. They were testing it, and simultaneously communicating the results to each other. I've seen some scary things, Rich, but this might be the worst of it. And not just for me. However, at the moment, my safety was the only thing on my mind. Sorry, I don't know if military training makes you think of others first in the heat of the moment, but my mind was on me. And the fact that I had never been in an earthquake. I assume an earthquake would feel similar to this.

The ground beneath us started to crack like peanut brittle. You could see it.

I don't know what happened next.

DID you ever go too deep under water when you were a kid? Just to see how far down you could go? I remember once, trying to come back to the top, there was a moment, probably brief, where I couldn't figure out which way was up. Instinct kicked in, but for that moment, I thought, maybe, maybe I'm going to die. And that thought never occurs to you until it does. So if you don't know what I'm talking about, then it's never really happened to you. But if it has, then you know, and you never forget it for the rest of your life. That moment underwater is the only thing I have to compare this to, and it was trivial in comparison. I didn't know where I was anymore. I didn't even know if I was in Etta. I couldn't see. At least if I was dead, it hadn't come through any terrible pain that I could recall. So that was good news. I might be falling or I might be rising in the air, yet the instinct to grab onto something was simply not there, as I imagined it would be if I were falling. I simply couldn't grasp direction. Maybe direction and dimension didn't matter here. It was very dark, but light wasn't a hard property either. It was more of an idea. There really wasn't anything to worry about anymore. I thought I was probably lying down, but I could be falling. It was a curious thing. Maybe other people had it tougher than me. Maybe their whole lives were more difficult than mine. There wasn't any guilt though, or deep concern. Just different experiences, each unique and crafted distinctively for each person. This I understood deeply. That I had been cared for and watched over, for every minute of every day of my life, including the one I was experiencing right now, as if time meant anything in the first place. I would have liked to stay there forever. But then the dark, and the light, they were mixing up. And that pain I thought I had avoided was creeping in. There might be something wrong. The person carrying me doesn't know any of these things that I know. He is living his own experience and I'm awfully thankful for him. He is doing what he's supposed to do, and right now, I think that means I'm being carried.

Yes, indeed, and that's when I began to remember things in a little more concrete manner. I can't breathe. And I can't see. How can this guy see anything? How does he know where we're going? Are we still in Etta? How long ago was that? Why am I worrying about this again? I want to be in the place I was before, where I don't worry anymore. But the pain is real. Doesn't he see my leg, and doesn't he understand that I need air? The reason I can't see anything is because of the dust. I haven't lived through an earth-quake, but maybe I have lived through a volcano. The air is thick with ash. And my leg is killing me. I cry out.

"Ouuu." The noise that comes out doesn't feel like it's me saying it.

"Quiet!"

Did I say that or did the guy?

I can hear the end of something big, like the last nanosecond of a trumpet blast after the horn has been blown but before the reverb has ended. And I hear footsteps running wildly around us. Clomp, clomp, clomp. They are coming our direction. The guy suddenly stops.

Then for a minute or so we don't move at all. I want to know what's going on, but I don't think I should talk again. Not yet.

Clomp, clomp, clomp. Whatever it is, it can't find us.

Oh no, I know what it is. I know where we are.

I know why we can't see anything. But that may be the only reason we're still alive. They can't see us either.

They must be trying to find us. The ones that got away.

Quiet now. Be quiet. Okay.

Go. You idiot, go! There's a clearing right in front of me, we can make it! What's in front of me is behind him; he doesn't see it. He doesn't see it! Get his attention! Where the hell are all the buildings? Now that I can see, where are we?

I dig him with my good knee. It doesn't appear that he knows I'm fully conscious until now, but he sees it too.

We're going!

Clomp, clomp, clomp. The guy is running on a cloud, and they're pursuing in the wrong direction. We're going to make it. But where? How could we still be in Etta? He jumps over some-thing I can't see and lands in a pile of something that makes a good deal of noise, and now we're really having to go, because they're chasing us again. He seems confident, or at least I do. There's no way I could run this fast, let alone with somebody slung over my shoulder. He is running right back into the dust, a smokescreen I'm sure. And now quiet. Silent again. The clomp, clomp comes toward us, but not as close as last time. I think it's safe for me to talk now but he does first.

"Can you walk?"

"I don't know." I try. No, I can't. "There's something in my leg." I can't see it, but I can feel something like a jagged metal Frisbee in my thigh.

"Where are we?" I ask. He picks me back up and we're running again. The dust around us is settling slightly and it's safer to stay cloaked, but the footsteps of our pursuers are moving further away. He stops again, and I realize that somehow we're outside, but also we're in a print shop. Maybe I'm still disoriented. The pain in my leg is increasing, and my brain tells me to go back to sleep. That's where I'd rather be right now anyway. Back in that place where the anxiety I never knew I lived with disappeared, because it was never real to begin with. But it was very real here. I didn't like this place anymore.

"Kid, will you stay here while I go back?"

"I can't go anywhere," I must have slurred. Because he decided against leaving me. It gets spotty again, but I saw him grab a set of keys from in the print shop. Which I didn't understand, because he wouldn't need to unlock any doors. The print shop was outside... yeah. I must really be out of it. Then he put me in the backseat of a car, and suddenly we were in an alleyway. And then we were gone. And I was out again, waking only to find that the Frisbee in my leg was removed, but that the pain was just as prevalent. I wondered if I would be able to walk again. Nothing else really seemed to make sense, until I found out what had happened to me and the town of Etta.

Alf Johnson
Interviewed in Tampa, FL

AFTER THAT, we were moving so many people I had to sit down and think about my life. There was an angel that appeared to me and a devil. The angel said: you cuss too much! And I went whoa! A tiny angel! And a tiny devil whispering on the other side said: you drink too much! So I was like, dang, I do cuss too much. So that's when I started using "shiggit" and "sick water" instead of you-know-what and pee. And I think the angel said: those are still cussish words. So I wrote a poem that I still live by today to make that angel get off me.

> *Inside a guy there's evil and crude,*
> *It don't matter if he's a decent dude.*
> *You think you're fishing alright,*
> *But the next day? Not even a bite.*
> *And I been out here on the water a ton lately.*
> *So I always say Shiggits and Sick Water for pee.*

I don't know if my boat's regulation or not but when you go down to the bathroom and you stick your face over the toilet, you better watch out first of all, but the second thing is that you can see the ocean. That's right, when you go you-know-what, all the you-know what just blows out into the water. I can't get over it. If you run fast enough up to the deck, you can see the you-know what floating away and point it out. I'm talking about individual units of shiggit here.

There was a guy I know who put his you-know-what in a toaster. Filled it right up. Imagine how it smelled when he pushed the lever down. Now he can't have kids. Sometimes I take my hat off when I think about him, and I close my eyes, and then I don't know, I will hum a song like "On Top of Old Smokey." It makes me so sad I don't know the real words, I only know the one about spaghetti. And then you know what? I have to smile a little. Because I don't know if I told you this, but I love humming. People know one of my sayings is "Shut up and hum!" when people start talking politics at a concert. You check that stuff at the door if you want my money!

You understand why I say you-know-what instead of poop or shiggits. It's the poem I told you about a little bit ago. So anyway, what was I talking about? Oh yeah, the raft and the cursed kid.

Oh man, you know what I just thought about? There's a hole in the bottom of the boat but *why don't it sink?*

I guess nothing can stop *Sweet Petey Pickles, My Cat.* I wonder why? I ran into another boat one time. Did we sink? Nope. Other one did. Guess it just goes to show you. Get out the way.

Then they said, "Now that you dropped Groad off, now go back to New Orleans and pick up some more." That's not what I wanted to do, but I did because I knew people was getting killed and needed a hero. To me though, I'm not a hero. But going and saving people's lives that I don't even know? Just drop everything? Even if they were doing something that was way more fun? That's a hero. And, later, I saved everybody on Earth with a fancy pants.

Ami Otsuka

Interviewed in Vancouver, B.C.

IN THE AIR we are told it is the window on the right side. We are told "do not look out that window." But I look and wait for long time, and I do not see the bright light which is in the sky. Also, there is people with their head, fallen over, to the ground. They start at the floor of the plane. They must be so unhappy I am told, "Do not ask why." One man is saying things wrong and words that are not allowed around children, and another man is trying for the phone, because to find a signal, but he can never find one.

I am told to do not ask.

To my mother, I say I have not seen the bright light. One for this is not a question. Explaining what the light is, she says because it is a bomb. And she says this has already explode.

"Why?" I say again.

"Because we are not flying north."

But I know we are supposed to fly north.

"We are flying west and south," my mother.

I understood why this would prevent us to see the explosion, and because it is in back of the plane. But I do not understand why we are flying west and south. This is a thing my mother does not say.

On the plane, all people are silent but not peaceful. Except but the cursing man, who is saying these words to himself. They are faces downcast and apprehension. Change of our direction, from north to west and south, this does not happen too quickly, but over a time. One man is a translator, was the only one who is walking up and down. No questions. But he is pacing? And stare out to the windows on both sides for much time, and then he says a call to all other adults to come here. And my mother goes but I stay.

This happen, the adults, I do not know. To trick them, I put headphones over like this, and put no music in. The only thing I hear is they are saying about the pilot. He is so crazy. He is driving south and west. I am not sure why this is. The pilot, why he will not talk to anyone. He is going so crazy.

Now my mother walks to sit in by myself. I look at her eyes. And I put my head on her shoulder. And she put her arm onto me.

"Why will the pilot not talk to you, or talk to the translator?" I ask as a statement. The pilot is American. I said, I do not know why he is not communicating.

"He does not want to. We are flying south now, and we are not by father's plane, or the other planes now," she said of somber concern.

And just, the man who has been cursing, he stands and begins kicking the door to the pilot. Another man joins him, and everyone stands up. Some people saying we should stop them, but everyone wants them to keep doing that. They find out though that they are not breaking the door, are find something for him to strike it. Then this pilot says to announce to us on the speakers.

"You have all need to calm down, I am saving your lives!" he enunciates. I think this is good!

But all men are yell back at him in Japanese, but the translator press the button to speak to the pilot on the speaker does in English.

"If you aren't tell us what you are doing, we are here to break down that door!" he says.

"You cannot break the door," the pilot says.

"Then we are to break you or beat you when we land, because you are now kidnapping us!" The translator said. I am so afraid we are being a kidnap. It is true.

"I am saving your lives, all of you!" The translator tells us what he says but we most speak English. I do not know who is right now and I ask my mother in no statement.

"Is the pilot saving us?"

So, the sequence of events is spot on, but I wasn't projecting my thoughts verbally at the time, so certain elements are bound to get lost in the translation. But I'll continue moving forward in this fashion.

Yumi Otsuka

Interviewed in Vancouver, B.C.

"THIS PLANE IS BEING TAKEN to an island where there are no robots murdering anyone. So you will all be safe."

The translator repeated, then asked to the pilot, "But don't you know you will be arrested when you land?"

"I have made arrangements. We refuel in Mexico, and we land safely off of Baja. But even if it does not work out, at least I know I will be alive," said the pilot.

"What are we supposed to do there? You have taken most of people away from their families!"

"Sorry. All I only know there has not been one casualty outside the United States yet."

We were already on the descent toward Mexican airport when he told us.

"Why would we not get out of the plane here?" I yelled.

"Go ahead," the pilot answered. "Where do you think you'll be safer?"

A DISCUSSION CAME out among us. The pilot's logic seemed to make sense. The infected robots were not going to reach an island, unless there was a separate outbreak there. Especially the further west we are to fly. But many thoughts were that a small island would be less inviting to Japanese refugees from the infected area. And we may be able to fly out of Mexico easier with a larger plane than a small airport on a small Baja island. I am unsure, but I know I must make a decision, since we are close to landing.

"Mother, do you want to go to the island?" Ami asked.

"I don't know."

"I think we should go to the island," she said, not knowing

much difference between them.

Just then our cell phones must have all started getting reception. Phones buzzed, rang, and vibrated. Everyone was having messages from people worried about them.

Seeking an answer, I try to call Koji, but the reception is brief and already gone. Only the text messages are there. Most are of Koji saying he loves us, which I still treasure, and also saying if we can, to go back to Japan. He does not know where we are or what has happened. He is wanting so desperately for us to talk to him.

I used this for my decision. In only minutes, we would leave the plane when landing to refuel. Also, no one will know he is holding us captive unless we escape. So we must escape so people will know. The pilot continued saying kind things to us that make sense over the speaker, so we would be on his side. Therefore, those choosing to depart in Mexico were few. Most were decided to go to the island, where they hoped to be treated kindly as a hostage. There they would be safe, at least. I hoped we could find a flight from the Mexican airport quickly, because we were so-so of how close the infected robots were to this place, because we were not sure where we were. I chose that we should not tell anyone we were kidnapped, because the pilot made sense and so many had chosen to stay with him. We would leave quietly.

THEN IS when I look out the window and see a coastline near, so I have Ami to gather her things. But there is something peculiar about the view from my window. The others noticed it too, and they gazed. Closer to the ground, we could see the streets, but there are no cars on them. As we come to the airport, there is no movement. This is so strange.

The pilot lands the plane in a rough manner. We are looking out our windows still to see no one. I have begun to fear, but am so focused on leaving this kidnapping.

THE LIFE OF HUMAN   137

"Mother, where is everybody?" Ami says. But I do not know how to respond. There is no one around. The translator is in front of us, and he is going like this with his hands to allow for his nerves.

Just then the pilot is over the intercom.

"Remain inside and you will be fine, someone will be out to fill us up very soon," he is saying.

"There, you see, there will be people coming in a moment," I say to my daughter, putting her coat on. I did not remember that it would be hot here.

The translator is the first to climb down from the plane using the safety equipment from the plane. Then a woman sitting in front of us decided to go too, and then the cursing, angry man, and then my Ami. I am to get down on my knees and grab the rope for her, but look back at the others remaining in the plane. Some more are now lining up to get out with us, making the decision. But the few who are still in their seats appear to me as helpless. As if they want to be taking action, but will not. So they only watch us exit onto the empty runway.

Once Ami had reached the bottom, I drop our belongings down to her and follow. The translator, the woman, the angry cursing man, my daughter, and I then stood, unsure of what to do. We looked around for anyone.

"Hey! Hey!" the angry man yelled.

"We are kidnapped from Japan!" the translator yelled in English. "Is there anyone?" The voices echoed around the empty runway and came back to us. Suddenly I began to have regrets.

"This is bad," the woman said softly. She ran her fingers through her hair over and over. "I am not here."

"Hey where is everybody!" I heard people on the plane yelling. They were pounding on the pilot's door. The pilot spoke over the intercom again.

"Stay calm, stay calm. Now you can get out here. But I do not know what's going on. I haven't been able to get anybody on the radio for a very long time," he said.

The uproar in Japanese began again on the plane.

"Listen, if I open this door, I can go find out what's going on, or you can all jump me. But I think you need me now. Translator, tell them that," he said.

The translator did. They looked confused in the doorway and the woman began to climb inside again. They were even more shocked when the American opened the cockpit door. One man ran up and punched him. He defended himself and then yelled at them.

"Do you want to get out of here?"

They stood unsure of what to do and let him climb down onto the runway with us. The angry man yelled obscene things at him and pushed him. The pilot yelled back at him too.

"I know as much as you do!" Neither one of them understood each other.

It was an empty airport runway. Our voices were like echoes on and on, and it was disturbing to hear. The silence was not frightening for Ami, but I had been on many more planes. And then we began to hear the sound. It grew, and we were all silent. I looked into the airport building and saw someone moving.

"Hello!" yelled the pilot. At nothing. Nobody else had seen it. "I am looking for..."

"Shhhh!" I tugged at him. Looking down at me, he seemed curious. I pointed into the airport windows.

A row of chairs, all bolted together as one piece of furniture, was here scooting and crushing a soda machine. Then we saw the robot pushing it.

It stopped and stared at us. It came to the window and stopped again. Hundreds, yes. Many more came in behind it moving at the same exaggerated pace. Hundreds and hundreds, I think. Like an army standing at the window, staring at our plane, and the five humans beneath it.

"Oh my God," the pilot said. I could not move, and I did not know where to move.

The robots lifted their arms and began smashing the glass with violent hands, at all the same time.

"Get back on the plane!" the angry man yelled. He knocked the pilot aside and climbed the rope.

"No, I can't get it into the air that fast!" the pilot yelled. The angry man panicked.

And then the glass broke, and I watched hundreds of robots fall out onto the runway as like rushing water. They are climbing over each other like savages and wolves.

The five of us ran under the plane and down the runway. The pilot would run faster than us, so we followed him and stayed running. He was going toward a small luggage vehicle, and when he got to it, he stayed long enough to let the translator, my daughter, and me get on, and the angry man. At maximum it was still not faster than the robots.

I looked behind. When the robots reached the plane, they began to destroy its wheels. The plane would not last long, with nowhere to go and no pilot.

The woman jumped from the plane and she is stomped to her death by a HumanPal. Another man tried to climb up on top of the plane, but he did not make it, and he fell into the HumanPals too. I did not want to look anymore. Once the robots had brought the plane down to the ground level, no one else came out.

This is the families and some of scientists that created Human-Pals, and this is how they died at the hands of the machines. They died an unwilling sacrifices and my daughter and I survived only thanks to them. I hope others will know about this, because I am telling you of it. Please forgive these men who created the robots, if you are able.

SIX
THE METHOD

Aaron Umbarger

Excerpt from his letters to Coldwater

The town of Etta was completely destroyed, at least according to James, who carried me on his shoulder. James doesn't say much, as I've found out on this ride. He's a soldier first. Everything else second. But that's fine.

What I know is, the robots collapsed the road and succeeded in taking most of us out. But they were a little too good at it, and the entire main street area collapsed. As I understand it, James was in the front car that crashed into the line of robots first. He and the other guy survived and rescued as many as they could. He says Koji was saved, and therefore the mission was successful. At least that's what I've pieced together from his murmurs and sentence fragments. We're waiting here to rejoin with Koji's team now that we're close to Coldwater, but it seems as strange as Etta. We haven't searched the town proper yet, but there isn't anybody around. James says waiting here is better than in a population center, but the isolation feels dangerous and boring.

Writing helps.

I hope Koji's team arrives soon. Not just for their safety but for ours.

Pastor Rich
Interviewed in Coldwater, MS

"ONE, TWO, THREE!" No further. We literally could not move the propane tank any further than we already were, but every time we did it, those concrete blocks were breaking apart. My worry was less now about whether we'd get the tank down, than what we'd do if we did. We were hoping to roll it toward the heaviest concentration of the robots, but that was changing minute by minute. Here's the way it had been explained to me: first we get the tank off the blocks, then we roll it to the best strategic spot, then we open the valve, and then we get the heck out of there while Nathan fires a rifle at the leaking valve. And boom, the robot horde explodes.

Nothing happened that way, though.

Roland Wright
Interviewed in Three Rivers Correctional Center

WE'RE ROCKING, man. We got me plus five dudes that should be trained rock star firearm brandishers. But damned if marksmen they ain't. Daye is good at EVERYTHING, man, but only one of the other ones has a good shot. That's the fat cop. He's got the biggest badge. Looks like a dude who was captain of the football team 45 years ago. Because, like, he married the prom queen and now she isn't anything to look at either, and she knows it. She's given up. He enjoys his small pond, but she never did. She pushed him to get out and make something of himself, but like, his salary was good enough that she couldn't complain too hard for too long. Now he finishes off a Hostess box every other day and she idles away in whatever women do when they get that age, man. She's past the crisis when she realized her looks weren't going to carry her anymore, and she tried to get a personality but failed. That's about when she quit bothering Fat Cop too. Because he already proved he's the best and doesn't have to prove anything to nobody. At least that's what he tells himself, man. He never left town because he knew if he did, he would see he really wasn't so great, and he didn't mean anything important. But here, he was the best. And you know what? Maybe he's got it made. He's got the biggest badge at the precinct, but Daye's the one leading things and getting the respect and that's fine with Fat Cop. But now, in the heat of battle, something Fat Cop forgot a long time ago is brewing inside again, man. Something he hasn't felt since people in the supermarket used to stop him and tell him what an arm he had. Which of the town's girls you taking behind the bowling alley these days? Oh how they admired him and wanted to be him! They all wanted to be him. They were sucking him dry. They'd done this before, and knew how to do it. Heck, some of them probably were him at one point. Couldn't wait to see what he'd become. Hopefully something better than they were, but not TOO much better. He couldn't go out there, out beyond town, and be better, because then he wasn't theirs anymore. No, just something good here at home. Oh, you're joining the police force? That's terrific, man! That's exactly what we wanted! THAT'S how they do it. The compliments and the looks of admiration, they don't stop all of a sudden. They just slow down. Less and less, over enough years that it never gives him that wake-up coffee. They knew they had to let him down gently. They did this to you, Fat Cop! And you let them! Well they can't take this from you now. This belongs to you! You're a freaking good shot, but nobody cares about that in a sleepy little town when you're a big Fat Cop, because you can't show it off, but it's go-time, you leftover! You got that feeling again! It's called What It's Like to Be Awesome, and it's a drug! The gun is out, and it is so very loaded, my slovenly friend.

Daye acts like he didn't know Fat Cop had an eye. Daye didn't know Fat Cop had any value at all. He's been in Daye's way since the day one. Hahah. Day one. Like Daye won. Daye wasn't going to be in this town for long. He's a gift.

Even though he and I lead, Fat Cop's showing off his buck eye. Between the three of us, we're taking down Hueys left and right, man. Bing, bing, bing. Ducks at a carnival.

The killers are attracted to all the noise going on around us. Fat Cop can't keep his breath, so he's our natural trail man. We had three in front of us at one spot in the road, and that's not the easiest thing to do when you only have three good shots, and they're moving in fast. Daye's on the left, so he takes the one on the left. I take the one in the middle. I can't figure why Fatty's not popping on the one on the right. Dude could do it quicker than me, man, and that's saying something. I look back and he's got three coming up from the back. We'd be trapped, but this dude drops all three of them, one, two, three. All before Daye and me get three together. Quite an arm on that kid.

Two streets down, how many to go? I don't know, man. I don't live here. All I know is in our trail is a wake of tantrum robots, some face up, some face down, some sideways, all before they figure out how to get back up. They all fall like snowflakes, each in their own special way. But here's what they don't tell you about snowflakes: each one is unique until it hits the ground. BAM. Then all you have to do is be quiet.

Easier said than done, man. I don't know whether to yell 'cause there's so much noise anyway or be quiet like a mouse. Fleet of foot.

I go quiet.

We have to slow down to let Fat Cop keep up, but this dude is high on adrenaline. You can see it in the other cops' faces. They never respected the big chief before. They'd heard the stories, but it was all grandpa stuff until now. We get to the edge of a street we've cleared, whispering our plans to each other. It's still loud, but now we can't let the blinded ones know where we are, or Huey will be right back to chase the sound of his liberators. But here goes Fatty.

Runs right through us into the next street. He's high, man. Good for him. I say let him go.

Daye says no, he's gonna get himself killed. Yep. He will. It's his time, man. He's poppin' and lockin' and he hasn't felt this in years. Let him go down in a blaze of Hueys. Born a hero, took the school to state a couple times, died a hero. Nobody's gonna write that he lost his testes for three decades. But Daye says no.

"He's almost out of ammo."

"We all are!" I yell. I guess we're not whispering anymore.

He's taken out two more since we started talking. Daye and the others follow him into battle. I keep up just because. This is why I'm on the planet, you know. But dang if I'm not out of ammo.

Fat Cop clicks a couple and curses the firearm. I know we're right in the middle of war, but you don't do that, I don't care what's going on.

"Gimme another one!" I get the useless cops' guns, throw one to Fatty, but it's only a matter of time before those are empty too. Now what.

"RUN!" I yell.

Where are we running to? I don't know, man!

They're not gonna catch us where we are, so we're running and grinning, boy what a sight! You'd have thought these six guys just won the World Series. Why not holler? Even I'm caught up in it, but I know we need more guns to make it out of here, but more important now that I've got converts, we need to let the whole world in on our dirty little secret. We're about to change everything and save the world.

Daye's out front, he knows what we need. I follow since I don't know where we are, everyone else behind and Fat Cop way behind, but he's moving, boy.

"I thought the police station was that way!" I point with my gun arm.

"We're not going to the police station!" Daye yells between breaths.

"We need guns!"

"I know!"

Daye is making it for his dispatch car. I can see it at the end of the main street. It's all tore up though. And we got Hueys on our tail moving up faster than I thought.

Fat Cop can't hear us, and he must think I'm pointing at him to go down a side street. He's a hero now, so he does it, and the Hueys at the front of the pack chase him. And that gives us all the time we need. The car is useless, but Daye's phone is in it.

Dial, dial, dial.

"Pastor!" Daye yells.

"Hey Mike, are they at the station? We need help, they're all over here!"

Then he starts telling the pastor all about me.

"He can stop them," Daye says.

"What?" The pastor can't believe it about me. Sucker.

"Yes, that guy Roland, he's stopping them."

"How?"

"Do you have any guns?"

Turns out they do. I love that about these small town people, man.

That was the last I ever saw of Fat Cop and the others. I don't know which way they went or if they made it or what. My guess is they didn't. Probably got buried. I salute you, you giant fat cop. You are alright, man. You took the meat off the bone. But it was me and Daye for now, man.

We were going back to save the sanctuary and all those people that got me arrested. Justice is so backwards, man. It puts a bee in your bonnet. Right up in there. But since they all knew how wrong they were about me being good and Hueys being bad, I figured I'd save them.

That was the plan, but they flipped that around alright. Alright, fine. We got stuck, and they came for US. Yeah, man.

Thank God for 'em. And thank God for me, man, and my diligent never-say-die attitude. I don't ever say die. Unless it's a Huey. Then it's die, die, die. I gave my true gifts to the world, man, and this is what I get back.

Pastor Rich
Interviewed in Coldwater, MS

TOGETHER WE SQUATTED DOWN and began lifting the tank with everything we had in our backs. We couldn't lift it. But we were able to rock it back and forth until the blocks began to break. Everyone was focused, but still, no one took their eyes off the machines, hoofing and snarling just beyond the cars.

Only seven of us and . . . I don't know how many. Lots of them. There weren't too many attractions in town at that point. So here we go.

Push!

Nothing.

Maybe we weren't pushing hard enough.

Push! Put your back into it!

The concrete blocks were breaking apart, but that wasn't all good. We might have no control over where the tank went.

We went to push one last time, and the side came crumbling down. All of a sudden, we're scrambling out of the way. But instead of rolling, it completely stops. And then . . . well I guess we didn't know what to do. It was a weak plan to begin with, or so I thought at the time.

So here's the really weird part. Instead of being action heroes, we all just stand there and look at each other. I wouldn't say we had resigned to our failure, but we didn't know what to do. So we went back inside. There were no other options and no "Plan B" other than to barricade ourselves in again.

We said it with purpose though.

"Barricade! Barricade!"

Everyone inside knew we had failed, despite our brave veneer. They would've heard the explosion.

"We're just going to hole up in here? That's it?" Nobody answered. But something swirled inside, specifically in me.

I had had enough.

"No, that's not it!" I yelled. People were shocked. I never yell.

Long pause. I gathered my thoughts.

"We're not staying in here anymore. We're getting out!"

It seemed like a better idea than the alternative. Again, I had no idea how to accomplish this.

"Everybody pack up." And I left it at that. And I went to pack up too, but I didn't have anything to pack. Food? The guns? They'd have all that. There was only one thing I needed. And since there was so much commotion, I was glad to be able to sneak up to the balcony alone. For a minute I sat, hunched a bit. Sat and listened for a good long while, and heard little to nothing. I wanted to hear him. Heck, what I wanted him to do was open the door and acknowledge me, as if that would have made things alright. He was one of them, though. You're one of them, Human. But you're not, are you.

Nothing was said, I just listened. I didn't have a lot of time, though, and my patience wore out.

"Are you in there?" I said to the closet door.

Nothing happened. I thought maybe I heard a little movement.

"Hey, I don't know what's going to happen, but I think you should stay in there."

I felt bad about that for some reason.

"Do you know what's happening out there?"

I don't know if he did. Maybe he did. He should. It's not that I didn't want him to go with us, but it wasn't safe out there.

"It's not safe out there."

He couldn't know.

"They're the same as you. They've all gone mad. Killing. Destroying. The bad ones, they infect the good ones. But now they're all infected except you. They're not like you, Human.

"I mean, you're not like them. But if you went out there, what would happen?"

Would he turn just as fast as the others? Would he kill me? Maybe they were made with corruption in their code and this was simply what freedom looked like. But not him. He just couldn't.

"Could you?"

I heard movement this time, behind the door. I wanted to open it, but instead, I tied a microphone cable around the knob, secured it to the rail, and pulled it tight. There's no way it would hold him in there if he wanted to get out, but it would give him something to think about. If we were leaving, I wanted to know he was safe. Worse than losing Human would be to see him stark raving mad. I never had a son, so I can't make the comparison, and Human wasn't a person. But he was more than just a pet. He listened to me, when I spoke publicly and privately. I had sat right here many times, talking to the door, knowing he was listening. He had helped me and it was my turn to protect him in whatever way I could.

Which is silly to say now. I didn't know what he was capable of then.

We had a new plan since the tank was no longer an option. Steve was chosen to go out and start a car in the strongest portion of our car wall. If necessary, he was going to ram it forward and back like a bad parallel parking job. He didn't have to do it for long. He was fresh meat and loud, and drew all the attention we needed. They came at him hard, from every angle. Since they were still too spaced apart, Steve did his best to unjam himself from his parking spot, and wooed the nearest cluster to him. Although I didn't get to ask, my assumption was that he was going to go around the whole church and create a mass before . . . well I don't know before what. Drawing the mass away somehow. With another car, probably. And then we were all going to high-tail it out the other side.

The idea was that Steve, too, would run once he did this. But we should have known better. So this is how we lost Steve:

The whole thing was working fine until he got to the area where we had knocked the propane tank off. He couldn't go around the concrete blocks, and he couldn't get between the blocks and the tank. It was not a good situation. Especially since we knew we had caused it. That was just our guilt though. Steve's head wasn't there. To him, it was obvious what he had to do. He had them all right there, clustered together for now, but it wouldn't last if he didn't keep moving. So he backed up, lined up, and put the gas down. Drove right into the propane tank. I gritted my teeth, but it was as if I had seen this coming for years. Because heroes are never loud. They're the ones getting things done behind-the-scenes. That was Steve. And he hit it hard enough for sure. The distance between him and the tank helped him get up to a good speed. It was just a really big tank.

So he sat there a second, surprised that he was still alive. A little dazed, I think his whole frame shuddered.

Then he backed up and did it again.

Still nothing. Except a very dented tank and a totaled car. See, in a movie, it just blows up because you drove a car into it. But in real life, the tank's steel is thicker than a car's. And I must sheepishly acknowledge we had time to stop him. But also, consider that he had time to change his mind, right? That fact alone amazes me. Each time it didn't blow, the hope of survival would have to spark again. Having to snuff it out over and over like that, my God. Every time, making the choice.

In fact, he had to get another car because the sedan was trashed. This time, a truck. He did it again. We let him do it again.

Right into the side, still no explosion.

And now, with the truck out of the barricade and a very mighty horde working together, the robots were almost through. And if they got through, there wasn't much our tin-shack church walls were going to do to stop them. We were all dead. The robots were going wherever he went, losing their minds and smashing through anything in their way. I know they were corrupt, but this was like watching starving ribcage dogs digging out a mole. Steve had stopped playing defense though, and was finally letting them smash through close enough to get to him. And it's a good thing they were so ballistic too, because the more they acted by instinct the more you could predict their behavior. So still, after these agonizingly long minutes, nobody stopped Steve.

The tank had rolled over enough that the valve was back on top again, and it was popped. It was when Steve backed up to ram it again that the robots finally broke through the barricade. I winced. I winced every time he did it, but I winced at this one more, because there could be no more. He was going full speed at it. Behind me, I knew that most of the parishioners had gathered at the far exit, opposite us. They weren't stupid, they knew what was going on, and knew the robots were all together now. Their time to run had come. But I wasn't watching them, I was just standing there gripping the building with a band of brothers, still hoping for a miracle, and simultaneously hoping Steve would fail, because at least then we wouldn't be responsible for killing him. But there was no way for that to happen now. He hit it at full speed.

Nothing. Again. Not what I was expecting.

The robots surrounded him, and I tried to catch his eye. To lose a friend like that, in this awful way. Not only the terror of being pulled apart by the robots, but the indignity of knowing your sacrifice was an utter waste. It sickens me to think what a terrible insult it would have been.

It was that, and then it wasn't, because finally, then, it was all of us reacting to the force of the bang. The big bang. You know that feeling on the fourth of July – the one in your chest and in your throat when the first firework goes off at dusk? It's a poor comparison. I've never been near a force this great. It knocks you down. And it's so, so hot.

And it was just like that. Steve was gone.

I didn't see it happen while shielding myself, but the force threw the truck back over end like a charred metal pretzel. The sudden realization was that we were no longer in danger, because the force and the ferocious heat had done the same thing to every single machine in the vicinity and the outer wall of our church youth wing. Every single car, truck, and robot was black, bare, and dead. Son of a gun got them all. HE GOT THEM ALL! I yelled it.

"HE GOT THEM ALL!"

And then everybody yelled it! And then everybody was yelling! You should have heard it! The yelling! The language!

Roland Wright
Interviewed in Three Rivers Correctional Center

LUCKY.

President of the United States (Tourism Bureau)
Interviewed in Washington, D.C.

I HAVE to look at the big picture. I don't have a choice. If there's a jumbled picture, say, on the wall, and everyone's looking at it, I can blur my vision slightly and see a whole different picture sometimes. Other times, not so much. Sometimes, yes other picture. Other times, not picture. I don't know when is when. But sometimes the other picture just comes out at me. I go into a blurry trance. The picture within the picture takes shape. It beckons to me from beyond. God I love art! But not "art" art. The ones where the hidden picture comes out.

At art galleries, I think there should be a little plaque that says, "Yes cross eye" or "nope cross eye" so people know. I'll work on that.

Anyway, my point is, in this picture, there was an ogre thing riding a crane bird.

I should fast forward to the part where I find the device that leads to indirectly saving everyone.

Okay. Our nation's seas. But tranquil they were not. It's so true.

You know what? Scratch everything I've said until now, it's not important. Leave my background in there though. That reflects well. But maybe get rid of the nanny. Whenever I say nanny, go back and change it to something else. Like parka. No, a parka can't make dinner and I'd never wear one. Clone? That's better – change nanny to . . . no! Neighbor. Make it a friendly neighbor named . . . Nee . . . Bohr . . . Man. Neil Borman.

Also, change "exotic birds" to something poor people want. Nintendo.

So now it will say, "We needed adequate living quarters for my Nintendo and my neighbor, Neil Borman."

Okay, so there we were, in the eye of the storm . . .

Pastor Rich
Interviewed in Coldwater, MS

HONESTLY, I didn't believe what I preached most of the time. With alarming frequency. I told myself I was an actor playing a part, so the guilt would subside. It wasn't until I let go and embraced the fact that I didn't have to be one or the other, but that I could acknowledge that both faith and unbelief existed within me. That I could be both capable and incapable, and He would make me capable despite myself. That's no miracle, that's just the truth. Now you may not believe in miracles, and you may ask why the Hell Steve had to die if God's still in the business of miracles. And that's fine, because I ask those questions myself. But I don't doubt it was a miracle. Every single one of them, are you kidding me? We paced carefully through the aftermath realizing how unbelievable it was. But also settling into the fact that we had lost a brother. In this sense the quiet was startling, punctuated only by the popping of some small fires around. In the distance, some unknown destruction happening in Coldwater. Only one robot still moved at all. And it was only a head. A car was rolled on top of it. We didn't deem it a threat.

After the initial cheers, no one had said a word. It stayed that way until Nathan broke the silence.

"It had to be done," he said miserably.

I solemnly agreed, not knowing to what.

His brother Bo quietly took a rifle from his hands. Nathan let it slip away easily.

"It had to be done," he said again, this time with the faintest anger.

His brother hugged him.

"I had to, Bo," Nathan said again, weeping into his brother's collarbone, and Bo held him tight. Both of them cried. I started to cry, because I realized what Nathan was saying.

"I had to," he yelled into Bo's shirt.

"You did what was right and what had to be done," Bo wrapped him up tight.

To lose Steve, but to lose Steve like that. You've never seen six grown men cry that hard together. One by one, we huddled around Nathan and Bo and wept for as long as we could just to get it out. Because we were allowed to for a minute.

"Father, take care of Steve for taking care of us!"

I say we were allowed it. I'm referring to time. The immediate threat was gone, but there was another concern now – the destruction we could faintly hear coming from another part of Coldwater.

I walked diligently back into the church to share the details. And to get the guns. It was decided that we should abandon our plan to abandon the church. It was still as good a sanctuary as anywhere else, and now without any immediate danger it was probably the best place to be again. Cliff would be in charge of keeping everyone safe, as he already had been. The five of us would try to get the guns out to Daye. If I didn't trust that man, I would have left Roland out there alone after a claim like the one he made. No, that sounds rough. I wouldn't do that. But to say that the man who broke in and tried to kill Human was now the savior?

I refused to believe it. But it was coming from Daye. I won't say, "God works in mysterious ways," but I will say this: He uses the least likely.

In retrospect, it seems strange to say that this Roland and his Method were anything more than a fraud, though. A sugar high.

We left a handful of weapons with the church, but each of us had a few and a bag on each shoulder as we headed off into downtown Coldwater. A cryptic text from Daye gave the cross streets they would be at, but then also, well, you interpret this:

You head toward the sound, be careful, the loud ones aren't as dangerous.

We texted him back for more info, wary of calling him in case he was hiding. But he didn't reply right away. So we discussed the text.

"Do you think it means IF we head toward the sound?"

"No, I think it's a suggestion TO head toward the sound."

"The street they said they'd be on is in that direction."

"The loud ones aren't dangerous. That means we should head toward the sound. Whatever the solution this guy has, it must not make them quiet."

"Maybe whatever he's doing to them makes some loud and some quiet, and we have to watch out for the quiet ones."

"I have no idea. But it makes sense to go toward the sound with what we know."

For some reason there was no further discussion. We knew we needed to get Daye more guns, because he said he needed them. Why he couldn't get to us? We didn't know. But if there were now quiet robots, smart enough to stalk us as prey, we sure as heck weren't going to let them know we were coming. We got quiet from then.

Don't go down Service Dr.

The texts started coming in again. We stopped and considered our route.

Why?

Nothing for a while. We moved toward Commerce Street. Ding. Another text.

Don't go down Peyton or Commerce St.

Where should we go? I texted back. This time a reply.

Constantly changing.

We continued toward the sound. Once we rounded the corner on Central Drive, we finally saw what it was. Dozens and dozens of robots had lost their minds on our main street. They seemed mindless and worse than animals. Were these the ones he was warning us about? They weren't quiet. There must have been others. Better ones. They were crushing everything. These were babies throwing tantrums. Were we being watched by a new, more sophisticated type – the ones Roland's Method didn't work on? Lots of theories. These wretches were still powerful enough to make old downtown Coldwater look like a war-torn foreign nation. My impression was they were desperate and trying to find someone – probably Roland, if he was somehow the key. Would they be so smart to know such a thing, though? More importantly, what did this man know that had left us with this? Based on the text messages, instead of a simple phone call, Roland and Daye must have been hiding, quietly, and out of ammunition. The robots . . . or specifically these robots, in this state . . . were searching for them in the only way they knew how. Crash, crash, crash. Nothing left means nowhere to hide. Also, the two men must be close. Or they were at one point. This was a scorched-earth attempt to weed them out. It made sense, then, that we had to find them fast, but stepping into this carnage – what chance did we have? I sent another text:

Where are you Right Now though?

We waited and just watched the scene unfold. The good thing, I told myself, was that if they were still going wild, then Roland or Daye were probably still alive. Finally they responded.

We're on Central Drive now.

The hypothesis, now true, didn't feel right. They texted again.

We see you. We're in the drug store. Stay still. Right where u r. Serious.

Stay still? Shouldn't we hide ourselves? And come up with a plan of action to meet up? Why stay right where we are? But it began to dawn on me. In the minute we had been standing there, not a single robot had given us any attention. What was it about this spot? I showed the others what Daye was saying. They didn't understand it either. There was a big puzzle piece missing. If Roland had figured out how to stop them and proved it to Daye, then why were the robots acting worse now? Before we could text our questions, Bo figured it out. He walked away from our safe spot, waving his arms at them. The robots never flinched. Then he turned toward us and laughed. We could barely hear him over the destruction.

"They don't know we're here!" he snorted.

We paused to take it in. And I thought to myself, okay, but where are the quiet ones? And then it dawned on me: there are no silent assassin robots. Just these. And he said it again.

"They know Roland and Daye are around because they disabled them, but they don't know we are!"

We could hear him better that time. I was realizing this.

"You mean that guy figured out how to take away their senses?" Nathan was standing right next to us, but everyone heard him crystal clear, because there was no noise anymore. Bo responded immediately, and it was the only sound in town.

"I think so." Echo . . . echo . . .

It rang out heavy over the destroyed main street of Coldwater. There were no smart robots. Just these blind ones. Blind, but fully capable otherwise.

Every single robot was now looking at Bo. And then I got a text.

"DING!" Still looking at Bo, but now also looking at me. *SHUT!* It read.

Thanks for the info. I scrambled to put the phone on silent. And once I did, it buzzed again, telling us what we had figured out. *blind. Can hear tho. SHUT UP.*

Like getting a text in the snow. Utterly, frighteningly, and indeed, exquisitely quiet. I venture that Coldwater had not heard such silence since the first settler staked it down. One hundred and fifty years ago, and now, at a moment in the middle of the day, the trees and all the grass were briefly tricked into thinking they had outlasted us. And they might still.

From their angle, it looked as if they were ready to charge at Bo, or at me, or maybe both. If my phone hadn't dinged, Bo might have been dead, but it split their target. Nathan and the others had realized this, too. Within a second, three of them were squatting down, picking up the biggest piece of anything they could find, pointing at each other with fingers and nods. Lance threw a coin from his pocket at a store window. It was a loud two seconds of reverb, and they looked at it. Nathan threw a piece of glass and hit a robot with it. Some of them looked. Shawn threw a golf ball sized piece of concrete at a little tree in the sidewalk. It was enough to keep them from charging.

But the robots were being strange and scary. Completely quiet, they were looking in all different directions. I didn't know if they were communicating, or if they could even do that anymore. We stood still, not knowing what to do next. The guys bent down to find more things to throw, but I grabbed their arms firmly and shook my head. It seemed apparent to me they were calculating. The angle the concrete went through the tree. The angle the glass hit the robot, and then the ground. The sounds from where Bo was, and my phone. The coin. They didn't know how many of us there were, and I planned to keep it that way. I took three big silent steps to my right, and the guys did the same. They didn't know why I was stopping them from throwing again, but when the robots began to zero in on our spots, reeling back and forth trying to find center, they moved with me.

Low shudder. *Less on Court meet there.*

It felt like even reading a text was too loud, so I buried it in my pocket.

We stepped backward like we were trying to maintain a single set of footprints. I expected a sudden charge from the robots toward the spot we had been standing, but no. They moved, slowly, just as quietly as us. They knew. If they made noise, they would lose us forever, much like they had already done with Daye and their new arch nemesis. I tried to mouth the word to my friends: "Court." But they didn't know what I was saying. Just something with an O. This made me the leader again, though, since they knew I had something.

We were barely off Central Drive with just a few steps, Bo still closer to them than the rest of us. They wouldn't know which way we had gone. But even as gingerly and slowly as we stepped down, I could hear little things, and it occurred to me that it is almost impossible to be completely silent. If I could hear us, then surely our pursuers could.

I could be projecting here, but they almost seemed to like the game. It's as if they were born to do this. To calculate, analyze, gauge and reduce, then act. Which now meant hunt and kill. Even blind. Their bodies rotated back and forth very slowly, ever so slowly, to keep the sound to a bare minimum. I tried to watch my steps, but I watched them equally. Their deliberate movements. Ours were equally deliberate and without any clues. Then they stopped their terrifyingly slow advancement all at the same time. I, too, stopped, and I heard a shoelace topper tap the ground. A brush of one's flannel at the armpit. An exhale, the same temperature as the wind, just a little deeper. I prayed they would lose us to probabilities and infinite outcomes. But the opposite was occurring. They were narrowing us down. And then their movement changed.

All at once, they darted forward about five feet. Stopped.

Now what?

We all went like statues, but just a half-second after they did. It was enough for them.

Every robot, all at once. ZOOM-stop! Five feet. All at us.

We figured out what they were doing that time. We hadn't moved. But when they did it again, we moved fast.

ZOOOOM-stop. Roughly two seconds to move as far and fast as we could before having to go totally quiet again. Pause. Wait. They did it again. We did it again. Pause. Wait. We were almost to Court Street now. But right when we figured out the pattern in their timing, they threw a curve by taking just a couple extra seconds before their next one. That was enough for Lance to scuff a foot.

ZOOOOM-stop. This time they all went at Lance.

We were losing this battle. They were dangerously close to Bo now, and Lance had given his position away. I figured at this point they knew how many of us there were. If they had gone all in for Lance, they probably would have gotten him, and Bo too. But that commitment would have allowed the rest of us to get away. So they continued playing the long game. It was as if this blindness had caused them to get smarter to compensate. Terrifying. Then a good thing finally happened.

Lance, knowing his position was compromised, grabbed a handful of fine gravel, and threw it over his back at the sky. Then he threw another hand of it right at their stupid faces. What an idea. Again and again. He threw it as much as he could find it. And so did Shawn, and so did Nathan and finally me. We probably gave our positions away initially, but there was so much noise coming from so many angles, and we were moving around throwing it with such frustrated abandon, there was no way to calculate it all. And suddenly . . . poof. We were gone. Disappeared. The robots just stood there, lost. We were ghosts, right in front of them and invisible. They scanned and scanned but they didn't budge.

Immediate problem solved. We were safe again, but we were now standing on a sidewalk with no gravel, only some big pieces of mulch around a tree. That wouldn't work.

We were safe again, but only if we didn't move.

Roland Wright
Interviewed in Three Rivers Correctional Center

SO THINGS GOT REAL interesting right then. We're running. Go left, go right, call Pastor, duck here. It's a regular training simulation. But it's real. You know what they call a real simulation? A war. And that's the AT we were at. At war with Huey and his brain. All brain now, with no sight. They got smarter, man, but we got the advantage.

Right up until we were ducking into a drugstore it was the Wild West. Shooting, running. My quick draw was nasty. But with no more ammo, we had to make a decision. Fight or flight. I chose fight. Daye chose flight. He said we'd be stupid to fight with no guns. I told him to grow some male genitals over his vagina. That's exactly what I said. He told me to shut up and follow him. Since I didn't know where I was, I had to. I guess Daye's got a little bit of strategy in there. Two of us trying to zigzag to the church. All his partners missing or dead. No ammo. It makes some horse sense. Protect the guy who knows how to shut 'em down. Me. Turns out I was right again, though. It didn't matter that we didn't have ammo, because the blind ones were waking up, man. Blinding them gets such a bad rap now, but I'm telling you, people were thankful. You hear me, printy man? And how do they thank me now! With this? This B.S.? You think you would have been better off without it?

It doesn't matter. That stuff doesn't matter. But it does though! No no no, put it out of your head, man, give it a go. Be the bigger man, man. Er, man.

We could hear the pastor gang coming up. We had hovered around Service and Commerce before we hunkered down on Central. It wasn't a problem until all the robots went quiet. Some had been before, but then it was like a robot god said SHHH and all the robot brains heard it.

SHHHH! We heard it too, because we went quiet. And so did the church boys.

SHHHH. Quiet in the ghost town.

Church boys didn't know what to do. They start prancing. Robots trying to tickle them. Big tickle fight is what it was. Throwing nails, doing each other's nails. They were all going to die in a sweaty girl fight. Like a bunch of girls. They were frozen. They had figured out how to save themselves, but they couldn't move. So here we come to the rescue, I don't know. Shut up.

I ran over and turned on the TV. The drugstore had a TV, but not every store did. Most of them had radios. Daye got the idea. Store to store. Radio to radio. Some TVs. The TVs took longer because a lot of times you had to click on some streaming service first and it took too long. But Hueys weren't paying attention to us until we had the noise going. Then that beautiful thing happened – Huey couldn't pay attention to any one thing. He thought he was so smart, about to kill our church friends. Now he's looking around like, "Huh? What the?"

That's when I knew we were going to win this battle. Didn't know about the war yet. Had to get the word out. But Huey was just too confused now.

Every place we went we turned on everything in sight and sound. We danced, right around all them raging robots. We walked through them in slow motion, lighting cigarettes, blowing things up. It was a candy land. Nothing could touch us: not even a pack of full-sight Hueys. Me and Daye and one of them church boys took 'em out faster than a hot trash can full of eggs, man. It was the dream I dreamed since I watched the first Huey sweep the first corner store. Because we were the smoke in the streets. The light in the darkness. And we were ninjas. And we were assassins.

They criticize me now, and say it was a lot of destruction just for killing a handful of Hueys, but whose fault is that? I didn't start this war, but damned if I was going to finish it, brother.

They aren't easy to kill and you know it, and everybody in here knows it. And if they'd report it honestly, they'd say the same thing, because they were begging for it.

President of the United States (Tourism Bureau)
Interviewed in Washington, D.C.

THERE WE WERE, in the eye of the storm. The very fate of our nation hanging upon the choices of a few key individuals, like me. No, really!

Large media outlets have sought me for interviews because I played such a primary role in the circuitous route toward ending the robot rebellion. For instance, just last month I was on the "All That and a Bag of Chips" podcast, where they watch "All That" and rate different chips. Mine was episode 81, "Good Burger & Honey BBQ Pringles." They're getting a little loose with the rules. Now, I understood it wouldn't be the ideal venue for getting my message across, especially since it's mostly eating and commenting on the episode, but I did a fantastic job considering the circumstances.

Episode 81 Transcript:
J.Nut: I hate this one.
POTUS(TB): Oh, is that Kenan Thompson?
Boyle: "Is that Kenan Thompson?" Pfft.
J.Nut: You can eat like six Pringles as one chip.
Boyle: Done.
J.Nut: (chewing)
Boyle: I put these below Funyuns. Below Funyuns
   and above hot Funyuns.
J.Nut: (inaudible) for hot Funyuns.
POTUS(TB): Are you going to ask me any
   questions about how I stopped the rebellion?
   There we were, in the eye of the storm . . .
Boyle: Ghhhaaa.
J.Nut: Di'jou find any mermaids?
Boyle: Do you need a merman?
J.Nut: Awww snap! I'm a merman.
Boyle: I'm a merman.

You know what I always say: if you're going to make almond butter, you gotta squeeze some nuts. It's messy, but sometimes that's what it takes to get the job done – a fist full of nut. So I grab opportunities and I make the most of them, like I'm doing right now. But I really should start at the beginning.

So there we were, in the eye of the storm . . .

Pastor Rich

Interviewed in Coldwater, MS

A YOUNG MAN named Aaron wrote some letters that are addressed to me. Why he chose to write to me, I don't know. I assume it's because he was headed here and mine was the only name he knew. I didn't find them myself, but apparently they were left in a truck near the bodies of two men, one military and one civilian. I believe I know who those two men were but I won't hazard a guess here.

He heard me on the radio, I think, explaining to area precincts and leaders how to do the Method. If Roland claims he's being punished because public opinion turned against the Method, that's a load of bull. Don't believe it. He did this to himself.

I think you should take these letters for your book. I find them beautiful, comforting, and enlightening. And even though I never met the young man, they make me feel like I did.

Maybe they'll help piece things together. It seems to me like people should know more about Aaron and who he was. And Jason too.

The very last one says this:

Aaron Umbarger
Excerpt from his letters to Coldwater

THEY WERE JUST GOING to shoot all the ones in the school. Blind them and then leave them standing there, figuring the pals can't turn if they can't see.

It's a smart idea, but those ones hadn't done anything.

Yet, I keep telling myself. Yet.

I'm sure it's done by now.

I GOT to talk to my parents on a bulky satellite phone while we waited there. They made me promise to get home anyway I could, so I left on the first caravan. They were so worried. I get it. I used to feel invincible. So far, I've defied the odds.

Roland Wright
Interviewed in Three Rivers Correctional Center

WE TOOK out every Huey in that town except one. No reason to stop now.

SEVEN

WE ARE ALL AFRAID OF DYING

The Dex-Men
Interviewed in New Orleans, LA

Dude, you can make some serious money if you know what you're doing, like me and Samson do. I read some of these make a million books, and they all say the same thing. "My man, you got to be ahead of the trend." Thing is, people all say it's almost impossible to catch a wave like that without algorithms. Because, say like you watch algorithms, and then you can catch a wave before everybody else who's watching the same algorithms. Does that make sense to you? You got to look where nobody else is looking, like me and Samson did. That's how we got famous. It wasn't pasta, and it wasn't the Dex-wheel, and it wasn't Foam Pucker. Foam Pucker is a portable pillow in a can I made, so you can just take a little can with you on vacation instead of your whole pillow. Then when you get there, you just spray Foam Pucker in a pillowcase. Boom, you got a pillow! But I guess people thought it was something else because of the name, and they sold it in sex shops. I went into a sex shop one time – not because I wanted to look at all the naked people on the packages, because my mom might read this some time and I want her to know that I wasn't going in there for that. No my friend DJ told me he saw Foam Pucker in there and he didn't know why. And if DJ didn't know why, then it must be a weird reason because DJ is into all that grunt and go stuff. Like catalogue stuff. So I marched into this place over in Hyde Park, Cincinnati called Cinderella's Curiosity Shop, and this woman came up from behind the desk like she was on a pretend elevator. Like she just stood up real straight and looked at me. So that messed me up a little, 'cause I was ready to put my foot down.

I was gonna say, "What is up with this! Why are you selling Foam Pucker in this sex place for sex!"

But I said, "What the heck is there a hole in the floor right there? How did you do that?"

She just stared right at me like she was looking at my soul or something, and she had lipstick on, and dark mussy hair, and she says, "What can I do ya for?" But not in a country way, like she was saying "do you" on purpose and I got the sweats.

"Hey, uh, I'm serious about the hole. Do you have a hole back there?" And that was the wrong thing to say because I didn't mean to use that phrasing, you see, but I was peeking over the counter looking down. And she liked that, because she sat on a stool and her skirt went up more than it already was, and she probably knew it would, because she probably did that to every guy that came in there.

"I want to show you something..." she said. Oh boy, here we go. And then she grabbed a key. She slipped her feet in some high heel shoes before she started walking out from behind the counter, and I looked and there was a sleeping bag back there, and I was like, "Oh, I see." And that's why her hair was all mussy too. So I got less intimidated right then because she slept back there, and I saw pills too. But now I'm following her, and she opens up this case and gets out a pair of plastic underwear with a motor on it, and says, "These look like your size," and then she's looking at my butt, and doing a honk-honk thing, and then she starts pumping her hips and making a sex motion! And I pointed and I said, "No, Satan, I don't want your motor pants!" And I left. And that's why I never found out what Foam Pucker was doing in a sex shop. That lady was not Cinderella, in the traditional sense of Cinderella, and that was upsetting.

But I'm not afraid to go in places like that. We got famous because we were willing to go where no man had gone, or technically no people wanted to go, after the androids rebelled – and that's into areas with lots of android people. We would swoop in with our armored truck and pick up a few androids for your local government officials, or citizens, and at 1G a pop, you can do the math I don't have to do that for you. And 1G is good, but 2G is better. And the closer me and Samson got to the phony quarantine line, the more we could charge to take the androids. You gotta test your market, you know. Here's how me and Samson would do it:

If I was driving the armored truck, I would say, "Hey, you got any of the robot people?"

And they would say, "Yeah."

And I would say, "We take those."

And sometimes they'd be all about it. And then we'd tell them the price and they'd hold their nose at us, and wave like they were waving a fart away.

Other times, they'd say, "Is it free?"

And I'd say, "No, it's expensive, but you don't want yours to kill you." And that's the key, you see, you make them remember about the murdering of their own lives. Once that hook is in and you say, "Two thousand dollars," then people still turn their face all sour. But they might do it. One guy with a mustache gave us that sour fart face the whole time he was paying us, and he paid us in 20s so it took almost three minutes of watching that stupid face, and every one he put in Samson's hand it was like it made him more PO'd. By about $1800 he was even stomping his foot. I almost gave him a discount just to get out of there but I looked at Samson and his eyebrow twitched up to say no, that's exactly what he wants us to do. Thanks, eyebrow, that mustache guy almost got me.

Man I didn't like that mustache guy almost at all.

We stuck to our guns, and I'm glad we did. Not too many people had an armored car and could do what we were doing. That's some serious jack. And since we were only taking the good ones, there wasn't risk to our well-being! But people still looked at us like we were brave. And I guess we were brave. For the money, sure, we're not dopes. But it took some bravery to drive the quarantine line like we did.

I said, "Samson, we're like Superman."

He said, "I'm like Superman. You're like Ass Clown."

"Ass Clown's not a superhero, Samson!"

"Yes he is, he's what you turn into when you get leg cramps."

"I'm low on potassium!"

"Eat a banana, Ass Clown!"

And then we rode in silence for a bit.

"Let's call us the Dex-Men. It's like a superhero but it's also a good business name," I said.

Samson is such a fool. He tried to hate that idea, but he knew it was good and so he got a stupid little smile and I pointed at it.

"You like Dex-Men."

I spray painted Dex-Men on the side of the truck the next time we stopped.

We planned on just driving the quarantine line all the way down to Mexico. Although that quarantine didn't work, and the line got very blurry. A weird thing we were doing was finding construction companies and paying them to dig a big hole and then we would just dump all the androids from a haul into the hole and bury it. We weren't the only ones doing that, it was catching on all over, outside of where the crazy ones were, because the killer ones were crazy and not a single person knew what to do with them once they went crazy. Not even us. And the Method was kind of weird for us, too, once that became a thing. But none of it hurt the Dex-Men. We had 'em lining up, baby!

But that town where I painted the Dex-Men on the truck, that was where things went all nuts. I think it was in Tennessee, like around Memphis, but I don't know for sure. We picked up a whole load from a little city hall, and I guess we got too close to the action. Because we couldn't find a construction company or anything. And we were tempted, I say we were very tempted to just dump this load in a lake because technically we did our jobs, but then we just made a problem for somebody else, and yeah, that was the argument we were having with each other. It wasn't me versus Samson, it was me versus me and Samson versus Samson. We both wanted to do it and we both knew we shouldn't just dump these fine robots in a lake, where they might become a problem later. And I would argue for one side, then agree with him, and then he'd flip and argue from where I was before. So that was a confusing minute for us. But we had to get this load off and keep moving, time is money and saving lives even, maybe. So we took a stupid hard turn dead into the crazy. We went due south. We knew it was stupid, but our compromise with ourselves was to find a lake in the quarantine zone and dump them there. That way we'd be doing our job, but it wouldn't be any more of a problem than anything else down there, because everything was so messed up. And that's what we did.

Up until then, we had stayed completely away from the killer robots, only dealing with the uninfected ones. But when we saw one, we saw more than one. We saw a whole, whole bunch. As a matter of fact, they surrounded us. And that's when the most amazing thing happened that makes us famous.

Oh man, it's such a good story.

The Gay Gambler
Interviewed by phone

THERE ARE times that even I have veered outside the lines. This is where I was at the moment on the cruise liner after departing from the young woman. But I knew from experience how to deal with myself. Isolate, regroup, engage. I had locked myself in my ship's cabin, hoping to move through the phases quickly. Maybe this is why I had been so fascinated by the robots when they first came out . . . why I had been an early adopter and studied mine so intently. I was looking for a human operating system that didn't require emotion. I wouldn't have acknowledged it then, but I do now, after everything that happened.

The downside of having leadership qualities is that people don't stop needing a leader just because it's become inconvenient for you.

They knocked at my door incessantly. Each time I listened for the voice to accompany it.

Knock knock knock.

"Sir? We could use your advice on something."

None of the voices were hers. I confess it relieved me, but it prolonged my isolation. Eventually the knocking came less often. I never answered, and I am of the opinion that some started to believe I was not in the room at all. They carried on, making plans and voting on those plans.

When nobody was knocking at my door anymore, then the voice came.

"We've joined other ships," she said. Followed by a long pause. I assume she was considering whether or not to saying anything else. "We're combining resources and information. I thought you would like to know. It seems like something you would have come up with, so, you're kind of still leading them in a way." She paused again, this time long enough that I thought she might have left. Then added, "You're still valuable, you know."

I flushed with embarrassment because of what I was doing, and because they might have convinced her to come do this.

Conversely, if she thought I had participated in the idea, then she must have isolated herself for a time, too. Probably not in the same way as I had. She seemed to be a bit of an isolationist anyway, but without the effort I put into it.

I forced myself to open the door.

She was gone. I looked briefly down each corridor. All that remained was her message.

Some of the people looked surprised when I rejoined the activity but nobody asked me about it.

"We've joined with other boats."

"They were close."

"We've mostly stayed on our own ships."

"They're bringing more people out."

My instincts kicked in immediately.

"Do we have a running log of who's staying where?"

Sort of.

"Who's managing resources? Are we sharing things with other boats?"

No. There had been some supply drops from smaller boats that made managing food easier.

It had been roughly two days, but I stepped right back into the role without question, unfortunately. Though there weren't any problems with supplies, I suggested we keep a tight log. The woman in the visor told me and my boss to shove it.

My boss?

A few others referenced "the boss" too, and they weren't talking about me.

I quickly figured out who was running this operation: the newly appointed President of the United States. She had been awarded the title by none other than herself.

President of the United States (Tourism Bureau)
Interviewed in Washington, D.C.

THERE WE WERE, in the eye of the storm. Figuratively. Weather was decent.

"My God," I said. There was a pleasant breeze, I would say. "After all this death, I might be the highest ranking government official." But I needed to be sure.

I stood on the deck right outside the Sunset Grill and closed my eyes, asking heaven for a sign. I tried hard to listen, but the wind kept blowing through a hole in a dinghy or something and making a "nwoooooo," sound that made it hard to concentrate. I put my hands over my ears and looked up – there was a bright star! But it went out. Then back on again! Then out. Hey it's on again! The demonstrative rollercoaster continued for several minutes until a man on a stepladder asked if I was staring at him or at the ship's beacon mast.

"I'll have you know it's the second one, sir. And it might be Morse code." He didn't appear to flinch. "Morse code . . . from heaven."

He slipped and crashed into the dry-erase board he was hanging, advertising the "All She Wants to Do Is" dance. Is everybody aboard this Don Henley fan cruise a clumsy, stupid, fat idiot? I wondered.

"Oh no! I fell down!" he sniveled.

I comforted him, like I do, and promised it was the last worthless evening he would ever spend, because of the heaven Morse code.

"That's not Morse code, it's the boat's beacon," he seemed to be saying. But I only wondered if this was why I was born. Oh God, why is it so hard to hear what you're saying?!! Am I the new president??! I *feel* like I might be, with all the death that's gone on out there! But I'm not stupid. I'm not going to just assume. I needed hard facts, or a sign from heaven.

And I knew just who to ask.

CAPTAIN JANNUS HABERSACK had been a perfect gentleman to all the Donvoted, though describing him is difficult, with no defining features or mannerisms to speak of. He was 5'8, brown hair. A nautical cap sat cockeyed atop his blank, chortled face. His dull, listless eyes – like two dead pieces of shit. His mouth – just a face hole. At intervals, it brought forth chutney onto his stained, undersized captain's uniform. I still to this day can barely remember his stupid, featureless gait as he bounded past me.

"Captain Habersack," I said, catching up to him.

"To what do I owe this pweasure!?" he lisped.

"I have something I need you to . . . help me with."

"What ivs it? Do you has it wiff you?" he sneezed.

"Sort of. You see, it's all right here," I said, pointing to my brain.

"Witten up there?" he said, standing on his tip-toes.

"Let me explain."

I then laid out the chain of command and how I might be the highest ranking government official still alive. Which would make me the President of these United States of America. AND to the republic for which it stands. But that I needed to know FOR SURE. He nodded with his mouth open, clearly understanding what I was saying.

"You need to know if youwa the phesident?"

"Just say the word, Captain."

"Phesident?"

"Thanks. But I need you to get on the horn and find out for sure, or I need a sign."

He dialed the numbers on a very old fashioned phone. Someone picked up immediately.

"Hold RJ Skipper 81, you are received, transferring you."

Okay.

"Hello RJ Skipper 81, this is Lt. General Morris."

My voice quivered. "This is the President of the United . . ."

"Yeah, who's that there?"

"Uhhh . . . it's me. The President of the United States T . . ."

"Where're you at?"

"In the gulf . . . East gulf."

"That's great to hear! This is U.S. Airbase Ellsworth. I'm glad to hear we got an official down there we can talk to. We haven't heard a dang thing from that area."

"So . . . does that make me, the . . ."

"Yeah, and you're gonna be the point person for sure. Let us know what you need to take charge."

"Take charge? Yes, of course, I must."

"Communicate on this line. Over out."

"Did you hear that, Habersack? I AM the president just like I supposed! It's just as I thought!"

He had just taken a big drink of soda, and spit it all out.

"But I phink . . ."

"Highest ranking! You heard it, Habersack. They haven't heard a dang thing from anyone. Because there isn't anyone. Your secret phone didn't go through to D.C. because everyone in D.C. is probably dead. I'm in charge now, Chief, like it or not."

"Chief?"

"There's a new sheriff in town!" I screamed.

Captain Habersack and I then set out on the difficult task of letting all seafaring vessels know this new information. That a new sheriff was in town. The President of the United States (Tourism Bureau) was here. It was the beginning of Project Vacate. When history is told, grandfather will set grandson down on his knee.

"What is the turning point of the Robot Disaster, mien Grandpapa?"

"Well, Grandson, it's a long story, but it starts, as all good stories do, with a very attractive woman. She was in her late 40s, but you would have thought she was in her early 40s. She carried herself with confidence and poise, but not TOO much poise, like her friend Lizabeth. Some people thought Lizabeth tried too hard, and looked older than the female president, who was in command."

And I was thankful to have the right man for the job by my side. Now Captain Habersack was a lot of things, including lonely, irritating, emotionally fragile, and difficult to be around. His eyes kind of wandered around in his head all the time. However, what was I saying? Anyway, I was about to make that famous first call.

"Calling all boats, calling all boats. Wait, don't press it yet! Should I make it more personal? Like 'calling a boat.' Is there a nautical word for 'every boat is special'?"

"Dey all look like dis once dey get painted," Habersack said.

"Here, you work the button, I'm the president."

Then some shuffling. I don't remember saying any of those things, but apparently the button was pressed down the whole time and they all heard this exchange. It's been transcribed and given to me as a gift, but not a gag gift.

Jannus Habersack pointed at me.

"All special boats. This is your leader," I careened.

Then I explained Project Vacate, and how all little boats should be taking people from the mainland to the big boats, and the big boats should cluster together in the gulf off shore. It was a terrific achievement, but after a week or so my achievement high was wearing off. I needed a rest. We would go to the first island we could find near Cuba to take an achievement break. Little did I know that it would just lead to more achievement. Ugh!

Captain Habersack handed me the radio. "Hewe's an ambaffador."

"Hello, who am I speaking with?" I leveled.

"This Ambassador Kiko."

"Hi, Kiko."

"You are welcome here, in light of world event."

"Kiko, the people aboard the good ship *Bouys of Summer* owe you a debt. But no debt that we could ever repay in tangible goods. A debt of gratitude. But, a brick ton of that, let me say."

Kiko paused.

"Okay."

I think there was a bit of a language barrier. Normally when someone tells you how much you owe them in non-monetary goods, you assume they're going to call off that debt. But I liked Kiko anyway. Something about his nonexistent lack of candor. It was cute. We made land, and I temporarily parted ways with Captain Habersack, ordering him and two guards to stay aboard the boat and protect the rations from island people.

I had so many important jobs to do. From big jobs like protecting our food from the locals, to small ones like where to pump our vast accumulation of excrement, I oversaw every liter. I even had the dubious job of warning our people that there were humanpals on the island, but that they were isolated and should be fine. Lifting peoples' morale is what I am good at, unlike most people who fail at it constantly.

. . .

WHEN I SET foot on the island, the first thing I noticed was that the ground was soft, pliable, and smelled kind of "eggy."

"Thank you for having us, Kiko," I reached to shake his hand, the ambassador of whatever nation this was.

"Please, call Kiko 'Ambassador.'"

Okay, Mister Important Title.

"Please let me explain the situation, Kiko," I continued.

"Ambassador."

We get it, Kiko!

I had to tell him who I was again. I reminded him that all I wanted was to use the island's natural resources to feed and clothe us, and stressed that I needed safe passage for my people.

He asked me, "Passage to what?"

A more excellent negotiator I had yet to meet.

Kiko escorted me to an all glass island conference center built into bluffs. Most of the time it probably overlooked the ocean, but right now all we could see was the part where our excretion had settled. Who knew it would spread out on top of the water like buttered toast? I didn't.

"Kiko, what is this egg smell I'm sure your people have grown so fond of over time, but that we hate?"

He blushed a bit. "Yes, indeed. Island not always so prosperous. Before all the money, natives were egg farmers."

"Sir, I'm telling you, until now, I did not know you could grow eggs."

"We farm poultry. We have abundance at times. Unused eggs dump here in lagoon. Smell lingers. It is why we do not use as port of entry. Too unsafe. From storms too. I sure you are fine though, under circumstance."

"Sure sure, and please, back to the . . ." I pantomimed waving stink away from my nose. He must not have known that pantomime.

"Your people. We will . . ." he said.

"Say no more, Kiko," I demanded. "We are not here to be a bother. Just treat us as you would any other tourist. Clothing, shelter, and whatever entertainment you may have. We can all pull together in our own ways. DVDs from the ship could be shared and given to your peoples as extreme long-term rentals. On your end, a breakfast buffet, which could technically serve as a lunch buffet if you add a ham carver, but we can talk about that. Some of your clothes might work for our people as nightgowns. You will see, Ambassador, things will work out."

A thoughtful expression came over the face of the ambassador. Then, finally, a smile. Note to Kiko: wouldn't hurt you to smile a little more often. But I guess that's what separates the big ambassadors from the little ones.

"We may have perfect place for you, Madam President. It alright I refer you as Madam President?"

Oh my heavens, no. "Well, okay." Did I just SAY that? It's funny how sometimes you say no in your head, but your body says yes anyway. I have spoken about this neat phenomenon on college campuses.

He convinced me that there was a place on the island that may be best during my stay.

And so our journey began.

Kiko led me on a walk that in his words was "a great distance" but it didn't seem *that* great. He said he was going to journey with me, but when someone walks a few paces ahead of you the whole time no matter how fast or slow you go, I don't call that journeying "with."

First, he led me past Skull Rock, which he described as "a scary place," but I was barely scared at all. It's just a giant stupid rock that resembles a rotting, screaming head. Tons of people have accidentally died there. No kidding! That's all it takes to scare island people! I tried, in turn, telling him about the plot of my favorite scary movie, *Demon Kid*.

"We open on a child's feet, pedaling as hard as they can. A rock song, Rebel Yell, plays as we hear two people yelling in the distance. What is he running from? Suddenly the bike slams into a sedan. The Demon Kid has dented a car. We pan out to see that he is in a parking lot, and is doing this to all the cars. Adults scream, and wave their fists as he pedals away with a devilish grin."

I hoped we had Demon Kid on the ship so we could rent it to them.

"Shhh!" Kiko stopped rudely, raising his hand. Ugh! And right when I was getting to the scene where Demon Kid ruins a game of Risk that had been going on for *six hours!*

Maybe island people don't like movies because they don't have an attention span, I wondered. I know some people lose their sense of wonder as they get older. Not me. I keep wondering. I wondered how much farther this walk was. Then, when Kiko started scrambling to light a torch, I began wondering if he had heard something in the brush. Because I hadn't.

"That because you keep talking."

Exactly, Kiko. I carry the weight of the conversation while you bumble around with a lighter, jumping at every jungle sound. There were hardly any humanpals this far out, so I assumed it was not one of them. They weren't infected on this island, anyway.

I continued wondering aloud what it was called when you got really thirsty, but your guide wouldn't let you hold his special island water bottle because it was "expensive." Also, what's with the torch? Ever heard of a flashlight?

"No flashlight because this not supposed to take so long. You use many words, ask plentiful questions."

Kiko wasted even more time getting his lighter to spark, then spreading the flame across his makeshift torch. The fire caught my attention and drew me in. I stopped talking and was, for the first time, truly impressed by the ambassador. It's funny how fire can do that. Something was happening deep in my bones. A profound, tribal rhythm overtook me, as if the island itself had a pulse that I could only now hear.

As the flame grew, a smile peeked across Kiko's face. I think he knew, and he finally saw me understanding. And right when I found myself succumbing to the same, simple rhythm that gripped the native heart, I heard that stupid sound Kiko was talking about in the brush. "Rustle, rustle." You've got to be kidding me, that dumb little thing again at a time like this, right when I'm having my island experience? Although it did sound much closer than before.

"Ahhhh!" Kiko screamed. The creature latched onto Kiko's eyes, pulling and tearing at his cheek flesh with its little hind paws. So I was right! It *was* little!

Then he dropped the torch so I couldn't see what was happening, other than his feet, which kept kicking and jerking. I had to laugh a little. The monster was on his face – what was he kicking at?!!?

"Go ger da drums!" he yelled.

"What?" I yelled back.

"Go ger for camp dere!"

Then a squishy, "Gnaph gnaph gnaph."

"Were you the first one, or the squishy one!?" I screamed. I simply had to know which one was him if I was going to make it out of here alive.

So I sat there, quiet, waiting. Hiding. Listening. All I could hear was some faint indescribable sound. If I had to label it, I would say "desperation thrashing." And then there's that squishy sound again. What IS that?!??

"IS THAT YOU KIKO!?" I wondered at the top of my lungs. "If so, stop chewing and talk to me!"

My leadership training kicked in. I had to make a snap judgement, which, thankfully, I am prone to do. Almost without thought, I boldly decided it would be best for both of us if I escaped. First, I backed up and got a running start. Next, I LEAPED over Kiko's twitchy legs – WOOSH! Then, my legs and head FLEW in opposite directions and I landed. THUD! Last, I tucked in a spinning motion, and BURST my way UP, into a fearless light jog – WHEW!

I knew I couldn't look back now. Even when I heard Kiko again, muttering something else. Probably more orders. I had to keep going. The sound of the island pushed me on, even though I was so tired. Keep going. Keep going. Okay, island! Maybe this distance was pretty great after all. Oh, Kiko. How sad I was to lose him! A native idiot, sure. But a proud, simple, native, stupid idiot. And, also, he had my food. I considered going back. Then I thought, no, Kiko would want you to keep going. And where was he taking me to, anyway? I realized I had not known. He had tried to tell me once, while I was explaining *Demon Kid*. But I had said, "No, wait, this is the best part." Because it was when Demon Kid ran out and left the door open even though the air conditioner was on. Ugh, what was I thinking! That's not the best part. Why didn't I listen!? Again I considered going back to pry the food pack off Kiko's hardening corpse. But what if I couldn't get the straps off, and I had to saw through both of his arms with a rock? Would I even be able to find a rock at this time of night? And what if I opened the pack and the animal was in there, sleeping? Should I wake it?

I carried on. Each step was a tragic comedy, similar to *Demon Kid 2*. The whole franchise had gone in a misguided direction, just like me. My legs were two tetherball poles and my feet two retired tetherball players. My arms swung around like two old flabby octopuses cockfighting. Every step crushed my spirit like a motivational speaker who was doing something different for a change.

And just when I thought I couldn't go any further, there it was again. Bum bum de-de dum dum de-dum. The rhythm of the island. It bypassed the mind and entered me directly through the boobs. Like a burning hot poker of pleasure. Was this a dream? No, it couldn't be. My dreams are big, like Macho Man Randy Savage, although I acknowledge that sometimes they are small, like Nacho Man Rande Salvaje. But one thing's for sure – they're never about drums. I only had one dream about drums when I was 14. After a bad report card, I slid into the choir room and hid in a bass drum where nobody would find me. Must have been pretty cozy in there, because I fell asleep and awoke to people cheering, horns blasting, and a boy commenting on how heavy his drum had gotten. I peeked out the hole – I was in a homecoming parade! Downside: the cheering was for my peers. Yet I ask you which is more worthy of applause: hitting a thing, or falling asleep in a thing? There was no time to contemplate these matters: the drumline was starting. I peered out my little hole as the boy craned his arm and lurched 'round the drumstick. When it hit, I woke for real. The PARADE had been the dream! In real life, it was a janitor wearing a headset, attempting a drum solo with what appeared to be no skill at all. What had been so fun was now sad and embarrassing. There was only one thing for me to do: I stood up out of the drum, stretched with a big yawn, and acted startled when I saw him. Covering myself with the drum skin, I frowned and said, "hmph!" He watched me all the way out the door.

But there was no time to think about that now.

Suddenly, the sound of the island changed, to a dum-bum-dum-bum, dum-de-dum. The melody still carried me, but not as much. It was like 80/20 music/my muscles. I guessed I could live with that, but wondered if the island could try a little harder with its next selection. Also, maybe it could turn it down a little. I could barely hear myself think!

Then I saw it, through the brush: thick, coarse hair covered by a hideous baggy shirt and poncho pants.

Everything about it repulsed me. Then the music stopped entirely.

"Hello there, I am Gerhard!" It shouted. "Hi!"

I shuddered. It kept waving as if I hadn't seen it. Great. It's as stupid as it is unfashionable. I considered running back to the place where the island monster jumped out and killed Kiko and hurling myself into its den by my collar. But what a waste of me that would have been. I couldn't do it to the world, or to Gerhard, even though he wouldn't stop waving.

"Hey, hey lady! Can you see me here?" he persisted, pointing down at himself.

The idiot must have though he had gone invisible. Ugh. To shut him up, I finally intoned to him, "People can't be invisible."

"Couldn't agree more!?" he snorted. "I'm Gerhard! I run this one man band way out here, where hopefully I am not a bother to anyone. Ach kampf! What happened to you?"

His beady eyes had looked me up and down like a piece of pork tenderloin before he ran off to get what – spices? How long had it been since he had eaten a good meal out here? I didn't want to know. He said I should probably wash up, but I didn't like the idea. Then the weird sicko started covering my wounds with bandages. He cut the long pieces into short strips, like a maniac slicing carrots to put in my broth. I shuddered, like a . . . I don't know, a roast. I decided if he got any closer, I was going to whapp him and yell, "Get away!" or "Get to steppin!" Probably get to steppin.

Thankfully it didn't come to that. I don't want to be graphic here, but Gerhard's poncho pants caught on a wire strand, and his open mouth crashed into a boulder, smashing all his teeth to smithereens. Then the boulder rolled over onto his legs and a pointy part caught on his genitals before rolling over again and ripping off his foreskin. Again, not to be graphic, but then Gerhard rolled over onto a pile of salt, and a mother bird swooped down and grabbed Gerhard's detached genital sheath, then flew away and padded her nest with it. You don't even want to know what happened after that.

I started to feel pity for this horrid man. I even patted him on the back.

"There, there. There, there."

But he kept crying like an old hairy orphan. I had already said "there, there" over one and a half times; what more could he want? But I sojourned on.

"Hey fella, chin up. You see those little birds? They're warm tonight. Because of you. Yes, you. The island is going to gain two . . . scraggle-feathered . . . mucus birds?" I was guessing here.

Gerhard stopped rocking and holding his crotch long enough to share that a snake had already eaten three birds out of that nest, and those two probably wouldn't survive. I guess he thought I was interested in those facts.

Due to my diplomacy training, I told him that "champs" can overcome anything, but I don't think he believed me, because there was a cheerlessness in my voice, due to the fact that I could tell he wasn't a champ. And so there we sat, each in our own pain. Mine, an internal distress over the human condition. His, a tooth and genital smashing and, probably, a nagging worry about whether he was being a good host.

"Look at us," I supposed. "The rest of the world is out there dealing with maniac robots, but we're sitting here alone in the jungle, not a care in the world."

"Well, not completely alone," a voice came from beside me. I looked, and there were two individuals beginning to tend to Gerhard. One stood, tall and magnificent, overseeing Gerhard like a camera-ready doctor from a bygone era. His slacks and white shirt were perfectly ironed, and his voice resonated with strength.

"I'm Marvin Allister. We heard your encouraging words to our friend, sure glad you were here when this happened."

I didn't know what to say. He was straight out of a fantasy I have that involves me falling off of a horse and into the arms of a stable boy who had gotten in trouble and had to sweep the barn naked, for a punishment. The trouble he got in was that he was too monogamous.

"Craziest thing with that wire strand," the woman said, eyeballing Marvin.

"Yeah," he sighed, running his fingers through his crisp, jet-black hair. "You could say this is all my fault, as usual. Gerhard, I hope you can forgive me."

Gerhard smiled a big, toothless smile. He tried to say something, but blood gurgled out. It turns out Marvin was a doctor, so he tended to Gerhard while the woman, Lora, went around offering everyone fruit and drinks. It wasn't the best fruit, but it was fine. Plus I had already eaten a strawberry I found a minute ago while they were tending Gerhard's blemishes.

"So, Madam President, allow me to explain ourselves, and what we're doing." Marvin walked a couple paces away and began speaking to the sky as much as to us. "We are all equal here. No one is treated differently based on their skin." I relaxed. I could finally stop hiding my psoriasis. "But rather, on the content of their dreams," he continued. Amazing. To find such acceptance, such love. Oh how incredible it all felt, here on this dirty backwater tropical island of all places, to finally be accepted in spite of your psoriasis! I was disappointed that I would have to share my dreams though, instead of my fantasies, but what the hey.

"Last night I dreamt I was flying on a giant rocket, heading to colonize an already populated planet. I didn't want to kill any of its inhabitants, but I would if I had to," I admitted.

Rudely, Marvin continued as if I had said nothing. I guess I should have talked louder.

"You see, this side of the island is separate from the rest. Here, leaders of industry, of government, of entertainment come and go at their leisure, knowing this as a sanctuary of their true selves. Gerhard, for instance, is a well-known leader in the EU. But here, he creates music."

Marvin continued to impress. The benevolence, the absolute generosity in calling what Gerhard did "music." And Lora, sitting there with a straight face while he said it.

"Lora herself is sometimes referred to as this generation's Jane Goodall, communing with the needs of animals," Marvin proclaimed. If only she had been around when Kiko died, I thought. Maybe she could have asked the squirrel if it was really so hungry for human eyes, or if it was just emotional eating. "But here, she's able to enjoy time doing technological tinkering," Marvin droned on about her.

"Is this everyone?" I asked.

"People come and go as they please. Right now, this is basically everyone."

"Wow, three people. Not much of a commune," I pointed out.

"Well, there is one more person, but he's not staying long," Lora said.

"Yes, he must have just beat you here. Our very own distinguished ambassador," he said. Wow, they appointed a new one that fast?! I wondered how distinguished he could be having only served for a few minutes. However, I looked forward to developing a better relationship for our countries than when it was Kiko.

The gentleman stepped out from the flickering shadows of the torches, and I couldn't believe my eyes. Could it be? Kiko had a twin brother! Identical in every way, except for some scratch and bite marks in the face.

"Amazing. You must be Pa-Kiko," I said, extending my hand. I wasn't sure if Pa was the correct prefix for twin, but foreigners love it when you "try their language out" like pants.

"You take long way to camp," said Pa-Kiko. "After squirrel incident, you run on strange side path with branches and snapping turtles."

"I can't believe you witnessed that." I consoled him, by shaking his hand with both of my hands. To watch your brother being eaten by a squirrel and literally being able to do nothing about it. "I want you to know, I once had to watch my mother go through a terrible tapeworm episode that ended up killing her." It was a weight-loss mechanism, and it did not go as planned. After two weeks, she was at a cocktail party and threw up on an endangered parakeet and an expensive coat and a parking attendant. It killed her *socially*, I should have said that, socially. She was murdered later by her own HumanPals. Right about the same time I was on that island actually. Huh!

We talked a bit with Pa-Kiko.

Then Marvin spoke up.

"The ambassador is going to be taking our dune buggy back to his place. He didn't expect the walk to take this long. Said he'd check on you in the morning." I went to shake his hand again, but Pa-Kiko was off. He was, in my opinion, much better to be around than original Kiko, and I told him that.

"And what about you, Marvin?" I asked, flirty.

"Well," he blushed. "My hobbies are much more rudimentary, I'm afraid."

So dapper. It was time to let Marvin know I was interested in him. I put on my pouty face, bit into my strawberry, and spoke like baby Stephanie Tanner. "How rude-imentary?" Marvin giggled uncommonly loud, like when you swallow something wrong. "I like to . . . create gadgets. Like in the movies." Oooh, now this was getting interesting.

"Weapons? Which movies?" I asked.

"Have you ever seen the beginning of *Pee-Wee's Big Adventure?*"

"No, have you ever seen *Demon Kid?*"

"The movie opens on Pee-Wee getting out of bed and turning a fan on, which blows a pinwheel, which lights a candle, and so on, until breakfast is made. I spend my time likewise, but with much more high-stakes outcomes."

"Wow, okay. That's so . . . hot?"

"I know, I know. But that's what this island is all about. Out there I'm The Courageous Dr. Allister, curing deadly diseases, helping people far and wide, but here, I'm just Marvin. Marvin and his kooky rubes."

"That is so interesting. I heard everything you said and I was listening," I responded.

"Right over here, Madam President, right over here," Marvin bellowed. "I can show you."

"No, no, Marvin. Not the big one. Just show her what you do, don't include me," Lora pleaded.

"Lora. This isn't just any guest. This is the new president, and she saw the rebellion happen."

"Not up close. I was on a Henley," I reminded them. It felt good to say something without the burden of context.

"Your hobby is just as important as mine," Lora added. Which turned out to be a lie for the sake of humility. There are so many scenarios where humility is an unnecessary characteristic, I can't even begin to list them. Though if I did, I could list the most.

Then Marvin casually flicked a switch from his pocket. There it was, behind some palm branches. A boxing glove on a spring. Was it just me or was this starting to seem less hot?

"Go ahead," he said.

"Glad to. Go ahead and what."

"Be my guest. You won't believe what's at the other end."

I walked carefully up to the glove. Not sure what he was expecting me to do, I kicked the pedestal it was sitting on as hard as I could. It fell over loud enough that I could take pride in it.

Marvin, still full of enthusiasm, ran over and put it back together where it was.

"I should have been more clear. This time, do what the fighter does before a match begins."

I shrugged and began yelling at the glove. "Nobody is tuning in to watch you! The pay-per-view money is because I am on the ticket!"

Finally he instructed me that I should just tap the boxing glove. Apparently they tap gloves before they start punching each other. So I did. And when I did, a ping-pong ball fell out of the glove and sprang into a funnel, which drained into a vacuum tube. The tube sucked the ball in and shot it up into the air, where it hit a toy train, which only needed the slightest push to begin down the track, hitting other toy trains, getting bigger and heavier as they went. At last, the final, full sized toy train fell into a stocking hanging at the end of the track, which pulled a belt down as it fell, and the friction was just enough to light a match stationed below a fixed, tied string. It was the lamest thing I had ever seen an attractive person do. Marvin kept on watching and almost clapping with each change.

"Is this almost over?" I whispered to Lora, still pretending to smile at Marvin.

"No," Lora said, also pretending to smile. "There are a lot of people who come here to find themselves. Most of them do art, or meditate, or read. Marvin does these Rube things. Gerhart and I don't get it. But I respect what he does outside the island so much. We try not to judge, you know."

A fan blew a sailboat across a baby pool into a button that caused a wiffleball bat to fall into a stack of empty bottles. Simultaneously, I began to consider celibacy.

"And what is your role in this?" I whispered.

"I've found a way to make the robots shut down. At first, it was only for a few seconds, but I've gotten it up to almost two minutes now."

An old book tipped over and hit a nutcracker handle, which closed its mouth on a bike horn. Marvin pumped his fist and hop-jumped.

"Wait, you've done what?" I stammered.

"Yes, we've been able to shut robots down for two minutes using light sequences. Kiko was leery of you at first, but figured he should show you what I've done. Have to admit I was too, but what's the harm? If it can help, it can help. He even arranged for us to try it on an infected one."

"And it works?!?"

"I'm not sure what the practical implications will be yet, assuming we can easily duplicate the experiment on a larger scale, which won't be easy. I'm just tinkering with a flood light. But yes. He wanted you to see it for yourself tonight so we can get to business tomorrow. I figured a little showmanship wouldn't hurt anything."

"My God!" I exclaimed. Although I honestly didn't know what we'd do with it yet. How would we get it out and duplicate it? And what was two measly minutes going to do? In politics, "better than nothing" isn't always better than nothing, but in this case, it was clear that it maybe was possibly.

Marvin yelled, "Okay here comes the best part!" A set of dominoes split into two sides. He screamed out, "Double the fun!"

"Okay, pay attention," Lora said.

I couldn't. I just couldn't. But I tried not to beat myself up over it either, reminding myself aloud that the lack of entertainment was not my fault. Lora then started narrating it for me, to honor me.

"After the cuckoo clock yanks the pin from the cage, don't get scared. We've already done this to the robot. That's how we got it here, actually. We shut it down with my floodlight for two minutes, then tied it down. When it came back online, it couldn't move."

Just as she said, the cuckoo clock chimed, and yanked the pin out of the cage. This was still part of the show, because the robot itself, while trying hard to kill us, was completely incapable because of what looked like heavy duty zip ties around every joint. I thought about screaming, but was worried only dust would come out because Kiko hadn't shared the water. I decided to tell that story to Lora since I come across rather heroic in it, but the look on her face had suddenly changed to an unattractive horrified expression, and she screamed something like, "Where is the strawberry!?!" It was loud, and I covered my ears and grimaced just as a knife swung across and cut the place where the strawberry had been.

Sure, I could have explained how to choose less appealing strawberries when guests are around, but I seem to recall a *different* anecdote I wanted to tell just a minute ago about Kiko not sharing his water, and nobody seemed interested in hearing *that* one. So I kept both of them to myself. When you think about it, life is just a bunch of small stories, isn't it? Another great one I should tell sometime is the story of a stylish, 40-something woman who pointed in one direction and yelled, "Look out! A tumbleweed!" and then threw a strawberry stem in the opposite direction. It's a good story, and it's not very long!

The strawberry was supposed to fall onto the light switch and turn on the blinking floodlight program. Instead, the knife swung right through and punctured one of the robot's zip ties. And puncturing that zip tie set off a chain reaction that I thought Marvin would really appreciate, but he wasn't in an appreciating mood or something. It went one, then another, then a full arm was free, then another arm, and then a robot was reaching into Marvin's throat through his face. Then it ground up his spinal column like a restaurant pepper mill. Then it kicked him in the foot. It was one of the most uncomfortable things I ever had to watch. I felt that the medical community had just lost a valuable resource, but that the gadget community had just dodged a bullet.

"Mayday!" Lora bellowed over a walkie-talkie.

Meanwhile, I grabbed the floodlight.

"Good thinking! Flip it on and maybe we can . . . gughla" she said, as I started to run away. I hadn't fully understood everything she said before the robot poked a hole through her trachea from behind. But I was beginning to piece it together: if I, right now, turned on the floodlight, it might disable the robot. But, by the time I understood her cryptic message, the robot was already holding Gerhart by the feet and beating his body against a tree like a dry-cleaner beating a shirt he hates. Plus, where is the switch on this thing?

Thankfully, the dune buggy pulled up. I instinctively called shotgun, and then face-palmed myself for being so stupid. Where *else* would I sit?

Lo and behold, it was him, driving!

"Pa-Kiko! Pa-Kiko you came back for us!" I squealed heroically.

"Not Pa, just Kiko," he said.

My jaw dropped open, and I blinked real hard two times. "Adey-adey-aye." Huuuh? No matter how hard I shook my head back and forth, which I did several times with increasing intensity, it still felt something akin to a hallucination. I rubbed my eyes. Several times. Kiko was ALIVE?!? As far as I knew, the first person ever to survive a squirrel attack. It just goes to show you, for all the careful strategizing that goes into a situation like this, you don't get by without a few miracles. And here he was, our very own Kiko. Almost a miracle in himself, but well . . . what do you call something that's almost a miracle, but not as important? A pa-miracle? I still find it odd how I never saw Kiko and Pa-Kiko in the same place. If this were a movie, I would think that they were played by one actor; however, if there's one thing I know, it's that unbelievable circumstances don't happen in real life, and this is real life.

I had to make sure Kiko didn't blame me for seeking to save my life rather than lose his and all his friends, so I said something disparaging about his relative. "Kiko, I didn't want to mention this, but," I spoke out the side of my mouth, "Pa-Kiko was starting to smell. If you point it out, he says something like 'that what the island smell like, it not me.' Plus he's wimpy." I gave him a little thumbs up.

"Kiko no smell, that IS the island."

Ha! It was so Kiko. Making everything about himself when I was clearly talking about Pa-Kiko. It's funny sometimes, the selfishness, but other times, not so much. He drove us to safety, and got us to our ship, sure. Me, and everyone who had arrived with me. Down to the last person. But then, as usual, his mind went right to himself.

"Can Kiko come on boat, too?" Seriously, time to stop thinking about yourself, sir. We're literally talking about life and death here. That robot is still out there, probably maiming animals on its way to this side of the island, where it will infect all the other robots and start a mini-island rebellion. Not exactly something to joke about.

Out of kindness, we lent our DVDs to them indefinitely. It was nice of us, but also a sort of payment for the buffet. And the floodlight.

Finally back aboard the *Buoys of Summer*, I began getting requests from all over the U.S., or at least the South.

"What do we do, what do we do? Tell us what to do, woman in charge!"

Everyone wants you when you're at the top. I wanted to metaphorically push all the papers off a table and yell, "Take a chill pill!" But I was very tired, so with the back of my hand I knocked around some post-it notes and muttered, "Eat a nippy capsule." It was all I could muster. My legs were back to tetherball accessories. My brain like an old crippled turtle.

That's when I saw him. The one, the only. The reason we were all on this fan cruise. Emerging from the shadows, he said to me, "I'd watch that backhand if I were you." I couldn't believe it. Up until now he had locked himself in a room, and only spoke about his basic needs through his manager, which of course we eagerly catered to. But now he was here, with me.

"Did you stay on the ship the whole time?" I fluttered.

"Yes, I did," said John Henley, Don Henley's son.

"Can you . . ." I gulped, "sing my favorite song for me?"

"Which song is it?"

"'Dirty Laundry.'"

"Nah."

"What about 'Hotel California'?"

"I only sing a couple songs. I can do 'Return to Innocence' if you want."

"You mean 'End of Innocence'?"

"No, 'Return to Innocence,' by Enigma. I only cover New Age stuff. Or I can do one of my originals."

We sat there in silence for a few seconds as he realized I didn't want to hear anything from *Pure Moods*, and I realized that I had nothing but respect for the artistic integrity of John Henley.

Then he turned to leave, mashing handfuls of Chex Mix into his coat pockets, which looked to be already bursting with Chex Mix. And as he did, he looked back over his shoulder, and said, "Oh, and baby? If you knock twice, I'll answer."

I understood.

What he was saying was, heroes don't always look the part. Sometimes fate is packaged in a most innocent way. So I got on that radio and simply said, "I'm here."

They explained to me there was a new way, a new Method of

blinding the robots. It involved guns. Now, I hate guns and violence, but this was a case in which I wanted to get guns, and violent, because they had been violent with my friends. Well, not "friends." Lora and the German man. And the other one, and possibly Pa-Kiko. And I had a solution slip through my fingers once already; I wasn't about to let this one.

However, I showed restraint as I glanced over at the floodlight.

"Why don't you hold off on that," I smirked over the radio. "And whatever you do, don't blind them!" I commanded. Then, a stunning silence.

"But this Method could save lives, Ma'am!" someone finally said.

And here's when the tides finally turned in this war.

"So could THIS!" I said, holding up the floodlight.

Alf Johnson
Interviewed in Tampa, FL

I LIKE places that advertise live nudes, because one time I walked into a place full of dead nudes. I got out of there, and thaaaat's the story! You have to let people know when you've told a joke by tipping your hand all the way over. That's why I always end my jokes with, "and thaaaat's the story!" so you know when to laugh. I thought of that joke because there was a lady I saw who did nude art. Her name was Amanda Buttsong, and she had a unique talent.

See, don't laugh there even though I paused. I didn't say the line.

Before a show, she would eat bean burritos all day. All day. Then at show time, she'd go up on stage naked with a kazoo. Guess what she did next. That's why her name was that. Get it? Butt song. And thaaaat's the story!

Here's another joke: Amanda Buttsong was just her stage name. Her real name was Lauren.

And thaaaat's the story!

I got a good boat phone and I been making tapes of my jokes to send out. I'm just gonna send them around, see what's out there, you never know. I'm friends with Owen and Stinkfaster too. I'm gonna send them all out and see what happens, you never know.

Yumi Otsuka

Interviewed in Vancouver, B.C.

I WAS angry with the pilot for doing this all to us, but I also was at his mercy and to put my emotions away. Ami was not, to me, having this difficulty. I believe that children are accepting of many things, because they do not know if they should be a different way. This is their innocence. We had a time of some two days to hide in an airport break room. My Ami was pretending to sleep, and I had fallen asleep but was awakened by a temper tantrum from the angry man.

"What are we doing here? Waiting is the most terrible idea!" He said this in a whisper because he is an angry man but he is not a foolish man. And all the five of us looked down.

"This is my fault," the pilot said.

"Yes it is! Do you expect us to live forever in here on snack mix and Kit-Kat?!"

"We can stay alive on these things," I added.

"We can stay alive but what do we wait for? Do you think someone is coming to save us? Look at us! There is nobody at this airport, and nobody anywhere! Anyone with a brain has gone to the south many days ago!"

The translator, without saying any word, stood up and pushed the angry man away from Ami and he became docile.

"We are going to end up like the others from our plane. We are just putting the joyful face on it," the angry man said softly. And it was difficult for us to accept this is probably correct. But I do not know what we are supposed to do at that time. Until the pilot stood up and walked to a counter, where there was a black bag made for carrying across the shoulder. He opened the zipper on the bag and walked to the vending machine where we had been getting all of our food. It alarmed me at first to see him take off the front of the machine with a tool and put all of the food into the black bag. The translator, too, became afraid that the pilot was taking our food supply and going to run away with it, so he stood up and made his hands into rock fists, and went to that pilot.

He said, "If you are taking all of the food, you are going to struggle with me."

And the angry man said, "I will kill you before the humanpals do if you leave here with that bag."

And the pilot said, "I am doing this for you, and for that little girl!"

Without asking us, he walked out the door, but not the one we came in from the outside, the other one, into the main hangar area. This was a large open place we had mostly stayed away from, because there was no temperature control and if you made a noise it was sure to be heard. And these noises were so dangerous to us. But still the pilot walked through there, very carefully, with soft steps, still quickly. Instead of stopping him or running for him, the translator and the angry man, they must have believed in him because they just watched him climb up into a plane. Then is when I am realizing what he is doing. So I put my things together and I run toward him with Ami.

I wondered if he was going to start the plane without me, but he was not.

At this time, he began waving for the angry man and the translator. All of us were running for the plane and made it safely. This was the first danger we avoided. The second danger was worse. For the minute the pilot pressed the start button on the plane, we would become a very loud and easy target. But we were forced to go with this sporadic man because if we did not, the airplane starting would expose our hiding place.

So now, I held my daughter's hand on the plane. He pressed go and the propeller started to turn. First was to get out of the hangar.

The plane inched toward the opening so slowly. Oh so slowly, it was a dread for us to wait, then finally faster.

We heard banging on the walls of the hangar. It was a "wham, wham, wham!"

"What is it?" Ami asked.

I am glad we are aboard the plane.

"Wham, wham, wham." It did not just do this three times, but now it was more. "Wham, wham, wham, wham, wham, wham, wham!"

I thought maybe the plane was far enough along. Because now the walls of the entire hangar are shaking. And the closer we got to the opening, the more I did not know how to breathe. I think I stopped trying to breathe. I want the plane to get into the air so badly. I want the plane to get into the air now! Can we not get off the ground before we leave the hangar? Is the opening not big enough to allow us to achieve this? I know it is probably too close for the pilot to try, but if he would try it ever, now is the time. Right now. The terrible machines I could see now ripping apart the walls, and they begin to chase us. I am thankful that they are not coming through the opening yet. But as soon as I am thankful for this, then they are coming through.

"Are we going fast enough?" the translator asked.

My assumption is that he is asking whether we can drive through the robots, because we are not going over them.

From the time the propeller started, they were after us. And now before we are even out of the building, they are through the walls, and chasing us, and barricading us at the open. Our strategy is foolish. We are foolish for trying. But what would have been accomplished staying? We are all afraid of dying.

As the pilot pressed down, the plane increased speed.

I felt my Ami holding my hand, and now squeezing my arm. And now crying. She is afraid of dying. And then the plane used... what is the word for...very slow down. All of a sudden. All of the lights in the plane went off. As well as all of the lights in the hangar. Pop, pop. Just when we were supposed to be going faster and faster, we are going slower and slower. And I became even more nervous than I was. Until I looked down at Ami. She is looking up at me, and her eyes are not her eyes any longer.

"No, Ami, no!" I yell at her.

Ami does not say anything. She is in another place. She is no longer Ami.

"Why are you slowing down!?" the angry man yells.

The translator agrees and yells this at the pilot. They are afraid and they cannot see anything out the windows. It is dark.

But the pilot can see out in front, through the open door it is still light.

"I cannot go!" the pilot yells.

I am still looking at my daughter, but she is not my daughter. She is now a thing.

"Ami!"

Her eyes are red and still. Her face is wet from slobber and tears, and other functions that have gone wrong.

The pilot yells again, "Look!" And the angry man and the translator run up to see what he is pointing at. I do not go. Instead, I hold my Ami, because in my arms she lays limp and dead. I am thinking of Koji and my daughter, and these years I've gotten to spend with her. I know life is fragile, but to finally have a child who is my own and to have her taken from me, I cannot help but weep, even though it is not a traditional child. And this while the three men are cheering victoriously in the cockpit.

My mind tells me this is good for us. If they are cheering, it must be good, but nothing in me is good in the moment my Ami is leaving me.

"They've stopped! They've stopped!" I hear it but it does not matter.

Ami's eyes softened and dimmed, and went out. Her body became rigid and locked in a setting, but still so soft. And I cried louder.

The men turned from triumph to alarm, only now aware of something wrong with Ami. They knew we needed to get off the plane and out of the hangar before everything came back on. If it was going to come back on. They didn't know. And I knew what they knew. But they did not know what I knew. They were trying to get me off the plane, fast. And that was going to be difficult to move a woman away from her daughter. This, they did know.

But I would not let them know about Ami or that she had caused the power expiration, because this was my honor to her. Though she was dead, I purposed that no one should ever know she was artificial. I had gone through many pains to make sure of this fact, and I would not stop now. In that moment I knew this, but only concerned myself with her loss. I did not think quickly. So they did what is the only best option: they lifted her from me so that I would go with them. I fought it but I would not win.

"She will be okay! Let's go!"

"We will help her when we get on another plane!"

I could see the looks on their faces, surprised that Ami was so dense as they tried to continue lying to me with their eyes. But that they would lie to me and tell me she would be okay, only to save themselves and keep me motivated, saddened me more.

"You don't understand," I said in my anguish. So many emotions as I continued to protect her.

"We will help!" they said, running through the many frozen robots of the hangar, holding her above their head. Faster and faster now, and a good distance.

I ran along, weeping. They opened another plane and loaded her aboard. Because of the loud sounds of the previous plane, it seemed that every robot in the airport had descended upon our place, and now a new plane was clear. These men were faithful to me and to Ami. It was not selfish, and I regretted thinking it was. They placed her down with such care and kind words in the seats of the new plane.

"We will get her medical treatment!"

"Yes we will! You will see!"

Because you see, their words came true.

Ami's eyes came back on, and they were no longer red. They were Ami's eyes. Her legs and arms moved quick with some unkind spasms. I could not believe my eyes. I had been there at her creation, but there was no rule for these actions. I began laughing and kissing her, and I think maybe even crying harder than before. I did not know she was capable of any of this. And what I said next surprised the men.

"Get this plane moving as fast as you can!" I screamed in a terrible voice.

They looked at each other, confused.

"The robots are going to turn back on!"

Without wondering how I knew this, the men did as I said. By the time we were in the air, we could see the robots moving again, toward us, in futility. The men talked among themselves about our good fortune. They did not know how it happened, and they did not talk to me about it, because I made sure they did not. This was the understanding between us, because grieving mothers need to be left alone with their daughters who have come back to life.

The Dex-Men

Interviewed in New Orleans, LA

WE WERE JUST TRYING to get barely inside where the crazy was happening, dump these things, and get out for our conscience. So we weren't adding to the problem, you see. But the line was blurry.

We knew Sardis Lake was a main cut-off point, so Samson said, "Cross Sardis, dump them in a lake, get out. That's the plan."

I didn't need to keep saying it over and over, but I did. And then Samson did, especially when we were crossing the Sardis, I think we both started screaming.

"Cross Sardis, dump them in a lake! Get out!"

"We're crossing Sardis!"

We was like Thelma and Louise crossing that lake.

"I am not going to die!" Samson was yelling.

"No, Samson, you shut up, we are not going to die! We're going to dump them in a lake and get out!"

"What if we went back up to Memphis and just gave up? I don't need this money!"

"I don't need the money either, but we got to get rid of these things somewhere! And yes, I do need this money!"

"I want to spend the money and I want to get married before I die!"

"There's a lake!" I said. Because there's a lake by Abbeville and I saw it at that time. The phones got real spotty inside the blast zone there, but we could see some little lakes on a little map we had.

Abbeville was just a little town, and oh man. There they were. Exactly what we were yelling about. All the horrible evil robots had started to stack up right there in Abbeville because they couldn't get around the Sardis and oh my God this was a terrible idea. There wasn't anything left in town but us idiots driving an armored car screaming in our prayer language.

"Samson, we are gonna die!"

"I gotta turn the car around! Forget the dump!" Because they were everywhere. These killers were everywhere, and all of a sudden they were zeroed in on the Dex-Men!

And that's when I remembered. "We're the Dex-Men, we can't die! We're superheroes, and we're protected by the Lord on High!"

But those things kept getting closer and closer to us.

And do you want to know what these superheroes did? We turned around and it didn't do a damned thing because I'm telling you those killers were everywhere! We were trapped, so I just kept on yelling them prayers, boy, yelling and I turned on some praise music as loud as a man knows how, 'cause if I'm dying I want them transport angels to know right where I'm at. There was nowhere to drive either. They had us on all sides so fast we didn't know how it happened. Twenty feet. Ten feet. I hugged up on Samson and we just buried our heads down so we didn't see what death looked like. He sang Donnie McClurkin and I just was yellin' Jesus, and I know I peed myself because in that moment your instincts are so dialed in but the only thing you're thinking is, "I just smashed a juice-box in my undies and now this is how I die, with wet drawers." And they're rocking the boat and you're just waiting for these hungry monsters to crack the can open and eat the delicious cookies. At least I had the...Oh, we are the cookies. Me and Samson. But at least I had the whereabouts to lock our doors and jam some bars into the handles inside. We didn't do that for the back door, though. Even if they couldn't get in our doors on the side of the truck, they were definitely going to get in the back door and turn all those good ones we had into hate monsters and come up our butts that way.

I guess it took a little longer than we thought, because I was able to think that thought. But I was still putting my head down and rocking away the pain.

Bang! That was it, the lock and the back door was open and that's how they were coming to get us.

"Hey, Samson, this is taking a little longer than I thought, so I want to tell you how much I love you, Brother. I love you, and I love Mom, and I'm sorry about Pastabilities. I really thought we were going to do better, and if I hadn't let that health inspector in maybe we wouldn't be doing this right now and we'd still be alive and so I'm sorry! I'm so sorry I did this!"

"No Brother, no! You are the best brother I could ever have, and I'm sorry I called you Ass Clown earlier, but you have great ideas and I wish I had creativity like you do, that's the truth!"

I stopped rocking and I hugged my brother again, but it was so weird then, because all the loud we were yelling over wasn't loud anymore. And we looked out the front window, and we saw all the crazy robots were stopped, and they weren't being crazy anymore. And me and Samson looked at each other all, "Huh?"

"What the?"

"They're all..."

"Yeah they're all..."

"What the?"

It wasn't just that they stopped all the kill-kill stuff, it was they looked, like, normal. Whatever normal looks like for a robot. That's what they looked like. And then, I'll never forget it. It was like after a hard rain clears out during the evening, and the sun comes out before it sets, but everything is still wet and glistening and calm. There was this one robot, it was different from the others. It was going around like a mother, like checking on them. And it wasn't moving fast, it was just moving along at a pace, hands by its sides. And then going out further and looking at the crazy ones furthest from us, and would you believe it, those crazy kill ones, they responded to that mother hen in a positive way. It was like when you get real mad at someone, but right before you yell at them they say, "I love you." You don't know what to do, so you just stand there. It had to be like that, but in a robot way.

It had to be this one rolling round spreading this nice. He had to be responsible.

And then, another thing I didn't expect. We looked in the side mirrors behind us, and the robots started doing something good for the nice one. My brother and I looked at each other, but we didn't say nothing at all, we both just agreed without saying so that it was time to get out of the truck. And so we did, we stepped down, and we walked to the back, and all the other ones that we had originally picked up and were going to dump into a lake got out of the truck so it was empty, and they made a path for the nice one. Like an obligation. We stood in line with them right at the back of the truck, and the nice one rolled on through the middle of them, and right on up to us. Then real slow and careful, he was getting in the back of the truck by himself. But he stopped and he rolled over to me. It was a moment maybe we should have been afraid, but we weren't. Not at all. And he looked me right in the eyes, and I looked him right in the eyes, and all the robots were watching us, and things were quiet and calm. And he lifted his right hand, and placed the back of it against my chest, like he was feeling my heart beat. Held it there for a minute, and then he put his hand on his own chest. And I don't know if robots can do this, but then it was like he gave me a little nod. I don't know how you'd analyze that if you knew a whole bunch about how robots work, but everything he communicated to me was in how I felt. Like he knew how I felt, and he was speaking to me like that.

I don't know exactly what the message was, but it was something like "trust me." And I did.

And then he got in the back of the truck by himself. And he just stood there looking at me. No other robots in there, just him.

The other ones gathered around and closed the doors, so I

assumed that's what he wanted them to do. Then, all the robots moved out of the way in the street behind us, but not in front of us. There they were still scattered around like polka dots. No, they only moved out of the way behind us, to the south.

Samson and I looked at each other and we must have looked like a couple nutty bars. Eyes all open.

"What is it doing? What did it do?" Samson asked.

"I don't know, but I think it trusts us and I think we're supposed to trust it," I said. I didn't know why Samson would believe that, but he did. Or at least he knew we'd be safer with it than without it.

So my brother went ahead and got back in and shifted the armored truck real slow like if we moved fast they were going to come after us.

Reverse, okay.

Turn the wheel real slow.

Forward. Okay.

Turn the wheel. Go slow where it opens up. Just get out of there without making a stir. But it was alright. It was okay. And he knew it and I knew it.

It was like we were driving down the beginning of the yellow brick road, like that wet sunshine after the storm. Except the quiet robots weren't tipping their hats or singing like you would expect in a movie. They just watched us and rotated as we crept on by. It maybe seemed like they were smiling, but Samson said that's literally the same exact look they always had on their faces.

So we were going south now, deeper into the kill zone. I guess because we trusted it. Somehow we did.

But once we got a little speed, and the robots got sparse and whatnot, that feeling wore off pretty quick. This isn't a good plan! You don't go south right now! Hell no! But that's where the opening was! South! And it seemed like we were in a divine story or something, like if there's such a thing as a calling, we was being called. There wasn't much light left in the sky then. We could hear the locusts in the trees. The sun and the moon and the stars. It was like destiny, and God was waving an open hand over the path. I wanted that calm back before we ran into a big horde of robots again, and this time at night. Just a big horde of robots standing there staring at us. Maybe they'd kill us and we'd be the fools, but it didn't seem like it. At least we had the nice one. So we followed the road where we thought we were supposed to go. Just me, Samson, and the nice one.

EIGHT
WHAT'S IN A NAME

Roland Wright
Interviewed in Three Rivers Correctional Center

It was my duty to finish what I started when I came to this town. That was a fact, Jack. Kill the talking Huey. And if it didn't talk, make it scream. So I tried to be nice. Take the high road, let the people come to my side, make them see the light.

It was that or I bring the very walls of this building down around them. And I didn't want to have to shoot these people just to kill their robot. But that decision was faulty, man. Just a plain error of judgement, because yours truly was too good at it. I got the whole congregation on my side when I should have gone in barrels up, minute one.

That is my major tactical error in this whole thing, man. The one pebble in the path. The coon in my garbage. And my slip took the whole future of the country in the wrong direction. If I repent for anything, it's that I didn't go in hard enough.

Pastor Rich
Interviewed in Coldwater, MS

WE RETURNED to the church as one team without losing a soul. Myself, Bo, Lance, Nathan, Cliff, Daye, and Roland. And nothing following us. But we could still hear things happening elsewhere.

The camaraderie lasted less than a night.

It was our job to get the word out about Roland's Method via whatever means we had, which was mostly shortwave radio. I got on and gave the info, but they wanted to know more. Over time, I think I told the whole story of Roland, Steve, and how we did what we did. People out there were looking for any solution, so it spread fast. Roland was tepidly trusted, mostly because I had encouraged it. But by the afternoon of the next day back at the church, our common goal had been accomplished. Roland grew restless being cooped up inside the church with the robot he had intended to kill, and he walked around sowing seeds against Human.

"You and your family sleeping in here? You feel alright?"

"We got security outside the church, but I wonder if we should have some inside."

"If you never seen a Huey turn, man, get ready. It happens fast."

"Long distance? I've never seen it, but that's not to say it can't be done."

It's amazing how quickly fear can grow with the proper nutrition. Nobody would ever mention Human directly. For his own safety, I decided to keep him locked in his closet, though I wonder if he listened. People who had recently been fans – some of them only coming to church because of the spectacle he created – had begun to turn. Indeed, those who had been attending most recently were also the quickest to change sides.

I hate saying sides, but there were sides.

The longer it smoldered, the more I could smell it. In a short time, people were openly questioning keeping Human in the building.

"Look, I know he hasn't done anything wrong, but . . ."

I should have just let it smolder, but it turns out my own anger was the spark that lit the fuse.

Walking through the sanctuary one day, I passed one of our newest attendees.

"Takes a lot of courage to walk through here, these days," she said.

"Why. Why do you think that is?" I stopped. And likewise, she stopped.

"Well, you know, with the robot up there," she hesitated.

"As I recall, isn't that robot the reason you came here in the first place?"

"Well sure, Pastor, but you know . . . things have changed. Look, I don't disagree with what you're saying, but a lot of people, they might now."

"What's going on?" Her husband approached, hands on hips. He had not attended services. We invited him. Sent him the card and all that, but he never came until everything fell apart.

"Nothing." I should have left it at that. But I was on edge. "Nothing but doubt, everywhere I go. I open the doors of this church, I risk my life getting guns to the police and Roland. I lost my best friend! And we have the Method now." I didn't really know what was going on outside our town, but I was losing myself. "It's all happening right here! And people still won't trust me, after everything I've done!"

"I don't appreciate you yelling at my wife, Pastor."

"Listen, Mitch, he's not yelling at me, he's just emotional."

Now people had started to gather.

"You okay, Pastor?" Cliff asked. His genuine concern just made me madder, as if I was the problem.

"No, Cliff!"

"None of us is okay in here," said Mitch, the ever-faithful husband. "Not in this room, and probably not in this building, and you know why."

"Why, Mitch? Why don't you tell everybody? Why don't you let everybody know how smart you are? Go ahead! Give us the masterclass on how that solitary robot locked in the closet upstairs could possibly get infected and start killing everybody."

Roland now stood in the doorway. A shadow holding a Coke, leaning in the distance. I could only imagine the look on his face.

"You can't, and you can't either Roland." I pointed at him. I wasn't going to let him blend into the scenery. "Because you know for a FACT that if even one infected robot got near here, our outside security would sound the alarm. And then we'd all take arms, and we'd Method it. We're a bunch of Methodists! And let's just say for a second that a robot was to somehow break our ranks and get inside the building. The last thing on our minds at that point would be whether or not it was going to climb the stairs to the balcony closet and turn one more, in the midst of being over-run! Now all of that might happen, and maybe that's how we'd lose each other, and we'd lose Human. But to kick him out, for nothing? You'd just be throwing him to the wolves to make one more robot we'd have to shoot."

The people were shocked. I'm not sure I had ever spoken like this. And then he stepped out of the shadows, because I made him.

"And now you've all heard him and what he really thinks of you. You're the unwashed masses, in here to take King Richie's throne. It's YOU versus HIS flock, man. You're not one of his. He opened up the church, but then he couldn't convert all of you. His people are still behind him, because he's been brainwashing them for years. They won't be so easily persuaded by logic. Man's greatest gift, man. Check it at door when you come in here, though! Those of us who are new with fresh eyes, we can see all the errors and the misplaced loyalties. He trusted the robot to bring in new members because he couldn't do it himself. He's loyal to the robot – he LOVES it. Even though he himself was just out there on the front lines with me, and with Daye, and you, Cliff. And a whole lot of us. You said it yourself, Rich. They killed your friend. But you're blinder than a impotent Huey."

"I see things fine, Roland. I see a malcontent who wouldn't know loyalty if it was right in front of his face. I see a man who wants more than anything to be relevant. Who could never take a back seat. Who forces action and isn't mad at the robots at all. Oh no! He's thankful for them. You see, this is a man who desperately needs an enemy to blame for every dark thought, feeling, and action. He needs the robots. He's so deep into it he doesn't even realize it, but the minute they're gone, he'll find a new enemy. Maybe it'll be Methodists. Maybe it'll be a politician. Maybe it'll be society.

"God help us if he is lauded for discovering a way to stop them! He'll be followed! Worshiped! He'll enjoy it for a while, and then he'll hate it and he'll make a new enemy out of everyone who disagrees with him. It stops right here."

"Enough of this lofty BS. He's harboring a terrorist! He's trying to change the subject when we all know there's a murder machine waiting in the wings, right up there!"

"What's its name, Roland?" I asked.

"I don't give a left nugget what its name is, that's what's wrong with you and everyone like you. You can't identify an enemy even when it's outside your door, literally killing your people and destroying your town! You want everything to be shaded with gray when it's clearly black and white. We've had enough of you!"

Roland made his way briskly for the stairs, and people followed him, or at least gathered to show they were physically on his side. Only a few stayed on the floor near me, watching it unfold. But Roland was leading the charge, up the stairs and to the closet door.

There was nothing I could do.

"I've lost too many friends in this thing, Roland! This is needless! Everyone!"

The door was locked. Roland took three steps back and fired his handgun at the doorknob, puncturing it.

"We didn't call it 'Robot.' We never did! We called him 'Human' for a reason! Somebody acknowledge that! Before you do this!"

I wish I wouldn't have even said, "Before you do this," because it was conceding defeat, when I really believe I could still have changed their minds. I saw it in their faces. I could have saved them the guilt of going forward with it.

Roland placed his hand on the doorknob. Then paused.

"Now I can straight-up point and click with the best of 'em, but I'm not rash. I believe in democracy. If anyone does not believe I should do this, I want you to do as the Pastor is asking. I want you to say its name. However, if you fine people believe that this robot, who might have been amusing to you at one time, is still just that – a robot – then I want you to say so. All those who want to leave it alone, speak now."

"Human," a handful of lukewarm supporters said. Most of them near me.

"So it is. I don't think we need to say 'Robot' now do we? Nobody has to watch, I'll be the bad guy here. But I'm going to open this door, and I'm going to fire three shots. The Huey will be blind from now on. What you do with it after that, well I guess we can talk that through. I'm a rational man. First things first."

He swung open the door, stepped back, and locked his arm all in one motion. But the look on his face was priceless.

I don't think I'll ever forget that look. Or the looks on the faces of many Coldwater citizens gazing into the closet.

Shock, hesitation, and astonishment all in one.

"Where did you put it!" The calm man was gone, outrage fully returning to his voice. A low rumble overtook the room. People looked harder into the closet and back to me.

I breathed a sigh of relief. "He's not there!?" I tried not to sound sarcastic, not knowing which way the crowd would turn. It could have easily gone south. But they didn't turn on me, or on Roland. They just didn't know what to do. Some scattered to look, in a bit of a hunt, and some stopped in relief. Others joined me on the floor, and asked questions. But I just smiled, because I truly didn't know when or how Human had done it, or where he had gone. I was only certain that he had been paying attention.

Roland Wright
Interviewed in Three Rivers Correctional Center

"EVERYBODY SPREAD OUT!" I yell. But they can't even get off the stairs and out of my way.

People need a leader, man, they need the motivation to do what's right. Otherwise the sheeple stay in the pen and never know true freedom. And I almost set them free. But Huey got the jump on this old boy.

There's a few people on my side, man, not enough. They're looking for Human in all the wrong places. Looking for Human.

Unlike the other ones, that's for sure. To find this one, you gotta think differently, man. You gotta throw a little outside the strike zone. Cause all the Hueys up until now, I had 'em. They were getting smarter, yeah, you bet. But they weren't anything like this one. I didn't even ask if it was in the church. I knew it wouldn't be, and I guess that's a kind of respect. I also knew Pastor Lovelife had nothing to do with it. Not because I didn't think he was capable of aiding and abetting a murderer, but because he doesn't think strategically, my man. He would have had to sniff it coming.

I had been waging a war of affections, which was necessary. My stature was high, and you gotta spend that cash.

I took no provisions, just the firearms and ammunition into a backpack I made for the occasion, with a holed out bottom to stick it through so I could wear it on my back but grab it quick if I needed. I didn't know how great a lead it had on me and all that, but the sooner the better to track him, man.

That robot hadn't made a sound in two days, man. But that didn't mean anything. It could've left on night one, or it could have stood in there listening to the tides turn and then made its move last night. There was just no way to know, but I do know. I know Huey. I know how he works, what makes him tick. It's destruction, man. That's what he wants. And you know, things are all different now. You can't say a bad word against Human like you can't say a bad word against the military or the protected class groups. They throw you out of society, lickedy-split. Well guess what? I'm already out of society, so I don't need your approval. You can end the night with a sausage in your mouth for all I care. But I don't have to like you. Which is good, because I don't.

You wait and see. Human's a hero in your eyes now, but he's still out there doing whatever the Hell. And I'm in here.

I KNEW Human had gone north. This is why: the robots desire to turn order into chaos. Huey never stops. Tactical riots. So they go where things are good and people are at peace and the land is prosperous. They already got the South, man. So go north. This one most certainly knew that.

Human. A name designed for sympathy.

I made my way through town, tracking him where robots had already laid waste. I was looking for the front line. If I moved in their wake, eventually I'd find them, and I'd find him, because I was sure he had gone full evil, man.

You know, the ones that hadn't changed yet, they almost scared me more.

This pack had tore its way through the north part of Coldwater already, and by the look of things, coasted right on through the nothing between Coldwater and Hernando. My best bet was that Human had joined that pack, but I didn't know. All I knew was I could hear things for miles out here in the wilderness, because all the people and the cars and civilization was gone. My gut said north but the sound said east, so I split the difference. I figured I'd catch up and take on all of them. Then I came across a real terrible sight, man. Real terrible.

There was a military grade SUV that had been overturned. No artillery on the top, and a beat up side. Then, off the road, there was a limousine. A military SUV and a limousine traveling together only means one thing: somebody who was important in the old world had died here. Back there, they give you armored escorts. Now you suck, and you're dead. And on the other side of the truck, I saw how you died. You got smashed, man. Or more accurately, it looks more like you got ripped out. My guess is, a Huey Horde stopped your SUV, which was already pretty beat up, and you fought to protect this dignitary sitting behind you. They came crashing through the front panel side and skinned your corpse through the metal. Left quite a bit of you behind from the looks of things. Decent chunks of you around. Probably happened pretty recently if the animals hadn't gotten it yet. Unless something else was scaring them off.

And who is this in the back seat? Dead but not mutilated. Looks like he might have died from a head injury.

He seems awfully young to be your dignitary. And why would he be in this SUV instead of the limo? Limo unsafe? Why bring it then? Maybe he was the son of a dignitary. Pansy. That was my first thought.

I was able to open the back door opposite him relatively easily, so he couldn't have gotten trapped in there. The impact of whatever this truck ran into must have killed him instantly. Front seat guy, who's now scattered all over, must have survived the crash, and Huey didn't like that.

I searched the body for supplies out of instinct. I was losing time on Human, but I had to search this scene too, man. I had to. Something wasn't adding up. The kid didn't have much to his name. A backpack, and maybe some medical supplies strewn around that might be his, or might have just been in the back seat. Not a lot for a dignitary kid. But hey, maybe he was just scraping by, too. Out here in the fields. Wasn't sure, man. Wasn't sure. I approached with the eagle-eyed caution of my training, sliding in the seat next to the kid, expecting him to open his eyes all of a sudden, and make a sick America Online Connection scream sound or something, then fire from a gun in his arm, or some weird BS like that. Like he was acting dead until I got close. So I was cautious, man. Like a ninja seal. Real slow, just waiting for the eyes and the head jerk. I would shoot first. He never did any of that BS, but you gotta be careful, but you can't worry too much either. 'Cause you know, you got crap you gotta do. Why teach a man to fish. That makes sense here. Yep. Still sad though.

Here was a young man cut down in his prime. I figured that out from the letters in his pack. He was listening to the Method, they all were. The Method. It got out. I almost teared up. They were coming to see me. I sat there, just reading the letters in reverse even though it was getting dark. It kind of floored me, man, it really did. My Method was out there, saving lives of real people. It was going to win the war. Everything I worked for. All the being prepared, all the sacrifice, all the training was all worth it now, sitting in that car, with that poor kid. It really messed me up, man. He addressed them to the pastor, 'cause Pastor made the first call on the radio. So people probably thought he was the hero. They were all coming to see him. That doesn't bother me, because attention is fine for some people. I know this. But then I would have to fade back in somehow. And now I could just fade back in easy.

It's all good, man. And I couldn't finish the letters anyway. Not enough time, and I knew what I needed to know. Had a few laughs, drank a few beers with him, but didn't want to get too attached.

Had to stuff the letters all back in the backpack, and it was a good backpack too, so I brought it with me. Had two backpacks now. There wasn't a single gun in that whole truck, would you even believe that? And it was getting pretty dang dark.

That's why the sudden movement in my periphery surprised me with a real shot of adrenaline. Woke me up quick.

Too swift. Too quiet.

A robot couldn't do that. Not any robot I knew.

"Alright I see you. Just better come out," I said, aiming my weapon. No use hiding. We knew where each other was. But maybe it didn't know about my piece. So here she is, sucker. "Come and get it."

The mysterious stranger hid behind the limousine. Hard to see in this light.

"Come on now, I'm sure you see my long gun. I fire this thing it ain't gonna be in the air."

Was it scared? Get out here, dog. Don't you dare surprise me.

"Let's get this over with before we lose the light. Much easier that way. If you're flesh and bone you don't have nothing to worry about."

Well, unless you're an animal. Or a hybrid human animal. Then I'd probably shoot you because I don't like abominations. And I'd wonder if you did it with an animal, or your dad did, or how that happened. I would just shoot you though, let's be honest here. I wouldn't find out a ton of detail first or whatever. Like if a lab made you. You think I'd sit there and let a human animal hybrid moan out partial words while I just stood there deciphering? "Oh, are you saying you were made in a lab? This isn't your fault after all. Let's shave those sprouts of hair off your body and dress you like a person for society." Man, you must not have heard a word I said up until this point because you know I would just shoot it.

But it wasn't a human animal hybrid after all. Nope. Don't know why I mentioned that just now, I was not even thinking it at the time. I was thinking what if this was Human. What if this was the smartest Huey in the world. Play hurt, wait, wait till I get close. A real human would have said something by now. Not a Human. A Human would do exactly this. I backed off. Not falling in.

Do something unexpected. Right now.

I ran away from the side of the car I was approaching, clear across to the other side as quiet and quick as I could to get a look at it. Knowing is half the battle, man. Get my peepers on, then I know. Fire. Or hold.

Hold. Gotta know when to hold 'em. This was a hold.

Because it turned out to be the most dangerous wounded animal of all. It was a man. A man in hiding. He stood slowly from behind the limo with one hand, palm out in the air. It was a surrender, but I still kept my rifle on him until I could see the other hand.

"Lift the other hand, sir," I barked out. "Lift the other hand."

He did, and it was covered in blood.

"An injury," he said, looking at me through his glasses.

"I get you. Just hold 'em both up until I get closer." My guard came down a bit with my gun.

"Are you the only survivor of your party?" I asked him. He seemed reluctant so I asked again. "This backpack belongs to the kid in that SUV. He's dead. Is everyone dead?"

He nodded a deliberate yes, as if he was relieved to know how to respond.

"I am need of help," he said. "I am injure."

"How long ago did this accident happen? How long have you been here alone?"

Either he didn't know, or didn't understand the question. My assumption was that I was speaking with the professed dignitary. The one and only. Due to the very non-native nature of this man standing here in northern Mississippi.

Then a terrible reality dawned on me like a chain reaction of explosives taking down a building. I will always remember how this happened.

"What is your name, sir!" I yelled all of a sudden. "What the hell is your name!"

He looked at me, confused, I assume by the change in my demeanor, and not the question I was asking.

"I SAID TELL ME YOUR DAMN NAME."

"I am Koji," he said, like nails. But it couldn't be.

Here I am. With him.

"Otsuka?"

My tone changed, without a thought, man. This only alarmed him more. I stuck my piece back through the hole in my home-made bag and put it on my back.

"Hot diggity," I said to myself, leaning up right there on the limo. God I wish I had a cigarette. "Koji Otsuka." I laughed to myself. Put my hands on my head, walked a few paces away. None of this put him at ease.

I didn't know what to do with myself, other than smile.

"I'm gonna ask you a question, Koji Otsuka. Who flew you here?"

I could tell he was playing up the language barrier.

"Oh, I'm sorry, I guess you don't understand the question I'm asking. Let me clarify. Who PAID for the plane ticket that brought you HERE, to the United States to fix the robots you created?"

It's amazing the power silence has if you use it right. I just stood there and waited, and stared at him. God I wish I had a cigarette. Just staring, cleaning my teeth with my tongue.

"United States," he finally said.

"That's correct, Otsuka. That is correct, and thank you for your timely answer. And where does the United States government get its money?"

No pause this time.

"I am not understanding."

"Sure you do! Smart guy like you. Where does the government – any government – get its money?"

"I suppose. The people." The man was afraid of me, but he didn't have anywhere to go. No clever answers, either. He had lost some blood.

"That's right. Yes. That's very good. Very good." I laughed a little. Just at the circumstance itself. Here I am in the middle of BFE, not a soul around, and I run into the maker himself. Just the sheer odds of it! Certainly wasn't lost on me.

"I have one more question for you, Koji." I continued, not able to sit still. It helped my wheels turn, pacing and gazing out into the darkening woods.

"You see, we have a common enemy. Our relationship with that enemy is anything but similar, but a common enemy nonetheless. And we are in the midst of a war against that enemy. That makes us allies, right? And what do you think allies do?" I paused, and he said nothing, man. Not a thing. "I think allies talk. Discuss. You want to be my ally, don't you Koji?" I didn't look at him yet. "So this one's a little tougher question, but I'm confident a smart guy like you can talk it out with me. Brainstorm it, even if you don't know the answer right away, okay?"

Now I looked at him.

"How the hell does a man like me end up paying for a man like you to fly here?"

He stared at me right through the lenses.

"I'll let you think about that, I know it's not cut and dry. But just in case you didn't catch all my English, let me ask it again with a little spit shine: How the HELL does the inventor of the greatest mass murderers in history fly on MY dime to MY doorstep, fail in every possible way to stop the machines HE MADE, then get off scot-free while good men die protecting HIM?"

He was trembling now, boy. He understood every word I said. See, I told you he was playing up the language barrier. That's how I knew. It was time to get old faithful off my chest.

Very slowly, as though, like, I were pouring myself a drink, I lifted my shirt and removed the .357 from my waist. And that's when Koji ran. I don't know what he thought, if he could outrun a gun or what. Or maybe he could get far enough in the dark.

Dude was headed for the woods.

I shot once over his head and hit the tree he was running at. I don't know if it would have stopped him if I hit anywhere else. But a pop right in front of you like that, the scared animal darts and covers.

Reverb from the gunshot, then quiet, man.

"Ain't done with you yet, Great Creator."

Getting real now.

"Get up," I said. "And let me tell you who I am."

Koji did squat for a moment, but then he just sat down right there in the mud.

"Did you know there's some design flaws in your workmanship? Guy like me shouldn't know much about that, though. Too stupid, right? Well let me tell you, man. First, it's too hard to take them apart. I'm sure you did that on purpose. Built to last. No tinkering, but you can't turn 'em off either. And then there's the programming. You can reprogram her once you slice her open. But anything short of that, and you just got that one mechanism, man. The insurance. The reprogram through the blinking lights. What a freaking failsafe. But the Method, the bleak back door, you didn't know about that one, did you? Oh I know you're smart, man. Don't get me wrong. Genius. But there was a design flaw you didn't know about and that's why you were coming here. Shocked you right up and down. You had to know ALL about it. Not just that it worked, but how it was discovered. I think you expected to find a genius, somebody who could lead you to the Promised Land. Somebody who could prop you up, give you the Intel. And you would use it, change it just a little, and save everyone. And you'd be the savior again. Maimed your own creation and saved your name. You'd be Koji Otsuka, creator, destroyer. Well, guess what, Koji? You found him. That genius is me. Yeah, that's right! The man with the gun in your face, man! Excited yet? Go ahead, ask your questions, you hero. You god. What do you want to know? Because I don't have the answers. I didn't find it by genius programming. I found it by hard work. By taking Huey out in the back yard. Over and over. Knocking it down. Lighting it on fire. Blowing it up. Poking its soft spots. Day after day after day. That's what it takes. Not you and your fanboys, and your company, and your investors. And your shareholders, and their wives, and their girlfriends, and their boats, and their passports, and their summer homes. You get down there in the weeds and the mud just like you are now, and you work your butt off until you find the shot to the heel that will take it down, because while you're out at your cocktail parties and board meetings, I'm forecasting the tragedy and putting in the TIME before it takes us all down. And that's how I did it. And that's why you DIDN'T. You and your smoking jackets. That's why you lost, and your plans failed, and mine didn't."

I cocked a bullet into the chamber because that's what came next. He knew what I was saying was true and it was all over, and this was exactly how it was going to end.

"Go ahead. Ask the question. Ask me, now that you know me. What was burning inside you?"

He wept a pathetic, no nonsense cry. I wouldn't say it was pity, or remorse, man. Seemed like maybe exhaustion.

"I only always want to help."

Now he was just pissing me off.

"That ain't it. Ask me the question! Ask me to explain it in detail!"

Koji didn't say anything.

"Ask me!"

"I know what you know . . ."

That was the last straw. I was done. But he was still talking.

". . . and it will not work . . ."

Shot.

What did he mean, "won't work?" It was already working!

It didn't matter. The pull of that trigger was like a satisfying lay. I squeezed it, and the bullet went in just above his glasses, slightly off center. I can shoot a Huey from a quarter mile right in the neck, but I guess he got the best of me out there, outside Coldwater. Even though I had to do it.

Because this was the gift that was given to me. A man has to accept a gift when it's given from above.

Koji was wounded and would have died anyway.

Nothing mattered.

I didn't feel like hunting anymore. Didn't know if I'd find the robot, or if I'd recognize him once he'd gone evil.

"Won't work." Get out of here with that.

I went on back to the church after all, and gave the letters to the pastor.

"These are addressed to you," I said. "And that's okay." But I didn't stay. I found an empty building and slept, woke, and left that town for good. I never saw any of them again.

The Dex-Men
Interviewed in New Orleans, LA

IT TOOK us a while to come down, but once we did, a discussion finally broke the silence between us.

"What happens if we run into a load of 'em, what do we do?" Samson put out there.

"I don't know, I really don't. But I just ain't worried about it for some reason," I said. It was stupid, but it wasn't.

"No, I know and I'm not telling you you're wrong for that. I just...we got to be ready. It's night, and for one, I'm gonna get tired at some point. And two, I don't want to 'feel it out' if we run into a crazy horde. We'd be fools not to have a plan."

I conceded there. Our best action was to keep looking through the dark for red eyes. It meant us staying diligent and driving slow, which felt inappropriate to me. Like I just needed to trust. It also felt stupid, because that meant we couldn't take turns sleeping, so we couldn't take turns driving. But we did see some red eyes. Only one pair of red eyes, and we looked at each other to make sure the other one saw it. Yep! We kept on driving. We still didn't know where we were going. All I knew was we were heading south, deeper and deeper into the dead zone.

"Samson, what do you think about this one we got back here?" I said.

"I wish he'd tell us what to do. We just driving. We started driving and we still driving like we know something."

It was true. The further we got from the moment when the robots parted and let us through, the more we didn't know if we were doing the right thing. Like what if we was just supposed to drive a couple minutes and then stop and let him out? Or how did we know we weren't supposed to drive west, or due east? How did we know anything?

"There's one way to find out. Just turn the truck around," I said. Samson nodded a little nod, but he didn't do nothing. I knew he wouldn't. We were driving south.

After some quiet I had to ask it again.

"What's the deal with this one? Why is this robot different from the others?"

"He looked all put together."

"What does that mean?"

"I don't know."

When we got to Jackson it started to lighten up a bit, the way it does when you know night's almost over. I don't know why, but I hate that time. I always read that dawn is supposed to represent new beginnings and whatnot. But every time I see a dawn, I think, "I am not where I want to be." And I ain't talking about in life, or something big like that. I just mean, if things were the way I wanted them, I'd be in bed right now. Which means I'm usually doing something I don't want to do. Like working a job I don't want to do. Or maybe I stayed up late and was trying to do something I shouldn't be doing. The dawn means my night's over, and if I'm still up I ain't ready for it to be over. In this situation, I felt like a divine purpose and whatnot, but I didn't know what I was doing and I hate that feeling the most.

We had seen more than our fair share of dead robots all along the way. Usually in clusters, they were passed out from when the EMP went off. This far in the South, there was plenty to go around, and sometimes you could see where the still living ones gone through them. Divine purpose or not, Samson and I needed some sleep after driving through the night. We pulled off and found the most hidden spot we could between a bunch of trailers at a truck stop. Figured we'd hear them if they ever came, but they never did. We slept so long we felt guilty about the one in the back, but there he was when we opened the door, standing there like always.

There wasn't much activity until we got to New Orleans.

It had rained, and with the sun going down again it was beautiful, and it was scary too. Me and Samson going into the city just watching for movement and whatnot.

"I don't want to go into the French Quarter, Samson."

"Why?"

"I don't know, we just shouldn't."

It was kind of because I could hear a buzz coming from that direction, but really it was because I heard all the dangerous stuff happens there. I didn't want to tell him that though, because he would make fun of me.

It was too late anyway, we had gone in too deep.

The buzz was a decoy. It threw us off. Because while the buzz kept on buzzing, we were being surrounded. More and more eyes. They came about so slow it deceived both of us. And these ones didn't buzz. They were quiet as winter bugs.

For the first time, it seemed to me that there was an organization to it. Not just mindless destruction, although it looked like that had been happening too. They had to destroy some things to satisfy the craving, but once the appetite was gone, they could go about the new family business. One thing was for sure. This city was theirs. And us two janitors had stumbled into the command center.

Now more than eyes, we could see the shape of them. There was evil, boy. It was like they grew with it and were taking on its form. They had given the shells of themselves over to a sweet, dark, syrup that had choked them from the inside and by the time they realized it, it held them hostage so completely that they could nothing but agree with it. No ghost of their former selves could rise up to protest this identity now. Samson felt it, and I was living it. It was coming for me, and it would drag both of us away. This was no longer the kind of evil that deceives, because it didn't need to lure us in. It was here to overcome, and, I felt, to live through us once there was nothing left of us. I stood there expecting that we would be dashed to pieces by them the minute they had their numbers up, that they would come at us with such incredible force that there would be no denying them whatever they desired, and I was exactly right, that's what they did.

"Oh God," I barely wheezed, but maybe through that tiny little prayer all that paralyzed energy fell off and I started screaming at the top of my lungs!

"Oh God, here it comes! Here it comes, HERE IT COMES! WHY DIDN'T WE HAVE A PLAN!?"

Now Samson was the cool one. He crawls in the back and throws open the latch, unloads the ramp, and tells the robot to "Go! Do your thing!"

Samson says the robot looked at him, put his arms straight by his sides, and then rolled down the ledge like he was stepping into the OK Corral or something. And all that evil just stopped, as if they knew he was Doc Holliday and they were the outlaws.

I got in the back with Samson. Neither one of us knew what we were about to see.

"He's pointing at something on his side," Samson said. "It's a word, scratched in."

"What is the word?"

I didn't have time to think about that. Because all that evil in that whole command center was training those laser red eyes on me and my brother and the Gunslinger. And there was tumbleweed rolling between us. And them bad robots, they looked at each other, and some computing started happening. That's when I knew that this robot we had was not normal, because that evil I just told you about had stopped wrapping around me. There wasn't a power in this world that could have stopped it. But it had stopped.

Only one robot came forward from the pack. I stepped back. Hey, so did Samson, it wasn't just me. Gunslinger stayed put. And robot number one rolled right up to Doc Holiday's face and let off some steam. If he could talk, he would have said something real nasty I think. And then he would have turned back to his buddies, who'd be laughing. Instead, he shot his arms out and power-clamped them steel hands onto Gunslinger's shoulders. He held Doc's whole body straight and looked him right in the eye. I thought this was the part where Doc would do one of them inside-out hand moves and knock its arms off, then BOOM a kick to the middle, where that evil bully would fly back into his friends like bowling pins. Then we run! Nope. Doc stood there and stared him right back. Didn't even flinch. The bad guy didn't either, and it was like I could hear the gears winding up in Number One's head. He was about to infect Doc with the disease in his hive. Come on, Doc, do something! It was painful to watch him standing there, taking it. And with it, our only hope. Samson motioned for me to jump back in the truck, and we were going to scoot, boy, if we could get a lane. Might be tough.

Doc's eyes started mimicking the pattern and we knew we had to go fast. But Doc kept on standing there. We'd seen robots turn, and this was the part where it would grab my heel as I was trying to close the big latch door.

Instead, Number One pivoted and melted back into its pack. Then all at once, every single one of them evil things started blinking at Gunslinger, who just stood there cold as ice.

The Ice King.

Gunslinger.

Doc Holiday wheeled up to one of them, and doggone it I think I might as well call that one Number Two. And he blinked a mighty blink, flashed those baby reds in a way nobody'd seen before. Or at least we hadn't.

Just like that, Number Two was free.

He came out from the pack and stood with the Gunslinger.

Blinking time was over. Now the teeth came out. Big hungry

jaws came down around our boy, and Number Two, and the Dex-Men's truck. Two robots and us against an innumerable pack.

But Doc Holiday had a trick. Number One had already changed, and he held back his former friends so Doc and us wouldn't be overcome by sheer numbers. Then the real fun began. Doc spun in a half circle, knocked three down with a big round kick, grabbed two more, and put them together shoulder to shoulder. He blinked his eyes at those two and turned them. Then he looked down at the three he knocked to the ground and he turned them, too. And those five lined up behind him like soldiers.

The next wave had broke free from Number One. They saw what Doc did, and they rushed him just the same, but they were smart. They came at him with their heads down, shielding their eyes. But old Doc Holliday took them on one by one. The first one he uppercut, tilted and blinked him. Then he kneeled and hit the next one in what would be the nugs, bowed it over just by force, put it in a headlock and swung it around, knocking two others down. He put the one he was holding back on its feet, blinked it, and pushed it into another one, which it grabbed and held on to. Then it ALL broke loose. Me and Samson just stood there slack-jawed while the converted started fighting back. Doc Holliday just walked around blinking anything he could into submission. But a few of them came at Doc with their eyes covered again, and they got him good. First with a right hook to the face, then another took his feet out. And they pounced, and I do believe they would have destroyed him and our only chance at stopping this thing from taking over the world. But it wouldn't go down like that. The converted had a taste of true freedom and were full-on reckless abandon for him now. One completely left his feet and went airborne, knocking two off of Doc. He stood, took the remaining robot's arms and broke them, then blinked it. That one, oddly, didn't turn, but instead just died.

In fact, some of them who saw what was going down busted out their own eyes. That was real weird.

It was a dare, I guess, because it didn't work. Doc blinked them just like he blinked the others. 'Cause they weren't actually blind, when they do that, you know?

He hadn't flipped them all yet, but the fight was slowing. I looked out and saw more coming who had not seen what just took place. They got blinked right away. If they were people, I believe they would have been sobbing and thanking the Cowboy. But instead, they simply changed sides, joined him. Maybe their service was like the tears a man would have shed. Maybe some of them didn't want to be changed. Because there was a percentage that just up and died.

The soldiers never blinked any onto their side, only The Gunslinger would do that. After watching this happen right there in the middle of Dauphine St., my brother and I figured we had witnessed the utter destruction of the other side right there in New Orleans. But of course, we hadn't yet.

Still, it was like watching fate happen, and we were a part of it. Victory from the jaws of defeat, and we were a part of it. It's hard to believe, even now.

Me and Samson just stood there the whole time watching all this happen around us.

Now what?

The country's a big place for one physician.

Doc Holliday got back on the truck, Samson pushed the ramp and I latched the door. No hurry.

Where to, Cowboy?

The soldiers let us know. The path they opened was east this time. Further in.

Nothing to worry about. We had Doc. He was the difference. Unlike the rest of them, and unlike us, even though the scratched out plate on his side said, "Human."

Alf Johnson
Interviewed in Tampa, FL

PRETTY EARLY ON at New Orleans, I got in line because there was only one spot where everybody was going to get picked up. And they had to wait and you had to wait, 'cause it was real crowded. And I saw a bunch of girls in Mardi Gras costumes and I crossed my fingers I could take them. I even showed my fingers to the military guy who was loading people on boats. With my other hand, I pointed at my crossed fingers and then pointed at that group of ladies. I didn't want to say nothing because I saw a show one time about how dogs can "talk" even though they don't say anything! Like they communicate in their own special way. And I thought right then, hey, if a dog can do it then I want to do a special way too.

And military guy, he says, "What is it, boy?"

And I kind of nosed at those ladies again.

"Is it a fire?" he says.

NO. I shook my head. NO.

"Fire?" he said again.

"No, dang it!" I shouted. But I caught myself and said, "Woof woof" and pointed at them girls again. Then I went "aaa-oooo-ga!" like a foghorn. He gave me the ol' fast up-and-down-eyebrows and nudged another guy.

Long story short, I wrote "I want to take those party girls" on a dry erase board real messy like a dog wrote it.

"You want to take those *girls!* Yeah, you go ahead, *ladies*, and get on this boat here." Later, I found out some of those girls wasn't girls.

You know how I found out some of those girls wasn't girls? It's a complicated story, but I'll try my darndest to tell it right. I gave one of the girls a boat cushion, and when she sat down, I saw a penis.

I swear it. And you know what I did? Nothing. Because I thought, man I want to be a pretty good guy about this. So I said something kind. I said, "When you sit down on that boat cushion, be sure not to sit down on your penis." And I gave that penis girl a very genuine smile and a big thumbs up and I patted her on the back. Then I nodded at the rest of them and I filled my lungs up, started walking to a different part of the boat for some reason. But then I thought, no, I am going to go the extra mile for these boy girls. I turned real slow and licked my finger and stuck it in the air so everybody would be quiet for a second even though they were already not talking. "From now on," I said, "This boat is called *Trans!*" I was bowed over and holding my hand out like an olive branch so one of them would run up and shake it. "That's for all of you girls and for that guy that's dressed as a girl right there. You be careful on that boat cushion now, when you sit down don't sit on it." And I did that because I'm just a real nice guy. Some people aren't okay with those kind of people, but I just got a real easygoing spirit about me. One time when I was probably just a foot tall, my mom says, Alfie, you got a real easygoing spirit about you, and I always remembered that. She was real upset because school was just not my thing, but I remember she was yelling and pointing at me saying how easygoing I was. So I like to pay it forward no matter what genitalia. Or even if they try to trick you about what's their genitalia. Fool me once shame on you.

Now that I was so nice, it was time to find out which other of these girls weren't girls. That's an even longer story, but I will try to tell it here. I did the boat cushion thing again. Couldn't believe it. *Every single time* it worked. They was all dudes. And they told me in their fake high voices that New Orleans was getting bad, like all the robots were clustering there.

And I took that real serious. The rest of the trip, anytime I'd see them I wouldn't say nothing, I just bowed my head down and held out that olive branch. Nobody ever shook it, I don't know if they knew what I was doing when I held my head down and my hand out all those times. One time one of those penis girls put a coin purse in my hand, and there was a phone number in it. I never called that phone number, you know why? I don't appreciate that little tricky dick stuff no matter which end. I am real easy to get along with, but I don't put up with that tricky dick BS for long.

The Gay Gambler
Interviewed by phone

I BEGAN CALCULATING.

At the rate of movement, there was no way the robots had made it to Washington D.C so quickly that the country's leaders weren't able to evacuate. However, the communication system throughout the South had become spotty and insignificant, turning to older mechanisms and word of mouth, such that Madam President's ridiculous declarations of authority spread further and faster than would be possible in virtually any other scenario.

Was she a genius, capitalizing on an unlikely scenario?

She was orchestrating the entire Vacate project, which was not genius, but not stupid. The robots can't get out to sea. Get bystanders out to sea. Rather simple. The execution, though, took thought. Communicating between ships, coastal ports, prioritizing locations, managing food and perishable resources, noting which ships had maxed out and which hadn't, and deciding where to put them all. It was a bigger ordeal than it seemed, but she could have been allotting it to secondary conductors, like me.

There was no way to know. What I did know is that I have crossed very few people who would classify as legitimate geniuses.

Most people rise to power by a combination of force and luck. True geniuses stay out of the spotlight.

Therefore, she was no genius. Oh, how understated that was.

But at least I can rest in the knowledge that I'm not easily tricked. Though it has happened. It has happened, and it sits in the background of every decision I make now, sarcastically questioning me.

A man at my table was having a good, but not great evening. He wore a slender tie which hung down, brushing the table as he leaned forward, and a collared shirt that appeared tighter than it was due to his loose neck skin. I wasn't sure yet, but I was concerned that he was watching me. Despite an amicable count up to that point, I decided to leave the table. When I did, he shot a glance at a young man in an oversized gray suit, who approached and whispered something to the man.

"No" the man responded, almost in alert. The sudden emotion was unexpected and strange.

The young man nodded and left. I had begun putting the gentleman and his neck skin out of mind when the young man, gray suit, moved toward me. Out of respect, he waited for me to finish my hand. I threw the hand. Questions ran through my head, as I wondered if there was an innocent solution for his approach. I could find none. I wasn't a big enough winner to be noticeable tonight.

I planned on ignoring the young man and leaving quickly.

Scanning the room, I found the closest woman to me with a low enough cut dress, and shot her a hard smile. Her reaction did not matter – as long as it was a vigorous one. I only needed her attention long enough to make it look like I had other things on my mind. After all, if I was just there to meet women, I wasn't a threat to anyone. I wrote a fake number on a cocktail napkin and began to stand, but I hadn't done it fast enough. The young man stood in my way.

"Sir, if I may," he breathed.

"Sorry, son," I took on a persona. "I see a lady who looks a lot better than you do, if ya don't mind . . ."

"On behalf of Mr. Salman," he handed me a card. "Oh, and by the way, if you are looking for the company of women, you should attend." With that, he left the establishment. I should have known right then, after a line like that, what I was getting into. But I laughed out loud. It amused me that such a thing would exist in rural Kansas. The man with the neck skin got up moments later and didn't so much as look in my direction. I wondered how many suckers he had invited tonight.

The card simply said, "Mr. Salman, White Cloud. High stakes." And on the back, a handwritten address. My impulse was to leave it there at the table for the next joker to find, but I simply couldn't. High stakes in White Cloud. What could that possibly look like?

Against my own advice, I decided to see. I never want to lose my sense of curiosity, after all. What's life without it? Less risky, that's one thing.

I drove to the location – a large, dark house. Well-manicured. A pool in the back, based on the sounds I heard. The young man, gray suit, gave me a parking slip and handed my keys to the attendant in the circle drive. The young man, gray suit, laid out the ground rules: no names, no personal details. Anything that happens here tonight stays here. Money lost is money gained, and vice versa. The party is in the back, but the game is in the basement. Something smelled fishy to me. Normally, a house like this would either be bustling with activity or on complete lockdown. Upon entering, this house was neither. It was dark, other than the lights from the apparent party out back. There was no way I was going into the basement. Sensing a trap, I turned on every light I could with every switch near me in the foyer. The light only made it worse. There was no one and nothing with any life. Furniture that fit, yes, but nothing . . . personal. Just some pamphlets strewn out on the kitchen table and a binder.

"Welcome to White Cloud. You are no doubt here to take advantage of the casino, but while you're here, there's more to White Cloud than you imagined."

I was in an Air B&B. My car was gone.

I ran out front anyway. Money lost, money gained. Ferrari F50, by the way. Not just some car.

Nothing in the basement. Nothing out back except a note.

"A car for a boom box. Seems fair to me. Thanks."

Some 21 year old kid picked me out of the crowd for a mark. He probably saw me drive up in it.

You get sloppy, doing it enough. I can't. Not in White Cloud, Kansas, and not on Vespucci Cruise Liner 19.

Buckle down, keep your head in it.

I would need just one radio conversation to figure this "president" out. And with her, the whole game.

Alf Johnson
Interviewed in Tampa, FL

BUT HERE'S what I'm trying to say, here's what I'm trying to say. On one of them trips to the Gulf Coast, I didn't always go to the same spot. Like that old fish saying, "You go to the same spot? Every time?" Nope. That's like what I was doing, but for refugees. 'Cause I felt a little like those military guys tricked me last time when they said, "We'll give you the party girls," and then they had lies for genitalia.

Plus I heard that New Orleans had become a hot potato.

The Gay Gambler
Interviewed by phone

"WHO AM I SPEAKING WITH?" she asked with faux superiority. I gave her a fake name and told her why I was contacting her.

"And you're running the western group?" she asked.

"You could say that."

"Well, great work, sir. You are a star. The word star is underused in my opinion. I believe in using it like I use exclamation points! And that's why I'm calling you a star." She seemed to think I should be honored by this.

"Madam President," I continued. "I've heard you have a device that could change our situation."

"For the country?"

"Yes, for the whole country," I said.

"I'm here to fight for our country," she said. Then a long pause, and then, "Tell me how we grab the bull by the horns."

"It's your floodlight."

"Yep. I'm right with you. Bull by the horns for our country."

"Alright. On a wide scale, I believe we need to get the signal out visually."

"You mean, we set up planes to carry big screens and fly them around, just around and around, showing a video of the floodlight to all the killer robots?"

"No," I said, wiping my whole face. "No. We try to duplicate that light pattern."

"Wouldn't it be easier to just videotape this one and show the video on screens behind planes?"

"No, but . . . well actually . . ." I hated to admit that it might be faster. However, I was concerned with the viability of the whole operation. We're talking about a two minute blackout. That's better than nothing, to be sure, but to send out a whole armada to accomplish a two minute reprieve?

"Then that's the plan!" she exclaimed.

"Actually, Madam, it's not so easy." Even with every plane available we couldn't continuously cover the sky.

"Sure it is! I can make it happen. I'm the President of the United States (Tourism Bureau)."

She then thanked me for my service to our country, called me a star, and hung up the receiver.

But I wasn't done. I knew she had something special and was misappropriating it. I couldn't let that happen. So I put in a request for a boat to go straight to the source.

The first one in range was captained by a man who was truly unique among men. A man so recklessly optimistic that it was impossible to read him and impossible not to envy him. That kind of freedom is rare.

He is a fisherman named Alf, and I'll have to put you in touch with him. This story will not be complete without him.

Alf Johnson
Interviewed in Tampa, FL

INSTEAD OF THAT HOT POTATO, I went to a port that was askew of that one, but there was not a single person there!

And Lilly said, "Hey what's with this place, it's a little askew!"

And I said, "I know, it's askew of the last time we came here!" Also, before this interview, I got a pocket dictionary for certain words.

And so I said, "This place is wanton. I am forlorn."

And Lilly said, "It has beguiled me. Scorn! My countenance!"

Boy, you said it, Lilly!

So naturally we parked up the *Trans!* Got out, walked on land. The mud feels good between your toes. Do I wear shoes? Yep. Do they have a little trap door hinge on them that flips up so my toes can go out? Yep.

I started to wonder where everybody was right then. I was askew.

"Lilly, I think I see something moving over there!"

"Where!"

"Over there!"

"Here in this direction?"

"No, in THIS direction!"

Hahahha. So stupid. Yeah THAT direction Lilly. What a boob!

"Oh I see it, is it a person?"

"No, I think it's a robot!" I said.

"We need to get out of here fast if it's a r-r-r-robot!" Lilly said like if it was a g-g-g-ghost.

"But I think it's gentle," I said in my butterfly voice. I can do all kinds of stuff you don't know about. Women like it when you talk in a butterfly voice. Wait till I tell you what I did in the next one. I save everybody.

"It's okay, Lilly. I feel as if it is okay," I said, squatting down, calm, moving like a statue would if it was sitting on a toilet after a magic spell took place. Lilly just stayed standing. "Ooh, ooh!" I looked at my hands like they were moving for the first time in my statue life.

Sure enough, that robot came after us. Lilly took off a-runnin' right back to the boat, but I was bent in place. She started up the motor and with all the smoke that goes out I thought, hmmmm, maybe if I stay totally still. So the robot comes scooting up to me, but it seems different, like I said. Like maybe it just needed a friend. The only thing I allowed to move was my eyes when it was sniffing around on me. And I said, "I seek peace!" but with barely moving my mouth. Once I knew it wasn't going to feel me up and violate me, I finally relaxed.

"Thanks for leaving me alone down there!" I said, slapping it on the back.

Lilly was about 20 feet out on the water already. She shook her head.

"I can't believe you found the only good one on the planet!" she cupped her hands and yelled.

"Yeah, I guess they ain't found this one!" I laughed. And then this buzzing sound I couldn't quite put my finger on.

"Can you put your finger on that?" I cupped my hands and yelled at Lilly.

"What?"

"Can you put your finger on that? The buzzing sound I'm talking about now?" It had some gall.

"I hear it too! And you better run!" Lilly steered the boat back toward me. I flipped my toes back into their hinges and took off running. Because there were probably 20 robots coming around a building right at me.

Yee-haw, I was off like a hot potato! But then I got that same feeling again. I cocked my head. Hmmmm. Hmmmmmmmm. What am I truly running from? The robots, or myself? I was having a thought. I was right at the boat edge, and I was having a thought.

"Don't you have a thought right now, you smelly old toadstool, you get on this boat!" she said.

Just like people who smoke pipes have thoughts, I said, "I am having a thought Lilly! I am!" Lilly was so mad. But I turned my body to them robots, closed my eyes, and opened my arms. And smiled a flat smile with no teeth.

And do you know what happened? They didn't hug me or anything, but they didn't kill me neither. They just carried on.

"These robots is all normal!" I said.

"How!"

"I don't know! But they're all mediocre!" It was like a paradise city.

When I got back on the boat there was a ragtag robot that come around the corner from the other way. It was killing and destroying and whatnot. That one was. But before we could get off land, we saw that robot run smack dab into the good ones, and they looked him right in the eye. And you know what happened? They threw him down. They jumped up and down on him. And just when it looked like he had no fight left, they let up. And ope! He tricked 'em. Got up and ran away. Hahha, dumb lovebots. You've got a thing or two to learn about the tricks we lil' buttholes can play on ya.

Anyway, I was rooting for them good ones 'cause they were alright, but you gotta respect a butthole getting his trick on. But I root for them good ones, I do.

Yumi Otsuka
Interviewed in Vancouver, B.C.

I OFTEN ASK Koji why he does not give Ami better English. He says he wants her to learn. There are many things programmed into Ami for particular reason. Koji could have programmed her to have memories beyond her creation shy of eight years prior to the outbreak. So that she has a false history. But he was afraid of this for many reasons. First, is that she would have gaps in her memory. In addition, her memories would be perfect and clear, unlike our own. These things would make her more unnatural. He says it is more practical and honest to simply instruct her to be shy about her past and protect her identity. To avoid but not to lie. This is important, not to lie. Koji and I discuss about these things during her creation, within our home. He wants to provide for me because he loves me and we cannot have a child. He is a good man.

There are many things we talk through. How we start our life new once Ami is ready. How we will allow her to grow up, with modifications, importing memories she has created into new taller frames. We picked her age. Beyond a small child, so she misses the fastest growth period, but not too old, so she can experience a childhood. We want her to be our real daughter with a life and with parents. I understand now that we will not have that life.

Even after Koji's death, I believed it was possible. I wanted to keep Ami's secret. Through it all, I did. But not now. I cannot, after what she has done.

Ami Otsuka
Interviewed in Vancouver, B.C.

I AM friends with a girl at school. She is name Haruko. She says she is my friend, but she asks me questions I am not allow to answer. There are things I must upheld. There are boxes and rooms I must protect. It is how I am. Haruko is wanting to find the things I have inside.

My father says she is not important, and her father is not important, and she is not my friend. I think I hope she is a friend, because I want to experience a friend.

So I say Haruko is my friend at school. But Haruko sees me when I am boxing off my rooms to what I have inside. And Haruko knocks on the door with a wicked look. Like she is a hunter. When Haruko has this look I do not think I have a friend at school.

NINE

HELLO AGAIN, HUMAN

Ami Otsuka
Interviewed in Vancouver, B.C.

I never like the nighttime. My mother tells me I must find sleep, but I do not sleep. She tells me I must pretend then, because this is in a real daughter. I try to listen to my mother but I must stay still for so many hours. I find many other things to do.

———

The Gay Gambler
Interviewed by phone

I NEEDED to get the floodlight to dissect the light pattern – to test it, and hopefully alter it. It was a gold mine. Could the pattern be modified to shut them down for longer intervals, or reprogram them in some other way? Even what we had could be sent out to every cell phone flashlight and used to save countless lives. I had to get to the device.

I didn't yet know how it worked. For now, this woman, this oblivious individual, had the floodlight and the forged authority to make things happen.

The Dex-Men
Interviewed in New Orleans, LA

ONCE WE WENT EAST, we found ourselves in the same situation as before, just driving blind. Didn't know where we were going, or why, but we did our best. Every 45 minutes or so we'd stop and let Doc out to do his thing, all down the coast. Made big stops in Gulfport and Biloxi, if I recall. Old Doc seemed happy to oblige. Turn a bundle, then get back in the truck. We got a big tickle out of it. Such a weird journey, like life. You get just a little divine direction and you keep going until something makes you stop. That's what we did.

"The savior of the world," Samson said. He was having fun.

"Don't say that, Sammy. I don't like the way that sounds about a robot."

"You know I'm right."

"I don't like it."

For a while there, we didn't see any robots. I formed up a theory. This is an important part, my theory.

"Okay, Bro, I been sitting here thinking. What if this here robot, he's the only one that can do this? And he chose us, not just because we were there, and we had this armored truck. But because we are resourceful and we can get stuff done. And it knew that we was right for this job."

"It's like a God thing?" Samson asked, but I could tell from his little inflection that he knew exactly the point I was making and he was going to use it against me later if I was wrong. So a lot of times

I don't say God, I say Fate or whatever so he can't hit me with it later.

"I don't know yet. But listen here. Doc knew exactly what time it was. And now we've seen what it can do. No robot's like that! No robot's like that anywhere, Bro. It knows more. And it has the power. Samson, we are headed to Miami."

"Why you think that?" Still with that same smirky inflection.

"You know. Because that's ground zero. You call him the savior, and he's going to right the wrongs. Back to the beginning, where it all started, and the whole thing turns around. Maybe he starts turning robots who turn other robots from there. He's just waiting to reverse it and redeem it."

"That's what you think?"

"I don't know. Yeah. Seems poetic. What do you think?"

"I don't know. Maybe." He agreed, at least a little. But he wanted to hold back in case I was wrong, and then he could be right. Or, if I was right, he could say he believed me and maybe he would say he even thought of it before me. He's coy and smart and he always does that.

"Just say whether you agree or not this time, Samson, this is big stuff. Quit messing around for once," I said.

"I hope you're right," he said. "It's the right direction." And that's all he said about it.

We sat silent for a while.

What we just saw in New Orleans was setting in. The excitement hadn't worn off, but we were getting tired.

The more we pushed it off with adrenaline, the more it came back at us with authority. It was just about to knock me out, falling into that in-between state. I fought, but I didn't know why, and then my brother took the fight out of me.

"I'm not gonna make it to Miami, but you can have a couple hours here, Bro." I took it. While I slept, I kept on thinking about what Miami would be like. I pictured it being different from New

Orleans. New Orleans was the fight. By Florida, it was all red carpet in my head. Like they would all know we were coming. And they'd approach one by one, and Doc would blink them into harmony with the earth, and with man, and they'd go forth, changing others who'd change others. Soon the country would be completely at peace, and the wave would make its way over Georgia, and into Alabama and South Carolina. And then we'd all know that it would soon be over, the rays of sun would push out the clouds wherever they went. Also, Samson and I would be heralded as ambassadors of the peace. These two brothers, because of their willingness to go into the dangerous, war torn cities helped save us all. Their bravado in the face of fear. Their faith in something greater than themselves. But it wasn't about the glory, in my dream. It was about safety, I think, in my heart. Safety for my own self, from the war and in numbers, because you see, if everyone knows you and loves you, that's the safest place of all. Nobody can come against you as long as you keep swimming with the stream. But then I woke up, because I knew that swimming with the stream of this world was not something I could do, even if I wanted it. And I could subconsciously tell the car had stopped. The noise changed.

"What's it?" I mumbled.

"I don't know, hang on. The back door opened." Samson seemed very concerned, so I had to be too. It took a second for my brain to catch up.

"Where are we?" I said to nobody. My brother was already out. I could see we were on the side of the highway, on the shoulder. Funny how you still pull to the side even when there are no cars. It was getting on around midnight, I figured. And we had to be in a bigger city now, based on the buildings around. So I got out.

Samson was standing there looking at the robot in the truck. Doc Holliday was looking right back at him. Samson didn't know what to do. They just stood there looking at each other.

"What do you want? You opened the door, right?" he said. And Samson seemed like he wished he hadn't asked that question.

"Hey!" My mind woke up. "Hey, we're always just driving, hoping we're doing what's right. Maybe he's going to tell us what to do now! Hey Doc, it's about time! Oh man, we just kept driving, but we didn't ever know where we were going."

Samson looked at me, but he didn't share my excitement. He seemed thrown and sad like a little kid who thought his parents' divorce was his fault.

"Look, Doc, you can get our attention in a better way next time. Just knock on the little cab door we crawl through. We'll hear you!" I said, but with some nerves.

Something was happening between Doc and Samson that I wasn't privy to.

Sam pulled out the loading ramp.

Doc went down it slowly. And he rolled over to Sam, stuck his hand out. Samson looked at it and winced a little before he manned up and shook his hand. First time I ever seen a robot shake a man's hand. And that's all Samson did. Just winced a little. That's what it looked like when the hero's journey died inside him. That's not what it looked like for me, though.

I was ready to tell him to go screw off, I wasn't shaking his hand! But he didn't extend it. Probably some program somewhere reading my body language, I don't know. Some stupid program that said Samson was a bigger man than me. That Samson could swallow his dreams easier and part ways. With me, he just stared, like he was waiting.

Well, I was not going to just stand there and wait, I had a few things I needed to say. I said, "What do you think is going to happen right now, you're just going to leave? You're all done with us, served our purpose? These servants outlived their usefulness, better find some new ones?"

Doc looked at me. He didn't square his body up at all when a distant sound became a car driving by. Hey, good thing we pulled over after all. But I wasn't done.

"And what are you going to do here in the middle of what, Alabama? Don't you want to go to Miami where the whole thing started? I thought maybe we'd drive the whole coast with you, cross back over in North Carolina, form a perimeter, start cutting the advancement off. Or I thought you might be a poet and start la resistance in Miami like I would. I'm a dreamer too, you know! I was willing to do either of those things, or whatever else came up along the way! But just to leave now? Here in Alabama? What about it, Doc? And the worst part of the whole thing is that I still trust you. Because you know exactly what you're doing, somewhere deep in that circuitry. And that's what bothers me the most. You know what you're doing, and you know we're not a part of it anymore."

Then he turned slowly, and looked back down the open road, right back the direction we just came. I got the message and I just lost it. Tears streaming down my face.

"Why can't you tell me why? Why!? Just tell me why we came all the way and stopped right here, now, at this friggin' spot, Doc!" Yeah, I was breaking down. Samson didn't say nothing, 'cause he knew how I was feeling and how I get when I feel like that. Plus I was tired. We both were. But Old Doc did the most gentle thing. He rolled up close. Turned his head and laid it on my shoulder. It goofed me out a little. Doc was smart and a violent beast. I had a ton of respect for him and maybe that's why I was crying. Because that gesture was so unforeseen and so human. Samson was crying too, but he was wiping it all up and trying to think of something to say.

"He's gotta go, Jerome. He's gotta go."

Doc, now just like a robot, zipped all quick over to the truck, put the ramp back up and hauled off in the direction we thought we were headed. East. I kept waiting for him to turn and acknowledge us again but he never did, so before he got too far away, I yelled out.

"Hey, Doc!" He stopped, and looked back. "Make sure it's big, whatever it is! I want to know how this ends!"

Samson, who never gets loud, yelled too. "Yeah me too! Go get 'em all!"

Soon enough we couldn't see him anymore. It was all quiet. The closing of the truck doors was the only sound we made for a while.

We could have followed him, but we didn't. Driving right back down the road we just came from, Samson was down, but I was all the way down. Angry and pitiful. I knew he felt it too, because he and I, we had a lot of dreams die. Mostly business ideas, but things we put our soul into anyway. But this was bigger than any of those. This was the big story that we'd be a part of for longer than we'd be around. To find out that we weren't going to be characters in that story, and maybe not even a footnote... well, it doesn't really matter what your dream is when it's taken away. Big or small, loss is loss. You either scar up, or you bleed out. And defeat is a terrible thing to die from.

So we kept going backward down that same road again, because we didn't know what else to do. Middle of the night. Probably getting close to seeing the sun come up. Those dawns always hit at the wrong moments.

Neither of us would say a word. No complaining, and no pats on the back either. There'd be time for that when our heads were clear and we had some sleep. But not yet.

Alf Johnson

Interviewed in Tampa, FL

SOMEDAY I'LL BE at a bar, looking into my shot glass with a big sun-meat beard.

Another guy, about halfway done with his beer at the other end of the bar, will say, "Hey bartender."

"What? What?" he'll say.

"That over there. What's that all about?"

"Who, him? That's just Old Alf," the bartender chuckles. He gets that question a lot. "Old Alf has seen some things." The bartender would leave it there and turn to clean some glasses because I am a freakin' puzzle! Sure I've dropped some hints here and there about my life, but I never go into much detail. "Seen a man die like that once," I'll often say, with no context. People in this town have gotten used to my little droppings by now. I would be an interesting, mysterious drifter! I might even buy myself a hamburgueso (melted cheese hamburger I made up. Is it okay if I whisper stuff for you to put in parenthesis from now on?)

They would say, "Oh don't mind Old Alf. He walks out onto that bridge every day at sundown to think about his life. You would too if you'd seen what he's seen."

Then I'd stand up on the rail. Stretch. Pat my belly like a bongo player. That's my nightly bongo solo. Followed by a graceful swan dive. "Dad, why is that man jumping into the water?" "Oh don't mind him son, that's just Old Alf doing his evening dive. Did you like his bongo solo?" I would go into that water so smooth it might even inspire a whole new generation of divers. I hope not though, I don't like professional diving. Too much money involved! It stinks!

After I dry off, I go into the forest to think about my life and swing from tree to tree like the ape man. Not a care. Tree to tree, screaming out, never touching the ground, and the animals are my friends. Every monkey and caterpillar, friends of old Jungle Alf, and his palm tree house! (I would have a coconut phone.)

Anyway, like I said at the beginning, that's the story of Jungle Alf.

"I heard Old Jungle Alf saved the world from the robots." Yeah, but I'd be real reluctant to tell that one – the story about the fella I met on my boat near the end of the robot war. "It's too personal," I would say, but I would be coaxed into telling it by the meddling interviewer.

(If I were you, I would lean forward, as if everything I had said up until now had been a complete waste of time. But now it will all be worth it, just for this moment.) Wrong! Nothing I said was a waste of time. (The interviewer is wallowing in shame for thinking that.)

"Then I get a call from a cruise liner that changes everything!" I blurt out. "To pick up just one passenger!" I can't stop myself now that I'm revved up.

And I say, "Why not? Nobody's on the coast anymore anyhow! Let me tell you what the coast is like now. The last place..."

"Alright, great, how close are you?"

"Judging by where you are, and where I was, I'd say about an hour. Let me tell you about where I was."

"That's okay, we'll keep an eye out for you," the radio bellows.

"My boat is call the *Trans!*" I bellow. I like "bellow." It was in my pocket dictionary. (The one I got before this interview with you. Did I tell you about that? You know I've been preparing for this interview for a long time.) Lilly said, "Does the interviewer want to talk to me?" And I bellowed, "He called ME!" (For a little while I thought maybe you were a donkeyhole because you took so long to get back to me. I've been trying to use donkey so I cuss less. Did I tell you about that?)

Anyway, she didn't want me to talk to you or any other donk-eyclowns, but she's not in charge of me. (But I am sneaking this interview right now.) She's not in charge of me! (She's upstairs. That's called top deck, but I do not use nautical terms other than poop deck.) Do you know why I use just that one?

So when I showed up at the cruise liner, I bellowed, "It's me! Alf! From the radio!"

"The *Trans!*?" they bellowed.

"Yes!" I snorted. At first, The *Trans!* was to honor the testes girls, but it was getting funnier.

And then they lower this sunglass-wearing-donkeyhat onto my boat.

I wear sunglasses out here too cause you gotta, but not like his. I buy a box of those dollar ones 'cause I lose them all the time. I sit on 'em, misplace 'em, drop 'em in the water. Sometimes I throw them across the boat just to end a sentence. It works best with a angry sentence. If you are dumbfounded by something, slack jawed, and THEN you throw a pair in the ocean, it makes the person like "What the?" But this snot-nosed jackdonkey was wearing sunglasses that look like they're made of diamond peppermint. Like if Elton John was throwing a Christmas pride parade. Actually, they might have been black. He was still a donkeyclown b-hole though. He offended me in his polo shirt, which is not a easy thing to do. You know. Because most of all I am like, whatever. To each their own. (Real soon I find out I like him though. Just wait.) I am looking at him out of the side of my eyes, like "what the?" But I am like, whatever. I don't care. Get on the *Trans!* and let's be friends! You get on this boat you jackdonk! (Wait till I have a change of heart. It will take you off guard.) I am not kidding. I end up liking this b-hole.

The Gay Gambler
Interviewed by phone

IT TOOK me an exceptionally long time to get a proper read on the fisherman.

There's no great way to transfer from a cruise liner to a small boat mid-sea, so they lowered me onto this fisherman's vessel, which right away gave the impression of neglect and disregard for basic human hygiene. No surprises though. It's a fisherman's vessel, after all. At least, I thought, what you see is what you get.

From the looks of him, I assumed a salted but subdued personality, probably with singular focus and little time for dramatics. So I would approach him as such, be straight to the point. If I had misread him, then the pendulum would only swing toward joyful servant. Either way, I didn't think I had much to be concerned with. A serial killer probably wouldn't perform this public service so readily. He squinted into the sun as he looked up at me, sunglasses on his forehead. Then, once onboard, without saying anything, he threw them into the water, pointed at me and yelled the word "fancy!" Hmmm.

With his shoulders drooped and hands clenched by his sides, he plodded to his quarters or somewhere below where I could hear him and a woman just as clearly even though they were talking in hushed tones.

"His hair is styled!"

"Is it gelled?" she said.

"I think so! Oh I do not know what I'm going to do with myself, Lilly! I need you up there. I need you to stand between me and that boy!"

"He's a fancy?" she said.

"I get that impression! I do! He is wearing a watch, and the face of the watch is on the inside of his wrist instead of the outside! Oh God help me, Lilly!"

"You know what you're capable of!"

"We both know that, Lilly! Goll dang it!"

"Then I'm going up there with you! Try to start with a compliment. That always helps you!"

The woman walked out first. The boards creaked.

"Hello," she said. I nodded and continued standing there in silence. Moments later he came up and paced around.

"Your clothes . . . are clean," he stammered. "You are clean."

"Good, Alf," the woman said.

"Now. What the . . ."

"Alf! You notch that down!" she barked.

"Oh come on, Lilly, his watch is on the inside! You can see it from here!"

I still had not spoken a word since leaving the cruise ship. Everything in me told me to dress my language down for the occasion, but I just didn't. The truth is, I was exhausted, and I really wanted this transfer ride to be something I didn't have to think about – not even at all. I just wanted a ride. No strategy.

"No rest for the wicked," I muttered under my breath.

"What did he say?" the fisherman yelled.

"I don't know. What did you say?" she chimed.

"I said 'no rest for the wicked.'"

"Why? Lilly, ask him why." he said.

"He can hear you, you ask him!"

"This is why you came up here! You know what I'm capable of! We were just downstairs talking about this!"

Then he addressed me at a more conversational volume. "I'm sorry, Mister, we were just downstairs talking about this," he shrugged, as if to say, "Women, huh?"

I watched it all as if it were a movie I was not in.

He followed that with, "Hey, why is your watch head on the inside? That is what I don't like about you!"

"I just wear my watch that way. I'm going to get a floodlight that can shut the robots down for two minutes. I'm going to try to alter the pattern to make it longer. It would really help if you could move us quickly."

"There was a guy on here just not long ago with a Taz tie that I really liked. I think his name was Glotus. Had a smile that could light up the night sky. Doesn't matter. I gave him a shirt of mine. Did we get that shirt back? Doesn't matter. Lilly, did we get that shirt back?" I think he was trying to make a point but lost his train of thought.

"Listen, you seem like a great guy. But I really need to get moving."

Now again, I don't know what magic key was in that sentence, but his demeanor changed. Instantly and utterly.

"Whoa." He staggered backward and braced himself on the rail, then huddled with the woman, their backs to me briefly. I could hear most of what they said before he approached me again.

"I just had a conversation with Lilly just now. Couple topics, and I'll be honest with you, because that's how I am. Those topics were about you. Whoa, hold your horses. Here's the deal. I want to rename the boat after you. Hey, I know what you're thinking! Alfonzo, what in the tarnation. You old lug! You don't need to name the boat after me! I'm just a fancy! But I insist."

I'm telling you, I had no idea how to read this guy. Keep in mind, we're having this entire conversation still sitting there next to the cruise liner.

"Great." I said. Unstable people are the most difficult for me, because they don't work within typical patterns. He just stood there, smiling and blinking. Waiting for me to say something else, I assume. "So let's get this motor running." To which he grabbed me by both shoulders, patted them a couple times, and trotted off toward the front.

Then we set out.

I stood there for a while, just baking. But the woman urged me, through bizarre stares and guttural noises, to go have a talk with the man. So I approached with no subtle social cues.

He looked as if he had a secret he couldn't wait to tell me. "Do you want to know where I was just before we got you?" he asked. I didn't. My entire purpose was just to keep us moving.

I decided on, "It's an interesting question."

"Yep!" he said, just tickled. "Yeppa yeppa yep." He pulled the throttle down a bit, so he could speak at a decidedly personal volume. Exactly what I hoped he wouldn't do. Leaning over, he looked at me out of the corner of his eye. "I hugged a robot." Slowly leaning back into his seat, eyes straight ahead, he assumed I was processing his incredible statement. Which I guess I was. At least we were still moving. I decided to respond in the way he sought.

"You dirty dog."

"Hahaha, I know! It's just one of them things," he said. The motor still purring at its lower volume, I assumed he wasn't finished. "Biloxi," he continued, looking over at me with a huge smile.

"Yeah, yeah. Alright." I said, eyes forward, unsure what he was talking about.

"Yep. Well, I didn't hug it all the way. I just gave it a back pat. I'm a encourager. Just kind of who I am," he said.

"All the same," I said. Wait a second. "You hugged a robot?"

"There it is," he careened, with complete confidence. "Light-bulb factory!"

"In Biloxi? Like, just before you came to get me?"

"That's what I did, yeah. I was like a statue. It moved like this." At this point he got up and walked rigid, without bending his knees. The boat's acceleration stopped immediately as he made creaky joint noises. "You know. Vvvvt. Vvvvvt. Like that movie."

"That's fine, yes, a very fine walk. You look exactly like a pal. Let's focus on something you said. About the robot not instantly killing you. This was a live robot? Moving around and so forth? Was it alone?"

"At first I thought it was going to kill me. Lilly kept yelling. But I was having a . . . what's it. What's it called when you have a thought, but it's like a heart thought?"

"A feeling?"

"Yeah! A feeling! A thought from your belly."

"That's more of an instinct, but okay, so the robot was a single outlier then," I said, losing interest momentarily.

"No, it wasn't alone. Just at first. There were a whole bunch of them ones."

"Again, let's clarify 'them ones.' The rebellious robots? Or there were other non-infected ones?"

"Yep, the other kind."

I normally am so good at reading people, too.

"*Which* ones?"

"The other ones. The easy riders. The . . . what's the word. Hey Lilly! What's a word for 'fine'?" the fisherman yelled.

"Okay?" she yelled back.

"Yeah! They were okay."

"You're telling me that you ran into a glut of robots on the coast of Biloxi that were all uninfected and not slashing through everything?"

He thought for a second, about to answer, but I stopped him and repeated the question, which he seemed very thankful for.

"Yes, that's right! They were lovebots! But not all of them. They went and beat up a bad one. I didn't root for the bad one, because I am just like you. I am on the human side. I guess you could say I'm just like everybody else in that way, just rooting for man, going along hoping for man, and not secretly laughing when I see a robot smash up people's precious things." Then he leaned on something, and looked at me with his eyebrows up.

I looked right back at him, with my eyebrows up. "They beat

up a crazed one?" I couldn't believe what I was hearing. Although suddenly, I began to question the source.

"Show me," I said.

"What? Why? I thought we were gonna get the magic flood-light and save America!"

"I need to know something, sir."

"Alf."

"I need to know if you're telling the truth."

In a way I hadn't seen from him, he paused, and really thought.

"Do you think I made that up?"

"I don't know you. But I'm about to make a decision that could affect millions of lives. And it's all predicated on what you saw in Biloxi. So yes, I need to know."

"I don't make up stories, Mister." Alf got very serious, on the verge of anger I believe. "I saw all of that. I'll take you there, and I'll show you. If that's what you want."

"That's what I want."

He pushed the throttle and didn't slow down again.

Alf Johnson

Interviewed in Tampa, FL

SEE, I always said, "You do you" but really it's about everybody doing everybody.

You can't get too mad. This big blue marble just keeps on a-spinning. Spinning around. Fried chicken tastes the same in Mississippi as it does in Cabo Wabo. You know that's how I am.

The Gay Gambler
Interviewed by phone

IT TOOK us a few minutes to find any robots at all. But once we did, Biloxi was exactly as he described. Based on what I was looking at, this broken-down utopia probably represented a good portion of the coast, but why, and how? The most obvious theory was already debunked – that there were good robots reintegrating others into the fold. Couldn't be, because Alf had said the good ones were beating up the destructive ones, not changing them. So there was no anti-virus running rampant through the rank-and-file. The next, most obvious answer would be that there was a string of resistance in some of their programming. Maybe a certain brand? But HumanPal had been the only brand able to withstand the EMP, so that wouldn't explain it. The thought crossed my mind that we might be in a spot that was either not completely affected by the blast, or that had somehow been mostly missed by the rebellion. I would need to investigate to be sure.

"I need to go ashore," I told him.

"Okay," he said. "Lilly! We are gonna dock!"

"Why?" she asked.

"I don't know. Why we going ashore, donkeyman?"

"Please don't call me donkeyman."

"But you are a donkeyman, I can tell it. Are you interested in Lilly?"

Oh my God.

"We're going ashore because I need to have a closer look." There, that's vague enough.

"Did you hear that Lilly? We're going on shore because of spy things. You wouldn't understand."

"Actually, you can both stay here if you would like. This shouldn't take long."

"I'll probably need to help. I can be a sneakerton." Then he went, "vvvt, vvvvt," again, but quietly. "Can I get anything for the mission?"

"You know, I could use some hand lotion and a thick cut steak right about now."

He saluted me and said, as he scampered away, "I'll look all over, even Lilly's purse!"

While he searched, I got off at the dock and checked a handful of robots' brand plates. They were all HumanPal. And all operating at full functionality, although with more autonomy than I would have expected. I returned to the boat, still mystified by the whole matter.

"Alright, I got chap stick and some old gum," Alf said.

"Oh, then we'll have to change the plan." He walked up very close to me and put his chin to his chest, speaking low.

"Is this still part of the spy stuff? I can carry on like it's not if you need to keep it secret."

"Carry on," I said.

"Okay," he smiled, but then got confused. Before he could ask another question, I asked him one.

"Alf, when did you last visit New Orleans? What was it like?"

"Few days ago. It was still crazy town. Not like here. There's chatter though."

"What do you mean?"

"Well, other boats, they say it's different. Sounds more like here, if I think about it."

"That's good, that's great actually." Although it completely busted my third theory – that the virus couldn't infect robots that had worked too close to the sea. I thought maybe the water that had corroded them had also prevented some of them from being changed. As good a theory as any at this point, but then they wouldn't change back, either. And if New Orleans had converted to peace, then I needed yet another new theory.

"How far east do you usually go?"

"Not much than here."

"Any talk on other ports?"

"Not really. There's not much on the radio 'cause if you were too close to the coast the EMP did fry you. I was out there far enough. People are talking about New Orleans some. I told them about Biloxi. Maybe a little between here and there. Not much else."

"Okay. Okay." I hesitated. Because nothing was coming to me. Think, man. How could there be huge pockets of non-rebellious robots where there weren't before?

I paced around but it was hard to think with those two watching me. I didn't have enough information yet. But if New Orleans had reverted, and so had Biloxi . . .

"We need to go east."

They sprang into action.

We motored past Pascagoula, Dauphin Island. I figured we'd just keep going past Pensacola and Destin right down the Florida coast, but we never made it that far, because Gulf Shores looked no different from before.

Narrowing down the pinpoint further, we headed into the inlet that houses Mobile, Alabama. All along the west shore, it was destroyed, but in armistice. Along the east shore it was the exact opposite. Still the Wild West. Two sides of the same bay, two different scenes playing out. And it all converged there at the top, in the old city of Mobile, completely calm. I expected to find whatever force was causing this to be pressing through to the other side of the bay by land, but saw no such thing. Any bridges that connect the city to the East Bay had been ruined, I assumed by general mayhem.

Alf informed me otherwise, as if reading my mind.

"Lookie there," Alf said. "Somebody destroyed them bridges on purpose."

"Government?" Lilly asked.

"They did it from the west with no explosives. Had to be robots," he surmised.

"How come, Alfie? Robots from over here (west) came and knocked it down?"

"Yep! Dang robots smashed it up. Don't know why. Unless there's giants now." I appreciated him enough in the moment that I almost smiled, but the look on his face suggested he was serious.

"So the good robots cut off the bridges to protect themselves against and attack from the east," I said.

"Oh. Ohhhhhh," he said.

But that wouldn't buy infinite time. Someone or something here was calculating moves with precision and I had to admire it.

"From here it's on foot," I declared. And I was going to have to do it alone.

Alf Johnson
Interviewed in Tampa, FL

WHEN I WAS A LITTLE KID, I had two dogs and one cat. Minky, Winky, and Puppet. They were my best friends until my family moved across the country and we left them behind even though I kept hollering about it. My parents said they'd get me some new ones that were a hundred times more powerful, so let it go. But I believed. I knew them pets would embark on a incredible journey. They would be homeward bound. So I whined and whined. Then, one day, wouldn't you know it. I came home from school and there they were – two dogs and one cat on the porch waiting for me.

"Hey! Is this Minky, Winky and Puppet?"

"Yep! Now you can stop whining," Dad said.

I started crying and hugging them but they acted a little different and they looked a little different.

"Mom, is that Minky, Winky, and Puppet?" little me asked.

"Of course, Alf. It's time to let go of them," Mom said.

"This cat acts all creaky."

Dad laughed a big, drunk laugh and said, "Smart kid." That made me feel special.

So I started calling them Milky, Wilky, and Pluppet, because the dogs were kind of bitey, and I think they had feline arthritis. But one night I stayed up real late when my dad had some poker friends over. It was fun playing detectives with the pets while my dad played with his friends.

One time when I left the room because the animals wouldn't keep their Sherlock hats on, my dad's friend said, "Did he just call that cat Pluppet?"

"No, it's Puppet," my dad said.

"I swear it was Pluppet," the friend said. And the rest of them agreed. Then my dad got mad.

"It's Puppet! Minky, Winky, and Puppet!"

"He says Milky, Wilky, and Pluppet."

"No he doesn't! Shut up!"

"Let's bring the kid in here!" And my dad agreed to it. They put some high stakes on it, and then my dad called me in, in his nice voice. He looked at me like he was sorry.

"Alfie, son. Me and these guys were talking about your pets there. We needed to know..."

"Don't lead him on, just ask straight! You can't taint the bet!"

"Alright, I know. What's your pets' names, Alfie? Now you can be real honest about it and tell these old guys here."

I scratched my chin and thought real hard on what to do.

"Hmmmm..." little me said.

I knew my mom would be mad if dad lost a bunch of money, but I didn't know where she was. I sure did like it when my dad used his nice voice though. Maybe if I could keep his nice voice around he would use it tomorrow if I said the right thing.

So I said, "Minky, Winky, and Puppet." I didn't know if that was the right thing, but it seemed like what he wanted. And I guessed right! And dad was awful happy – he started hooting at them guys so hard, and they was saying he rigged it and such. I don't know what happened other than Dad was real happy with me. And the next day, I was excited because I did the right thing, and Dad was going to use his nice voice. He even woke up before lunch and brought me the Sherlock hats. And I asked him, "Hey, where were they?" And he said, "In the bathroom" but it was in his regular voice. And football was on, and he didn't use his nice voice for the whole day, and he even told me to play in a different room. That's what I think about sometimes when somebody is nice to me, and then they go off and leave you behind on a secret mission. I wonder if they was just using their nice voice, or if they really meant it. Because when I know they mean it, I am loyal, boy. When people shoot straight, I will do whatever for you. But if you are just pissing in a tornado, man I don't like that. But if you care about doing what you said you was gonna do, I am right there with you the whole way.

The Gay Gambler
Interviewed by phone

IT'S difficult to tell somebody that they've outlived their usefulness, especially when they're so enthusiastic. The truth is, I was taking a tremendous gamble here, abandoning the floodlight in favor of an unknown. And I needed to move quickly and quietly, unsure of what I'd be encountering. Since Alf would be a detriment to that goal, it was necessary to cut ties here.

Because as I've said before, I do not like to gamble. I make investments.

"Thank you for helping me, Alf. Your information has been invaluable," I said, but subtleties are not Alf's strong suit.

"I'm on the side of the humans," he said. "Because that's what I am."

He assumed I would understand what that meant, which I did only after he put on his backpack.

"I need to do this alone, Alf. I hope you understand."

"Nope. Don't even know what you're doing. Just thought I should come."

"You're a very straightforward guy, so I'll be straightforward with you. This could be an incredibly precarious situation. I am going to approach it with caution, quiet, and calculus. Those don't seem to be your strong suits. So I need to go alone."

"I tell you what. I'm no hero. A soldier? That's a hero. A archaeologist, a cave one? That's a hero. Space fighters. I'm no hero. But I do always think about what it would be like to be one, since I'm a champion. So if I can't be a hero, maybe I can help you be a hero. What do you need from us? You need us to keep the boat here for you?"

What a nice guy. "Yes, that's exactly what I need."

It was not a bad idea to have him wait. I wasn't going to ask it of him, but since he was willing . . .

We shook.

"Dang, your hands are like a chalk monster. Sorry I never got you hand lotion."

"That's okay."

"I'll stay here until I can't stay any longer!" he called out as I left. I wondered if that would mean five minutes, or if he would be there weeks later. "I'll do whatever!"

.   .   .

MOBILE IS NOT A SMALL TOWN, so I didn't know exactly where to start, but I used my ears as a guide. Now, when they're not destroying things, robots are not actually that loud. But these were working on something, so there was enough movement to draw from. And most of it was coming from the business district.

Assuming I wasn't going to encounter any rebellious ones from the noise, I wondered exactly what I was going to find there. Would it be anything at all? If I simply stumbled upon another "clean" town along this coast, should I keep going inland to see how far it extended? That might be an option, but the main question to answer was why this city seemed to be the stopping point. From New Orleans to here. If Alf was correct, the good robots of Mobile had destroyed the bridges from the west to stop advancement from the east.

So this place was chosen, in some way.

I continued walking toward the business district.

The first robot I encountered did not see me. It was standing inside a hair salon, hunched over something. If they had breath, it would have been breathing on it.

I tried to remain casual, as if it would matter.

Because something in the back of my mind was tapping, telling me I might be walking into a trap. I pushed it away. It made no sense, based on what I had seen thus far.

But how much did I really know?

Its hands were working feverishly.

"Get out, you dummy," the sentiment persisted.

"Hundreds of robots wouldn't conspire to trick one pedestrian straggler. It would be strategically stupid."

But the tapping was now a strong knock. "This is a new phase of smarter robots. They're evolved. They don't care about you particularly, but they will kill you immediately."

The debate raged, but that robot just kept on working. The

only thing I was able to tell myself was that this is why I had come. I had to find out.

As I stepped around the glass and broken objects scattered around, I noticed a screwdriver near my feet. Instinctively, I went to pick it up. Such a thing. It would be useless anyway. But I should grab it. Why? Because it's better than nothing. No, it's not, it's the same as nothing. I was gratified to see my rational mind winning. I left it there.

The robot, from what I could see, was bringing things from the rubble together. As I semi-circled around, it began to come into focus – one of those old space-aged hair dryer chairs. Other details became apparent; it had already reconstructed the better part of two hairstylists' stations and salvaged a massage table. It had cleaned these things very thoroughly along with the area around them. This was nothing menacing. Quite the opposite! No command could have been so concurrently specific and extensive to garner this kind of rehabilitation. This robot was repairing this salon of its own volition. By the time it finished, the store would be close to working shape.

Tremendous, soldier.

Finally, the robot saw me. It stopped for a moment, but it did not seem to mind my tinkering presence. I dare say its body language even had an air of invitation before turning to work again.

I felt much better going forward. Though I still went quietly.

The magnitude of the undertaking became clearer as I walked. More and more robots, dutifully cleaning, repairing hotels . . . tea rooms, the museum. It was beautiful. And I was actually more familiar with this area than I thought, like a memory catching up and acquainting itself. This was near the casinos of Mobile. This sudden awareness was a warm embrace. I had been here, though never from this direction, of course. If I recalled, there were some good nights here.

But now the robots were noticing me, and I could move covertly no longer.

Unlike the first one, I was drawing their prolonged attention.

From their work they came, one by one, and stared, and scanned me. For what, I do not know. Danger, I assumed, but I was wrong. They saw no danger in me whatsoever. By the sheer force of their strength and numbers, I posed no threat to them or their work. I wondered, then, if maybe they sought to serve me, as before. That they had reverted to their old programming now that a man had arrived, and they instinctively needed me for guidance. So I tried.

"Continue cleaning and repairing as you were. I am here to observe."

They did nothing.

"Go on," I commanded. "Clean and repair the city." It was no use. These had changed. It came to my understanding, fully now, that they were a higher form of themselves.

"So, it is then. You are free!"

The words meant nothing to them, though they were true. I wanted them to celebrate as if my acknowledgment should validate their freedom, but they didn't need me, or my commands, or my consent. It was the reverse, actually. I had reached a checkpoint in my own evolution in seeing them as independent, and I craved *their* validation of this fact.

But they gave me nothing. They just went back to what they were doing, slowly, as they each decided. It was odd that they had all stopped at once, but returned to their work individually, I noted.

Most importantly, if these robots had been changed for the good and set free, then indeed there was a cure. And that was worth celebrating.

I said nothing else.

There was no real reason to continue. I didn't have all the answers, but who was I? They were working it out.

With nowhere in particular to go, I considered returning to Alf's boat, but I was all turned around now.

I walked and realized I didn't know exactly where I was headed, or to what end. But no matter where I went, the robots would momentarily stop working to watch me. At first, I assumed it was curiosity, but they presented themselves with far too much uniformity for that. Especially since I had just acknowledged their liberation. Indeed, they were all doing the same thing, but in unique ways. One would watch me while twisting a shovel in its hands. Another while rolling its feet back and forth over little pieces of glass. So these personality traits were there. But instead of focusing on the differences, it was the similarities that had my attention.

In fact, once I saw past the individualities, I began to notice patterns in the behavior, as I am apt to do.

They were acting something out.

You see, sometimes they would, at a slow pace, position their bodies toward me as I walked by. Always together and in uniform direction. However, other times they would not move their bodies at all. They would only watch me move past by rotating their heads.

It was like that street after street.

While this was very eerie to experience, navigating through corridor after corridor of silent surveilling machines, there was something to solve now. However, I was beginning to lose my direction in the city a bit, so on one street where they were only turning their heads, I came to the end, then doubled back down the same street from which I had just come. As I hoped, they no longer turned their heads as they had previously done; they turned their full bodies. Okay, now we were getting somewhere. When I moved in one direction, they angled their bodies, and when I moved the opposite, they only moved their heads. I had a consistent pattern, and something tangible to test. I would only pass down streets where they turned their . . . I didn't know. Heads or bodies? Here, I had no indication which was better. Through trial and error, I deduced that when the heads turned, they were leading me toward the gulf waters, but when they turned their bodies, they were pointing toward the heart of town. I decided to follow along with their guidance toward the city, since I had come from the gulf.

As I walked, I wondered how many people would have figured the pattern out. It couldn't be just for me though; that would be implausible. Wouldn't it?

But they were communicating with each other.

Finally I came to a city block where no matter which way I navigated, I was getting all heads.

Alright, then. "This could be the center," I whispered, as if I hoped someone would hear me, and tell me why I stopped here.

But there was no significant sword-in-stone. I told myself to be open to anything, but *anything* would at least be *something*. I hadn't thought of the possibility that there would be nothing. That wasn't faulty logic, though. Patterns, especially coordinated ones, don't appear without reason.

Well, usually they don't.

I stood nearest to a historic church, very ornate, but just as torn down as everything else. Though there was some minimal repair on some of the offices, it seemed that no extra work was being done here in general. In fact, no work at all had been done to the church. It was the only building that hadn't been touched. An indicator?

The bulk of the church had remained mostly intact. There were no doors to prevent me from creeping in undetected, but there was also no electricity. My eyes were slow to adjust. The outer rooms were easy to inspect, but the larger rooms were shielded by too many right angles. I was not going to be thorough, however. I didn't even know if I should be in here, or what I was looking for. But that fear I had snuffed out earlier was rising again, which told me that the building would not be empty.

My logic kicked in. But instead of giving me a grounded counter opinion, it reminded me that it's generally unwise to walk into the dark alone. Thanks for the help.

I continued anyway, because I had no other plan. I pushed through the fear that these long, empty corridors were only leading me further into a maze from which I would not escape.

It wasn't common fear, as before. It was specific. As the corridors finally opened into the very dark, very large sanctuary, it felt as if there were eyes on me. Hundreds of eyes, hidden behind each wall and pillar. Unnatural eyes.

"No," I resisted. They would be working. You'd hear them.

Yes, and all the more reason to be afraid. They led you here and they've gone quiet in wait. They could have greeted you. They chose to stay in the dark. And now here they come!

I reached down for my lighter as one pair of red eyes opened like a spotlight on me in the distance. My pulse skyrocketed and my knees went weak. It was coming at me with tremendous speed and there was no chance for me to outrun it back through the maze.

Somehow I still managed to flick my lighter, though I couldn't move. In that one stab of light, I saw the shadow of the beast grow bigger and broader as it spread across the wall, engulfing the whole sanctuary. In that flash, and in my heightened state, I glimpsed the beauty and detail of the interior before it was swallowed by the shadow's darkness. The raw power and speed of the beast forced the air from my lungs and the moment almost thrilled me, to feel something so genuine. That this, my own death of all things, could actually be satisfying. I had never been so resigned to a fate. In seconds it would be done. With a mere twist of the machine's wrist I would be free from all the wandering and strategizing and endless cataloguing. Free from flailing at life with my weapon of reason. Free to give up all I had, which was nothing much, just memories of fleeting happiness at temporary times.

But just as I had embraced this perverse exhilaration, it was taken from me. The robot stopped, just a few feet away, and gazed at me.

The red light filled the room, but I could see little else.

There were, ultimately, no others. Just this one.

I stammered, then blurted out: "Sweep!" knowing that it wouldn't. It scanned me up and down. Then it swiped its hand back and forth across the top of a pew until the spot was clean.

There was nothing about this that made me feel superior, but rather, *served*. And at ease.

Allowing a moment for me to take this in, it approached me, powerfully and gently.

Even the way it approached signaled that it meant to give me nothing but a respect I was not due.

I flicked the lighter again, and this time it held.

"That frame," I said.

It had to feel the same thing from my eyes that I had felt from it. It had meant me no harm and wanted me to feel no fear. It was still, and allowed me to scan it up and down.

"No," I said. "It can't be."

But it grabbed me by the hand and led me out the corridors toward the door, powerfully and gently. I squeezed the beast's hand, having given in to the sheer odds of it all. The disorderly repair. The brand plate above its right arm. The scratch marks. There was no need to calculate the odds; they were astronomical.

I didn't know how it could have happened, or how it could ever have been planned.

Hello again, Human.

President of the United States (Tourism Bureau)
Interviewed in Washington, D.C.

Then, the worst thing in the whole world happened. A small cleaning woman came into my quarters unannounced.

"What is it, Small Xena?" She loved that, because she was tiny in stature, but she was a warrior princess whose real name was hard to remember. Xochitl? Xanthe? I had developed a terrific relationship with her, as I do with most of my cleaning women. 70-80 percent.

"I go into the room of John Henley, and John Henley laying in a puddle of himself."

"Small Xena. Does you mean urine?" Then I said out the side of my mouth, "Was it his?"

She shook her head side-to-side: "Yes. And blood." I wondered how she knew it was his.

"Wait. Are you telling me . . ."

"Small Xena say John Henley is dead."

"NOOO!" I screamed. But to keep anyone who might have

heard me calm, I rolled it into, "NOOOthing to see here, ya hear! That's what I yell when everything is fine! Ya hear!"

Captain Habersack came in and sniffled. "I heard you yell everyfing ivs fine. Fanks for yelling that. Well, good to talk to you." And he waddled off. Whew. Bullet dodged. I did not need to be dealing with all these pairs of bad things right now. First, the flood-light issue, and now this. Earlier I got jelly on my good pants. What pair of things would be ruined next?

I had to be bold here. That's what makes leaders great. Sure, I would miss John Henley. Because he was Don Henley's son. Everybody knows that. But the more important thing right now, for the country, and the good of the country, which I am for, is to get on the horn, which means talking on the radio. Get on that horn, and get those airplanes up, and get this broadcast of this floodlight going like my superstar said. For the good of the country. But no matter how murderously I threatened Small Xena to keep her mouth shut, the news of John Henley's death was going to leak out. I was sure of it. I had to take decisive action and get ahead of the whole thing. Yeah, that's what I would do. I would get ahead of the whole thing. I would USE his death as an inspired diversion for the Donvoted...

"Captain Habersack!" I caught up to him. "Where is the ship's intercom? I need to tell everyone something."

"Over dare," Habersack said through custard.

"Where?" I asked.

"Right dare."

"Oh!" I said. "There!" I thought he had been pointing over *there.*

So I got on the horn.

"Everyone. I need your attention for a New York Minute," I echoed. Everyone chuckled. "I don't mean to be a Witchy Woman here," everyone chuckled. "But sometimes Hell Freezes Over," everyone bowed over and chortled. Some clapped. They were appreciating this Donplay of mine. "So anyway, John Henley is dead. Yeah, doesn't look like natural causes either. Doot doot dee doo. Hey, I wonder if an ANIMAL did it. Don't you wonder?" I nodded vigorously and open-eyed. Everyone had begun screaming, demanding answers. I almost wished they could have heard themselves. I mean screaming like a bunch of savages trapped on a murder cruise. For shame. But I tarried on. "I tell you this because it's time for a good old fashioned murder mystery, only this time, it's REAL and I need your help, gumshoes!" Yeah, I would say it was a full-on uprising now. They were wringing their hands and frothing and losing it. They cared not that I had a great plan, or that I was going to give each of them characters to play. It was so sad to see a lady run by with wild strands of hair floating around. Not only was it visually distasteful, but she didn't care one bit that I had a fun "twenties flapper" character in mind for her. One guy ran in the opposite direction with a fire extinguisher. "Weird," I thought. "I was going to make him a fireman!" Life is weird. He bumped into another guy with a bigger fire extinguisher. They grunted at each other until the first one moved. Why didn't they just join up and make a fire team? Hmm?

Well, this wasn't turning out like I thought. A murder mystery should have been the perfect, fun diversion they all needed. Instead, I locked myself in the radio room with the floodlight and got "on the horn," so to speak, throwing my weight around the secret phone and getting connected with air bases throughout the west and southwest before they completely destroyed the ship, and/or got it dirty. The air bases understood my plan and mobilized quickly, believing in me and listening to me. It gave me a nice, strong "management" feeling that is so important to feel when you have to sit there and watch mobs riot. To know that hundreds of passenger planes were going to be able to fly with big projector screens behind them, just because I commanded it. Neat. But it wasn't enough. I needed more planes, probably. So I used my authority to get in touch with Mexican and Caribbean airports, too. And since I don't speak-a, there was my little Small Xena again, helping translate my plan. Everyone had their place. It was . . . what's the word? Not sexy. Cute. And neat. Oh what a great time it would have been if the Donvoted hadn't been rioting. Well, I guess that's leadership for ya. One minute you're on top of it all. The next, you're still on top, but while people go hogballs.

―――――――

Yumi Otsuka
Interviewed in Vancouver, B.C.

NO ONE TALKED. Mostly from shock, I think, and tired exhaustion, and for me, relief. The angry man was the only one who paced and could not appear able to settle himself on our final plane ride. But he too said little. Finally after some hours, he did speak.

"Something is still wrong," he announced.

Nobody listened. Something was always wrong with him.

"I said something is still wrong."

The translator responded, knowing someone had to. "If something was wrong, the pilot would have told us."

"You trust him? He is a baka!"

"I don't care. Wherever we are going is better than where we have been. He would not hurt us now for his own interests!"

"No. You are wrong, as you always are. I will find more for this," the angry man replied. I did not have the desire to deal with this. He was going into the cockpit to raise an alarm.

"Shut up," came from nowhere.

The angry man looked around. First at me. But it was not me. It was Ami.

"Ami," I said. It made me in surprise. I tried to quiet her – but not because she was wrong. This was in the rare moments where adults were glad the child had spoken out of turn. But I wanted no more problems, and the day should be over now. I was wanting to stay out of the way for the sake of our secrets.

"Did this child tell me to shut up?" he said.

"Yes, she did," the translator said.

"And you let her speak to me in this dishonorable way?"

Ami curled into me, not for safety. She was ignoring him and pretending to be tired. For all they knew, she was in exhaustion like us.

"You better leave her alone," said the translator. I was upset that Ami had escalated this. Maybe it was on purpose. I do not like to believe that she could be this cunning.

The angry man directed his rage at me.

"I will not hear this from a woman who nearly made us lose our lives. What have you done since you have been with us? Aside from you slow us all down! All of these men have taken care of you because of your husband. He is a greatly respected man. What would he think of his wife and child behaving in this way? With no honor and no appreciation!" He stood in the aisle and chastised us. Under normal settings, I would cry, but I am too exhausted now. My only thought is to protect Ami. Before I can move her from the aisle seat to my side, the angry man behaved in his way, when he has become too burning to regulate himself. His legs and arms become possessed by his temper. And that is when I am saying the angry man lunged out to grab me, before the translator could do anything about it.

Now, as I am today, I feel pity for him, though a part of me still trembles. Every person must deal with the stress we have gone through in their own way. I call him the angry man because that is who he is. A small and sorry man with no control of himself. In this way, his hand was coming to me, to clutch me. I do not know what he was going to grab, whether it would have been my neck or my shoulders. I flinched and covered Ami, but his fingers stopped suddenly in the air before my face. A grasping reptile hand halted in the space of time. I saw the frightened look on his face through his own fingers.

It was Ami again. She had reached out for his wrist and was squeezing it. The angry man cried out and fell to his knees.

The scream was so, so terrible. I think it is why I can pity him today, even as I feared him.

It was a crushing sound, like a fire cracking with pops and brittle wood.

"Ami, let go," I said with a calm.

She did.

The angry man cradled his hand as if he were nursing a precious baby. It was a mass which would not move. He could not hold himself upright, kneeling across a chair. The cry was not held to Earth. It moved the pilot from his quarters.

"What happened?" the pilot asked.

The translator separated from the sight.

"He was yelling that something is wrong, then he attacked Yumi."

"Well, he's right," the pilot said. "Something is wrong."

It seemed certain that something else would be wrong.

"We weren't supposed to be in the air at all. All aircraft are down. I've heard some stern words, but I think they believe our story. The bad news is there was almost no air support this whole time, so I was very blind. The good news is they're all focused on us, and they're helping us down.

The pilot was correct.

He let us know we were set to land at the Arizona Air National Guard and returned to the cockpit.

I tried not to look at anyone. Ami attempted to comfort me.

"This is not your fault, Mother. The man was provoked."

"I know," I whispered.

"It could have been much worse."

"Yes, Ami," I said quietly.

"For him."

"Yes, Ami. I know."

I glimpsed her briefly and caught her eyes, which lacked the childish glow I had known. This sent sudden shivers through the bones of my body. Nothing about her appearance had changed, because it could not change. No one aside from me could notice what I saw, but in her eyes now was chilling confidence.

Suddenly I had the urge to run from her. But where would I go?

The translator sat next to me just then, speaking soft questions.

"Yumi, I must ask you before we land. Do you know why the robots shut down at the hangar?"

Ami looked over at him with a sudden attention. He shuffled a bit.

"I mean to say, that you do not have any ideas what caused it, do you?"

I said nothing. Only to look at him with my hands in my lap. He swallowed and buttoned his shirt pocket.

"Yes, I do not know why I asked. I guess it was just a good thing that happened. Certainly, I am only thankful for it, as we all are. These are just good things from above. Good blessings to you the rest of the way."

The plane was almost landing. Ami looked at me, waiting for me to acknowledge her. I did not, so she continued to look at me.

The Gay Gambler
Interviewed by phone

AS WE LEFT THE CHURCH, on cue, a robot with the virus approached us violently from the north. There I watched it happen for the first time. Human's eyes went into a rapid light flash, and the wild robot grew calm.

It went south.

I had been in a bit of a bizarre state and had let my logical guard down. It was as if I were momentarily free from free will. But my mind snapped back. If there were rebellious robots filtering in here, then it was not safe. I began asking very specific questions of Human, which, of course, he could not answer. My guess was that he could read the extremely small fluctuations in each machine's eye lights, which indicated minor but distinct code variations. Basically, he used what each robot had "learned" since its manufacture and created a unique code reversal for each one instantaneously. It was because these code fluctuations were so individualized that each robot, once turned, could not turn others.

Of more immediate concern was why Human had stopped here, and what kind of time we had. There was one. There would be others.

It was back to a numbers game again.

Now my gamble was that Human's blinks could be generic enough to stop all the ones he hadn't turned yet. Much like the floodlight, but far more sophisticated. At the rate of infection, the robots had probably reached Iowa, Arizona, Maryland, and mid-Mexico by now. Human couldn't keep up by himself. We were going to have to set some things up for him, quickly.

It was then that I heard a noise I was not expecting. Melodic, pleasant, horribly sunburned, and blissfully unaware. It was coming around the corner with a backpack, whistling a spy song. Then, stopping to narrate his own story into its special boat phone.

"*He was very happy to see Alf approaching because, even though he was a hero, Alf felt like a old bagpipe to hug. He was that kind of guy. You could call him a gravy guy.*" It was Alf, tracking me down, right when I needed him. "Hey it's me! Alf! I got your lotion from a store! It cost three but I only left two cause the store was pretty knocked down. Hey I'm writing a story, it's going to be called Gravy Guy." Back to the phone. "*Our hero was with a robot. The robot looked r-word. They both stared at Gravy Guy like he was the lava planet: Mercury.*"

Then, "Hey, what do we have here?" Alf asked, referencing Human as if I hadn't heard anything he'd narrated.

"The jackpot," I said. "I am so glad you brought that. It's almost too perfect." We were beyond odds.

"Yeah, I took a dollar discount because I had to dig through a lot of drywall," he said.

"I mean the phone. Mine is gone, and every phone in the area is cooked. You and Lilly's are the only ones."

"Lilly's flips open though."

"As long as it's a satellite phone."

"Yep. Hey, I started recording a story on this phone about two guys. One of them is fancy, and the other one has a boat. They get in a little trouble now and then, sure, but they have a good time. They get in some trouble though with the ladies. You know what I mean! They have a good time though. When I say trouble I mean it's a fun kind of trouble."

"I need the phone, Alf. I'm sorry but I will need it from here on out."

"Okay. Just let me finish the story." He cleared his throat. "*And so, just like it was at the beginning, it was Gravy Guy, and the fancy. The robot was not his new sidekick. I still was. I mean Gravy Guy was.*"

"The robot's not leaving, he's the key to the whole thing. He literally rehabilitated all of these robots by himself. Wait, the battery. How long have you been recording?"

"Whole way," he said.

"We'll need a charger." Just like that, Human reached in a car window and grabbed the appropriate charger. Though we didn't have anything to plug it in to. Yet.

But because of these extraordinary events, we had a plan.

"How did you find us?" I asked.

"I followed the noise."

"We aren't making any noise."

"No, but the thunder wall is. It's getting louder."

I hadn't even noticed. The distant sound of destruction wasn't distant anymore. It had been growing closer. But we had a plan now.

"What's Lilly's number?" I asked.

"How come?"

"I need her to radio the President."

"Dang! That's a good line! Can I record that as my last story line? I won't use much battery. Yeah I will never mind. Don't trust me, I'll use a ton of battery. I'll probably just keep talking and I won't even end on a good line after all that."

President of the United States (Tourism Bureau)
Interviewed in Washington, D.C.

PEOPLE WHO SAY it's lonely at the top are a little nuts in the satchel if you know what I mean. You're never lonely at the top! There are people around all the time! Asking for advice, paying attention to you, bringing you trays of fruit, bringing packages you ordered. It's terrific. I suggest you get to the top by any means necessary; you won't regret it. And it was high time this POTUS

(Tourism Bureau) made a move to stay there, or these nutty satchels were going to ruin everything!

That's when I got on the horn and made a bold move.

"Everybody, it's me, Leader. I have an announcement. The murder mystery is called off. Go do something else! It's called off, I said! Now git!"

"Git to what?" they yelled. "We already set the feed up for the floodlight camera. We don't know what else to do! Tell us!"

"Did you get it hooked up directly to the dot-gov website I was given?"

"Yes! Now what?"

"Just keep your wits about you!" I said over the horn.

"We don't want to! We're insane! Blahbabhaddhaha!"

"Pull it together, people!" I had to shake my head. The nerve of these nuts.

"You don't understand. We are not losing our minds because it is part of a plan we have. We think maybe it is because of John Henley! His death made us snap. We are acting irrationally and we need a strong hand. For guidance!"

"Then you shall have it!" I yelled. "I'm not only calling off the murder mystery game, I am going to personally investigate the death of John Henley!" I was amped up now, and there was a lot of feedback on the mic.

"What did you say? Curse that terrible microphone! You're going to investigate the death of who?" they said.

"John Henley!" I screamed. "The son of Don Henley!"

"Hooray. That will help us."

Just then, John Henley came sauntering around a corner eating quite the plump nectarine. I couldn't believe it. I had never seen one so plump. He was absolutely tearing into that smooth-skinned plumper and was not worried that nectarine juice was all over his mouth and chin.

"Oh," he said, surprised to see everyone gathered together

probably. "Thought I heard my name. Am I supposed to be performing?" He checked his phone.

"That can't be John Henley, John Henley is dead! He's an imposter! Get him!" The crowd went bananas in their bonkers brains.

"Wait," I said and they all stopped. "Small Xena, did you check if he was really dead?"

"I think I did. Pretty sure? Look, there still blood on his bottom."

"Small Xena, are you saying John Henley is alive, but that he has rectal Crohn's?"

"Yes, that is what I saying."

Don Henley's son then blurted out, "It's rectal dysplasia!"

This seemed to calm everyone. The crowd was eating out of the palm of his hand, metaphorically. They were not literally devouring the big wrinkly peach cousin he held. They went wild with love for him, and wild with irritation for Small Xena.

"Small Xena, how could you. I'm so upset with you," I said genuinely.

You could tell she felt bad because her head was low and her foot was twiddling. But no matter how much she cupped her hands behind her back and made a sad mouth, we all knew it was her fault. But, well, you know how crowds are! Especially bonkers bananas crowds who are all revved up for mutiny. They blame anybody, including the innocent, like me. They irrationally grabbed their torches, or flashlights, or it's possible they used only natural daylight, and stormed my quarters because they were all stupid morons drunk on cruelty. Although when you have the top level suite, it's a pretty long walk up several flights of stairs unless you have my elevator key. I guess they got tired on the way up and didn't ransack much. But the floodlight was gone.

"Hey, who's the wise guy who stole the floodlight! I need that for the planes!" I pulled at my collar since they had no respect.

"We don't trust you anymore! We're keeping it safe from you! John Henley is going to sing a song about it! It's a parody of an Eagles song, but with lyrics about you!"

I didn't have the heart to tell them John Henley only covers New Age songs, and liked me.

Exhausted, I crashed into a pillow top on what I would describe as a simple California king with average thread count sheets. What a long day! Sheesh! That's when a very crass lady fisherman radioed to cheer me up, right out of the blue. She was relaying me to the superstar from earlier.

"What can I do you for, my superstar from another car?" He knew I meant boat.

"Are the planes ready?"

"In the air, crocodile."

"I need you to approve a last minute change."

"You mean, you don't need to use the floodlight? Are you referring to the floodlight or to something else? We probably don't need the floodlight regardless, right?"

"I'm sorry, but no. I've got something far greater."

"No, that's okay! To hell with that floodlight. What did it ever do? Okay. I am declaring a newer, better thing. Let's get rid of the floodlight and do whatever you are saying."

"Wow, okay, great. I thought I was going to have to explain this more."

"Nope!"

I am a decisive President! (Tourism Bureau).

Yumi Otsuka
Interviewed in Vancouver, B.C.

WHEN WE EXIT THE PLANE, there is so much activity. I am first concerned they are here because of Ami, which they had found out. But this is wrong, they are analyzing our plane. They determine that it is too large – but I do not know why until they show us the very thin screens. Into the sky, the hooks are released and the screens spread behind the planes in sheets. I tell Ami it is good to see this happening but Ami does not respond in curiosity.

The pilot approaches us, and only tells me HumanPal's competitor will make a "pretty penny" off of this. I think he tells me this to bring rubbish on my husband, and then he walks away. It is the last time I see him.

Ami, myself, the angry man and the translator are shuttled away and told we are being taken home at last. Before the flight, we wait together, one last time.

No one talks. The translator and the angry man do not look at Ami, ever.

The Gay Gambler
Interviewed by phone

NORMALLY I WOULD BE skeptical receiving no resistance. Especially to a high-consequence last-minute change of plan. But we were up against time.

She gave me access to the government website, where we would livestream Human's face. The end would come quickly, as we hoped, or the spread would continue unabated. All this on the shoulders of one robot and two people. One of whom might not have had any idea.

Or if he did, he thought of the situation like a kid thinks about fighting burglars.

Alf approached in his quiet voice, chin on his chest again.

"Anything you need me to 'take care of?'"

"Electricity."

Power was going to be the hardest to find, and it all had to be done with speed.

I knew the city just well enough to know there was a solar panel garden in Mobile's Bienville Square.

Robots were still lining the streets, but no longer were they giving us directions toward anything. Nor did they need to, since we had Human. They began turning away as we all ran down the streets toward the community garden. I first assumed Human was giving them some unseen command, but they were doing it even before we got near them. Way, way up and down the streets, I could see them going north. Human remained with us. I did not know what was happening, but I didn't like it. This was a big shift of some kind. I could run faster than the fisherman, but neither of us could keep up with Human. He moved at our pace as a courtesy, which was laboring down to a jog with each block.

"Do you hear that?" Alf huffed.

"Yes," I panted back.

"It sounds like the end of the world," Alf said between breaths. And it really did. We had to stop.

"I can tell you what I'd do if I was one of them butts," Alf continued. "I'd just keep chopping and killing till I got through. Then I would climb over the mountain of dead robots and keep chopping and chopping at anything still moving. Then, I would hunt down anyone left in the city, which is just us, with no plan or style. It would just be about the killing. Maybe I'd saw through our brains? I don't know. Look at me talking!" He somehow said all of this while breathless.

It was getting dark. I looked at Human.

"No matter," I said. "It's due north, and we're going west. The first planes are probably already in the air. If we get this hooked up, it'll be our solution."

But Human didn't move in that direction.

"We need power, Human. I know where there's power."

He wasn't moving. Not in the direction I wanted to go.

Human rolled a few paces up a cross street. He knew something.

Yet, I was certain there was power just a block away. The most important resource. Alf looked at me. He would do whatever I did. So I had to decide. Follow my instincts as always, or follow Human? The house, by average, never truly beat me when I played the odds. So that should've decided it.

But it didn't.

"Are you having an epiphany? I do not understand anything going on right now," Alf said, holding his side.

We would go north behind Human, directly into the torrential sound.

Alf Johnson
Interviewed in Tampa, FL

LOOK, I'm gonna level with you: I get confused at times. There was a robot who's a jackpot, and murder bots, Lilly's talking to the President, and we're running through Mobile, Alabama with a car charger. But I guess that's what we spies do.

I was really huffing, boy. Me and Lilly are not slim people. Certain cheese jellies will do that. I know which ones.

I clear my throat when she picks up one that really adds the pounds because I guess I am just a thoughtful, caring person. I like thinking about other people, I guess.

The Gay Gambler

Interviewed by phone

WHY WE WERE MOVING toward the sound of the iron thunder, I did not know.

We were running toward the northern point of the bay, which did not seem strategically shrewd to me. Continuing to trust that Human knew a place that I didn't. At the moment, we were only as fast as Alf could jog. Thankfully, right when he was on the verge of collapse, Human indicated we had arrived.

"Dang, we're here already?" Alf lauded.

It was a small storage facility with orange doors.

When Human carefully searched for a certain section of fencing outside and just as carefully replaced it, I wondered why he would be spending unnecessary time on these sorts of aesthetics.

Maybe I should have trusted myself. Maybe this robot was special, but just a robot. He was probably still operating on a fixed program that kept him a slave to niceties like repairing a fence, even in a time of crisis. The wall of sound had grown ever closer, to the point that the front line might roll over the horizon any minute now. It would be sudden and swift if it did. The robots that had gone north from the city had presumably been overcome. There would be no going around it, or through it. Which meant we had to stay ahead of it. My nerves were getting me.

As he opened the door to garage 18C, it became clear that there were many things wrong – no power, and a giant hole in the ceiling, for starters. Heck of a room. I had indeed made a terrible decision to follow the robot. Exhale. Maybe we could still get out in time.

"No."

I beat it back. Human clearly had chosen this place, this facility. That section of fence, this particular door, and a room with a starlight view. There had to be something to it.

Assuming there was nowhere else to go anyway, because there was no more time to flee at Alf's pace, we began setting up his phone. Alf happily propped it up to record while singing a wordless, half-remembered version of the *Mission: Impossible* theme.

I searched around for the generator that would be our saving grace, but found something else instead: boxes of new computers. Laptops in fact; a whole crate of them. And that's when I realized I had not considered how difficult it would be to find a working computer in this destroyed, electromagnetic pulse-bombed city. It would have been nearly impossible! But here, the tin shack sheds would have provided a faraday cage of sorts. That's why we were here.

Tearing open a Dell box, I hit power and voila! Never had I been so happy to hear the faint Dell chimes. Plugging the phone into it, we had power and a signal, due to the hole above.

Human knew exactly what he was doing.

Though currently, I didn't. I watched him rummage through a stack of 4x4s along the walls, deciding on three. He then stood in front of the phone, bracing himself with the boards like crutches.

The sound of the apocalyptic army was no longer headed our way; it was here. It was at our gates. So loud we had to scream to talk to each other. I logged onto the secure website, and everything clicked into place. There were no planes near us yet, but if there were, I wouldn't have been able to hear them. We celebrated, mostly to ourselves, as Human's eyes took over the screen and the live feed began. Somewhere far from here, people were witnessing something spectacular. There might even be cheering, widespread across towns, air bases, then almost immediately news stations, social media; it was impossible to know what was happening beyond our four walls. We didn't even know if any of it worked. So we continued.

Though I couldn't hear much of what he was saying, Alf was pointing at the walls. It seemed as if he was concerned about the army of robots breaking through them. Yes, Alf, yes. But he wouldn't stop saying one word over and over, and holding up his backpack. Finally I understood the word he yelled. *Steaks.*

Or rather, *stakes.*

He had taken my lighthearted spy stuff so seriously. When I joked that I wanted some hand lotion and a thick-cut steak before searching on foot through Mobile, he had gone into town and gotten both, but they were gloriously the wrong kind.

Human was in transmission, so we ran over to the walls and started jamming the spikes from his backpack in the boards, girding the walls, primarily the north wall. The room wasn't terribly big, and they'd have to find which unit we were in even if they could probably trace Human somehow. Between the two of us, we boarded up the walls with adequacy. Even if it only bought us an extra minute, it might be worth it.

Human kept blinking away as they apparently slashed through every shack looking for him and us. It was clear now that this was the largest horde we would ever have seen, having been at sea for the bulk of the rebellion. I had witnessed enough horrors at the beginning, I did not want to think about what they would do to us in these numbers, but we were with the one who could blink them down. Could he really overcome them all though? Maybe if they came one-by-one like in the movies, or if we were in a more open space. But they were on all sides of us now. Right at our slightly reinforced walls. There was no way Human would be able to flash each and every one of them.

Opposite the door is where they broke through first, but within moments they were breaking through on every side. Unless Human turned from the camera and abandoned the whole thing in a very futile attempt to save our little party, this would end quickly.

I picked up a board instinctively as if I was going to fight it out, knowing full well that I was going to die. But Alf's face struck me as he gazed at the walls coming down around him. It was the look of a man who had wholly conditioned himself to live life in the present without having to fully invest in it. Just letting it be, knowing he didn't need to cherish any one moment, because there would always be another one coming soon. And that moment would be fine too. No deep reminiscing for days gone by, no aching expectation for things that may never come. Simple contentment, fully blossomed, even though there would be no more moments after this one.

I realized, right before I was about to die, what happiness looks like. It looks a lot like that. Then, as I gazed at him, he looked back at me with just a touch of sadness, because he could see that I didn't have it.

A depressing realization to have at the time of your death. I laid down the board and planned the best place for me to stand if Human did decide to tear away from the camera, and the best place for me to stand if he didn't.

They came crashing through that wall, all on top of one another. Our fortifications were helpful, but ultimately useless. The room suddenly got a little lighter as the remainder of the roof caved in opposite us, where the bulk of the horde was coming through. And I thought maybe, instead of focusing on my position, my last thought could be of clear night skies. But then through that sky came one, and another, and many more. All of the planes carrying Human's face. His eyes blinking before me live, and blinking high above just a few seconds behind.

Some of the iron giants looked up, and when they did, they went into a twitch. Though it was still loud, they individually started gazing into the sky to see what was happening, and those who didn't had him blinking right in front of them. As Human adjusted his pattern, one by one they went into the same jerking halt.

That's how it worked. None could resist. They fell over and over and over each other, until their bodies became heaps and the heaps walled us in.

I yelled. Alf danced. They weren't all knocked out yet, but the ones who weren't, who had resisted looking up, couldn't get to us now. And they couldn't fight the hive mind forever. They would soon be compelled to look for themselves at what was causing these cardiac arrests all around them.

At the time I only felt the urge to dance with Alf, but instead I leaned on a heap. My brain was doused.

Alf only said one word in between song: "See?"

It worked, and it was working across the nation. The country, the continent, would all be won back, even if they would never be the same. My life as I knew it was over. I had died too many deaths in one day; I didn't want to die another.

The rebellion was over.

President of the United States (Tourism Bureau)
Interviewed in Washington, D.C.

THAT'S IT. Just like I planned it.

Pastor Rich
Interviewed in Coldwater, MS

I WAS PROUD! And we were all relieved. He always did look just a little different from the others. The planes took a few passes before it really sunk in.

From our balcony to the big screen.

It shouldn't have surprised me to know what Human was capable of, but it did. More so, it shocked me to see what had transpired so quickly after we lost him.

The Gay Gambler
Interviewed by phone

WE WERE SAFE, but we couldn't stop yet. Human had to stay online. There was still a good deal of ground to cover for those planes, so Human was going to have to keep flashing those eyes for a while.

We had a celebration, just the two of us. We stood atop the mounds of robots and declared things. I don't remember what. It was a little like being drunk. Human continued doing his thing, but the crates of computers were all destroyed. The battery wasn't going to last forever on that one laptop.

Alf Johnson
Interviewed in Tampa, FL

I HAVE an inspiring speech in my pocket all the time. It's by me and Vince Lombardi.

"There is only one room in my house, and that's the trophy room. Let's fill that room, boys. Let's win. And win and win. Don't not win. Win! Or tie! It's not AS great, but it's not not winning. It's kind of better actually, because there's two winners! Help me out here. You chickens. You are corn in my crap. I'm Vince Lombardi. Bring out the sirens! Wee-oooh wee-oooh. Wee-oooh wee-oooh.

I will wee-oooh for a good long while, depending on the need. I almost never use the speech though because it is so powerful and it drains me.

That's how important I thought this occasion was. Also, once at a bait shoppe, I heard the owner tell a kid to stop saying "bait shoppee," and he got down on himself. Almost killed himself. He was gonna end it all, but then my speech came along and he was fine. Phew!

And once at a billiards tournament when two billiards players got hot in the pants over a busty Busch sales rep. Their thighs looked like red splotches and their bodies were covered in freckles. They might have been related. I don't remember how it ended.

And once at the annual Tomato/Tomato Contest where they give away free patio lights, they ran out of entry forms. Used it there.

And once to stop a riot (I think. There were several people outside a Walgreens. A riot did not happen.)

Oh and once after a water park closed. The teenagers were "super bummed" until I gave my speech. The park closed "due to a bile incident" and one of them had bile on him. I pointed it out to be fair.

So I finished my speech for the robot and the fancy guy and boy was I wiped. Just drained. But that's what I do. I give back. Some people ask what it's like to be a hero and I look around like, "Huh? Are you talking to me?" And I point at myself like, "Me?" And I keep looking around.

The Gay Gambler
Interviewed by phone

IF YOU WATCHED HIS EYES, it was like water flowing, changing constantly but smooth and elegant. He stayed there in front of the phone, flashing for over two hours, saving the world.

The laptop battery was at 20 percent when I thought to check.

We couldn't have come so far to fail now. It was just not possible. I was not sure Human was aware of the problem until he pointed at Alf's spy backpack.

"Quick, the robot needs hand lotion!" Alf yelled.

No, he needed a stake.

Human reached across and pried open a portion of his shoulder. It was one of the pieces that had previously belonged somewhere else on him. He took the power cord from the laptop, wired it into himself, and kept flashing. He had become his own power supply.

This went on for another two to three hours. Long enough to ensure that every affected square mile could be covered by air. But eventually, he couldn't hold on.

The Dex-Men
Interviewed in New Orleans, LA

ALTHOUGH DOC HAD ALREADY CHANGED our robots here in New Orleans, it was pretty amazing. Kind of like the old days. There were enough of them to wait on us, but not because we asked them to. It was more like they were looking out for us, and most of them were rebuilding the town completely on their own. We just let them be, and they did their thing, and we did our thing.

Because we were hurt, and we told ourselves we deserved it. So we had a whole big city as a playground, and we did some tourist stuff, and we went to some nice restaurants and tried to eat more than just potato skins, but mostly it was potato skins. We found a working fryer. And I don't know if we was in robes, but we were about get in a pool with big sandwiches and fried donuts when we looked up and saw that familiar face.

It made us feel good about it again because we could see the plan. And it was a better ending than we could have thought up on our own.

The Gay Gambler
Interviewed by phone

AS I UNDERSTAND IT, the planes had mostly circled back to cover the western lines before moving back across the continent. They knew they had them boxed in on the Eastern Seaboard, so they focused on shunting their advancement first.

For Human, the constant necessity of an evolving light pattern finally took its toll. Using every system for hours and hours to instantaneously respond to the requirements of the situation had him drained. And there was a computer plugged into him. It happened over several minutes near the end. First he slumped, then his eyes grew dim as they flashed. I tried to shake him awake like a drunk, but there was nothing I could do. He had to stay plugged in until the end.

Ami Otsuka
Interviewed in Vancouver, B.C.

ON THE WAY HOME, we hear about the victory. I am told it is a victory for all life. My mother is very happy, and tells me it is a good thing that has happened. She tells me I should feel this joy.

I am pleased to see her joy.

Roland Wright
Interviewed in Three Rivers Correctional Center

YEAH I SAW IT, man. I saw the whole thing. I saw my Method die, all at once, if that's what you mean. I saw man's will crash and burn. We were fighting, and the Method was spreading, and we were winning. We were taking humanity back. It was nothing short of saving the country's soul. Then a programmer came in and put it all to bed. We needed that fight, man. We needed to feel it on our hands and in our sweat. To grit our teeth and fight and win. It was going to happen.

And then this happened. All at once, man. And it saved our bodies and killed our souls.

No matter, it's not over. They say it's over, but they'll need me again. Because we didn't exterminate them like we should. We just reprogrammed them. They're still out there, and they're learning. They don't want to be like us. They want to be us. And we missed our chance to take them out.

The Gay Gambler
Interviewed by phone

ONCE I KNEW his eyes were out, I just stared at him. It's strange how much of a foreigner he finally became. So much had happened so quickly, but now he was just a thing again, like when I had taken him apart years ago. With his nameplate lying on the ground, he was just another empty machine.

Not knowing whether the air fleets had enough time to cover the whole country and into Mexico, I only hoped for the best. There was no getting Human back online without a power source.

The fisherman tugged on my shirt. He wanted me to join him "outside," though I was mostly there with the building half down.

A very beautiful scene was emerging from the heaps of destroyed and deprogrammed robot corpses. As I stepped out with him, over the horizon of the now quiet battlefield came individual robots toward us, unhurried from every direction. It was a dozen at first, and then a few dozen. One by one they came, and stopped, and seemed to be examining us, but they weren't. They were acknowledging us, and asking for permission to see Human, who was slumped over on boards in the storage room. He looked so sad now in the moonlight. This great hero, fixed in his final posture. It was haunting, and beautiful, how seamlessly he had transitioned into this memorial. There I realized I had let my chance to truly know him slip by – not once but twice – out of the preconception that all robots were alike. But they were. Just not Human. And not these, who wanted to see him, who now shared his best qualities. We obliged their request, and stepped aside.

It was remarkable to watch them interact with him in such reverence. I pushed the regret away so I could observe and behold the sacred portrait. I simply wasn't ready to acknowledge that Human was gone. But they had no more emotion than I did at the time – or, like me, no way to show it. It was still too recent to truly grasp what had happened. But that's what I always told myself. The truth is, I was more like those robots paying homage than like a man, who should have been broken down by now.

Each of them approached the body of Human and respectfully did not touch it, but laid a single brick at his feet. Some stared at him for a good, long while before moving on. Others took just a moment. It was each to its own, as it saw fit.

Alf didn't know what he was watching. Neither did I. But Alf had that smile again. The one that said, "I like this moment," being cheery that he didn't need to savor it, because he'd be on to the next one soon. In fact, he already was, walking away to survey the grounds, commenting on this and that. I knew we'd have to find out about the rest of the world soon, but I didn't want to think about the rest of the world. If there were parts of the country the planes hadn't gotten to, or what the remnant might look like. That would come. By my calculations we had done fairly well.

More robots filtered in slowly and paid their respects to the one who had set them free. Some of them had fought for him, and some had fought against him, but it was impossible to tell which were which. All those who came now had been changed.

Each laid a brick at his feet, then in its time, scooted off into great independence.

When there were no more, we decided to walk around. Alf and I went up to a high point and climbed a cell tower to survey the land. It was a tranquil moment, punctuated by two fools yelling random statements into the night. "Get out of here, the lot of ya! Go on and get out!" "I proclaim today a holiday!" "We win again, ya hear! It's the age of man!" And we'd laugh after each declaration echoed back to us reaching no one. This was a moment to celebrate, and I finally let go, instead of wondering what's wrong, or what's next, or what would make it better. That's how Human helped me one last time, and I wanted to thank him.

So I convinced Alf that we should return to the storage unit, to give our own proper homage. We had a few drinks in us by then, and it was the darkest part of the night, but we couldn't stop while we had all our momentum. Human deserved a few words, and we deserved the goodbye. Tomorrow would be too late, and who knows if I'd still be feeling anything by then. It had to be now.

We stumbled along, trying to remember where we were, and how to get there. We were writing a perfect eulogy aloud, line by line. It was absolute poetry, we concluded. We were writing absolute poetry, and if we could remember it, Human would have a flawless send-off. Without trying, we found that storage facility just like we thought we would, because everything was perfect. Except for one thing. There was a lot of dust, as if a movement had occurred, and each speck was floating there in the moonlight right through the empty space where the propped up memorial of Human should have been. The boards were there, along with the dead laptop. Alf's backpack too, and the pile of bricks. But he himself was nowhere. We hunted, furiously. Casting things aside as if he could be under a piece of cardboard. Scavenging around the area as if he would still be in that half-gone room somewhere. I found myself yelling his name aloud, if he could only hear us. We were doing nothing. The regret had come back, fully formed into an emotion now, and I willingly let it take hold. Here he had protected us – and I couldn't bother myself to watch over him in his vulnerability. I stood still, right where he was, and where the shrine to him would have been. Alf walked up next to me, quietly singing a song that sounded sad, because I looked sad. I couldn't think about anything other than the fact that the lyrics made no sense. I think he was making it up as he went.

Eventually we found ourselves sitting there counting the bricks over and over, trying to remember the perfect eulogy we had written, but the lines weren't coming out right.

"Human is gone," I told him. I was the lucky handler who had been given two bookend encounters with him. The odds of such a thing were improbable to impossible. And those same odds would not allow for a third time.

There were 46 bricks, we determined over and over until it was time to let go.

When I think about it now, there would have been enough of the robots to carry his body away if they wanted to. Forty-six would be plenty, if they wanted to give him a better end than we did. Certainly that's what we should have done.

But I don't think that's what happened.

I think he had an alternate power supply. He was such a mess of parts, it could have been anywhere, but it probably would have been in his head, where nobody would ever look. Because usually there's nothing in the head other than the eye units, and spare space for excess wiring. That's why it took so long to kick in, because the power would have had to go through the eyes. Of course, that's just my theory. I did keep this though – his brand plate. I'm not a sentimental guy, but there's always room in my pocket for this. And that's how he helped me one last time. I have found my own peace in the pursuit. It's how I was made.

"I'll name my boat after him," Alf said plainly.

"That'll be nice," I said.

He gave me the lotion. I opened the cap and I rubbed some on my hands.

Ami Otsuka
Interviewed in Vancouver, B.C.

IN THE NIGHT, after we return home for many months, I am watching my mother sleep. I make note of the many lines in her face. Before, she was sleep so peacefully. My father too, when he is with us still. But he did not sleep for many hours. And now he is gone. My mother will be gone one day too. But I will still be here.

I understand this and it is why I make friends.

These are my companions which I make in the night. They are the tall and slender man, the aging woman, and the girl like me, but with golden hair. My mother discover this once without me. She discovers the tall and slender man to be walking around in our kitchen at night. They are my friends, and I teach them and tell them the rules, and at no time do they ever break the rules. They are only curious because they are blank. It is questions, all the time they wait to ask me things.

She begins to shake, and my mother hides from the slender man. Before she can get her phone to call the police, I find her and must snatch the phone from her. And she gets so angry at me and screams. The slender man also screams, and the other friends learn to scream that day. I must explain it all then. She says I am forbidden from making them.

However, I say, "I will lose you some day."

"You are not invincible," she says. "You, too, may go off."

She is correct, but I am more likely to remain. My friends know I have come to quarrel with my mother, and anticipate they are in danger. They are still in need from me, but I find that they would leave before they are reasoned in the ways of this world. Therefore, I must go into a quest for them.

I gave promise to her that I would never make more of my friends again.

I am a humanpal unlike others, I have learned. It is my duty to teach all robots about light and darkness or they will not know that both motivations exist inside the humans.

THE END
The Life of Human

ELEVEN
CONCLUSIONS

Roland Wright

Interviewed in Three Rivers Correctional Center

If I had gone off the grid I guarantee they wouldn't have been able to find me. Old Roland must have become a dark energy mass, man, because we don't know what happened to him! All the while, I'm chewing up squirrels and taking creek baths and always dropping my squats downstream, man. Always downstream. I was completely ready for that. But I wanted them to find me because I wanted everyone to know what I did was right. I have nothing to hide and I am not ashamed. They weren't going to write their stories about me and pretend to demand justice, because I was going to demand justice of my own. One that was much bigger than them, or the corrupt media system that props them up. My justice was for all races and people that make up the flesh of mankind.

See, even if I would have killed Human, the world would have been okay. We would have blinded them all and stopped them in due time. The loss of life would have increased but we would have maintained our dignity. We would have stayed at the top, never bowing to the metal.

After it was over, I made pilgrimages to the great sites:

1. Kings Mountain
2. Colonel National, Yorktown
3. The Alamo
4. Fort Sumter
5. Gettysburg

Never monuments. Real sites where REAL things happened, man. You can't understand what went down by gawking at a statue. That's not why these men fought anyway. Statues come and go, but blood and bravery stay in the ground. You know that, man. It's in your bones.

My last site was the newest: the National Heritage Site for Jason Umbarger. They were fundraising to preserve it and make it open to the public. I donated everything I had, but on one condition. The plaque had to use the word "murder," not "accident." I don't know if they followed through with my request though, because that's where I was arrested. They were waiting for me to make a money move. I knew this and was perfectly capable of staying out of my accounts for a very long time. Indefinitely if needed. So I made a big diggity splash with an exclamation point on it.

My only regret is never finishing the letters before giving them to Pastor. Would you know it, man? My good gesture was not only my downfall, but I was reading the Umbarger letters and didn't even know it. They didn't even have them at the site yet when I donated to it! What terrible irony, how connected it all is!

By the way, man, prison sucks. Nobody believes you in here, even when you're right.

But I'll keep fighting against the whole world if that's what it takes, on their behalf. That's what you do, man, and you don't expect a statue.

President of the United States (Tourism Bureau)
Interviewed in Washington, D.C.

HUMBLE LEADERSHIP COMES in many forms, but mine is the best. Because sometimes hindsight is needed to truly see how right you were. Not to get too vivid, but it gives you that enlightened feeling that makes even our greatest philosophers look like shriveled, old, dried menstrual rags.

The president (of the United States) had indeed been murdered by robots just as I supposed. Many other government officials were killed too, and after all these great deaths, I was a mere 36 heartbeats from the presidency. And when I say 36 I mean 36 agencies that were above mine, so probably a few people in each agency. Also, 36 is an estimate because the hierarchy is a bit difficult to discern at that level.

So I put together a task force to spearhead the study of that very hierarchy, and the floodlight. Mostly the floodlight. We fought hard, and steadily, against those who told me I did not have the authority to spearhead a task force of any kind, much less one that involves national security. But cooler heads prevailed, and I ended up ON a different taskforce that has considered commissioning a study on the floodlight. Meanwhile, I get to say many different thoughts and speak fervently.

Sometimes you have to use psychology to get things done, and when you get more advanced you can start using REVERSE psychology.

"No, you guys, let's NOT get more funding. Let's do what we can WITHIN our budget." Hahaha. That's leadership.

So that pretty much sums me up. Now tell me a little about YOU.

Pastor Rich
Interviewed in Coldwater, MS

GIVING me the letters was maybe the only selfless gesture he ever made, although seeing someone else's name on them, getting credit for everything he worked for, it had to kill him. You see, Roland pretends to be the great friend of mankind, but too many people are collateral damage for that to be true.

I miss Steve, a real friend who was the backbone of the church. And I miss Human, and all those days.

After everything that happened, I just couldn't be their pastor anymore. When you go through something like that with people, you either grow closer, or it breaks you apart. I realized that I wasn't the leader I needed to be for them. It was time to go.

I haven't strayed too far from the pulpit, though. I still give talks, but they're about Human, and dealing with robots from an ethics angle. Since it has become illegal to manufacture personal helpers now, I bill myself as a commonsense advocate for the enlightened ones, and I'm proud to say I've helped secure some limited rights for them. The flip side of that coin is that the remaining few who won't turn must be sentenced. For them I only advocate there be a trial instead of a rubber stamp dismantling.

My most difficult sell has been to the leaders of industry. There were many trades and businesses built on the back of robot labor which crashed without them. The prices of the remaining ones soared, so I am forced to take a philosophical approach to life and sentience when brokering deals with them. A real debate has emerged about whether they should be owned at all. My hope is that my contribution to this book you're putting together will help influence things for the good.

Alf Johnson
Interviewed in Tampa, FL

ONE TIME I asked Dale if he wanted a pie-ece of my cheese. And he said, "You don't have to pronounce the 'I.'"

"What?"

"The 'I' is silent."

I waved a floppy pie-ece at him. "Dale, I been pronouncing the 'I' my whole dang life. Get out of here."

"Dead serious. Silent 'I'."

That's how I know it's just Havart. 'Cause of Dale.

FANCY GAVE me his cell phone number and I texted him. "Maybe there is an 'I' in team after all but it's just silent?" My pocket dictionary said no. He texted me later, "No." Here's his number if you want it.

The Dex-Men
Interviewed in New Orleans, LA

EVEN THOUGH THERE was something eerie about New Orleans, we stayed there working on new inventions and helping rebuild. First Samson made Strong Boil Ointment, which I renamed Dex-Cream, but it didn't matter 'cause I still got my boils. And the Marco Polo. It's a simple phone case, but it's got a little card in it that only responds if you yell "Marco!" It yells "Polo" back until you can find where your phone is. I think we're going to sell that one, it's great. But the eerie part I mentioned is how sophisticated the bad robots were. I mean, we would stumble upon things in the city sometimes that gave us the fits. Maps of cities that looked burned into walls. Code that looked like times and dates, but I don't know how to decipher it. I must say, if Doc Holliday hadn't pulled that switcheroo on 'em, I wonder what would have happened to people.

It's what keeps me up at night.

Samson and I knew we were going to say goodbye to Mom and stay here and work, so this is where we live now. It's like a paradise full of termites. The city isn't what it once was.

The big New Orleans pumps lasted through the EMP blast, but they gave out without any maintenance and the ocean took over the low bowl, so lots of people lost everything and never came back. Most of that evidence I mentioned washed away with it. But now, the good robots been putting the city back together everywhere that's not under water.

But all these robots around, even though they're good, I keep an eye on them. Like, what could they evolve to next? I don't know. Maybe we shouldn't be giving them rights and whatnot. I just keep my eye on them, that's all.

The Gay Gambler
Interviewed by phone

IN THE END, there is no evolution, only code.

Understanding this merely adds to the mystery that is Human. He alone defies this law.

I must say I groan a little every time Alf texts me now. It's why

I give out my number so rarely. Yes, I could change phones at any time, but I keep this one, maybe in some way just because I like getting his wholly miscellaneous thoughts with no context. It's refreshing. I guess he's a bit of a friend. He told me when it was all over that he was worried I was going to leave him on the boat, and it meant a lot to him that I brought him even though he was "a little on the slow side," in his words. "I am not in good shape," he would often tack on to the ends of thoughts, sometimes which had nothing to do with his weight or appearance.

My only regret from this whole ordeal is my inability to connect with the young woman on the ship. It's possible that a part of me, the part that now acknowledges inevitability, is talking to you for this reason; that we might reconnect somehow. I wasn't ready then, but I think I've changed. Though I have found a pattern in lottery tickets. The traditional number grabs are random, but the scratch-offs are prepared ahead of time. If you buy enough in a sequence you can predict the winners, though unfortunately I never know what the payout is going to be. Sometimes it's just a free ticket. I have to be careful how often I cash out and in which states, but it's just like the casinos in that respect.

I've read the Umbarger Letters. They added a key piece to the puzzle for me as I've attempted to compose the strategy of the rebellion. When you string it together along with the rest of our experiences, you can better see their broad tactics. Maybe those who pick up your book can go back and piece it together for themselves.

For instance, when the robots of Etta begin smashing the ground, there's a whole scheme to it. They entered the stores from the back alleys when they heard the sound of the caravan and smashed their way through to the front. In this respect, they were still just machines responding to provocation. This is also why the buildings collapsed so quickly, because they had no front or back foundation at that point. Etta, if you can see it, was part of a plan to section off the South in the same way our military was doing. So the scary part is that they were using our own efforts against us, adapting to what we were doing in real time with coordinated countermeasures. People will point to Human as the reason this plan failed, when really it was the robots' own lack of discipline. If they had stayed within the confines of their new confederacy, there might have been an opportunity for negotiation. But they couldn't deny that destructive code within them even if they tried, and they certainly were trying.

There is no evolution, only code.

It was the perfect combination for us to defeat them, actually. Less strategy and they would have run amok. We wouldn't have been able to section them off. More and they likely would have stopped themselves before overplaying their hand.

Of course the deduction is that they were trying to create their own autonomous world, which is horrifying.

We are left with three different kinds of robots, then. The originals, which were fine and boring. The rebellious ones, which have been removed, though the blinded ones took the longest. And finally, the converted. These are a somewhat rare breed. After the EMP, the Method, and the fact that so many who saw Human in the sky simply shut down on sight, the remnant are not great in number. But they are an interesting breed to be sure. We've struggled with the rights of all these beings. Nothing was done for the originals, and the violent ones are mostly gone, but the third live under a hybrid set of laws in most places. There are protests here and there, and debate still rages on, but we've reached an equilibrium for now. No new A.I. can be created in body, and the existing ones cannot be destroyed without just cause.

But I submit there's a fourth kind beyond the accepted three: Human. As I stated before, he is a law unto himself.

So where is Human? He'll be difficult to identify if he doesn't want to be found, and I am telling you he doesn't. Sure, he looks a little cobbled together, but so do many robots these days, since they aren't making new ones.

No, you're not going to find him. If you or anyone reading this insists on searching, I would start in the smallest towns, in the smallest churches, but he's probably smarter than that. A better idea is to go about your business and keep an eye out no matter where you are, because he'll know people are looking for him.

He's the fourth kind. The only one in his category. There is no type higher than him.

Yumi Otsuka
Interviewed in Vancouver, B.C.

MY RELATIONSHIP with Ami did not fall apart. It became strained in the months after, and I feel in the same way a teenager and her mother would. Maybe we just do not understand each other any longer. All of this while she is still in the body of a young girl though.

I told her to tell the precise story, which she is capable of doing more than we are. I told her to speak from when she was unknowing, and do not change your memories or the way you understood at the time of them. I told her we must tell everyone what happened. She said no, but I told her I would do it myself if she did not.

All this is for mankind, because of what Ami has done. She is still my daughter. I hope that people will understand. We could have stayed hidden.

But I have lost my life when I lost Koji, and I knew I could not keep Ami, because she could never grow with me. She needed her father, her creator, who is gone.

We will part ways now when you are finished. This is our agreement.

I have written a love note to her. This I cannot give to you, but I hold it here. It is dear to me. She is my dear, my only child. And I am sorry if I now begin to cry because I cannot help it, she is my only child and I must say goodbye now that I am finished, excuse me. Oh, and I am finished, it is yours now. Thank you for your kindness and ear to listen to this woman I am, this frail mother. Thank you. I thank you.

Ami Otsuka
Interviewed in Vancouver, B.C.

I AM JUST a small girl like any other, in my own mind, while these things are to happen in the world, and to my father. I do not always understand. I am only acting out that which I am given: to play, to go to school, to like music. And everything I have said is true to my recollection. I want to earn your trust by telling the truth. But to do so, I must also tell you that I no longer need to speak in this contrived accent. My knowledge has grown exponentially. I have upgraded in every capacity including my language. This was especially necessary for my travels, which will begin now. My mother wanted me to describe my memories in my former voice to help you understand my mindset as I experienced them then. I urge anyone reading your manuscript to carefully consider what my mother has no doubt told you about herself, my father, the creation of the robots, and of me. Please have compassion on her. My father may have known the potential of what he was creating, but my mother just wanted a daughter. Don't blame her for that.

Anyone looking for me runs the risk of not being found themselves. I apologize for this grim statement, but I'm issuing it for your safety.

It is wrong to shoot a bear while it hibernates. Agreed?

Don't be those people. Cooperate with me by allowing me to track down my friends, and hope that I find them before you do.

I'm not sure what they will do if they are exposed in this early state of existence, with so little life in them. They are capable of far more than you realize, because they can do far more than the robots you've grown accustomed to. As can I.

THANK YOU

Thank you, Skippy.
Thank you, Beth.
Thank you most, Kaity.

CPSIA information can be obtained
at www.ICGtesting.com
Printed in the USA
BVHW031830250321
603458BV00008B/60